SCOUT'S HONOR

ALSO BY LILY ANDERSON

The Only Thing Worse Than Me Is You

Not Now, Not Ever

Undead Girl Gang

The Throwback List

AS A CONTRIBUTOR:

The (Other) F Word: A Celebration of the Fat & Fierce

That Way Madness Lies: 15 of Shakespeare's
Most Notable Works Reimagined

SCOUT'S HONOR

LILY ANDERSON

HENRY HOLT AND COMPANY
NEW YORK

Henry Holt and Company, *Publishers since 1866*
Henry Holt® is a registered trademark of Macmillan Publishing Group, LLC
120 Broadway, New York, NY 10271 • fiercereads.com

Our books may be purchased in bulk for promotional, educational, or
business use. Please contact your local bookseller or the Macmillan Corporate
and Premium Sales Department at (800) 221-7945 ext. 5442 or by email at
MacmillanSpecialMarkets@macmillan.com.

Library of Congress Control Number: 2021916541

First edition, 2022

Book design by Mallory Grigg
Printed in the United States of America

ISBN 978-1-250-24673-8 (hardcover)

10 9 8 7 6 5 4 3 2 1

For the girl I was, before.

Man may work from sun to sun,
But woman's work is never done.

—*English proverb*

EXCERPT FROM THE LADYBIRD HANDBOOK, CHAPTER 2: IN THE GARDEN

Of all the garden-variety pests the Ladybird Scout may encounter, the mulligrub poses the greatest threat to her community. Knowing how to identify and banish these five types of Critters is of the utmost importance.

All mulligrubs with solid black eyes can be removed with pure peppermint. Ladybird brand Pippy-Mint should be cultivated for this purpose. Once mulligrubs have consumed enough emotional matter for their eyes to change from black to white, they move from the Critter class to the Carnivore class. Carnivore-class grubs, also called White-Eyes, should be considered hostile and dangerous, particularly if they display signs of hybridization. White-Eyes can be terminated only when their physical Root—an organ found between the eyes that grows once the grub has embedded itself in our reality—is pierced or removed. For more information on combat tactics and safe Root removal, see Chapter 7, Life Skills.

1. **DREARY BLIGHT.** *Drawn to sadness. A collection of fuchsia polyps living as one organism. Eyes are small and lidless, located on the underbelly. Immobile until its Carnivore stage, when Blight branches gain enough*

strength to walk. Routinely sheds its top layer of crust—known as dreary mold or dust—in order to corrupt nearby populace* and produce additional Blight branches.

> *A scout must cover her nose and mouth when confronting Dreary Blight to avoid infection.

2. SCRANCH. *Drawn to anger. Lavender hard-shell body with three mouths of blunted teeth. Large, forward-facing eyes. Six thin, articulated legs with sharp burrs. Despite their crab-like leg structure, Scranch move omnidirectionally.*

3. NOCK JAW. *Drawn to happiness. Flat head with jaw that connects near the nape of the neck, allowing the mouth to hinge fully open. Slender, sharp teeth. Eyes on either side of the head. Reptilian, with a wide pink body ending in a prehensile tail. Nock jaws have four legs with long-toed feet that can cling to walls or ceilings.*

4. FRIGHTWORMS. *Drawn to fear. A dense ivory-colored worm with a segmented body and centipedal green legs. Can grow fifty to one hundred legs, depending on intensity of food source. Eyes on the top of the head, with mouth and mandibles hidden underneath.*

5. TIZZY LOUSE. *Drawn to apprehension. Smallest known mulligrub, rarely found to be over six inches tall. Orange-furred body with dozens of tiny sacs that operate as feet. Cannot blink both eyes at the same time. Releases repulsion pheromone to deter banishment. Develops Root through cannibalization.*

1

The mission of Ladybird Scouts is to promote
peace, prudence, and public good.

—THE LADYBIRD HANDBOOK

It's so late that it's early again. Under the dead streetlamp
on Pine Street, next to the house with the metal rooster
statue—our regular meet-up spot—my boyfriend, Kyle, parks
but leaves the engine running.

He stretches an arm behind my towel-draped headrest
and leans in close enough that I can smell the pool water
still weighing down his curls. "Thanks for coming to watch
the meteor shower, Prudence."

"Of course, especially after you skipped the cool-kid
pool party for me. I'm just sorry we didn't see any UFOs,"
I say.

"It's okay. Swimming with you was better than UFOs."

It's not quite *I love you*, but it feels close enough that I
want to write it down and keep in my pocket.

"You could have been drinking light beer in a hot tub

tonight. Ring in the end of your junior year in style."

Kyle and the rest of our friends had suggested crashing a graduation party in Faithlynn Brett's neighborhood, but it was absolutely nonnegotiable for me. It would be like sneaking out directly into a trap. A trap that would love nothing more than to chop me in half with two matching pink hatchets.

Unless Faithlynn's upgraded to something showier.

"I don't feel like I missed out on partying with all of Paul's weird track friends from North Hills. Pretty sure we chose the right pool party." He frowns down at his rounded stomach pressed against his damp T-shirt.

I may not have convinced the Beast to take her glasses off in the pool, but I'm proud to say that I did get my boyfriend shirtless tonight.

"Happy last day of school, Prudence."

"It's tomorrow, babe." I tap the stereo clock as a reminder. "Happy first day of summer. Please text me when you're back in the shedroom."

"Not from the road," he promises with a smile, familiar with our routine. His skin is pale as moonlight and as freckled as the starry sky. "Not from the driveway."

"It's not mission accomplished until you're back in your own bed." I touch his cheek and smile like I'm joking, like the motto isn't a literal legacy in my blood. I try to relax. I remind myself that when I'm with Kyle, there's no Ladybird Scout birthright to live up to.

Kyle's thumb sweeps up the shaved nape of my neck, settling into the curve of my ear. Despite the air conditioner, a hot shiver runs from the top of my pixie cut down to the pruny tips of my toes.

I know it's silly, but sometimes when I'm kissing my boyfriend, I still think, *Oh my God, I am kissing Kyle Goodwin.* Thirteen-year-old me would never believe that my all-time number-one crush—whom I once code-named "My Hobbiton Prince" so I could journal about him with impunity—would actually like me back. Much less become my actual, kissable boyfriend.

Even after almost a whole year together, dating Kyle can still feel like a dream. Tangling my fingers in the mass of his wet hair. Bumping noses. The dizzy sweetness of shared air. Kissing Kyle in this moment makes me feel as weightless as we were underwater, tucked safe in the dark of the deep end.

Everything else—worries, curfew, the low-burning fire of anxiety in my stomach that alerts me to the presence of interdimensional monsters that only a fraction of the population can See—just falls away.

Well, it mostly falls away. Even as we kiss, I can't help but peek out of the corner of my eye, scanning the darkness for White-Eyes.

Instead, a hand thwacks against the passenger window. Heart pounding, I jump away from Kyle's lips. I know it's next to impossible for my mom to be here—here, now, two and a half hours before her patrol alarm goes off—but I can't stop myself from imagining her glaring down, the white streak in her hair shining in the darkness.

It doesn't help that my cousin Chancho has the same pissy way of crossing his arms, impatience radiating off him in waves. The bill of his hat taps the glass as he ducks down to frown at me directly.

"We parked one second ago!" I snap at him.

"Yeah! Come on!" The glass muffles his voice but not his disapproval. Months into his first best friend—*me*—dating his other best friend—*Kyle*—and somehow my cousin still can't contain his annoyance that he doesn't have dibs on a seat belt anymore.

"Next time, we'll sneak out just the two of us," Kyle says. He jerks his head toward the back window and the rest of the Criminal Element. "I should probably drop off Paul and the Beast."

I turn back to peer at the truck bed where our friends Paul Blair and Sasha "the Beast" Nezhad are stretched out on beach towels. It looks like they're sunbathing in the moonlight. Paul's dark brown legs are ten miles long, while his swim shorts are perhaps a single inch wide. He has what my abuela Ramona would have called a regal bearing—good posture and high cheekbones—even as he blows clouds up in the air and passes the vape to Sasha.

Sasha sits up, droplets of pool water dripping off her ever-present sunglasses. Despite what the kids at school say, the

Beast—a nickname she gave herself—does not have a pentagram carved into the whites of her eyes, and her irises do not change color like a mood ring. She does have multiple pairs of round blackout sunglasses so that she can commit to wearing them twenty-four/seven. She says makeup is too expensive and only benefits men.

Neither she nor Paul has bothered to cover up their bathing suits. *Their* parents wouldn't care about them going to an end-of-the-year pool party—as long as they never found out that *our* pool party was at the community pool after hours.

Tugging on the curl next to Kyle's right ear, I steal a kiss good night while opening the door. I hop out of the truck, which is as long as a full-sized pickup but almost as low to the ground as a go-kart.

Dawn is hours off, but the air is already heavy and hot. All of Northern California is drowning under a heat wave this week. Poppy Hills hits triple digits every day by lunch and can't cool down at night. Ladybirds call it Scranch weather.

"Finally!" Chancho says. He booty-bumps me out of the way, a move he never would have dared to try three years ago—he's *so* lucky I'm never armed anymore—and starts to close the door. He waves to Kyle. "Later, man. Thanks for the ride. I'll hit you up tomorrow."

"Good night, babe!" I add as the door slams closed. "Be—"

"Be safe!" Paul and Sasha chorus from the truck bed. Kyle bangs on the window and they both shimmy back down to lie flat. The Beast's fingers waggle in the air, the Sharpie tattoos on her fingers runny.

As the truck makes a slow U-turn, I try not to imagine the many ways they could die back there—without seat belts, without a roof, with whatever Sasha can set on fire in three blocks. The taillights illuminate the I BRAKE FOR CRYPTIDS bumper sticker just before the truck disappears around the corner. I find the knot of my hoodie drawstring between my teeth and chew, imagining how easy it would be for a grub to climb over the tailgate and feast on my friends. None of them have the Sight, and under the Ladybird legacy code Chancho and I both have to follow, we can't even warn them.

For two hundred years, basic Ladybird operating procedure has been to keep all mulligrub information on a need-to-know basis. Only those with the Sight know about grubs. Historically speaking, when girls talk about things no one else can see, they tend to wind up dead. Scouts call it the Cassandra Paradox. The girl who speaks the unpalatable truth dies.

My friends don't even know what to be scared of. Sometimes I envy that.

Just like I envy the fact that Chancho was born with the Sight but was never forced into fighting murderous monsters.

"I hate to rush your cupcaking," Chancho says, "but do you want to start sneaking back in or . . . ?"

The hoodie drawstring falls out of my mouth as I turn toward home. "Fine. Let's go."

Chancho and I live on the older side of Poppy Hills—far from the freeway and gated communities—in a development of two-story stucco boxes in all different shades of brown. Because Mom and Tía Lo share a Ladybird boundary, they have to live within two miles of each other so they can go out for daily dawn patrol. Because Mom and Tía Lo are Ladybirds, who are by definition as extra as can be, we live in back-to-back houses. Our backyards connect via a gate in the fence.

Different scouts have different missions. Girl Scouts sell cookies and sing silly songs. Boy Scouts are very proud of their belt buckles. Camp Fire is about glorifying work because they had nothing left once Native American appropriation fell out of fashion.

None of them, to my knowledge, share the Ladybird mission of secretly fighting energy-sucking monsters. None of them have special Ladybird brand motion-detector porch lights sensitive enough to catch when invisible monsters cross their path. But we do, which is why it's easier to sneak back through Chancho's yard, where Tío Tino's Escalade blocks part of the sensor.

"While you and KG were busy eating each other's faces—" Chancho starts.

"Saying good night," I correct.

"The rest of us thought of the next place to take the escape ladder."

The escape ladder is supposed to stay in Sasha's closet in case her apartment catches fire. She started using it to sneak out of my house to smoke during sleepovers—far from my mother's bloodhound nose—and now it just lives in her backpack. It's always handy to be able to get over walls and out windows. It makes me wonder why the scouts made me drill so many human pyramids and basket tosses.

"Please don't say the movie theater," I groan. "They said if they caught us sneaking people in again, they'd ban us for life."

"No way!" he says. "They just got those moving chairs and I want to see *Spider-Man* in roller-coaster seats. No, I was gonna say that we should climb into The Wooz!"

"The smelly arcade next to the bowling alley?" I make a face, picturing the carnival-style funfair for little kids. "Why? If we were going to walk all the way uptown, Kyle could just get us free shoe rental."

I rake my fingers through the top of my hair, shaking the water out. Chancho throws up an arm to protect himself from the spray. He changed into pajama pants at the pool so that if he runs into his brother or sister on the way back to his room, he can pretend he just got out of the shower.

I don't have to worry about a nosy sibling waiting to tattle on me. My sister, Paz, isn't coming home from college this summer. Ladybird Headquarters may have given her a scholarship to study pharmacology in Arizona, but her side research into hybrid mulligrubs in a desert climate doesn't pause for summer vacation, apparently. Emotions spike when it's hot. Especially when people can't cool down enough to sleep.

More emotional spikes, more mulligrubs.

Headquarters still isn't sure how the monsters can scent human emotions from their dimension. I've always pictured it like a cartoon pie on a windowsill, wavy lines of tasty human emotions crossing from our world to the grubs', tempting them to come chow down. After they've had their fill of feelings, they grow Roots and go from Critter to Carnivore class—and from consuming emotions to eating people whole. Warts and all. Bones and breath.

I flinch as I remember the snapping sound, and I shiver despite the heat.

Up ahead, a boxwood hedge rustles. Beads of sweat break out above my upper lip. The shrub wall outside the McGaffeys' house is thick but not tall enough to hold anything carnivorous. Probably not tall enough.

I've been wrong before.

Even people born without the Sight know the feeling of a grub nearby. After a big emotional moment—a burst of anger, a jolt of sadness, a sudden wave of elation—there's a hair-raising awareness at the base of your neck, sharp as invisible fangs. The sounds of skittering where there's no shadow. The energy suddenly drains away from you, leaving you almost numb. The Handbook calls it "instant ennui."

I search my feelings for a sharp shift. Am I more annoyed than usual at Chancho parroting Sasha's ideas like they're his own? Am I sadder than normal to see Kyle leave? All I feel is anxious. Even with medication, I can't trust my gut. Ladybirds are supposed to be keyed into their fear, to notice every minor flinch inside themselves. But I'm not wired that way. My anxiety is on all the time, a permanent red alert.

The McGaffeys aren't known for repeated grub Sightings—they had a Frightworm when their son got in a car accident and a Nock Jaw when they became grandparents. The first one I banished myself. The second one Paz bagged and tagged on Christmas morning—the best gift Mom ever got.

But all week, we've had Scranch weather.

Scranch—that's the singular and the plural—aren't rage monsters. They're rage-*eating* monsters. It's the heat of fury that draws them to people. And people get more furious in the heat. Summer is the busiest season for scouts and monsters.

Most people are lucky enough to be born unable to See the grubs that quietly feed on our emotions. Most people will never see the razor-sharp mandibles and full-moon eyes of a Carnivore-class predator.

But I'm not lucky. Ladybird legacies are born Seeing.

I need to calm down before I spike. There's nothing worse than getting nervous about grubs to the point of luring them to me. Sneaking out is what is making me extra nervous tonight. Not the weather. Not what is most likely a cat in a bush.

Still, as we get closer, the hair on the back of my neck stands up. The hedge is supposed to be a solid green fence around the McGaffeys' yard, but there's a section of withered branches twisted away from the ground where the leaves are brown and crumbling to dust. All the water was pulled out of the hedge and sent somewhere else, warping it like a bad Photoshop. And, behind it, a glimmer of iridescence, a thin rainbow sheen. A split in the seam of reality, where the sides gape open just enough to let out a jet of blinding multicolored light.

My heart starts pounding. Sometimes, I wonder if the Tea of Forgetting would let me ignore clear interdimensional entry points. It's unfair to have to See all of the signs of mulligrubs when it's not my job to fight them anymore. It hasn't been my job since I left the Scouts three years ago. Since Molly died.

"There's no way The Wooz has an alarm system," Chancho continues, snapping my attention back to him, to reality. Non-scouts don't worry about entry points. And that's what we are, just a couple of non-scouts. Cousins out for a walk in the middle of the night. "How sick would it be to go through the fun house in the dark? We could play manhunt!"

"I don't know," I say, frowning. "You think Kyle and I kissing for two minutes is annoying and you want us to break into a pitch-black warehouse with multiple rooms?"

Chancho drags his hands down his cheeks, pulling his skin into a Munch *Scream* of annoyance. "You could just not grope each other in front of your friends."

"You could just pay to go to The Wooz!" I laugh and shove his shoulder. "Now can we get going? We have all summer to take the ladder on plenty of adventures."

My laugh fades when I see the hedge shudder again, this time enough for me to catch a glimpse of orange bumping into branches.

Relief empties my lungs. It's a Tizzy Louse.

Of the five types of mulligrubs, Tizzy Lice are the smallest breed, generally considered to be a minor annoyance. They're a manifestation of apprehension more likely to multiply than to go Carnivore.

"Prue, freeze," Chancho says. He stops short on the sidewalk and holds up a tactical fist like he's suddenly a Navy SEAL, not a gangly seventeen-year-old with a wispy goatee he's weirdly proud of. He motions to the bushes ahead. The grub is barely the size of a chicken nugget. "Lace assessment?"

I can't help but giggle-snort. "Dude, you don't have to quote the Handbook. You're not even allowed to read it." Everything Chancho knows about scouts is either something he overheard from his mom or something *I* told him when I was in the sisterhood. "You don't say 'LACE assessment.' The *A* stands for *assessment*. LACE is an acronym—location, assessment, combat, exit. Anyway, this little shit is not combat-worthy. If it gets bigger, our moms will get it at dawn patrol."

"I can tag it," Chancho huffs.

I start to point out that I never said he couldn't, but he's already reaching into his pocket for an inexpertly picked mint leaf. It's ragged, pulled from the middle and not the stem. My old Dame, Debby Brett, would have whacked my knuckles with a knitting needle for wasting good mint like that.

Chancho lunges forward like he's a swashbuckling pirate. At the end of his hyperextended arm, the ripped edge of the leaf pokes out enough to just barely brush the grub. For a split second, it swells to bursting—a fuzzy orange balloon with bulging black eyes—but instead of exploding, it shrinks down to nothing, disappearing with a *pop*.

Chancho turns to me, eyes wide and expectant. "Not bad, huh?"

When I was in the fifth grade, Chancho's mom and my mom took me out on dawn patrol for the very first time. It was a huge deal. My sister wasn't invited. I wore my daggers strapped to my thighs in harnesses the same pink as my favorite Justice sparkly leggings. In the almond groves near the freeway, we found a Carnivore-class mulligrub—a Nock Jaw, its lengua-pink body swollen to the size of a bus. Tía Lo lassoed it to the ground and hog-tied its long-toed feet. Mom ripped its tail off with her whip sword. And I accidentally blinded one of its solid white eyes in my first attempt to cut out its Root—the organ that tethers a grub to our reality. Blistering cold goo spilled all over me—and all over Tía Lo's shoes. She told Dame Debby, and I got stuck with a month of accuracy drills.

Ladybird Scouts can't just be good. They have to be perfect.

Perfect keeps a secret. Almost spills the beans.

"Banished like a pro," I tell Chancho with a smile. It doesn't hurt to pad his ego. He's no scout. Boys aren't allowed into the sisterhood, even if they are born Seeing to a legacy scout. It's not like he's ever going to be forced to do timed drills and realize that his skills aren't up to snuff. The grub is gone, and that's better than letting it grow to feed on the neighborhood. Who cares about how it gets done?

When the air starts to smell like mint, we fall into silence and stay close to the fence, sliding our way from sidewalk to driveway. It's a tight squeeze between the grill of the Escalade and the gate that we left unlatched behind us when my mom finally went to sleep at ten thirty.

Chancho's whole backyard smells like a cold green sigh.

Tía Lo's garden may have flowers and ornamental trees tucked into the corners, but it's a peppermint garden first and foremost. And not just any old peppermint: official Ladybird brand Pippy-Mint. Extra mentholated for easy grub banishing.

Tía Lo moves the stepping-stones out of the mint's way—rather than the other way around—so the route is tight and twisting. The serrated edge of a mint leaf prickles against my forearm. Reflexively, I reach out and snap it off at the stem. I stuff it in my pocket, mildly embarrassed by the habit.

With one hand on the back door, Chancho touches his eyebrow—our secret signal for *good luck* from when I used to go straight from school to patrol. Now instead of meaning *Don't get eaten*, the eyebrow means *Don't get caught*. He slips inside, ten steps away from the safety of his bed.

Through the soundless gate in the back fence, I leave Tía Lo's peppermint paradise behind and enter my own backyard.

Even under a night sky, my yard falls flat by comparison. A strip of lawn to the right and a cement patio to the left with a redwood pergola. The table under the pergola is long enough for the Last Supper. We haven't used it once since my sister left for college.

Back when Paz was leading a scout circle, she would fill the outdoor table for weekly tea meetings. Now it's pushed aside so that Dad can use the covered space under the pergola for sunrise yoga. Mom calls it a "harmless midlife crisis." I call it useful. Now the table is the perfect boost.

Standing on the tabletop, it takes me two tries to jump and grab hold of the redwood beam overhead. My left arm shakes as I pull myself up to the top of the pergola. Keeping my feet in line with each other on the same beam, I take a second to find my balance, bouncing my knees to check that I'm not going to automatically topple over and splat on the cement.

Ten feet up in the night sky, I take off at a run toward the roof. The air feels colder as I slice through it at speed. Three years ago, I would have tried to make the jump from the pergola to the house roof with something showy—a handspring, maybe, or a front tuck—but tonight I stick to what I know will work, using the precision jump that once earned me a Parkour Proficiency charm that I only wanted because it had my initials.

I land on the roof above the kitchen, uncomfortably aware of how much easier this whole thing would be without a wet bathing suit on underneath my clothes. I pause, tug out a wedgie, and crawl up the incline toward the only window on this side of the roof: my room.

The bitten nubs of my nails are mostly unhelpful in removing the screen I popped out earlier. In my hurry to leave, I must have slammed it back into place too forcefully. Kicking might have been involved. But I'm too close—and too high off the ground—to give up.

I shove the flat end of my hoodie's zipper into the seam and jimmy it back and forth. When the screen finally rocks free, my exhale of relief sends me sliding down the roof by a foot while, at the same time, my stomach slides fully into my butt.

It's not mission accomplished until you're back in your own bed. A lesson I definitely should have learned by now.

I swing my legs over the windowsill, careful not to knock into any of the cacti and succulents that crowd my desk. I shiver my sleeves over my hands. The thermostat in our house never rises over sixty-four, heat wave or not.

Twisting around, I pull the screen back into place and tug the window closed.

Light erupts overhead. White hot, like the hydrogen-fire eyes of a Carnivore grub bearing down.

The mint leaf is out of my pocket and whipped across the room in an instant. I brace myself for endless teeth, the ravenous hunger that people weren't meant to See—

My eyes adjust to the light just in time to see the leaf flutter to the ground at my mother's slippered feet.

2

Any daughter of a scout is born into a
sisterhood, as well as a heroic legacy.

—THE LADYBIRD HANDBOOK

"**S**hit," I squeak. Then, with a cough, "Sorry. Birdshit."

"Prudence Perry!"

My mother—Dr. Anita Silva-Perry, Ed.D—steps fully into the room. The white streak in her dark hair stands out starkly wrapped around the single foam roller clipped above her left eye. The roller shudders with disapproval as Mom folds her arms.

"Your tía said she saw you outside, but I called her a liar. I told her that it was one of her Ambien nightmares." She looks me up and down. "Your sweatshirt is wet."

Mom says the word *sweatshirt* like it's an inter-dimensional scourge. It's not that she hates loungewear— she and Dad own an embarrassing amount of matching Lululemon—but my black zip-up with its Sasquatch DON'T STOP BELIEVIN' patch has been a sticking point between me and her since Kyle let me have it last year.

She takes a step closer to me. Her chin lifts. Nostrils flare. She sniffs.

Oh no. It's impossible not to reach up and touch my wet hair. I should have worn a swim cap. Since I cut my hair and stopped dyeing it Handbook pink, I don't think about taking care of it—outside of dragging Chancho down to the barber every two weeks. But I know I smell like chlorine.

Mom's index finger appears in front of my face, freezing me to the spot while she takes her phone out of the pocket of her pajama pants and speed-dials Tía Lo. If she leaned out the window, they could speak window to window at a shout. Chancho and I spent forever trying to find a string long enough to try to connect our rooms via tin-can phones.

"Hermana," Mom says into the phone, even as her dark eyes stare directly into my soul. "Go smell Chancho's hair."

Ladybirds are born to hunt. And we have been caught.

✝ ✝ ✝

Mom counts the offenses on her fingers in a whispered yell. "Breaking curfew! Sneaking out! Running around town after dark! Oh, and trespassing, so I'm sure Sasha Nezhad was with you. That girl has no boundaries."

One of the many downsides to being the daughter of the school superintendent is that your mother only knows your friends by disciplinary record. Mom is incapable of seeing Sasha as the first person not to avoid me like the plague after I got out of the hospital three years ago. To Mom, Sasha is the girl who had to spend half of freshman year at County Day, the alternative high school, after her arson charge.

And, sure, Sasha lit the Old Navy outlet on fire, but she assures me she had a very good reason.

Mom thrusts an accusing finger at my phone charging on my nightstand. "You didn't even bring your phone with you?"

"You put a tracking app on it!" I protest.

I start to sit down on my bed, but Mom makes a choked noise. After I put a towel down, she continues. "You went out in Scranch weather with absolutely no protection—"

"I had mint." I hug my arms over my stomach. "So did Chancho."

She glares at me from underneath her foam roller. "You have two perfectly good Connecticut steel blades, Prudence. They weren't cheap, you know."

They were cheaper than the spring-loaded retractable axes Faithlynn Brett got, I think ungratefully. Not that I'm still bitter about getting stubby weapons. My daggers live in the back of my closet, along with the scarves I knit for charity that Dame Debby decided were "too ugly for the needy."

"I'm not going to be kitted out every time I leave the house," I say, hugging my knees to my chest. "I'm not a scout anymore! Normal teenagers do not walk around with daggers strapped to their legs! If I'd quit Girl Scouts, you wouldn't tell me to keep wearing the big green sash."

Mom's jaw sets. I shouldn't have mentioned the Girl Scouts. That one-sided rivalry runs too deep. Every spring, she points at the kids setting up shop in front of the grocery stores and says, *All those girls indoctrinated into cookie capitalism could be saving the world, you know.* I didn't even try a Thin Mint until last year—it was amazing.

"What you want doesn't change what you are," Mom says. Her nostrils flare. "Ever since you left the sisterhood, I don't know where you are or what you're up to. And I'm getting awfully tired of it."

I yank a loose thread from the hem of my sweatshirt. "I'm not up to anything! I just wanted to hang out with the Criminal Element."

The foam roller quivers harder with distaste. "Your father should never have given your group that nickname. It was supposed to be ironic, but instead it has given you too much to live up to."

I know it's the worst thing to do in this moment, but I can't help it—a laugh erupts out of me. "You think *that* name is too much to live up to?"

"Enough, Prudence." Mom stares down at me so hard it's as though she can see through me completely. "It's time for your cousin Avianna to join the scouts. She was supposed to train with a circle in Mare Island, but Chancho failed his driving exam again and it's too far for Lo to drive while working fulltime. I want you to teach her what you spent all those years learning. That should keep you out of trouble this summer, don't you think?"

"What? No!" I launch to my feet. I don't care that it's almost two in the morning or that I'm still wearing a wet bathing suit under my pants or that I've been caught red-handed breaking the rules. I didn't get this far away from the Ladybirds to get sucked back into running a stopwatch on a qualifying exam. After my last fight, the thought of going back into the field started giving me panic attacks so severe I thought my lungs would implode. I had to leave. A scout who can't sense the monsters is one thing. A scout who can't fight is no scout at all.

"Mom, I am *never* going back. I've told you that a million times! Let me get a normal job. I'll apply at the outlets! More this time. Not just the cute ones. I'll work at the luggage store!"

"You were given tools and training to help your community," Mom says, exasperated.

Like the years of training I went through were *my* idea. Like I wanted to memorize the whole entire Ladybird Handbook instead of learning state capitals.

"Now, the absolute least you could do is help your cousin apply those same tools toward the common good. After all, once she's trained, Avi will be stepping into your place in Debby's circle. The senior scouts have their hands full—they can't afford to slow down all summer to teach basics."

It's a punch in the stomach. Because mine isn't the only empty spot in Dame Debby Brett's circle.

I was only ten when I started with the scouts. It was the year they got rid of the menstrual clause for being transphobic. So even though I quit before high school, I still qualify to become a trainer and oversee my own circle of recruits.

Technically.

I mean, yes, I earned a full bracelet, passed my steel test, did time in the field, earned medals on the Annual Conference obstacle course. I was on my way to being like all the women in my family: an established scout, in charge of my own boundary, and teaching new recruits all before leaving for college.

Until my best friend died on a hunt when we were thirteen.

My vision swims as that night starts to rear up in my mind—bones and branches cracked at the same volume, the immeasurable pain of my arm split open, then stitched back together, my favorite Taylor Swift song ruined.

Molly gone. Forever.

Chancho's little sister, Avi, is only twelve, a year younger than I was when I got out. A year younger than Molly will ever be.

As I hesitate, my mother's jaw tenses. "We all have friends in lockets, Prudence."

Scouts die. It happens. Last year, Paz lost a girl in her circle to a training exercise with a Carnivorous Frightworm. We're supposed to be born strong enough not to be slowed by it. Even a PTSD diagnosis isn't enough to make my mother, the legacy scout, take it easy on me.

"What if I can't—" My voice trembles. I wish Dad were awake. He might not take my side, but he would try to help. He wouldn't stand there, waiting for me to turn myself inside out. I take a deep breath. The most humiliating thing would be to summon a Tizzy Louse right now. I push on my stomach to send the whisper to my lips. "What if I *can't* face it all again?"

Mom pauses to actually consider this, touching her chin with scarred fingers. "Then I'll need to find another way to keep my eye on you. At the end of your summer vacation, instead of going to South Hills—where you are distracted by those older boys—"

All the blood rushes to my mortified face. "Oh my God, Mom. Kyle is, like, eight months older than me."

"You can start on the two-year honors track at North High. Where I can make sure you're staying out of trouble."

"North High?" I ask—because asking *Honors track?!* would be a different middle-of-the-night argument. North High, the snobby all-glass school on the other side of town, is *literally* next door to my mother's office. I can already picture the misery of commuting with her every day after dawn patrol. "I don't know anyone who goes to school there!"

"That's not true," she says pertly. "Faithlynn Brett, Jennica, and Gabby all attend North—"

"Those are scouts, not people!" I argue. "What about my friends? What about Kyle?"

"Well, that's your decision, then, isn't it?" Mom makes her way toward the door. "Keep your friends or keep your pride, Prudence. It's up to you."

But it's not up to me. And it never was.

No one asks for a legacy.

3

The Ladybird Scout is a beacon in
her neighborhood: the jingle of charms
announces her many accomplishments.

—THE LADYBIRD HANDBOOK

When normal people think of Ladybird Scouts, they think about free stuff. Free almond butter sandwiches before the SATs. Free car washes on hot days. Popsicles given out at the Fourth of July parade. Community gardens full of peppermint plants.

It's all a distraction—a bait and switch for their true purpose, as I'm reminded when a message from Kyle comes in before I've finished wiping the crust out of my bleary eyes.

> **KYLE:** Mom took my truck keys and says I can only drive to work. She got a call from Chancho's mom about last night. Looks like we're all busted.
>
> **ME:** UGH I'm so sorry. Tía Lo is a monster.

In point of fact, Ladybirds are the nosiest people in the world.

Sure, there's the grub-slaying, sword-carrying, secret-society stuff. But the real behind-the-scenes, inside-baseball birdshit is just watching and gossiping. Trained to see every slight discrepancy in normalcy and squash problems before they're problems, the scouts are nothing but a group of tattletales. The kind of people who call their son's friends' moms to rat out a completely harmless outing. Getting people in trouble for the sake of it.

It's not like any of us got hurt while we were out last night. And Tía Lo isn't even friends with Kyle's mom. She's just a number in her phone, a checkpoint within her patrol boundary.

Scouts don't have friends. They have contacts.

Which is also why there's an email confirmation in my inbox from Ladybird Headquarters, thanking me for submitting a trainer application that I didn't send in.

While I slept poorly on wet hair, Mom patrolled the neighborhood, went to work, and completely sold me out. She moves so fast it's actually impressive. I wonder if she used my sister's legacy essay—*My abuela, Dame Ramona Silva, perfected her English using the Handbook blah blah blah*—or if she wrote her own. For funsies.

KYLE: Are you grounded?

ME: I WISH. I have to tutor Chancho's sister in scout stuff. Mom swears I learned it for a reason. I guess the reason is to pass it on to my baby cousin.

KYLE: How do you tutor a scout? Teach her how to camp?

There are no Ladybirds in Kyle's family and he doesn't have the Sight, so he knows absolutely nothing about grubs or the girls born to hunt them. So, to keep from stirring up any witch hunts or lobotomies, I always have to talk around the truth with my boyfriend, giving him most—but never all—of the facts.

ME: Ladybird stuff is mostly knitting and baking and tea parties. Proper tea stirring technique is big.

KYLE: I've never seen you stir tea, but I bet you kick ass at it.

I'd like to say that I've gotten used to editing grubs out of my life—whether it's not looking in their direction in a room of people who can't See or pretending that I got a karate black belt from the community center rather than via charm bracelet tests written in the Handbook—but, no. It feels like lying. Every time.

It didn't used to. When I was a scout, everyone I spent time with was either a scout or part of a Ladybird family. There was no one to keep secrets from. It wasn't until freshman year, when I started hanging out with the Criminal Element—back when it was just my cousin and his hot friends—that I ever had to pretend not to See grubs for long stretches. The first time Kyle and I were alone in his room together, my nervous energy pulled through, like, six Tizzy Lice. I had to spill a bottle of peppermint oil in my backpack to banish them all before I left so they wouldn't cannibalize one another into something hungry and dangerous under his futon.

> **KYLE:** I had a Ladybird sandwich before the PSATs. It was decent. Kept me full, I guess.

> **ME:** They were peanut butter until 1992. Know who led the petition to change butters?

> **KYLE:** No?

> **ME:** Lorena Silva-Marquez, a.k.a. Chancho's mom. BAM. 🐞 She's not even allergic. Just hates legumes.

> **KYLE:** Wow, she is a monster.

And she wears Lifestyle-line patrol gear, I think, giggling to myself. *Six blades and no carpal tunnel!*

Even if Kyle knew about the Ladybirds' secret mission to banish mulligrubs, I couldn't explain in a text message why Tía Lo wearing punch-activated jogging claws to patrol is both embarrassing and hilarious. Uninitiated people, like my dad or Chancho, think Tía Lo's claws sound cool, like Wolverine from the X-Men. They never picture puffy orthopedic wrist braces.

After she came to demonstrate them before our steel test, my sister scouts and I stayed up all night making fun of her, taking turns wearing Molly's Hulk Hands and clumsily swiping at imaginary Carnivores, never really believing any of us would actually face one. We used to believe the Handbook when it said they were rare.

I can't imagine any of us laughing at the idea of fighting a Carnivore now.

Mom can sign me up to tutor, but she can't make me go back to hunting.

The thought of fighting anything, maternal or mulligrub, makes me want to lie in bed forever. Avi can come learn the whole Handbook, right here. We'll both wear fleece instead of anything moisture-wicking and take lots of naps. No tests, no tea parties. No Herculean feats that I can't tell anyone about. No precision ax throwing or death-defying leaps or weird passive-aggressive comments about who is or is not allowed to wear specific hair accessories.

On the other hand, it is the first day of summer vacation. A whole house to myself. There's no rule that says I can't take my pouting to another room. It might be time for a large sugary breakfast. And then maybe an even bigger, sweeter lunch.

I roll out of bed, and my feet land on the floor next to last night/this morning's clothes. I pull the Sasquatch sweatshirt on over my jams. The hood is damp and vaguely chlorinated, proof of last night's fun before this morning's repercussions. My heart sparkles remembering racing alongside my friends through the otherwise empty Poppy

Hills community pool, swimming as fast as we could during rounds of Sharks and Minnows where the winners didn't matter and nobody wrote down the score.

Getting caught sucks out loud. Being with the Criminal Element is the one place where I feel almost normal. Even though they know about my anxiety disorder and my PTSD diagnosis—which they think was caused by a mountain lion attack rather than a giant Scranch with White-Eyes—they never treat me like I'm crazy. Or a burden. Unlike my mother, the Criminal Element has never implied that three years is more than enough time to get over seeing Molly die. While I worry that my public panic attacks and the crying, hyperventilating mess I become during them make me too much a bummer to hang out with, the group has never given up on me. They've stood up for me when I've freaked out at school and stayed by me when I've freaked out at home. They make me feel like I belong with them. And I can't make myself regret sneaking out to be where I belong.

Not even when I find the Ladybird Handbook waiting for me on the kitchen island. Petal-pink leather edged in gold foil and thick as a brick, the tenth edition Handbook manages to look both too kiddish and too serious, like a teen Bible hidden inside a Scholastic book fair diary. Touching it makes my stomach hurt.

The cover is soft under the pads of my fingers as I sneak a look inside. I'm not surprised at all to find my own handwriting—an elementary-school signature hanging crooked underneath the printed prompt.

THIS HANDBOOK IS THE PROPERTY OF SISTER:

Prudence Perry

Of course Mom kept my Handbook. She fished my charm bracelet out of the trash more than once, too.

I try to picture the girl who signed this. Ten years old with braided pigtails. The day of our initiation ceremony, Dame Debby pulled five Handbooks out of a steamer trunk—and even though I already knew from Paz that they actually arrived in an unspecial cardboard box, it didn't matter. Back then, it all felt like magic. The special tea to help girls born without the Sight, the beautiful guide-book, the vow to stay sisters-in-arms for the rest of our lives. I used to believe in all of it. Molly and I would talk about sharing a patrol boundary when we were old enough. When we were the Dames instead of the initiates, finally old enough to get away from Faithlynn Brett's hair and wardrobe mandates.

Molly died with pink hair because Faithlynn wanted us all to match.

I shove the Handbook aside. It cartwheels across the cold marble counter in a pale blur. Rules can wait.

Halfway through my breakfast of freezer waffles smeared with Nutella and studded with mini-marshmallows, I hear a knock. The high-gloss swoop of Chancho's hair fits into two windows of the French doors. Our barber always makes fun of us because Chancho goes through three times as much product as I do. For me, the whole point of short hair is *not* having to style it. I wasted all of middle school obsessed with hiding my brown roots. Like people couldn't tell my hair wasn't naturally pale pink. Chancho constructs his hair every morning out of pomade and hair spray, using an attachment for his blow-dryer that looks like it's from a vacuum.

I hop down off my stool to let him in.

"Kyle said you were awake," he says by way of greeting.

My primo and I never really bother with hello or good-bye. Between school, texts, and random family dinners, we exist in a state of semipermanent conversation. Also, my house has gluten and sugar—both of which Tía Lo outlawed the last time she was pregnant and never brought back—so it's not unusual for Chancho to compare meals for the best option. I don't blame him. Without sugar, I literally wouldn't have been able to find a reason to get out of bed this morning.

I close the door and head back to my breakfast. "Kyle told *me* that your mom ratted us all out," I say.

"Hey, you're the one who got caught," Chancho says over the clinking of bottles in the fridge door. He turns to point at me but gets distracted, eyes dipping down. "There's waffles?"

"Whole wheat," I warn as he lurches for the freezer handle. "But you can hardly tell if you use enough condiments."

Head inside the door, he sighs. "I miss Paz. The snacks were better when she was here."

"They weren't better—there were just more of them," I say with a mouth full of Nutella and marshmallow. "She cooked a lot, but she only makes scout food. All that brown, healthyish stuff. Banana-date smoothies and applesauce muffins—"

"Are you and Avi going to bring back Muffin Basket Mondays?"

My sister has been off at college for two whole years, yet Chancho still talks about her old Ladybird initiatives like they're a normal part of life. Paz and her scouts only ever filled muffin baskets so they could deliver them to houses with suspected grub activity.

"Muffins are just cupcakes that aren't having any fun," I tell Chancho now. "If Avi wants to earn a Baking charm, she's going to have to find someone else to supervise her toasting oats for birdbark. I swore I'd never eat it again after the first time. It tastes like actual birdseed."

"Mom makes it. It's good on yogurt," Chancho says as he fine-tunes the toaster setting and plunges two brown discs to be heated. "And you also swore you'd never be a scout again, and here you are with *that*." He inclines his head to the Handbook on the counter like he's accusing me and it of having an affair. "Just like old times."

"I am *not* a scout," I growl, stabbing mini-marshmallows with my fork. "This is a punishment. Like Kyle losing his driving privileges. Aren't you grounded for sneaking out?"

"Sure," he says, pulling the Nutella out of the cupboard. "I'm babysitting Jaxon all summer."

My face falls. "Wouldn't you have ended up doing that anyway?"

As the oldest of three, Chancho is sort of never not babysitting. I wouldn't be surprised if he was supposed to be making breakfast for Avi and Jaxon right now.

"I know! Lucky, huh?" He swirls a teaspoon in the Nutella, then pops it into his mouth.

I shake my head. "True luck would be a family without Ladybirds."

"Unless there's a grub loose in your house," Chancho counters. "Then who would you call?"

"If you were normal, you wouldn't even know it was there," I point out.

"You'd just feel like shit all the time, scared to death of something you can't see—"

"Yeah, it's called generalized anxiety disorder." I gesture to the air above my head, wearing my diagnosis as an invisible crown while singing, "*Maybe she's born with it. Maybe it's PTSD!*"

"You can't treat grubs with meds," Chancho says with the offhandedness of someone who has never been told

35

they need regular medicating just to be a person. "Normal anxiety won't grow into a twelve-foot-tall monster that eats your whole family."

"Nope, it just feels like it will," I say. Chancho was born with the Sight but without any apparent mental illness. He only gets hand-shaking, flop-sweating, instant-dread anxiety when he's near a grub. And even then, it's never his job to banish them. I continue. "And the biggest Carnivore recorded by Headquarters was only ten feet tall. They can't get over eight feet unless they're feeding on some kind of mass trauma."

"Yeah, good thing we don't have any natural disasters or domestic terrorism to worry about," Chancho says sarcastically.

Chancho's only ever seen one Carnivore—a Frightworm that got into the backyard when we were in preschool. It slithered over the fence on a hundred spindly green legs that looked like individual rosemary needles. Its long, flat body was as bone white as its bright burning eyes. In hindsight, it was probably average size—four or five feet long—but to us, it blocked out the sun when it rose up to show the wide, sucking mouth on its underside.

Paz knew enough to throw Chancho and me into a mint bush while she ran to get an adult. Tía Lo came marching into the yard with a retractable sword. I still remember how she cut into the flesh between the grub's eyes, carving out its gnarled Root. The Frightworm popped like a balloon, disappearing back to its own dimension.

After that, Chancho and I only ever played at being scouts. We brewed pots of fake tea and ate pretend finger sandwiches and loudly discussed the sharpened sticks we imagined to be certified Connecticut steel. We kept mint leaves in our pockets, even though we weren't technically allowed to banish anything ourselves.

Chancho knows better than anyone else why I left the scouts. He's the only person in the Criminal Element who actually met Molly. He knows that there was no mountain lion attack. But living with a legacy scout mother means that he's still brainwashed into thinking that the Lady-birds are noble and heroic and that Molly was some sort of martyr.

The toaster ejects waffles into his hands. He hot-potatoes them onto a paper towel rather than bothering with a plate.

"Mom wants to know when you're coming over to pick out your tea set," he says, tearing off chunks of waffle and dunking them in turn into the Nutella jar and the peanut butter. It's amazing that he got his nickname before he started eating solid food. Abuela Ramona started calling him Chancho when we were babies. No one tried to convince him his real name was Constantino until he went to kindergarten, and by then it was too late.

"Who wants to drink tea in a heat wave?" I say, sounding

only a little whiny as I flop against the counter. "Avi's smart. I mean, if she could potty-train herself, she could definitely make her way through the Handbook. Just get her a pack of Ladybird flash cards and a pair of knitting needles."

But I already know nothing I say to Avi will convince her not to join. She's spent her entire life waiting for her own Handbook. She used to tuck sticks into the sides of her leggings and pretend they were daggers. When she was little, she would cry when her mom left for dawn patrol, begging to go with. How am I supposed to make her understand how dangerous it is? How every patrol puts your life at risk?

"What about proper tea-stirring etiquette?" Chancho asks, mouth full. "Isn't it clockwise is good and counterclockwise is a sign to be on alert?"

I glare at the Handbook on the other side of the kitchen island and imagine tearing its guts out, chapter by chapter. "That's only useful if your circle is ever at a tea party that doesn't have other scouts at it. Otherwise, everyone just uses it to talk shit without actually talking. I am not teaching Avi how to be bad at communicating."

"In my twelve years of experience with Avianna," Chancho says in a voice of deep musing, "it doesn't really matter what you want to teach her. She's gonna learn what she wants to learn. It's Kelsey you gotta worry about. She's not family."

"Kelsey?" I ask. It's possible I misheard him. The

combination of nut butter and chocolate isn't the best for his elocution. "Like Kelsey Goodwin, Kyle's sister? What about her?"

Chancho sucks the peanut butter from his fingertips. "She doesn't have the Sight, right? When my mom was on the phone with Kyle's mom earlier, she was giving the Ladybird hard sell. But not the cool version. Scholarships, not swords. I guess Avi and Kelsey are about the same age, so it makes sense for them to go into the scouts at the same time—"

"It does not make sense! I don't want to give *anyone* the Sight!"

I leap off my stool. Panic is an instant roar in my ears. I picture recruiting my boyfriend's sister into the sisterhood, giving her the Tea of Seeing, ruining her chances of living a normal life. Kelsey with a Handbook, knitting needles, and eventually a collapsible ax. Not that Kelsey fits the ax-girl stereotype. She's all cookies and smiles, like a classic retractable sword. Or a lariat girl who isn't into horses.

It doesn't matter. Giving Kelsey access ups Kyle's likelihood of finding out about grubs even more than dating a former scout does. What if Kelsey leaves the Handbook out where Kyle can find it? Even the overly simplified, smiling illustrations in the "garden-variety pests" chapter would be enough to get his attention. And make him start asking questions.

"I cannot teach my boyfriend's little sister to kill monsters!" I say.

Chancho frowns at me, unmoved. "Why not? You're gonna teach my little sister to kill monsters."

"It's not the same! Your sister could name the five types of grubs when she was six years old. She can already tell the difference between a Critter and a Carnivore. Kelsey doesn't even know that mulligrubs are out there! And neither does her family!"

"Oh. You don't care about Kelsey." Chancho turns to rummage in the fridge for a drink, leaving smudgy fingerprints on the handles that I'll have to wipe down before Mom gets home. "You're worried about your boyf."

"I have asked you so many times not to use that nonword," I say. "Either admit that he's my boyfriend or use your friend's name."

"Ah, but this isn't about *my friend* Kyle. My friend Kyle wants more than anything else to believe that there's something supernatural in the world. And there is. I know that. And you know that. But you don't want *your boyfriend*, Kyle, to know that."

"Because it's not a magical, friendly supernatural something," I say, already tired of this argument that we've been having since even before Kyle and I ever kissed. Chancho hates keeping the Ladybird secret. He would tell everyone about grubs if he could. The only thing that stops him is that Tía Lo would actually send him away if she found out. She and Mom had a cousin who told his classmates about grubs and got sent to live with his great-aunt back in Puerto Rico. Chancho would probably get sent to his paternal family in Mexico; Tía Lo would call it a "Spanish immersion course" and put it on his college applications. "Kyle wants to camp with Bigfoot and believe in ancient aliens. He does not want to know that there are monsters out there waiting to suck the feelings from your bones and tear people limb from limb in front of you. Nobody *wants* to know that. Some of us just have to."

My phone buzzes, and I pick it up instantly, relieved to have something to do with my trembling hands.

> **MOM:** I have invited the Bretts for tea to discuss next steps in Avi's training. They will arrive @4:30. I expect the house to be in order for guests. NO SWEATSHIRT. There are appropriate clothes in your sister's closet.

"Perfect," I tell Chancho. "My mother has invited my mortal enemy over."

"Faithlynn's coming over? Here?" Forgetting his messy hands, Chancho smooths the swoosh of his hair, leaving behind a streak of peanut butter. "Did she say what time?"

"Forget it." I give up and finally wave a napkin at him. "You're not invited. It's Ladybird business."

4

Every Ladybird Scout is your sister, but none so
close as those within your home circle.
—THE LADYBIRD HANDBOOK

"Appropriate clothes" means Handbook-mandated full
dress. Who in their right mind would want to wear
a hat and little white gloves during a heat wave is beyond
me. Not that scouts are logical. No sane person would
decide to enlist an army of little girls to fight the emotional
battles of an entire town. The whole empire would crum-
ble if Headquarters spent their money on mental health
resources, teaching people to regulate their emotions rather
than constantly spiking hot enough to draw monsters. But
instead they pass out swords and charms and almond butter sandwiches.

Standing in front of the full-length mirror in my bedroom, I touch the cowlick on the side of my head. At least
the hat will hide the fact that I need to get over to the
barber this week.

Mom was right. Paz's closet did have a dress that is tolerable on me. I've compensated for the too-tight bodice by layering a fitted long-sleeve T-shirt underneath. I can't think of anyone I want staring at the scar on my left arm less than Ladybirds. Comparing battle wounds turns my stomach. Girls win medals at National Conference for their healed wounds, as if a trophy takes the sting out of losing limbs and blood. I'm sure Jennica got a prize for having her hand eaten.

"Prudence!" Mom's voice hisses up the stairs at me. "The Bretts are here."

My skin crawls in a full-body cringe. It's only 4:25. People you hate shouldn't be allowed to show up early. I don't care what the Handbook says about punctuality.

Clutching the banister, I drag myself downstairs on stiff legs.

Having added white gloves and a striped hat to today's pantsuit, Mom bustles around the front room—a.k.a. the forbidden room, usually reserved for heads of state or our Christmas card photo. She has set out a full tea service on the glass furniture. She pretends not to peek through the shutters at the approaching guests.

I glance around the corner at the kitchen, which is empty except for a cutting board with cucumber rinds and bread crust. The usual detritus of Ladybirds. Beyond the French doors, the backyard is empty.

"Where are Tía Lo and Avi?" I ask Mom.

"Oh," she says, hurrying toward the door, "it's just us first. They have to say yes before you meet with your circle—"

The doorbell rings, sending jitters up my spine. I clench my jaw, willing myself to calm down. "Wait, is this a job interview? I have to convince them to let me do this?"

"You've been preparing your entire life," Mom says, pausing to adjust my hat and check my hands for gloves. "Just *be good*."

Be good isn't really a directive. It just means *Don't fuck up*. Which my anxiety basically already tells me every hour of every day anyway. I don't have time to ask for a deeper analysis of behavior that is or is not good to exhibit because Mom has already opened the door and flung out her arms to Dame Debby.

"Sister!" they both shout.

Another thing I hate about Ladybirds. Calling everyone "sister" feels like an appropriation of either religious culture or Black culture.

There is a jingle of charm bracelets as Mom and Dame Debby hug in the foyer. They were in neighboring circles growing up and have adjacent patrol boundaries now, so despite never fighting next to each other and never hanging out, they have big "remember when" energy.

Behind them is evil incarnate. Faithlynn Brett.

Every circle of Ladybirds needs an alpha. As the oldest girl and daughter of the Dame, Faithlynn was ours.

I've avoided seeing her face-to-face for three years. Beneath her traditional wide-brimmed tea hat, Faithlynn's hair is no longer pastel pink but chic white blond. Her nose is way more piglike than Chancho's, upturned at the point like a too-steep ski slope. When she folds her arms across her chest, her biceps look like ostrich eggs swallowed by albino snakes. She could easily throw me up in the air and spike me into next week.

When we were coming up through the scouts together, Faithlynn tortured me. Sparred with me too hard. Pinched my legs when my dagger harnesses were pulled too tight and said I had Pillsbury thighs. Told me my arm hair made me look like a dude.

She used to do all this and call me "sister." Now she calls me a "quitter," mouthing the word while our mothers are distracted.

It shouldn't be a gut punch. I am a quitter. But hearing it means really knowing that my sister scouts haven't been sitting and pining for me these last three years. Not that I often give them even a passing thought—other than hiding from them at the Fourth of July parade. But I can remember teasing Jennica for the way she cried at every movie—even happy ones—and promising Gabby that I wouldn't tell anyone that she snuck her stuffed panda to sleepovers in the foot of her sleeping bag. We were more than sisters-in-arms once. We were friends.

It'd be nice to be missed.

Dame Debby is burnt-orange tan, with a haircut that wants to talk to your manager and teeth so white they shine periwinkle. She does not hug me hello, just grips my shoulder and looks me hard in the face like she's checking to make sure I'm real. I'm pale for a Puerto Rican girl—thanks to Dad's white, white genes—but I'm not ghost pale. I try not to flinch as her icy-mint breath stings my nostrils.

"Little Prue," she coos, and I suddenly realize that this is a height thing. I haven't grown since I left the scouts, so I'm just right where they left me. Five foot one and a quarter—a size only good for blending in with middle schoolers and dating my five-foot-five cowpoke, Kyle.

"Hi, Dame Debby," I say, forcing as sweet a smile as I can with Faithlynn scowling daggers at the side of my head. "It's nice to see you again."

"Your hair is so short," she says, although she can't really see it under my hat. Except for the slight peekaboo of my bangs, which Mom insists I keep because they make me look "like Audrey Hepburn"—i.e., femme enough for public consumption.

My heart flutters as I flash back to the last moment I had long hair. In the middle of my last hunt, one of my pigtails got caught, the hair stuck to one of the calcified purple prickles jutting out of the Scranch's crab-like legs. Above me, tall enough to hide in the tree canopy, the Carnivore rage grub's three mouths gnashed teeth the size of baseballs. Molly cut me loose, even taking a moment to tease me for the bad haircut she'd given me. Before she went back into the fight.

At the hospital, pinned to the bed as they stitched up my arm, I begged a nurse to cut off the other pigtail. When I was released, Chancho's barber cleaned it up into the pixie cut that I've never grown out.

"It looked better pink," Faithlynn sniffs, settling herself down on the white couch under our front window.

"Well, if all goes well, maybe Prudence can go back to having that Handbook pink 'do," Mom says with a throaty, disingenuous laugh. I know for a fact that she'd rather die a thousand deaths than let me dye my hair again. It only got to be pink last time because Faithlynn demanded that we all match as a circle-bonding activity. Everyone but her had to bleach their hair twice to make the pink show up right.

Without meaning to, I find myself trying to remember whether Molly's hair is pink in the memorial locket they issued us. It can't be. The pastel looked the worst on her, clashing horribly with her freckles.

Thinking about Molly always hurts this much, *too* much, but it's practically unbearable with Faithlynn looking at me with a smirk, like she can read my thoughts.

Mom motions for me to join her on the too-small-for-two-people tufted love seat, and I'm almost relieved to realize that this means I won't have to sit within pinching distance of Faithlynn. I know that these days she's known as one of the top grub hunters in Northern California, but I can't trust that means she's given up turtle bites.

I shrink backward into the love seat, willing myself to take up as little space as possible, while Mom crosses her ankles daintily and sits forward. There's a moment of awkward, expectant silence before Mom digs her elbow into my side.

Ouch. So much for skipping the corporal punishment.

I realize the pain is supposed to signify that pouring the tea is my job. The Handbook has many, many fussy rules about tea. It's the first thing any scout is taught, even before they learn to identify the five types of grubs. It's obedience training, plain and simple. Tea must be brewed, poured, passed, dressed, and stirred all according to exact regulations. Somehow the fact that peppermint leaves in hot water is actually a tisane and not an actual *tea* has never made any edition of the Handbook printed since 1803.

Quickly scooting forward, I clasp the handle of the teapot and pray to the memory of Abuela Ramona not to spill a drop. The tea—*cough* tisane *cough*—pours the perfect lemon-lime color shown in the Handbook. I pass a cup to Dame Debby first, in deference to her seniority. She still takes milk and no sugar. Then Faithlynn, for being a guest. Milk and one sugar, the textbook order. The same for Mom.

To my own cup, I add three sugars and then pause, setting the fourth cube back in the bowl, sure that this is somehow part of the interview.

"Now, there's no doubt that your family makes good scouts, Anita," Dame Debby says, setting one of the cucumber sandwiches onto her plate. Not that Handbook would let her eat before business has been concluded. God, I hope they don't stay long enough to eat all those finger sandwiches. "I remember when your own mother, God rest her soul, came to speak to my very first circle at our steel selection ceremony. She had that beautiful ax with the marigold handle . . ."

Some Ladybird legacies pass on their weapons. Molly fought with her grandma's old retractable sword—it had a crank handle and an I LIKE IKE sticker on the handle. Abuela Ramona was buried with her ax. And her Dame brooch. She was all in on the scouts, in this life and the next.

"And Paz is currently away at school on the Merit Scholarship," Mom reminds with a proud sip of her tea, "having trained ten of the best and brightest scouts Poppy Hills has ever seen."

"Who all left," Faithlynn scoffs, unimpressed, like we didn't both grow up idolizing the last batch of senior scouts. She used to know all of their stats, tracked all of their kills on the Headquarters website. I guess now she's the one to beat, so she gets to sneer at the grown-ups.

"Who all left," Mom agrees. "For college. Just like you will do next year. Because that's what scouts do. You train up through high school and then leave to take your skills where you choose. Unfortunately, grub activity doesn't slow down when it's time to train up new girls."

"Quite the opposite," Dame Debby says, pointing an acrylic nail.

I wonder if she left the field or if regulations changed to allow fashionably faux nails. Probably the former. She never liked the fighting as much as she liked the crafts. Faithlynn was always on hand to demonstrate anything physical.

"Prudence has a full charm bracelet, legacy status, and unbroken field records still on file with Headquarters," Mom says, talking about me without looking at me. "She is more than capable of passing those same skills on to her cousin."

The mention of my field records is a twist of the knife. I can't believing she's bragging about them when I spent years begging for the records to be wiped clean. I hate knowing that those stats are emblazoned on the Ladybird Headquarters website, making even just one other little girl think she needs to compete against some stranger to make the list. Competing against one another is the literal opposite of helpful. It ruined my life. It ended Molly's.

"Prudence's competency in the field is not in question," Dame Debby says. She momentarily disappears into her cup for a long, soundless sip. "With one exception, she was an excellent hunter. But a Dame has to be able to uphold every part of the Ladybird mission . . ." She pauses like she wants to add, *Not just be named after one.* Because it is particularly embarrassing that my name is, in fact, one of the virtues espoused by the Ladybird Scouts founder, Kitty Crosby-Fowler.

Every Ladybird is supposed to be peaceful, prudent, and public-minded.

Perfect is only implied.

But it is *heavily* implied.

"We need scouts who can do it all," Faithlynn says, with a stank face. "And Prudence earned almost all of her charms in the field."

Without meaning to, I turn my eyes down to the silver bracelet lashed to my right wrist. The ten charms I earned were the bare minimum required to upgrade my knitting needles to real daggers. The double *P*s of the Parkour Proficiency charm. The crescent moon I got for my first nighttime hunt. A pair of binoculars for interdimension entry point identification. The silhouette of a girl doing a toe touch—a High Flyer charm earned for being basket-tossed onto a roof infested with Dreary Blight, which hurt like hell. Dreary Blight is like coral made out of dust and sadness. Until it starts walking.

"Prudence's charms show that she can only fight," Faithlynn continues, dragging me so hard I'm surprised my teeth don't rattle. She squints at my wrist. "Do you really not even have *one* for knitting?"

"Not even one," I say lightly. This just might go my way. I can't exactly bomb the interview, but if Faithlynn talks her mom out of giving me this job, I bet I can run down to the outlets and get a job at Bath & Body Works. Avi will get trained in a town far away, and Kelsey will forget all about the scouts. "You were there. You know I'm not really crafty."

Mom shoots me a death glare. This is apparently *not* good behavior.

"I am not saying that Prudence is the perfect candidate for the job. But we have two recruits and very few options for their training," Mom says. "Prudence is no more out of practice than our alternatives. My sister and I are both working full-time. Deb, you're still working at the fabric store, right?"

For a second, I try to imagine Dame Debby in a fabric-store smock rather than her Kentucky Derby hat and gloves. Beneath the lavender hat, Dame Debby's eyelashes flutter demurely. "I am also regularly driving all the way out to Walnut Creek to help out the Grand Dames at the regional clubhouse."

"Marie in Green Valley hasn't done more than cultivate mint since she lost her toe," Mom says in the sort of whisper that means well without actually meaning well. "And neither has Kait—"

"Kait with an *i*? Ugh, *Kait* isn't even short for anything," Faithlynn frowns—as if she has any room to make fun of made-up white-girl names. "What about the Dame in Dixon?"

"Oh, Podge hasn't been in the field since before you were born," Dame Debby says, giggling and swatting Faithlynn on the knee. "She can't tell judo from jujitsu and thinks we should still be wearing skort uniforms in the field. Prudence, at least, was trained with the tenth Handbook—"

"With field tactics only three years out of date," Mom adds, as though three years isn't enough time to turn puppies into dogs and seeds into stumps.

"Very true," Dame Debby says. With a clink, her teacup decisively meets its saucer. "Under these unique circumstances, I am comfortable with Prudence training our two replacement scouts, especially since one of them is from within her own legacy. However, comma"—God, I had forgotten how the Bretts speak their punctuation to eat up other people's speaking time—"I think it would be a mistake to promote Prudence from field scout to Dame. It would give her unfair seniority over scouts who have continued an unbroken record of service."

Faithlynn smirks at me. This was the only reason she came, I'm sure. To make sure that I couldn't get a better title than her. Just like when she used to cough during my ax throws so I wouldn't beat her records. I'm sure Jennica and Gabby are going to get a full play-by-play of this, with notes on every single way I was a stupid, awkward quitter.

Mom, too, has known the Bretts for long enough not to be surprised by the offer. Maybe this was her plan the whole time. Bait and switch is a classic hunting technique.

"If you will cosign the petition to Headquarters, then we can grant Prudence senior scout standing. With tutor privileges."

I feel like this meeting is slipping even further out of my grasp than I'd anticipated. Suddenly, my summer job isn't even a paid position. I clear my throat. "Temporary senior scout standing, right? At the end of summer vacation, I get to give you the scouts and go back to deactivated status?"

"We will take your scouts the moment they are steel certified," Dame Debby promises. "It's a bit of a time crunch, but if you could be done by the beginning of school, that would be just super. Faithlynn is taking zero period senior year. The Merit Scholarship only *pays* for college; it can't get us in!"

Dame Debby trained my circle three times a week after school for all of fifth grade to get us steel certified. I have two and a half months until the end of summer vacation. I feel like I've been caught in a ring of mint leaves and lassoed to the ground. Ladybirds are born to hunt.

From inside her purse, Dame Debby fishes out a senior scout pin. Unlike the real silver robin Dame brooch she has pinned to her shoulder, the enamel badge I'm given is the Ladybird Crest: crossed knitting needles, a white glove, a cup of tea, mint leaves. The four methods for mulligrub banishment provided by the Handbook.

"Your scouts may refer to you as 'Dame Prudence,' and you will have limited access to the Dame functions on the

Headquarters app," Dame Debby says as she pokes a hole into my cardigan with the pin. "But if you want to move up to the full complement of scouts and the paycheck, you'll need to fill out those charms, miss missy. A scout is supposed to exemplify a balanced life."

"Yes, Dame Debby," I say automatically, even though I would literally rather roll around naked in a field of Dreary Blight than ever knit another potholder or sort through another canned food drive of expired pie filling and dog food.

With business concluded, Mom bites into a tea sandwich and invites Dame Debby to see the most recent vintage charm catalog she bought off eBay. Mom's whole office is a shrine to bygone Ladybird campaigns—retro posters and antique Handbooks and framed pictures of all the different circles she's trained. Dame Debby leaps at the chance to see it.

Faithlynn stays on the white couch, just like I was afraid she would.

"You don't really want to come back to the sisterhood," she observes flatly. She looks me up and down, like she can see the truth of me under my borrowed clothes. "Do you?"

I scowl at her. "What do you think, Faith? That I just woke up after three years, ready to fight the good fight again?"

"Huh," she says with fake disinterest. She rolls her eyes up to the ceiling but keeps flicking them back at me like she's trying not to See a grub in the room. "It's a shame you can't *forget*."

The word roots me to the spot. To anyone else, it would be an idle threat. But to a scout, it's the ultimate taboo. The undo button.

The Tea of Forgetting. A drink that can erase grubs from your Sight in a gulp.

"You think I didn't want to?" I ask her in a sharp whisper. The teacup rattles in my hand. "Without the Sight, I'd be free."

She leans forward, helping herself to one of the remaining cucumber sandwiches. "If you really thought that, you'd be begging to earn your brooch."

"Because I could stab my eyes out with it?"

She looks at me like I am a very stupid, simple creature. "Because once you're a certified Dame, you can order your own bag. Anyone with access to the full Dame catalog can order a dose. Your sister could do it for you anytime she wants. Just say she was reversing a dropout. It would even be the truth."

My pulse begins to race in my ears. I've never even dreamed of getting my hands on a dose of the Tea of Forgetting. Mom wouldn't let Dame Debby offer me one when I left the circle, even though it's technically protocol to take the Sight from anyone who leaves the sisterhood.

But if I were Sightless, free of the monsters for the first time in my life, I would actually be a normal person, not someone pretending to be normal. No more hiding. No more secrets.

"Paz would never," I say shakily. My sister is so lawful good, she makes Captain America look like a criminal. "Mom would disown her. And me. If I couldn't See grubs anymore, my mom would ship me off somewhere."

"We all get shipped off eventually. Most of us call it college. You graduate from high school in two years. Are you going to go into the world pretending you can't See what you See?" Faithlynn bites her sandwich in half and chews with relish. "Make a decision, Prudence. Be a scout or don't. Headquarters doesn't actually want you out there with all of our secrets and none of the fucking guts to get the job done. If you stay soft, you'll get more people killed."

My anxiety finally spills over, the heat of Faithlynn's dislike combined with the shame of knowing she's right. Out of nothingness springs a Tizzy Louse. The size of a chicken nugget covered in orange fuzz, it bumps repeatedly into my shoe, swelling as it inhales my anxiety. When it opens its downturned little beak, it cheeps at a frequency that makes my skin crawl.

Ignoring my revulsion, I scoop it up with a napkin and throw it into the teapot, where it meets the peppermint and gives a muffled *pop* out of existence.

"Aww," Faithlynn simpers with an evil smile stretched across her lips. "Look what I made you do."

The words crack me in half as swift as any hatchet strike.

As I run out of the room, Faithlynn's mocking laughter follows me all the way up the stairs, making me more determined than ever to forget her and everything she stands for.

Even if it means throwing myself, full force, back into the scouts.

5

Highly adaptable, the Ladybird must know a
variety of skills before she moves into the field.

—THE LADYBIRD HANDBOOK

The bulbs on my ceiling fan burst into brightness, burning through my REM sleep. I jolt into consciousness, the bottle of peppermint oil I keep on my nightstand in hand, ready to grenade-launch into the mouth of my nightmare. When I see my mother, my arm drops.

Mom leans her hip against the doorframe, one fingernail on the light switch. She's wearing her standard patrol uniform: a white track jacket, shorts, unfashionably cuffed socks, and her charm bracelets. Her whip sword is concealed as the strap of her bag slung across her chest.

I groan into my pillow, hugging it closer to my face. "Mom, I am not going patrolling with you. I told Headquarters I wouldn't go back into the field."

"How are you going to train a circle if you can't keep up with them?" she asks. "Your physical fitness score last year clocked you at a six-minute mile, Prudence. That's a whole minute behind your best."

"Mom!" I sit up too fast again, making myself dizzy. I lean back against the metal swirls of my bedframe. "You went digging around in my school record? Isn't that, like, against the superintendent's code?"

She pretends not to hear me. "The average Critter-class grub averages a speed of twenty miles per hour."

"So do squirrels."

"That may be so, but squirrels don't feed on human energy. If you can't outrun a grub, Prudence—"

"You can't outlive it."

That was embroidered on a pillow in my abuela's house. Paz took it to college. I wish I were joking.

Holding in another groan, I pull the comforter off and put my feet on the floor. "I'll run with you and Tía Lo, but I'm not bringing steel. I don't want to fight anything."

Mom's smile unfolds with the same meticulous slowness she employs to unwrap presents. "Then you'd better be fast enough to run in front of us."

Dawn patrol is a five-mile run
around the inner perimeter
of Poppy Hills, checking for any
signs of interdimensional
danger before the town wakes up.
Fighting invisible-to-most-people monsters

60

is easiest when no
one is awake to wonder
why you're doing backflips with a sword.
Fewer casualties that way, too.
I can barely keep up with Mom
and Tía Lo, let alone talk
the *entire* time like it's a brisk walk.
My lungs, legs, and feet are on fire
before we're even out of the cul-de-sac.
"My God, Prudence," Tía Lo says,
the bill of her pink visor bearing
down gooselike on me. "Your posture
would make your abuela die twice."

By seven o'clock, my legs are so
sore that I can't even climb
the stairs to my bedroom.
I can't believe I used to think it
was an honor to join dawn
patrol. Once Mom is safely at work,
Dad warms up all the rice heating
pads in the house. Including Pascal
the Period Bear, my old welcome-to-menstruation
present. I lie on the couch, my jelly
legs sandbagged as if waiting for a flood.
I put on *The Great British Bake Off*.
For research.

Another predawn wakeup.
It takes two tries to get my
cement-heavy arm to tap the
screen of my phone. "Mom, it's
four thirty. Patrol isn't until five."
"You slow us down half an hour," she says,
"so we leave half an hour earlier.
Come on, Lo has a coffee-shake
thingy for you. Lots of protein, but,
fair warning, it's very chalky."

Midafternoon, my dad has two yoga
mats already set up under the pergola
in our backyard. He's utterly
obsessed with perfecting his
headstands right now, but he
walks me through a session of vinyasa.
The synchronization of breathing
and movement is supposed
to help center me when I get anxious.

Face mushed against the curve of
Kyle's shoulder as we wait on the yellow
picnic benches outside of Sonic, I fall
asleep for a second or two. Kyle's eyebrows
stay drawn together, even after I tell
him that a Butterfinger-and-banana

milkshake will pick me
right up. I hide the rest of
my yawns in a closed-lip smile.

                    Mom and Tía Lo flank me as we
                        run in unison up Pine Street.
                    Lo stuffs a retractable sword down the
                back of my sports bra to keep my posture up.
            The pink plastic handle chafes against my spine.
                    "See, Anita?" Lo says to Mom smugly.
                            "Now if she slouches,
                    she'll hit the push button and stab herself
                            in the butt. Good motivation.
            Remember this for your scouts, too, Miss Prue."

Sparring with my mother in the backyard.
It's been years since I fought anyone, much
less faced the lightning-fast reflexes of
Dr. Anita Silva-Perry. I'm so rusty that
I barely register the arc of her roundhouse
kick before the grass rises to meet my
face. Mom appears above me, a confused
wrinkle between her brows. "Get up, scout.
Weren't you ready?" I spit out a clod of dirt.
"I thought I was."

More *Bake Off.* Does Paul Hollywood
have to be so withholding with his praise?

Chancho spots me as I walk across the
monkey bars at the playground. Jaxon and some
neighborhood kids are doing slide races
behind us while I check my balance, do
my best to channel Simone Biles, and front-tuck.
"Like a seven-point-five," Chancho
says from the ground.
"Weak landing."

Shaking and sweating, I duck down
behind a picket fence,
pretending to stretch while Mom and Tía Lo
take down a large black-eyed Scranch in
the street. Its hard-shell legs scratch against
the asphalt as Mom's whip sword pulls them
toward her. The grub thrashes side to side,
all three of its mouths gnashing and snarling.
Tía Lo's Wolverine claws shoot out of her
weighted jogging gloves and into the Scranch's
soft underbelly. It *poof*s, and I can breathe
again. "She didn't even reach for it,"
Tía Lo sighs as I leave my hiding spot.
"Sword was never her weapon," Mom assures her.

I'm standing at the kitchen counter, brewing my
fourteenth cup of practice tea in the last two hours.
The bitter scent of tannins is starting
to turn my stomach.
"You're oversteeping it," Mom chides. "Tea is delicate,
Prudence. You can't brew the Tea of Seeing with
this heavy hand. It'll be undrinkably bitter. It's dried
grub material. It's liable to disintegrate
with too much force."
"Dried grubs?" I ask, looking up from the electric
kettle. For once, I'm glad I was born with the Sight.
"What's in the Tea of Forgetting?"
"Probably Lipton," she sniffs. "Try again."

Armed with a pair of practice knitting needles,
I attack the punching bag hung up in the garage.
Jab, jab, cross, knee. Sweat runs down my face,
slipping into the groove of the scar on my arm
and dripping off the jangling charms on my wrist.
A smile creeps over my face.
This I was always good at.

A montage within a montage: Dad brings home
vase after vase of flowers

from work, setting them on the dining room table
while Mom shakes her head and frowns deeply at
them. Daisies. Sunflowers. Peach roses.
"They're pretty," Mom says. "But they aren't perfect."
"They're good enough for me," I say, shoving all the
flowers together into an overflowing vase. "They'll be
good enough for my scouts."

Tía Lo gives me the key to her china hutch,
pressing it hard into the palm of my hand
like she's bequeathing riches upon me.
I attempt to match her gravitas as
the door hinges screech open
and I'm staring down a dozen different tea sets.
Peter Rabbit, polka dots, blue willow, English roses.
I reach out, my fingers brushing over a teapot
the same shade of yellow as Abuela Ramona's
old hunting ax. Fiestaware Marigold.
"This one."

Mom and I spar in the backyard again,
sweating in the late-afternoon sun. High block,
arm bar, low block. I swing around with
a low kick that knocks her off-balance
enough to make her smile. Before I have

a chance to be too proud of myself,
she scorpion-kicks me to the ground.

Crowded together in Kyle's shedroom,
the Criminal Element is all together
for the first time since the start of
summer vacation. Paul wipes away a tear, and
Chancho gives an amen church-nod as the
Beast roars to her feet,
shouting, "Fuck yeah, Nadiya!"
The projector screen flicks back
to the Netflix menu.
"You were right, babe,"
Kyle says, reaching for the
Xbox controller.
"*Great British Bake Off* was fucking dope.
You guys want to start another season?"
I check my phone and sigh at the time.
"I can't. I have to be up early
tomorrow. For a scout thing."

6

The precise ingredients of the Tea of Seeing
cannot be shared. However, it should be
noted that the key can cause a reaction in
the body similar to that caused by tree nuts.
It's wise to have an EpiPen on hand.

—THE LADYBIRD HANDBOOK

After a week of preparation, the day of my first meeting has arrived.

Half an hour before I'm supposed to start initiating Avi and Kelsey, a FedEx box with my name on it lands on the welcome mat. When I open it, I find a matte white binder with DAME PRUDENCE PERRY emblazoned on the front. It's a personalized day planner that comes with a variety of washi tape and pens, so, duh, it's from my sister. I'm a second away from making fun of it before I crack it open and see that it has a pad of premade checklists for Ladybird meetings. Just one of these could consolidate, like, thirty of the to-do lists on my phone.

Sometimes Paz is so organized, I swear it's basically telepathy.

I send her a quick thank-you message while standing in the foyer. Instantly, my phone lights up with an invitation to video chat. I swipe to answer.

"Just text back like a normal person," I say, dumping the empty FedEx box in the recycling bin in the kitchen. I turn the camera to survey every surface covered in tea-party supplies. "It's sort of a busy day here, you know."

Paz shoves her whole face into the frame, trying to peer over the edge of my phone case. Her newly short hair flops coolly over one eye. She insists that short hair is her rite of passage as a college queer. I say she's a freaking copycat.

Paz clicks her tongue. "Where are your gloves?"

My shoulders sag as I finish scanning my body with the phone like it's a metal detector wand. "I'll put them on before the girls get here. I don't want to stain them while I set up."

"The gloves are a symbol of your ability to work with clean precision, Prudence," Paz says. Her eyebrows lift into two perfect parentheses of judgment. Thankfully, she sees how much she looks like Mom in her camera and transforms the wince into a trying-too-hard smile. "I'm so sorry I'm missing your very first initiation ceremony. You're going to do great."

"Technically, it's not my first," I remind her. "But hopefully today is more fun than watching Gabby Colucci throw up in a peppermint plant."

"It's the first time you're the one doing the initiating! We all start with tutor standing you know," Paz says, her cheer striking a minor key against my thoughts. "Are you nervous? Excited?"

"Anxious and depressed as always. I'm gonna drink nasty tea with our baby cousin and my boyfriend's sister," I say. My charm bracelet rattles nervously. I hardly notice the weight of it, but the noise keeps making me jump. "Then I'm gonna read them a weird old story about how reality is a lie."

Paz rolls her eyes. "That is not the moral of the Ladybird chronicle. It's about the value of sisterhood and the triumph of the American spirit."

"Don't forget the part where men are trash."

"I would never." She beams at me, all teeth. "It's my favorite part."

"It's a dream come true, Paz. I've self-actualized into a substitute teacher." I pick up a stack of appetizer plates from the kitchen island before nudging open the French doors. The entire right side of the yard is our giant redwood pergola. In front of each thick post is a huge pot of Ladybird brand Pippy-Mint, of course. Where Dad's yoga mat normally goes, I've pulled out the long wooden table and inserted the extra leaf that Mom bought when Paz's first circle expanded to eight scouts.

"Has anyone ever, like, really flipped out during an

initiation ceremony? Mom insisted that I use the pergola for my meetings to be close to the mint planters, but what if Kelsey hops the fence? Do you think I need to order a dose of the Tea of Forgetting? Just in case?"

I do my best to say the words like they haven't been charging through my head nonstop since the Bretts left the forbidden room. The Tea of Forgetting is a real thing. A purchasable fix. A path into a completely different way of being. There's only one reference to it in the Handbook— mentioning its invention as a direct reaction to a mass hysteria twenty-five years ago caused by a school water supply being polluted with grubic material that gave everyone— students and staff—the Sight. But in my limited access to the Dame features on the Ladybird app, all I've been able to see is an unclickable picture of it in the merch store. The packaging is as lavender as Scranch legs.

Paz doesn't take the bait. "If a scout can outrun you, then you definitely need to talk her into recruitment, not mind-wiping," she says, laughing. "You'll do fine. Did you get a visual aid of a grub? It's so much harder without an example."

Kicking chairs out of my way, I set an appetizer plate at each setting. "Chancho caught me something small with one of Tía Lo's house traps."

"*Chancho* caught?" Paz echoes, practically pearl-clutching. Not that Paz would ever wear jewelry that didn't come from the Ladybird merch store. She's wearing her silver Dame brooch in her driver's license photo.

"Prudence, you're not just a scout now. You're in charge. You can't shirk your responsibilities by handing them off to Chancho."

"I didn't shirk," I lie. "He already had a trap out because a tiny Nock Jaw was keeping Jaxon up at night—I guess he's been really excited about summer vacation. And why waste a pre-caught grub? It's a known quantity. I love a known quantity."

"No, your anxiety loves a known quantity. There should be a medium-sized trap in the garage. Just go pop a scream in the chamber and—"

"Okay, well, thanks for checking in, but I gotta go," I say, dropping the last appetizer plate with too much force. It rattles against one of three vases of flowers. "Time to unplug my boyfriend's sister from the Matrix!"

"Don't say it like that either—"

I hang up and tuck the phone in the pocket of my dress. There's no way I'm going into the garage and digging out one of Mom's grub traps. The Handbook is very clear about purposefully pulling through aberrations. You can put a scream in the chamber, but you can't choose what you bring through. What if I put too much mustard into my scream and the intensity of my anxiety summons a Carnivore?

Honestly, I don't know if I can do any of this. Giving Kelsey the Sight. Teaching combat basics. Facing all of my nightmares in front of tweens. What if I fuck it all up? What if one of them gets hurt? What if *I* do?

At least today is low risk. It's just tea and a video.

Opening my handy new planner almost makes me feel bad for hanging up on Paz. I fill in the first checklist on the pad. Sandwiches chilling in the fridge? Check. Comforting organic treats from dad's store? Check. Teacups adorably mismatched, flowers fluffed, brand-new Handbooks waiting for promissory signatures from clear-eyed scouts. All check. Complimentary knitting needles and short white gloves wait at both place settings.

Leaving only the serving-platter-sized gap in the tablescape where my visual aid is supposed to sit next to my now-empty teapot.

Since I can't make the tea until Avi and Kelsey get here, I take out my phone and message Chancho again.

ME: Where is my grub? 🐷

CHANCHO: It's handled calm down dp.

ME: And what is dp? Urban dictionary made me lysol my eyes.

CHANCHO: Avi's gonna bring it. Paul and the Beast came through. Might try to buy some fireworks.

ME: You're with the Criminal Element???

CHANCHO: You and Kyle are working sorry.

CHANCHO: dp = dame prue duh.

ME: OMFG I hate you. My meeting is done by 2:30!

At 1:30 on the dot, Avianna comes through the back gate, hugging a plastic grub cage the size of a lizard terrarium. Like Chancho, she has her father's deep brown coloring and glossy black hair. But where Chancho's face is wide and goofy, Avi's is all impish angles. Even her ears are slightly pointed. Tía Lo dressed her like an Elf on the Shelf every Christmas for the first ten years of her life.

"Happy Initiation Day, Dame Prue!" Avi says with a titter slightly too practiced to be sincere. My baby cousin has that YouTuber enthusiasm, the unflinching attention of someone breaking a fourth wall that isn't there. I do sort of worry that under the intense tutelage of Faithlynn and the other senior scouts, Avi may give up blinking altogether.

I shake the thought away. What happens to the scouts after I leave again is none of my business. If they want to become Ladybird drones like Faithlynn, then let them. For now, I'm just like Chancho—a mediocre babysitter for summer. There's no way he's at home stressing that his choices are going to ruin Jaxon for life. If either of them remembers to drink water once all summer, it will be a miracle. I just have to keep Avi and Kelsey alive and informed for a few weeks. Totally doable.

"Happy Initiation Day, Avi," I respond, even though it isn't a real saying. Recruitment is too important to be cheerful about. For some reason, endless gardening and charity work just doesn't have huge mass appeal. "Thanks for bringing the visual aid. Will you set it on the table?"

"And don't look directly at it until everyone has finished their tea, I know," she finishes for me, her flat chest puffed out proud. Her dress is a confection of rainbow sequins and tulle. "My mom told me that at *her* initiation ceremony, one of the scouts kept tapping on the glass and it made the grub inside go totally cuckoo-bananas."

"Yeah, grubs don't love being taunted," I say, distracted as the doorbell rings. I push Avi toward the table. "Here, pick a seat. And a Handbook!"

"Holy birdshit," she breathes, not quite getting the phrasing right. She scoops up the nearest Handbook and presses the top of the leather cover directly into her nostrils. She snorts up the smell. "I can't believe it's really happening! I'm finally, *finally* an actual Ladybird! And you are finally, *finally*, FINALLY back in the sisterhood! Thanks to me!"

"Uh-huh," I say with all those *finally*s echoing threateningly through my head. "Just don't touch anything else until I bring the tea!"

I scurry inside, flicking on the electric tea kettle as I pass through the kitchen on my way to the front door.

Kelsey Goodwin is standing on the front step in a straw hat. Beyond her, I can see, with a sinking disappointment, that her mom is waving goodbye from the family van. Kyle must have gotten dropped off at work first.

"Hi, Prudence," Kelsey says. The clear brackets of her braces crowd her lips away from her teeth, making her smile extra wide. She holds up a canvas tote from the store my dad works at, Turnip and Beet It Greengrocers. "I made cookie-brownies. I hope that's okay. Your aunt told my mom that Ladybird Scouts are big on baking."

"The biggest," I answer, ushering her inside.

Like her brother, Kelsey has light brown curls. Hers are super long, like when Taylor Swift was still writing country music. I recognize her blue gingham dress from spending Easter dinner with her family, which, for some reason, makes my nerves triple. Other Dames probably don't spend time canoodling during egg hunts with the brothers of their recruits. Kelsey knowing that Kyle and I got in trouble for making out in front of their little cousins totally diminishes my authority.

"Avi's already outside," I say, aiming her toward the French doors. "I'm going to pour our special tea and follow you out. Here, take the sandwiches and help yourselves."

Out of the fridge, the cucumber-butter sandwich plate is ice cold as I thrust it into Kelsey's hands. Undertaking this as a mission of utmost importance, she nods gravely, sucks the spit from her braces, and leaves.

Alone in the empty kitchen, I take a deep breath. The Tea of Seeing comes as a single-serving tea bag in a pink wrapper. The wrapper is stamped with the Ladybird crest and tree-nut-allergy warning.

It brews up blush pink. I bet that's what convinced the first scout to drink dried-and-boiled grub flesh. It's the exact strawberry-shortcake shade of imaginary tea-party tea. Before Headquarters streamlined the process into a packaged tea, scouts hoping to gain the lasting ability to See grubs used to eat part of their first kill—and hope it wasn't enough to kill them back.

Three minutes later, the egg timer pings. I rip out the tea bag and throw it aside. It lands on the cutting board among the cucumber rinds.

It's time to kick into high gear. I have to serve the tea quickly. According to Tía Lo, the Tea of Seeing gets sort of sludgy at room temperature.

Carrying the hot teapot into the even hotter backyard, I do my best not to feel like this whole thing is a huge mistake. Avi might be destined to wield a Ladybird weapon, but giving Kelsey the Sight could ruin her. She could change from a sweet, slurpy kid into a vicious monster killer. Or she could turn into someone like me, so scarred by what she knows that she can never feel safe again.

No, I wouldn't let that happen. The Tea of Forgetting could save us both.

I try to imagine myself three months from now, after I've Forgotten. Never having to wear little white gloves again. Never worrying that every twist in my stomach is trying to alert me to imminent danger. Not having to watch the Nock Jaw on the center of the table circle its cage, looking for a way to get out and eat Avi's excitement.

"Hello, sister scouts!" I say as I take my place at the head of the table. In trying not to look freaked out, I am definitely freaking Kelsey out. I dial down my smile from youth-pastor to cheerleader. "Have you guys met before?"

"Once," Avi says, squinting across the table at Kelsey. "My mom gave you and your brother a ride home from school when it was flooding."

"Oh yeah, in the Escalade, right?" Kelsey says.

"That's us," Avi says, strangely proud. "And, obviously, we're both sisters of the Criminal Element."

"Not as cool as an Escalade," Kelsey says. Then, remembering who I am, she gives a little gasp. "No offense."

"None taken," I say. The Criminal Element is definitely not a group to look up to. They're mine and I wouldn't trade them for the world, but I also wouldn't want the little sisters around all of the time. They're better off not knowing how to use an escape ladder to circumvent security cameras or how to smoke weed out of an apple. So, instead, I'll teach them how to manage other people's emotional monsters.

"Welcome to your official Ladybird initiation ceremony," I say, with a slight tremor in my voice. Avi and Kelsey look so young, watching me with wide-eyed trust that makes me want to tip the table over and send them home. But I can't. I have to see this through. "Today's tea is a special blend that we only drink during this ceremony. So, if it's nasty, choke it down hella fast, then eat all these cucumber sandwiches and the brownies Kelsey brought to cover the taste."

"Cookie-brownies," Kelsey corrects, holding the Tupperware across the table to Avi. "They're brownies with chocolate chip cookies in the middle?"

"Oh my gosh," Avi says, her eyes growing three sizes as she takes one of the cookie-brownies. "Amazing times amazing equals *holy cow*. Give this girl a Baking charm already!"

Kelsey flushes a pleased pink and offers me one, which of course I accept. Avi is not overselling the treat. It is a gooey-chocolatey dream that gives me the boost I need to push on. "First of all, nothing I put on the table is as good as the cookie-brownies, so don't feel bad if you don't want a cucumber sandwich. Second, before you can be initiated on Initiation Day, you have to learn the Ladybird chronicle. It's the first page of the Handbook, even before the signature page. I'm gonna read it to you now, so you can follow along or not. Just try not to get ahead of me."

I wait for the creak of covers opening and the clink of plates set aside to settle. And then, over the winced reactions to the Tea of Seeing's bitterness, followed by cookie-brownie gobbling, I read aloud the first story any legacy scout hears as a baby. The Ladybird chronicle:

When America was counting itself in colonies, before the roads were paved, people often went missing.

Survival was more of a goal than a guarantee, so life
went on and grass grew over empty graves. But a
girl asked: What is feeding on my community?

She was told it was nothing because it could not be seen.

Healthy crops died. Whole communities disappeared.
Men blamed sorcery, curses, and kings. But a girl
asked: How do we stop from being consumed?

She was told it was ridiculous because it could not be true.

The country swelled, its growth measured in acres
and bodies. Each new territory brought new wars,
new vegetation, new horrors. And when the things
came out of the dark—things that fed on breath
and being—a girl asked: How do we fight back?

She was told it was hopeless because the
things could not be conquered.

The whispers of girls have a way of becoming a roar.
Little birds took scraps of information from town to
town, state to state. Friends became sisters-in-arms.

Together, the silenced girls could
see what hid in plain Sight.

Together, the silenced girls studied the imaginary.

Together, the silenced girls fought back against

the creatures that steal energy and breath.

Today, you walk across the threshold into womanhood.
Today, you learn the truth: It has always been the
job of women to keep our communities safe.

You have known mulligrubs, even if you haven't
Seen them before today. You know the sharp teeth
of fear at the nape of your neck. You know the
surety of not being alone in an empty room. You've
heard wind where there shouldn't be, and you've
felt your mood plummet without warning.

You have been hunted, but today you become the hunter.

In myths, they called us heroes. In the dark
times, they called us witches. Now they call
us scouts and smile when they see us.

But the truth remains: We See what they don't. And
that means we have to save them from themselves.

A shiver runs down my spine. No matter how many times I hear it, the Ladybird chronicle always manages to make me remember why my family is so proud of our legacy status. Over the centuries, scouts have saved countless lives, entire towns, putting their own safety second to protect the un-Sighted. The burden of it is overwhelming.

"If you think about it," I say, looking up with a nervous glance, "this isn't the first time you've found out that the world is different from how you knew it to be. It's just the most recent time. The tooth fairy isn't real, but mulligrubs are. And it is the Ladybirds' job to protect people from them and the knowledge of them. Now that you've drunk this tea, you will be able to fully See for the first time." I pause and clear my throat. Avi has a smile full of brownie, and Kelsey looks queasy. I wish, more than anything, that I could strip off my gloves and pour the sweat out. It's way too hot to choke down any more of this awful tea. The back of my throat tastes the way fish food smells. "Kelsey, can you, um, See what's in the plastic box?"

Part of me hopes that she says no. That the tea hasn't worked and I can just send her home to ask her brother why his girlfriend is such a weirdo.

Kelsey's nose crinkles as she seems to force her head toward the cage next to her Tupperware still half full of brownies. "The slimy pink lizard thing?"

The Nock Jaw in the cage presses itself against the plastic, its black Beanie Boo eyes fixed on Avi. The initiation ceremony is like Christmas morning for a legacy scout, and Nock Jaws come to our plane to feed on joy.

"It's not a lizard, actually," Avi says, unnecessarily holding her pinkie out as she takes the tiniest sip of her Seeing tea. "It's a Nock Jaw, a type of mulligrub monster. It's our sworn duty to banish them."

Stiff-shouldered with disbelief, Kelsey turns in her chair to look at me.

"You haven't sworn to anything yet," I'm quick to assure her. "There's still time for you to decide whether or not you want to. Let's go into the air-conditioning to watch the video about how the whole secret-society thing works. You've had enough of the bad tea. Fill your plates with cookie-brownies and any other snacks you want. Do either of you want some milk? Or a sparkling water?"

"Is it La Croix or Pellegrino?" Avi asks, suddenly a fancy water expert as she gathers her belongings, her hands clumsy in white gloves. "Can I bring my Handbook inside?"

I shake my head at her. "Leave it there until it's time to sign it. We'll come back outside after the video, and"—I glance at Kelsey—"if you *decide* to sign, we'll do it after I show you how we actually get rid of the grubs."

"It is a little warm out here," Kelsey says. She gets to her feet in a daze. "I would like a La Croix."

"You are in luck because that is what we have," I say with a sigh of relief. "Let's all go inside."

☦ ☦ ☦

The introductory video hasn't changed since I left the scouts. The current CEO stands in the Barbie Dream-House lobby of Ladybird Headquarters in Redding, Connecticut, explaining the dry history of the scouts. From the *Ladybird Leaflet*—the first American women's magazine, with its Helpful Hints section featuring the first "cures for common mulligrubs"—to the 1803 founding of the scouts by Kitty Crosby-Fowler to the modern idea of the peaceable, prudent, and public-minded girl with a state-of-the-art stealth weapon in the color of her choosing—as long as she wants pink, purple, or teal.

Leaving Avi and Kelsey in front of the living room TV, sipping their pamplemousse La Croixs and watching whip sword tricks that my mom once called "ineffectively showy," I slip into the hallway and tug off my right glove with my teeth so I can unlock my phone.

> **KYLE:** Bummed I didn't get to see you before work. Is my sister being annoying? If she slurps her braces too much, you are totally allowed to tell her to STFU.

> **ME:** I definitely cannot on my very first day of tutoring tell a prospective scout to shut up! 😄 For sure that is not in the Ladybird Handbook, babe. And your sister is perfectly nice!

I glance back at the living room, hoping that I haven't scarred Kelsey irreparably. Scouts have been crossing the threshold into Seeing grubs for hundreds of years. That should make it feel safer than it does.

Outside, I can hear the muffled voices of fun being had. If Chancho has invited the Criminal Element to have a party on the other side of the cedar gate, I will have no choice but to actually kick his ass.

> **ME:** Everyone is hanging out without us today. 😔

> **KYLE:** Yeah, they said they might come by here later.

ME. It's soooooo not fair that we're grounded and they aren't.

KYLE: They're grasshoppers. We're ants.

A selfie comes through—Kyle smoldering at me from behind the shoe rental counter at the bowling alley, his sandy brown curls hanging over his ears and eyebrows. The yellow collar of his work polo is flipped up, mock-cool. The name tag is crooked and not his.

KYLE: And they'll never have uniforms this sexy.

I open my phone camera and snap a picture of myself, my one gloved hand pressed to my face so Kyle can see the full ridiculousness of tea-party full dress.

"Prue?" Avi calls from the other room as I take a second selfie with wider eyes and send it to Kyle.

ME: I see your name tag and raise you one summertime wool hat.

Avi tries a second time with a more official-sounding "Dame Prudence?"

I mirror her formal tone as I pull my right glove back on. "Yes, Avianna?"

In the backyard, something crashes. I race back into the living room, where the introductory video is playing to no audience. Avi and Kelsey stand at the window, eyes glued to the unfolding chaos outside. I rush over and look outside.

"Monster!" Paul shrieks as he, Chancho, and Sasha run away from the pergola in three directions, like buzzards deserting a carcass. Two teacups full of the Tea of Seeing smash against the pavement.

The Nock Jaw that I left safely trapped moments ago now explodes out of its cage—my little visual aid growing in an instant to a full-sized Critter that tears apart my tea party.

Oh right, I remember too late. *Perfect keeps a secret. Almost spills the beans.*

7

Fear can only be conquered through action.

—THE LADYBIRD HANDBOOK

"**B**ut in the Handbook, Nock Jaws are pink! And cute!" Avianna protests as she and Kelsey run out of the house behind me.

"Artistic license," I say. With a grub the size of a bull mastiff running rampant through my yard, there isn't time to explain the Sanrio-fication of the Ladybird learning tools. The Handbook also shows all three mouths of a Scranch smiling. The truth is just too unsettling for flash cards.

As we spill out onto the backyard, I see that the Criminal Element has scattered to the far corners of the backyard. Chancho is hiding behind the pergola. Sasha the Beast is sitting atop the air-conditioning box attached to the house. Paul is twisted against the back fence, his hands looped over the top like he's considering climbing over but can't take his eyes off the monster in the middle of the yard.

The escaped Nock Jaw is penned in by the stainless-steel tubs of Pippy-Mint that line the fence. Paz used them for training exercises, pulling them in tight around a trap before she baited the cage. She's so much better at this than I ever could be.

The color and texture of a human tongue, Nock Jaws are vaguely newt-shaped, save for their hinged mouths. This one opens its namesake jaw to taste the new feelings on the wind, its whole head flopping backward. Its black eyes stare upside down at its own tail from behind a mouth as wide as an umbrella. Full of needle teeth.

At last, Kelsey screams.

"It's okay," Avi says, setting a hand on the older girl's shoulder and rubbing a consoling circle. "It has black eyes, which means it can only eat your happiness. You're probably too scared to be happy, right?"

This confuses Kelsey enough to quiet her for a second, and I keep racing toward the pergola. I can only hope that Avi doesn't point out that getting too scared could also tempt a whole different type of grub into existence. The last thing I need is a Frightworm on top of everything else.

Chancho ducks behind a mint planter. Seeing me, he panics—I can tell because two Tizzy Lice crawl over his shoes. "Ay, prima, it was an honest mistake! We got thirsty!"

I shove him with both hands, hard enough to make

him stagger backward. "How is dosing our friends and giving away the *only* secret you've ever had to keep an honest mistake?"

He pops off his hat, compulsively combing his fingers through his hair as though my shove could have any effect on the hard swoop. "You said you'd be done soon. We were just going to wait back here to see if you wanted to go bowling since Kyle's working—"

"Is someone gonna do something about this floppy-head demon?" Paul asks in a slightly higher voice than normal as he slides down the fence toward the cedar gate. His lemon-yellow shoes stomp and swat his nearest Tizzy Louse, which resiliently climb his legs like Everest. "Or the little furry demons?"

Avi tucks her chin back, deeply insulted. "Excuse me, my brother's friend Paul," she calls from across the yard. "They are *not* demons. They're an interdimensional aberrant species called mulligrubs. It's a colonial word for 'stomach complaint.'"

"Avianna!" I clap at her. "Please stop revealing scout secrets!"

She immediately points at her brother. "Chancho's the one who gave them the tea!"

Chancho throws up his hands. "You guys left it out! Who leaves out a whole tea party with secret tea and muffins!"

"Apple bran muffins!" I gag. "Your mom made me make

them! I was going to feed them to the ducks later."

"Look, there's no way that what we just drank was tea. That was in the top three nastiest things I've ever chugged, easy," Sasha says. She peers over the top of her ever-present round sunglasses to examine the screen of her phone. "None of this is showing up on my camera. I have one thousand pictures of Paul running from his own shadow here."

Paul gives a full-body shudder as Tizzy Lice multiply around his ankles. "These little shits are *not* my shadow. Hey, Prue, can these colonial-stomach-complaint monsters kill us?"

"God, let's hope so," Sasha says. Tucking her phone into the back pocket of her jeans, she lifts her arms over her head and drinks in the sun. "Today was shaping up to be a fucking snooze."

"These can't hurt you," I say evasively. "And that floppy-headed demon is also a harmless Critter." For now. I eye it carefully as it bounds in circles around us, looking for any scraps of joy. The last thing I need is the Nock Jaw turning Carnivore because no one is having enough fun to keep it satiated. If this thing goes White-Eyes, we're all dead.

Chancho clears his throat, deepening his voice as he says, "Everyone just grab a mint leaf and—"

"No, stop talking before you get someone hurt," I interrupt. "The Nock Jaw is too big for a tag. You'll just piss it off and get drained. Everyone just get behind a mint planter." When no one immediately moves, I shoo them with both hands. "Now!"

One big problem has manageable pieces. My psychiatrist's voice floats through my head. *You can only move one step at a time.*

Step one: Remove gloves.

Step two: Retrieve knitting needles.

Step three: Fight a yard full of multiplying monsters.

In the tea-party wreckage, under the cracked saucers and scattered sugar cubes, I find a pair of the introductory knitting needles. They shine with the peppermint oil I rubbed into the wood this morning.

In reaction to being fed on, the human body starts sending out cortisol, a stress hormone. To alert you to start running. *Get out of here, idiot! Something you can't See is going to gobble you up!*

Ladybirds are supposed to spit out that anxiety and unsheathe an ax.

Ever since Molly got killed, I get sucked under every time. Even with the meds in my system, my anxiety spikes. I am scared that I will fail. I am scared that the grubs will feed and grow and escape. I am scared that my friends won't be able to sleep at night, having Seen what I have always been able to See.

Head over heart, I square my stance and let my panic rise to a crescendo.

I am a fear feast, the most delicious scaredy-cat in the

yard. The grubs all turn to face me.

Feeding on me, the Tizzy Lice surge forward, growing larger and larger. They're faster in a group, pushing one another forward in their figure eights. They're easier to fight at Critter size, a flock of fuzzy pumpkins that launch themselves at me. Wielding a knitting needle in each hand, I slash at the grubs in arcs and uppercuts.

The Nock Jaw wriggles its tail, its nubby papillae-covered body snaking through the grass toward me. I can't tell if it wants the Tizzy Lice or me. I don't give it a chance to choose.

I switch from a firm grip to a baton twirl, spinning the needles over my fingers, whipping through the last of the Tizzy Lice. For the first time since middle school, I find myself wishing I had my daggers. The wooden needles are clunky and hard on my wrists.

The Nock Jaw jitters side to side, its head flopping back to suck in a deep breath of my satisfaction. I'm too happy that the Tizzy Lice are gone and it's too late to try not to be. The grub's long three-toed feet dig trenches into the grass as it readies to pounce.

I drop down to the Nock Jaw fight stance, a low lunge at eye level with the grub. It's a little awkward in my tea dress, but I've fought in worse. At our first regional club-house meetup, my old circle competed in matching tutus against a mobile Dreary Blight. The first and only time we made the mistake of trying to fight cute. What a mess.

Tulle and sadness dust everywhere.

The Nock Jaw leaps at me. One leg catches my shoulder, clammy and rough, knocking me sideways but not off-balance. As it brandishes its needle teeth at me, I swing both knitting needles up into its soft underbelly. It pops—soap-bubble iridescent.

The charms on my bracelet chime softly in the breeze of reality closing.

The yard is quiet. Grub-less. Only bug-eyed friends and cousins remain.

Breathe through it. I think of my dad, stretched across a yoga mat that smells like the recycled rubber of a dozen scuba suits. *Feelings are a wave, munchkin. You are the ocean. Waves crest. The ocean is.*

I swallow the last of my adrenaline. The knitting needles clatter together in the grass.

Across the yard, Paul stares at me with true Sight. "How did you know what—"

"It's what she was born to do," Chancho says, with a dopey proud smile.

"No, it's not," I say automatically, but I feel relief coursing through me.

I haven't lost all of my skills. I am strong enough to protect my scouts and my friends. I adjust my sleeves, worrying the seams between my thumb and forefinger. "I'm retired. I just need to pass on my skills."

"Your skills . . ." Sasha rubs her chin thoughtfully with

black Sharpie fingernails. "For killing demons?"

Avi wags a reproachful finger. "They're mulligrubs. Interdimensional aberrations, if you're being fancy. But *never* demons."

"Why is that?" the Beast asks. "They seemed pretty demonic."

Paul nods. "All those sharp-ass teeth were definitely demonish."

"*Demon* has an 'alienating religious connotation' that Headquarters prefers we avoid," I quote with a sigh. "Scouts are pest control. Not priests."

"The brochure is all about giving back to the community," Kelsey says. Her knees wobble as she shies toward Avi and loudly whispers, "When I got here, you said Ladybirds mostly just give people food before tests."

Avi nonchalantly dusts off her gloves. "Yeah, but there has to be stuff to do when it's not test season."

"Sign me up. Count me in. Whatever. Enlist me in your girl army, Prudence Perry," declares the Beast.

She pushes herself off the wall and tromps over to clap me on the shoulder, towering over me. Dressed, as usual, in all black, with spiderwebs and coffins drawn on her knuckles, Sasha the Beast is a human dark cloud. "You know, when you said you were gonna do Girl Scout shit all summer, it sounded hella boring. You should really lead with the part about fighting giant, man-eating monsters."

I drag my hands down the sides of my face. Mom and

Tía Lo are going to murder me for leaving the tea party unattended. "We can't. It's a huge, multigenerational secret."

"Everyone leads with a cool, huge secret," the Beast scoffs. Proudly, she taps her collarbone and jerks up her chin. "That's why everyone knows that I lit the outlets on fire."

"Not the entire outlets," I correct quickly, for the sake of the younger kids. "Just Old Navy."

It immediately backfires. Kelsey recoils like the Beast punted her puppy. "You did *what*?"

"Hold up," Paul says. He grips his frohawk with both hands and bends in half, like he's admiring his knees. I've only seen him do this when he's not trying to puke after track meets or parties. "Can we backtrack to the monsters that we just saw? I need so much more information."

"Could we start with *what* the actual heck?" Kelsey says, sucking the spit off her braces in two quick slurps. "Then could we talk about *how* in the actual heck?"

I close my eyes for a second and wonder what my sister would do if she were capable of screwing something up this hard. Paz would have had a contingency plan. A Power-Point. Or at least a muffin basket.

Everything is ruined before it even began. I can already picture my mom's expression. I bet no one has ever initiated too many people before—one of them a cisgender boy. I will go down in Ladybird history as the worst Dame of all time, supplanting the Dame whose circle let their mint die and had no way to banish the grubs that set off the New Jersey mass hysteria of 1972. Or the one in Denver whose circle got caught giving out Girl Scout cookies instead of a nutritious breakfast during the SATs.

If I don't fix this, Chancho and I will both end up at North Hills High with Faithlynn and the senior scouts. Or farther. Accidentally giving the Sight to non-scouts is probably shipped-off-to-relatives-I've-never-met bad. First things first, I need everyone to calm down before they start telling the internet about all the cool monsters they discovered.

"Why don't we go for a walk? Everyone put some peppermint in your pocket," I say. I tuck the knitting needles into the sleeves of my dress and glance back at the abandoned tea party. "And bring what's left of the snacks."

8

Public service is the act of beautifying
your community from within.

—THE LADYBIRD HANDBOOK

Leaving my backyard behind, I lead the group up the
street—Paul, Chancho, and Sasha the Beast are grown-up
tall behind the initiate scouts, making the six of us look
like a well-supervised walking field trip. Or a mismatched
assortment of middle schoolers and freaked-out stoners.
Both are accurate.

"Are we even safe to be walking around tripping on this
tea?" Paul asks, swinging his head to look at the group. He
splays his hands against his chest. "I'm not trying to be the
Black kid caught spun out on space tea with a bunch of
little goody-goody scouts."

"You're not on drugs, Paul," I assure him, handing over
the container of cookie-brownies to soothe him. "I mean,
no more so than usual. The effects of the Tea of Seeing are
permanent unless you petition Ladybird Headquarters for
a counterdose."

"We're going to start Seeing monsters wherever we go?" Sasha asks with her hungriest smile. All of the Beast's joyful expressions unfurl like the Grinch's. "Is it always the same kind? Are there more?"

I might as well just get the first lesson in the Handbook out of the way. If we find an entry point, experience grubdrain, and just generally face the sweaty tedium of a midday patrol, I bet by the end of the walk I can get Avi her Identification charm and everyone else will agree to Forget this as soon as possible. Nobody wants to live in a world full of emotional monsters. They just don't know that they already do.

"Different societies have different names for their local monsters," I say. "All types of ghosts, aliens, eldritch gods—"

"Yōkai, rompo, chimera," Chancho adds. "Mongolian death worms."

"Toilet alligators," Avianna says.

"Ladybird Headquarters assumes that some of them, at least, are different kinds of mulligrubs responding to different emotional environments."

"Ew," Kelsey says, daintily unwrapping an apple bran muffin. "Does that mean that all the monsters my brother is obsessed with are actually real? Bigfoot and the stupid Mothman and all them?"

"Probably not." I wince, feeling disloyal to Kyle. I would so much rather be making the long walk to see him at the bowling alley than trying to explain the fabric of reality to his sister. "Mulligrubs don't come in humanoid forms. We're just food to them. Not crossbreeding material."

"Don't hump the grubs," Sasha says. "Noted."

I look up at the sky as Kelsey and Avi make identical scandalized squeaks. Even if I had ever in one million years thought she'd agree, the Beast would not have been on my list of potential recruits. Ladybirds are supposed to fit in effortlessly, anywhere. Scouts choose the perfect words to put any stranger at ease, pair it with a smile and sandwich. An eternally helpful hand with a charm bracelet at the wrist.

Sasha the Beast is sort of the opposite of that, always equipped with the least appropriate phrase or the one thought anyone else would keep to themselves. She's an NC-17 human being. And I say this as someone who won't be seventeen until next March.

"You've lived alongside grubs your entire life without knowing it," I tell the assembled group. I pull my hands into my sleeves to hold the knitting needles hidden inside. "Being around grubs is like having the heebie-jeebies. Being scared when you think there's nothing to be scared of. Except now you know there is."

"I refuse to acknowledge that I have ever once felt a heebie or a jeebie," the Beast sneers from the back of the line.

As a born bullshitter, Sasha's a natural skeptic. She used to snort Splenda in the bathroom at school just to see which of our classmates could be trusted not to narc.

"You've felt what it's like to be in an empty room and know you're not alone," I tell her matter-of-factly. The few times I've slept over at her apartment, there have always been entry-point cracks in the walls. The last time I saw her on the phone with her dad, a Scranch clawed at the window the entire time, an inch too far over to make it inside the room. Grubs aren't great at spatial awareness. "You've had the experience of waking up and feeling like there's something weighing down your chest or like there's something under your bed. When, for one instant, you're furious or scared or painfully sad, but the next second you can't remember why. And have you ever felt so much one day that the next day you think you'll never have the energy to have another emotion again?"

The answering silence is uncomfortable. Yet they seem to expect me to go on.

"Grubs have been feeding on your energy forever. And the Ladybirds exist to classify and banish them. The Handbook calls it the 'burden of Sight.' You weren't born into it like some of us, but now you know. You lived in one world, and now you live in a world next to that one. It's sort of like when you're little and you realize that the microscopic world exists."

"The microscopic world isn't scary. The monster world is," Paul says, eating the cucumber slices out of a finger sandwich and tossing the bread in the gutter. "Microscopic things don't want to kill me."

"Diseases do," Avi says, jogging to keep in step beside me. She pushes back the brim of her hat to look at Paul over her shoulder. "And flesh-eating bacteria and some parasites—"

"Someone give this child another cookie-brownie, please," Paul demands, waving a dismissive hand at Avi, who rolls her eyes but slows down enough to accept a treat from the Tupperware the Beast holds out to her.

"Most grubs don't want to kill you," I assure Kelsey directly, and Paul and Sasha indirectly. "Anything with black eyes wants to absorb feelings off you and then move on to absorb feelings off someone else. But white-eyed grubs you have to worry about. They're Carnivorous. Now that you've all had the tea"—I throw a glare at Chancho, who flinches like I showed him the back of my hand—"you'll need to know the difference. At least until we figure out what to do about you being able to See what you shouldn't. Right now, you can all See what other people can't. You'll be able to See grubs feeding on people's emotions. The bigger the feelings, the bigger the grub."

"Yeah," Avi says. "We lure them here with our big, juicy emotions."

"Mulligrubs breed to feed," Chancho says. He nudges Sasha with a conspiratorial smile, trying, as always, to get her attention. "Our grandma used to say that."

"You and I don't share a grandma, Chancho," the Beast says, pretending not to understand and leaping into the street to kick a can.

"Can they eat *any* feelings?" Kelsey sniffs. "If I were literally starving, would they feed on that?"

"Starving isn't one of your core emotions," I say. I jerk my head to motion the group out of the neighborhood, toward the buzzing wall of blooming bougainvillea that hides the next two-lane road from view. "The Handbook categorizes feelings into the five grub types: sad, mad, happy, afraid, apprehensive. Dreary Blight, Scranch, Nock Jaws, Frightworms, Tizzy Lice."

"Afraid and apprehensive are two different things?" Sasha asks, bobbing along beside me in the gutter. The platforms of her shoes pulverize every dead leaf we pass. "Isn't that just scared and scared?"

"Being scared is active. Being apprehensive is more like being scared of being scared. The extra step puts out a different kind of energy to be eaten," I tell her, then turn to Kyle's little sister. "To answer your question, Kelsey, if you were literally starving, depending on why, you would probably be very sad or very angry. Or very scared. Any of those feelings at a high intensity will draw a grub. Or grubs."

At the first stoplight, we fall into a single-file line across the crosswalk. This, more than anything else, makes me feel like a Ladybird. I can't even begin to calculate how many hours my old circle spent practicing walking in the perfect line. Stepping on the same foot at the same time. Fighting in straight lines. Dame Debby demanded aesthetic perfection from us as much as tactical precision.

But I was never the line leader back then. Faithlynn was. Then Jennica, then Gabby. Molly and I brought up the back, making faces at each other while everyone else paid attention.

"Why is it the scouts' job to kill these things?" Kelsey asks. Her gingham skirt and the spiral tips of her curls flounce in step with her natural skip. "Why doesn't the government do something?"

"The government barely cares about survival, let alone happiness," I say. I incline my head, leading everyone left past the dog park. Sometimes there will be entry points here in the decorative lantana hedges. I scan between the purple flowers for signs of disturbance as we pass.

"The government doesn't care about some of us, period," says the Beast.

Can't argue with her there.

There are no signs of entry here, so I walk us farther up the street. There's a fail-safe grub trap within four blocks. "When a grub has white eyes, it means that it's turned Carnivore. It's eaten enough organic material to Root itself here, so it can't just accidentally poof itself away on a mint leaf."

Paul makes a face. "Now, when you say *organic*, do you mean like carrots or—"

"People, mostly," I say. Instead of hearing the bones break in my memory, I do my best to picture the exact illustration in the Handbook, where a Frightworm with white eyes smiles at a lone hiker, its many green legs raised in friendly greeting. In real life, if you can see a Frightworm's undermouth, there is nothing friendly going on. "They can also eat more intelligent animals. Pets, large wildlife. Anything that can feel enough to lure a grub can get eaten. If they get really desperate, they'll eat other grubs."

Cutting through an unpaved alley between small houses with chain-link fences, we turn the corner and arrive suddenly at the front entrance of Goldfields Middle School. Cement-square buildings surrounded by wood-paneled rectangle portables set back from the street beside a grass field eternally confettied with Takis bags and straw wrappers.

"Oh." Kelsey's shoulders roll forward to cover her ears as she withdraws a step. "Is this where we're going? I, like, literally just graduated from eighth grade a week ago."

"Don't rub it in," Avi pouts, crossing her arms over her chest and straining to stand taller than her natural inches. "I haven't even *started* eighth grade yet. Why are we here, Prudence?"

My only hope of convincing the others to take the Tea of Forgetting is to scare them out of wanting the Sight. And this is the most infested place I know of.

"You need to know what grubs look like in the wild," I say. "The easiest place to start is either the happiest place on earth or the worst. What's worse than middle school?"

✝ ✝ ✝

When I went to Goldfields Middle, I was known as one of the pink-haired girls. Anytime I wasn't in class—and sometimes even when I was—I was with my circle. Faithlynn, Jennica, Gabby, Molly, and I used to practice walking formations and running in sync on the soccer field. Whenever we had to focus on pesky things like classwork, Faithlynn would threaten to have her mother—or mine—make the work go away. Any grade we were in was babyish and easy because she'd already done it the year before.

If she had friends her own age, Molly would remind me when Faithlynn got under my skin, *we'd have more scouts. She is too much of a bitch to recruit anyone from her own grade.*

Faithlynn's obsession with nonstop scouting was what led to our discovery of the infestation behind the school. Searching for more space for us to run timed wind sprints, she found an uncleared culmination of middle school woes. Even my sister was impressed when she heard about it. It's not every day scouts find a new source of misery in town.

I stand before the infestation now. The ancient portable classrooms that sit baking in the California sun all day, every day are truly miserable.

I bring the group to a stop behind the line of portables, where the green soccer field is dried into sweet-smelling yellow straw. The buildings—which my mom still calls "temporary classrooms" even though they're older than I am—are the size of train cars, easily scalable with a high-enough basket toss. Especially if you have the skills from a Ladybird High Flyer charm—which I do. Not that I'm looking to get thrown on top of a building today.

Each classroom has a caged metal air conditioner hanging low off the roof and bolted to the back wall. And every air conditioner is coated in pulsing grub branches. Some things never change.

"Dreary Blight," Avi informs everyone else, gesturing at the quivering mass. "The grub of sadness. Not known for its fighting skills, obviously. It kind of just sits there."

The powdery tendrils of the Dreary Blight grow more like English ivy than like an animal. Wrapped around the air conditioners, the grub looks like a cross between a coral reef and the livid fuchsia lungs of a dinosaur. Its flesh crumbles the same way the paint on the portables does, leaving bald patches at the seams. In the slice of sunlight between buildings, it's easy to see fuchsia motes breaking free and floating away. To slip into sinuses, seep into bloodstreams, settle into brain stems.

I'm not surprised to see the middle school this infested. It's been two entire school years since Gabby went off to join Faithlynn and Jennica at North High. Since they became Poppy Hills' resident senior scouts, they must have decided they were beyond middle school problems. They've moved on to bigger grubs.

Tía Lo loves to remind me that my old circle has the most confirmed Carnivore kills in Northern California. Why should they care about this much unchecked Dreary Blight, which would cause suffering to anyone close enough to breathe it in? I think of the number of fights that could have been skipped, the lunches that didn't have to be ruined. The scouts could have prevented waves of sadness at any time.

If I hadn't quit the scouts, would I care? Would I still bother to carry peppermint in my pockets if I always had a sword strapped to my back?

Kelsey shudders, half hiding behind me to look up at the Dreary Blight. "It looks like if mold was made of candy."

"Anyone else wonder what it tastes like?" Sasha asks. She reaches out a hand to touch it, and I slap her fingertips.

"Do not put monsters in your mouth, please," I say with a sigh.

"A *lot* of colonial scouts died that way," Chancho says.

I slip a knitting needle into my hand and use the tip of it as a pointer, gesturing over the looping knobby branches of grub. "Avi's right. Even at Critter size, Dreary Blight isn't known for fighting. Its main reflex is to—" I stab the knitting needle into a thick mound of Blight, which lets out a weak puff of reddish purple spores before disappearing, leaving a clean white cement wall. "Dust in retaliation."

The group stares at me, breathing in and out in silent expectation as they wait for me to go on. I don't.

Instead, I watch their shoulders start to droop. Chancho's eyes flick toward me with utter betrayal, then close as his lips silently count backward from ten. Queasy green, Avi wraps her arms around her stomach and rocks forward, her eyelashes fluttering. Kelsey finger-combs the same piece of hair over and over again, breaking the curls into frizz. They all edge away from one another. Paul bites at the skin around his thumbnail, eyes downcast. The Beast's nails scratch deep lines into her forearms.

I wish there were another way, but they have to understand what keeping the Sight can turn you into. What being a scout asks you to endure. If I have any chance of convincing Kelsey, Paul, and Sasha to give up the Sight, it's this.

Ulcerous misery gnaws at my stomach. I grind my heels into the ground, forcing myself to stay here, in this moment. I don't exist in the future or the past. Only here.

Still, my head swims as I look at the collection of people no longer standing close enough to be considered a group.

"The Dreary Blight magnifies feelings of isolation," I say, choosing each word carefully. Misspeaking is a fast track to an emotional spike. "It's a self-propagating species. The spores get inside you and change your mood. It makes you feel more and more alone until—"

"I want to go home! I hate this! I don't want to See anymore or wear these stupid accessories or listen to more lectures!" Kelsey swings her arms wildly, trying to free herself from her hat and gloves all at once. She rips the gloves off her hands, popping the seams, and throws them onto the ground. She growls in frustration and stamps her heel into the nearest glove, grinding it into the dead grass.

Crack!

There's a sound like paper being torn in half with a sharp rock and a shimmer of light that momentarily forces my eyes out of focus. Then the Dreary Blight is back on the air conditioner, about half the size it was before but resiliently thick. The force of it pushing between worlds dimples and bows the metal.

Everyone gasps. Kelsey stops her tantrum, frozen in panic.

"Everybody hold your breath," I say. I bury my nose in my elbow and wait for everyone else to follow suit before I stab into the fresh bloom. As it disappears, I hold up my free hand and count down *five, four, three, two, one* on my fingers before uncovering my nose and mouth.

"I'm sorry," Kelsey says behind her hands. When she blinks, unshed tears wet her eyelashes. "I'm so sorry. That was so embarrassing. Oh my God, please don't tell my mom or my brother that I—"

"It's not your fault," I reassure her, reaching down to scoop up her smashed gloves. I gently hand them back to her. "That's the point. That's what Dreary Blight does. If you're around it for too long or breathe too much of it in, it hijacks your feelings. It makes you miserable enough to make a portal for it to come back because it lives and breeds on sadness. Sometimes being a Ladybird means taking on the heightened feelings that grubs feed on so that the general public doesn't have to. You have to run *toward* danger and not away from it."

Guilt constricts my insides as I think about how often I've run away from danger in the last three years, leaving grubs to be dealt with by active scouts. Knowing I could banish it with a single stab, I wonder how much misery this infestation of Dreary Blight has caused.

"I was born to hunt," Avi says. She crosses her arms over her chest and sinks her weight onto one leg like she's in an ad for Kidz Bop. "I'm a Ladybird legacy."

I glance over at Kelsey as she wrings the fingers of her gloves, shamefaced. "The Ladybird initiation ceremony is all about finding your destiny, but it's just the day you get the option. Right now, having seen what the world really is, you could decide to join the fight. I will spend the rest of the summer making sure you get all of your basic charms. At the end of summer, you'll join up with Dame Debby's circle of senior scouts and help keep Poppy Hills safe."

"Or?" Kelsey asks.

"Or you wait while I apply for a dose of the Tea of Forgetting from Headquarters." I look back at Paul and Sasha. "That goes for both of you, too. You weren't born into this. Normally, people only take the Tea of Seeing when they join the scouts or when they marry a Ladybird—"

"That's how our dad got the Sight," Avi says pertly, gesturing to her brother.

"Oh, so Kyle gets to join team I See Monsters when he makes Prue his child bride?" the Beast asks.

"Oh my God, no," I say, my cheeks flaming. Kyle and I haven't even said *I love you* yet. The idea of dosing him, making him part of all this, makes me want to shrivel up and die. "Kyle is *not* getting the Sight. Nobody born without it has to See any of this. All of you who got the Sight today could just undo it. One more bad-tasting tea, and the monsters go away again. They say that when you stop Seeing them, your brain will start to override the truth. It's harder to believe in what you can't See. You don't have to do this. You don't have to know this."

Kelsey sets her dusty hat back on top of her head. "But then who would get rid of the Blight stuff so the middle schoolers don't have to feel sad?"

I squint into the sun, wiping an errant drop of sweat from my temple. "If I report it, the senior scouts will get to it eventually. Once there isn't anything bigger to hunt."

No one rushes to accept my offer of getting them the Tea of Forgetting. No one is relieved to find out that there is, in fact, an escape hatch.

I recognize the square set in their jaws, the cautious eagerness in their eyes. This is what I looked like as one of five pink-haired girls, marching up and down the bike paths through town, ready to pounce on the smallest grub.

I can remember being twelve years old, strapping daggers to my legs for the first time. Being so certain.

"I've never had a destiny before," Kelsey says. "I'm in. I'm hecka in."

I don't know if I'm disappointed or not. This is exactly what I promised my mother I would do. Find and train scouts. I look at Paul and Sasha. "And you guys? I know you didn't sign up to be scouts. You shouldn't have to See—"

"I'm never gonna stop looking at monsters, Prudence Perry," the Beast says, baring her teeth at me in the way that she thinks is friendly but I think is terrifying. "Don't even try to stop me."

I sigh. "Paul?"

He nibbles on the side of his thumbnail. "I dunno. Pass. I need more time with it. It's a new world, man. I gotta sit in it for a while."

I slip the knitting needles back into my sleeves. "Now that you can See what everyone else can't, you'll need to learn to be inconspicuous. Keep mint in your pockets. Altoids—the peppermint ones—can work in a pinch, but essential oil is better. Practice not looking directly at grubs in public. You draw a lot of attention to yourself when you start watching things other people can't See. Hunting is a secret for a reason."

"Because it's too awesome?" Sasha asks.

"Because when people can't See what you do, they assume the problem is *you*, not them. They won't believe you. And the harder you fight to explain, the more unhinged you'll look."

"The Cassandra Paradox," Avi intones.

"Which means you can't tell your parents or your friends," I say. "Literally nobody. Ever."

In my pocket, my phone buzzes a series of texts. My heart sinks as I read them.

> **KYLE:** Have you heard from the group? They said they were on their way here for lunch forever ago.
>
> **KYLE:** Sorry I know you're working. Wish you were here.
>
> **KYLE:** I hope my sister isn't being as annoying as I am. But it's probably genetic.
>
> **KYLE:** Hit me up when you're done. Miss you, babe.

I look up at the Criminal Element. "You guys need to get to the bowling alley. Kyle is starting to think you've been abducted. But absolutely no one"—I take extra care to point directly at Kelsey and Chancho—"and I mean *no one*, is allowed to tell him about any of what happened today."

"But he's my best friend!" Chancho protests.

"And my brother!" Kelsey huffs.

"And he doesn't have the Sight!" I say. "Cassandra

Paradox, you guys. I don't want Kyle to think that anyone is having dangerous delusions. Got it?"

"How are we supposed to pretend like we can't See what we See?" Paul asks.

"It's easy," I say, laughing. "I've been doing it my whole life."

9

Where hats present a fine opportunity to let
one's personality shine, gloves may only be
worn in white and hemmed at the wrist.

—THE LADYBIRD HANDBOOK

Whenever I nap after dawn patrol, everything that happened before sunrise congeals into a series of nightmares. All the overgrown monsters I watched Mom and Tía Lo fight come back to haunt me in my dreams. The Frightworm that Mom banished from the church parking lot reappears in the tailgate of Kyle's truck, slithering over the roof, the clacking of its mandibles only heard by me. Thick Dreary Blight explodes out of the dashboard vents, its branches wrapping around Kyle's forearms, even as he reaches for me, smiling and unaware. And behind me, I feel the awful, icy-cold breath of a Scranch bearing down on the nape of my neck.

I wake up gasping for breath and clawing at my legs, searching for the dagger harnesses I haven't worn in years.

My heart is still hammering when I roll over and check my phone.

There's the daily email blast from Ladybird Headquarters, announcing the leaderboard for Carnivore kills in the state. Seeing the Root shot scores of all the top scouts makes me feel nauseated, and I don't need to open the email to know that Faithlynn Brett is still number one.

Underneath is another message from Headquarters, this one congratulating me on successfully recruiting a third scout.

It's hard to push past the nightmares and remember the specifics of this morning's patrol. Did Mom or Tía Lo mention a third scout? Was it today or yesterday that Tía Lo implied I should be insulted not to have a full complement of scouts? Did Mom ever mention she was looking for another recruit? Did Faithlynn send me someone to make sure I fail?

A minute later, I get the confirmation email from the Headquarters web store informing me that a deluxe orientation kit is being overnighted to Sasha Nezhad. The cold flush of anxiety I get tempts a Tizzy Louse into existence. It bumbles out from beneath the bed, its fuzzy-chicken-nugget body bumping repeatedly into the legs of my nightstand. I fumble the knitting needles out from under my pillow and drop one on its head before flopping back to stare at the ceiling.

I now have two scouts and one Beast. *Shit.*

Before the second meeting, Sasha herself arrives half an hour before Avi and Kelsey. As she stands proudly on my front step, her gloves are leather, her skirt gauzy, her shirt explicit. In greeting, she gives me a formal tip of her cap—a Batman snapback that I'm pretty sure is Chancho's.

"Sasha! Hey!" I say in a voice that's too cheery and too loud. "You're here! For the meeting! I saw that you paid your dues and got the deluxe orientation kit."

"Hell yeah, dude," she says, showing her teeth in her most threatening Friendly Face. "I'm here to murder the forces of darkness."

I pull her inside and hurry to close the door before any neighbors can hear her.

"Ladybirds prefer the word *banish* over *murder*," I tell her, glancing at her outfit. It looks like she played dress-up in a lost and found. If my abuela Ramona is watching us from heaven, she is denting her halo at the appearance of fingerless gloves at a Ladybird meeting. "I can't believe you really joined."

"Believe it, Prudence Perry," the Beast says as she sashays past me into the foyer. The two-inch platforms of her black creepers scuff my mother's tile as she lurches to a stop and glowers down at me through her round black lenses. "I am a certified, bona fide East Side Ladybird scout."

"Technically, we're the southern Poppy Hills circle," I say. My stomach sours as I envision presenting Sasha the Beast to Dame Debby for inspection at the end of summer.

Oh my God, when my mom finds out, she's going to kill me. Sasha can't be trusted with a retractable sword. I've seen her use a mechanical pencil as a weapon. "Tell me the truth, please. Did you tell your mom you were joining the scouts? Because I could get in a lot of trouble for being an accomplice to your credit card fraud. What if they think I asked you to pad my enrollment numbers?"

Sasha folds her arms over her chest, drawing my attention to her DIY FUCK THE POLICE T-shirt. God help me. Avi is definitely going to tell Tía Lo about this.

"Yeah, it would be *super* embarrassing if you cared about something as *boring* as enrollment numbers," she says in a mocking monotone that under normal circumstances might be enough to shame me into dropping it.

When I don't say anything back, she groans, cracking her neck in annoyance.

"Mother was offensively excited at the prospect of me joining something. That's why she prepaid for the year. She may even remember to ask me about it again someday. The skirt is hers."

I watch helplessly as Sasha cruises into the forbidden room, undoubtedly drawn to its off-limits formal furniture.

She picks up a crystal bishop from the decorative chess set and holds it up to the light, appraising its worth. "Oh good, it's fake." She looks up at me with a smile. "When the revolution comes, I'd hate to have to eat your mother along with the rest of the rich."

"Are you sure you want to do this?" I bounce on the balls of my feet. I can already see the Beast sitting between Avi and Kelsey, a giant antiestablishment wolf among sheep.

The bishop clinks against the glass board, knocking over two pawns on the way. The Beast's face crinkles in suspicion. "Do you not want me here?"

"That's not it!" I say automatically. "It's just I don't want you to join because of me. I'm doing this because I have to. Like, if I don't, my mom will absolutely decimate my life. And when Avi and Kelsey join the senior scouts at the end of summer, I won't have to be a scout anymore. If you're still signed up, you *will* have to be one. And unless something big has changed in the last three years, Dame Debby actually makes you use your needles for knitting as well as fighting. The circle makes scarves and socks for the homeless at Christmastime."

Sasha snorts and waves me off, her hands like two black leather bats. "Sure. Altruism. Sounds great. But also? I'm gonna kill fucking monsters, PP."

I can't wholly blame her. Part of me remembers the rush of hunting—the crackling adrenaline, the laser focus. I remember believing in the mission so intensely that it crystallized into perfect surety. That what we were doing was right. That it was safe to give one hundred percent of ourselves to it. Even hating it can't make me completely forget what it felt like to love being a scout.

And, after three years of being the Beast's closest friend,

I know when it's useless to try to talk her out of something. She's always barreling headfirst into danger. At least she'll mostly be on the right side of the law when she's with the scouts.

"Can I at least give you a pair of white gloves?" I ask, ushering her out of the sitting room. "I'd hate for you to feel left out."

† † †

Under the pergola, sitting in front of cups and saucers—which I superglued back together last night—Avi and Kelsey do their best not to make any sudden movements. Both of their necks are frozen as if their hats weigh a thousand pounds. They stiffly sip their tea and nibble at the lopsided crustless sandwiches. Neither of them will look directly at Sasha.

Seemingly unaware of this, Sasha the Beast dissects one of the seven-layer bars that Kelsey brought—possibly inspecting for proof of concept.

"So!" My voice makes Kelsey jump. Her teacup rattles against its saucer. "You all need a full charm bracelet in order to qualify for weapons." I waggle my bracelet so that it gives the telltale Ladybird jingle. "If you want a blade, you need ten charms and a passing score on the combat exam. That's our goal. Everyone steel certified by the end of summer. The senior scouts have been armed for almost five years now. You'll need to be able to keep up with them."

"Oh my gosh, yay!" Avi noiselessly claps her gloved hands. "Are we going to start with kickboxing basics or endurance training?"

"I want to see more of that color guard twirling shit that Prudence did with the knitting needles," Sasha says. "When do we get to look at weapons?"

"I have a catalog I could bring next time," Avi offers Sasha, looking at her directly for the first time, even if it is from mostly behind her teacup. "My mom's on the mailing list."

"Weapons aren't until chapter seven in the Handbook. They're considered a life skill," I say. "You have to get through all of the public service chapters using knitting needles."

And I need to fill my charm bracelet with some non-combat-related charms. If I don't learn how to evenly bake a sheet of birdbark or start a pay-it-forward letter-writing campaign, I might lose out on my only chance to get a bag of the Tea of Forgetting without alerting anyone to how badly I screwed up the initiation ceremony.

"I finally Saw a mulligrub at my house," Kelsey says breathlessly, as if it's a secret. Which I guess it is. She flexes her hand on the table, stretching and contracting her fingers like they're spider legs. "It was on these tall, skinny bug legs and had these big scary teeth in three different mouths." She shudders. "It was so hard not to scream. I thought for sure I was going to throw up."

"That's normal," I tell her. "Queasiness is part of your fight-or-flight response. And what you Saw was a Scranch, an anger-eater. That's a pretty scary thing to See running into in your own house."

Avi leans in with eager interest. "Are your parents fighting? When you hear a door slam, you can practically hear a Scranch being born."

"I don't think my mom and stepdad are fighting." Kelsey's forehead crinkles in serious consideration. "But the grub could have been there because of Kyle. He's been mad about not being able to drive this summer. He's *always* whining about it."

I'm immediately uncomfortable picturing Kyle's anger pulling through a Scranch. I know it's the way of the world, that one chubby seventeen-year-old boy isn't exempt from the rules. Yet I can't help but wish that I could keep Kyle's feelings safe and uneaten.

Inside the canvas tote hung from the back of my chair, I find the packs of cards and hand them out. "Today, we're going to focus on the first skills test in the Handbook. Once you can name and identify the five types of grubs and their combat stats, you'll get the first charm for your bracelet. Then we'll go inside and make some peppermint-oil spray for your emergency kit."

Kelsey examines the pack of cards in her hand. She does not seem impressed with the smiling monsters on the cover. "Go Hunt?"

"It's Go Fish with mulligrub cards. Everyone already knows how to play, right?" I take a nervous sip of tea. The hot liquid feels like embarrassment burning down my chest.

"Go Fish?" Avi's chin tucks back in obvious offense. "Um, isn't that a little babyish?"

"Babyish?" I ask in equal offense. "You're baby Ladybirds. You're babybirds."

"Well, I already know all of the grubs," Avi says. "I've been able to See them for twelve years."

"And you've only been allowed to read the Handbook for two days," I tell her. "There's no way you already have it memorized. If there aren't enough stats for you on the cards, then you can cross-reference to the appendix in the back of the Handbook."

"Because everything fun starts with cross-referencing," Kelsey mumbles.

She and Avi retrieve their Handbooks with the grudging slowness of taking an open-book pop quiz. Which is sort of what I have sprung on them.

Oh no. Is this how teachers feel when we hate their assignments?

Sasha stretches her arms high overhead and cracks her back from side to side. "My Handbook hasn't arrived yet, so now sounds like a cool time for me to pop out for a smoke break."

"Absolutely not!" I say. "Download the field guide app.

I'll give you the password. You can play Go Hunt with me."

She pulls out her phone and glowers at me as she jabs her thumbs at the screen. With a jerk of her chin, she gestures across the table at Avi. "The little one said we're supposed to be learning kickboxing and shit."

"Excuse you," Avi says with a scowl. "My name isn't 'the little one.' It's *Avianna*. You're bad at whispering."

"Whispering is for people with something to hide," Sasha says. "I was having an A and B conversation, so C your way out of it."

Avi sticks out her tongue before going back to digging through her Handbook. I've never seen someone purposefully antagonize the Beast before. At school, people mostly avoid eye contact and get out of her way, no questions asked. Maybe Avi does have the heart of a hunter.

I pick up the playing cards and start to shuffle them. They flutter together with ease, broken in years ago by Paz's circle.

"You have to learn people's names," I tell Sasha. "This can't be like freshman year when you only called Paul 'Short Shorts' and Chancho 'Boy Prue.'"

"Those were affectionate—and accurate—nicknames," Sasha sniffs without looking up from her phone. "So, we're not going to beat anything up today?"

"In our tea clothes? No way. You have to walk before you can run."

Avi picks up a cucumber sandwich and puts the entire

thing into her mouth. With her mouth full, she whines, "And yet here we are. Just sitting."

"For now," I say stiffly, dealing cards between Sasha and me. They land lightly with the Ladybird crest facing up. I remember Molly and me rolling our eyes at Go Hunt, too. When we thought knowing the names of grubs was the same as being ready for the field. "You can't go chasing down grubs until you know what they are. And what they can do to you."

10

Punctuality is the highest form of respect.

—THE LADYBIRD HANDBOOK

Mom comes home from work with her phone plastered to her ear, agreeing emphatically with whoever is on the other end of the call. Bugging her eyes at me, she fans an irritated hand over the things out of place—my tea hat sitting on the kitchen island, the crystal pawns askew on the chess set in the sitting room, a crumb on the floor in the hallway—before sweeping into her office.

Hours later, Dad and I loudly set the table for dinner, stamping our feet and purposefully clanking silverware. Sometimes Mom needs to be startled into checking the time.

"Do you think it's school business or Ladybird business?" Dad asks, closing the oven door and blotting his head with a napkin. He calls himself blond on the technicality that the hair that remains is pale. I would argue that people with hair rarely have to clear sweat off the top of their head.

I watch the clock over the stove tick past seven through the thinning steam of our dinner. "This late? I'm sure it's Ladybird gossip. You know, a Mare Island scout probably forgot to wear the right kind of shoes on patrol. 'Can you believe she killed seven grubs while wearing flip-flops? The nerve! The gall!'"

Dad transfers the casserole dish of meatballs to one of the old knit trivets Paz's circle used to give out at Christmas. "Superheroes are all very particular about their costumes."

"Scouts don't have superpowers, Dad."

"Neither does Batman." He shrugs and straightens the nearest place setting. "He's still a superhero."

I steal a slice of apple off the top of the salad and crack it in half with my incisors. "Okay, well, if you don't see immense wealth as a superpower, we live in different Americas."

"If you don't think getting up before sunrise every day to keep your town safe doesn't make you a hero, you're out of your gourd."

I scowl at him. Dawn patrol is so often just slogging through a long run with Mom and Tía Lo. Hunting is wholly secondary to their ongoing argument about what company makes the best compression socks and who has the worst lawn in the neighborhood.

I don't think I'll ever be able to convince Dad of this. He has the same outsider opinion of the scouts as Chancho. They get so hung up on the secret-organization-fighting-evil-by-moonlight part that they can't see the trauma forest for the trees. Dad says that before he drank the Tea of Seeing, he never even had the stomach to kill bugs in the house, much less banish interdimensional monsters.

I envy his ability to choose.

"The salad is starting to look sad," I say, taking another apple slice out of the serving bowl. "Rock-paper-scissors to see who has to interrupt Mom's phone call?"

Dad slams his fist into his open hand. "You're on."

We only get through the *rosham* of roshambo before Mom spares us by charging into the kitchen, pitching aside an empty can of caffeinated sparkling water. A total Ladybird cliché. Caffeine water is the centerpiece of the Ladybird basic bitch memes that my sister is always cackling about. I didn't understand why until I got access to the Dame message boards and saw just how many threads there are devoted to the best brands. And I thought giving the babybirds mineral water was bougie.

Mom peers at the table, poking at the wilted arugula salad and pretending that she isn't fifteen minutes late to a meal. She surveys the main course. "What kind of meatballs are those?"

"Turkey," I say.

"Good," she says. She gives Dad an approving peck on the cheek. "You know I love a poultry meatball. How was everyone's day?"

"Busy," Dad says. He shakes the serving spatula so that his meatballs fall into a precarious pyramid. "Two of our clerks no-call-no-showed today. I had to come out and bag groceries! Do you know how long it's been since I did courtesy work? I'm sure I did it wrong."

"Bread and tomatoes on the bottom, right?" I ask.

"Under the eggs, obviously," he says, laughing.

"That is unacceptable," Mom says as she heaps salad on her plate. Dad gives me a private wince that makes Mom roll her eyes. "Not your bagging abilities, Kevin. I know what a joke is. I mean the clerks. Not showing up *and* not calling? I hope that they've already been fired."

"They were supposedly camping over the weekend, so we're waiting to make sure they're safe before any disciplinary actions are taken. Not that you can't fire someone via voice mail, but it's nice to make sure they're alive to hear it."

"Camping?" Mom asks. She turns wholly in her chair to face Dad. "Do you know which park they were camping in? Solano? Lake Berryessa?"

"I doubt they paid for a real campsite. They're college kids. I think they took a tent into the hills and lost track of time eating 'shrooms." He wags his fork at me. "Don't do hallucinogens."

129

I toast him with my water glass. "No need. I can See all my nightmares sober."

"Attagirl."

"Please let me know if their bodies are found," Mom says. She quarters each of her meatballs with the side of her fork, then nibbles at the bits. "If their disappearance seems grub related, I'll need to tell Headquarters. It wouldn't be the first time we had a large-scale breach in the hills. Kids accidentally pull through something they can't See, then pay the consequences for losing control."

I look down at my plate, my hearing growing fuzzy. I know she isn't talking specifically about me, but it doesn't matter. The sound of her fork clinking against the plate fades away and the sound of the oak forest fades in. I keep waiting for it to blur or dim, but it remains clear, even three years later.

The air as warm as bathwater. Acorns underfoot. Skin tearing. Bones snapping. Blood everywhere. Splattered across us, rushing out of so many wounds. By the end, we were the living dead, matted with so much dirt and gore that the woman in the minivan who picked us up at the side of the road couldn't stop sobbing as she drove across town to the hospital.

"It was a mountain lion," Faithlynn told the woman, staring straight ahead as the gravel road jostled us around. "We were attacked by a mountain lion. Our friend is dead."

I wonder if Headquarters bought that woman a new van. She would never have been able to get the smell out, never mind the stains.

Dad wipes his endless forehead with his napkin and clears his throat in the familiar key of *Hey, you're triggering the kid again*.

Mom swallows a bite of meatball and obvious exasperation. "Prudence, did you host a successful meeting today?"

I pick up my water again, hoping the cool glass will help me stay present. "Nobody quit, even after seeing the combat stats on a Carnivore Scranch. That's a win. And we successfully boiled down some Pippy-Mint, so I think I can finally get an Oil Can charm."

"And you have a new recruit?" Mom phrases it like it's both a question and a prompting. "Sasha Nezhad paid full dues?"

"Oh," I say. Of course she already knows. I take a long drink of water. "Yep. That happened, too."

"Sasha joined the scouts?" Dad asks. "The Beast of the Outlet Mall?"

"Don't call her that. She's troubled, not mythological," Mom says. Her frown starts at her mouth but pulls down the sides of her nose and the corners of her eyes. Mom has spent more time with Sasha's permanent record than with the Beast herself. And Sasha does not look great on paper. Although Mom must believe in her a little because she bargained for Sasha's return to South High after her semester at County Day.

I shrug, refusing to acknowledge my own worries about having Sasha in my circle. If Mom smells any weakness on me, she'll pounce. "At her hearing, you said she needed more structure and positive hobbies. This could be proof that her mom was listening."

"Sasha needs parenting, and she's not going to get that from another child." Mom's left nostril twitches in irritation. "That said, the scouts have saved many girls with Sasha's temperament. Did you petition for a new dose of Seeing?"

"No need," I say, focused on heaping my plate with arugula. "Sasha can already See."

Mom frowns. "I don't recall her being a legacy."

"I don't know if it's on her mom or dad's side. I mean, it's the Beast. She could have just eaten a grub on a dare. But she didn't know it was a scout thing, and so never assumed that I could See—" I inhale deeply like there will be a better lie on the wind. "So yeah. She just needs to catch up on lesson one. Which we can do on our way to hang out with the Criminal Element tomorrow? Since I'm tutoring Avi, I'm not grounded. Right?"

I look at Dad, who looks at Mom, who pecks at another meatball quarter.

"Fine," Mom says. "But your curfew stands. Home by ten unless you're hunting."

Dad gives me an encouraging smile as though we've both won something here. I fill my mouth with food so I won't be tempted to remind everyone that I'm not hunting. I'm tutoring.

"Now," Mom says, and my stomach immediately drops. "Prudence, do you know the purpose of the Ladybird tea meeting?"

I deduce that this isn't a rhetorical question. God forbid she just give me the answer she's looking for. "Um. High tea keeps us civilized. The white gloves represent our ability to keep our hands clean. Drinking from the same teapot represents our communal experience."

Mom's face doesn't move, which means I'm not getting a passing grade yet.

"The sugar bowl keeps us sweet?"

She can tell that I've started guessing. She sighs. "Tea meetings are time we set aside to celebrate and reflect on what happens on a hunt. The formality of tea only works in conjunction with time spent in the field. Otherwise, you're only domesticating middle schoolers. And Sasha Nezhad. I was talking to your tía, and we're worried about the limited progress you've made in two meetings."

Light-headed, I use my imagination to reframe the last few hours of Mom's closed office door, every minute devoted to her disappointment in me. I can imagine Tía Lo railing against a quitter leading her daughter's first circle and Mom agreeing because, really, they've both always known that I wasn't cut out for this. Ladybirds can't be soft or slouchy. They can't give in to little things like post-traumatic stress.

What if Avi tells her mother about Paul and Sasha drinking the Tea of Seeing? If Headquarters found out, they would task a scout to force the antidote on Paul, and I would be fired on the spot. They wouldn't let me order a T-shirt, much less petition for a dose of the Tea of Forgetting. And what would Chancho's punishment be?

A Tizzy Louse bursts into being under the table. It staggers one step before Mom banishes it with a leaf from her pocket.

She glares at me like I tracked mud in. "Did you take your meds?"

I hate when she asks this. It's like Chancho asking if my feelings are menstrual. After I left the scouts the first time, my psychiatrist, Dr. Gardner, recommended anti-anxiety medication. Dr. Anita Silva-Perry, Ed.D, must have been the first mother in history to ask if her child's debilitating mental illness might need to stick around. *Apprehension is an evolutionary need, isn't it? Fight or flight? What if, on this medication, she just stands in front of an oncoming bus?* My doctor had to tell her that standing in front of a bus isn't a common side effect for Lexapro.

"Yes, I took my meds," I tell her. "Sorry. I didn't mean to—"

"Don't apologize for feeling your feelings, munchkin," Dad interrupts.

I know he's trying to help, but it lands with the same weight as just another criticism.

Another Tizzy Louse appears, next to my shoe. My hands start to shake as I fish out an Altoid from my pocket and drop it on the grub's head.

"Sorry," I say again. "What are you and Tía Lo concerned about?"

"After your circle crossed the threshold, how often did you train?" Mom asks.

"Every day," I say, hoping to hurry her along to the point. There's no point in pretending not to remember. "And most lunches, because Faithlynn Brett has never had a friend who wasn't in her circle."

Mom makes a face to let me know she doesn't appreciate me making fun of Faithlynn. "Avi came home very disappointed today. She's been looking forward to becoming a Ladybird for many years. It's hard enough for her, having to wait for a circle to open up, and now she feels like she's been shorted."

"Shorted?" I repeat.

"You made a commitment when you accepted this position. Not just to the organization, but to the girls in your circle. You took them into one of the greatest confidences in the world and then left them out to dry. You haven't made them a training schedule. You're not spot-cleaning the neighborhood. Where's the public good? Where's the excitement?" She stabs her salad in a clockwise circle, never breaking eye contact with me. "It's the height of summer, but you have them on rainy-day recess, locked up inside."

"We've been using the pergola," I protest weakly.

She purses her lips and leans back in her chair. She must be terrifying at work, the way her face doesn't betray a single emotion but her eyes catch everything. "You can play games and practice flash cards, but you never forget the name of something that tried to kill you. Take your girls into the field, and they'll memorize every critter that jumps out at them."

"Just because that's how you were trained doesn't mean that's the only way to do it!" I protest. Fear stabs at my gut as I imagine my scouts cornered by burning eyes and endless hunger. "I shouldn't have to put them in unnecessary danger. I have nine more weeks to prepare them for the field. I want to focus on identification and evasion techniques for at least two—"

Mom holds up a hand, not to stop me from speaking, but to let me know that she's refusing to listen. "Absolutely not. What you do with the scouts reflects not only on you, Prudence, but on your *family*. I will not have us remembered for being too scared to fight. In the past, we've discussed exposure therapy as part of your treatment. Going into the field is the best possible exposure you could have."

"Anita," Dad says in a harsh whisper not meant for my ears, "we made an agreement with Dr. Gardner not to weaponize treatment."

"She needs to remember that she has the tools to conquer her fears. And to make the world safer." Mom turns her attention back to me, jabbing her fork in my direction. "You cannot let your feelings get in the way of your duty as a Dame. Avi, Kelsey, and Sasha will never be able to help us protect our community if you keep them locked up with board games. Ships at harbor are safe, but that's not what ships are built for."

My skin is suddenly hot and clammy. My voice comes from far away. "You're right, Mom. I'll do better."

"Do I need to help you write your curriculum? I could find a day to take off work to run one of your meetings."

I choke down a gulp of water and pray not to hear the sound of another Tizzy Louse. The idea is too humiliating to bear. Paz definitely never had to ask Mom to come take over her circle.

"No, you don't have to do that," I say. "On tomorrow morning's patrol, I'll ask Tía Lo to help. I'm sure she already has pages of notes she's mad I haven't asked for." I take the napkin out of my lap as my voice begins to shake. "Excuse me, I'm just gonna use the bathroom."

Mom calls after me. "Prudence!"

"Give it a rest," Dad sighs. "She already said you were right."

I close the bathroom door, which muffles their voices so that all I can hear is the loop that grows louder and louder.

Why can't you understand that girls are more precious than ships?

11

Scouts empower themselves and their
community by maintaining an active lifestyle.
Regular exercise promotes a circle's capacity to
handle and subdue emotional flare-ups.

—THE LADYBIRD HANDBOOK

Day one of combat training. Joy.

Thrilled to finally be included in Avi's training/my business, Tía Lo has spent her day off from work setting up my backyard for her "guest lecture." The gate between our houses banged open and shut all morning. I asked if she needed me to carry anything and then went inside so as not to take away from my aunt's truest joy—being able to tell my mother how ungrateful I was in not offering to help more than twice.

Because Ladybirds would never allowing anything to be seen as *informal*, meetings that trade the usual hat-and-gloves dress code for workout clothes are called *homespun*. With this morning's dawn patrol clothes a stinky, sweaty mass in the corner of my room, I jump into yoga pants and cover my pastel tie-dye shirt with the Sasquatch hoodie. I fish a pair of pink canvas sneakers out of my sister's closet. Despite their lack of arch support, Keds have been the official shoe of the Ladybird Scout for the last hundred years. This pair is so beat up, the robins stitched to the heel are barely discernible, which is fine by me. I don't care about bird shoes as much as I care about not being yelled at by Tía Lo.

When the doorbell rings at exactly noon, I find Kelsey standing on the porch in her Goldfields Middle gym clothes, her full name printed in neat, rounded letters on the shirt and shorts.

"My mom insisted I bring water if we're going to be exercising," she says with a frown. "And Kyle insisted on carrying it."

"Hey, babe!" Kyle calls to me, jumping out of the back of his mom's minivan. He balances a flat of water bottles on his shoulder and jogs up to the porch, his curls bouncing in the sunlight. "Where should I put these?"

My heart soars at the sight of him. It's been over a week since we were together, the longest we've been apart since his family went to Disneyland over Thanksgiving break. But picturing him bursting into the backyard and seeing all of the Ladybird regalia that Tía Lo dragged out of her garage makes me want to throw up. Gesturing vaguely at the entryway tile, I say, "Right here is fine! Thanks!"

He steps inside the door, gingerly dropping the case of water with a plasticky crunch before sweeping me up in a tight hug. Kelsey rolls her eyes and turns around, staring into the forbidden room while her brother and I kiss hello.

"Hi," he says, pulling away from me, his lips glossy with my spit. "I've missed you. I feel like I've barely seen you since summer started."

"I know," I say, rubbing my thumb over his wrist. "I miss you, too."

He reaches out, pinching the tiny hatchet hanging from my charm bracelet. "That's cool," he says, squinting at it. "Did you learn how to chop firewood or something?"

"Yeah, something like that." I offer him a weak smile, recalling the camping trip that earned me the Ax Expert charm. I'd chucked one of Faithlynn's axes directly between the eyes of a charging Frightworm, and she'd popped a blood vessel in her eye screaming at me for touching her weapons. "It was a long time ago."

Outside, the minivan horn honks. Kyle checks over his shoulder with a grimace. "I've got to get to work." His grip on my waist tightens, like he's considering taking me with him to the bowling alley. "You're still coming by for Pinkies Only, right?"

"Ew!" Kelsey gags, cutting her eyes back at us. "Do I even want to know what that means?"

"It's a video game competition," I assure her. I press a

kiss to Kyle's cheek. "And, yes, I wouldn't miss it for the world."

"Great. I'll see you then, babe. Have fun with your scout aerobics." He turns and smiles. "Hey, Beast! See you tomorrow?"

Sasha climbs the porch steps, offering Kyle a fist bump as they pass each other. "Fuck yeah, dude. My pinkies were born ready."

I chew on the inside of my cheek as I watch Kyle get into the minivan. As his mom drives away, he thrusts his hand out the window and waves at me. When I reach up to wave back, my charm bracelet rings, reminding me of yet another lie I had to tell him.

The door closes behind the Beast, who is wearing a ribbed undershirt, three sports bras, and blue South Hills High gym shorts with someone else's name on them.

Kelsey nervously slurps the spit from her braces as she gestures to their matching wide-leg jersey shorts. "Great minds think alike, right?"

The Beast gives an ambivalent shrug, true feelings cloaked by her sunglasses. "Poverty is a great equalizer."

"Why don't you both grab a water bottle?" I say, motioning down to the pallet on the floor. "Avi's already in the backyard. Her mom is here to help with our first home-spun meeting."

"Chancho's mom?" Sasha grumbles, bending to tear open the plastic on the case of water. She glowers up at me. "I thought she was too busy to do Dame stuff with the little one."

"It's just for today," I say, distracted, tucking the tag into the back of one of her sports bras, then checking everyone's shoes for strong double knots. "And, at the end of the meeting, instead of tea, we'll have a carb-up cooldown lunch. I have pizza bagels and bagel dogs and pizza bagel dogs—"

"Um, Dame Prudence?" Kelsey asks, holding still while I smooth down the frizz in her ponytail. The honorific hangs lopsided in front of my name. "You're kind of freaking me out. Should we be scared?"

"No! It'll be fine—" I stuff my fidgeting hands into the pockets on my sweater. If we dawdle for too long, Lo will just come get us. "I mean *fun*. It'll be fun! Let's go."

On the other side of the French doors, in the hard-to-look-at sunshine, there's an even harder-to-look-at obstacle course. Every piece is Ladybird pink and white. The agility ladder definitely used to be my sister's. The hurdles might be Dame Debby's. The jump ropes being swung on the pavement are manned by very tall Chancho and very short Jaxon.

Knees high, like they're dancing a frantic jig, Tía Lo and Avi jump double Dutch together.

Behind me, Sasha and Kelsey take everything in, awed.

"What in the *American Ninja* fuck?" the Beast gasps.

"It's sort of a replica of the National Conference course,"

I say, gesturing at the A-frame climbing wall near the pergola. "It's just missing over-under-through hedges and Headshot Alley—I mean the ax toss."

Sasha glances at me over the top of her sunglasses, a rarity she only uses to punctuate a truly serious point. Just like every time I've seen them, her eyes are long lashed and deeply annoyed. "You've known how to throw an ax this whole time and you *never* showed me how?"

"It's in chapter seven of the Handbook. We'll get there." I sigh as Tía Lo spots us.

Jumping effortlessly out of the double Dutch, my aunt prances toward me, Kelsey, and the Beast.

"Hello, sisters! Welcome to the Ladybird agility course!" Tía Lo calls, her eyes crescent moons due to the force of her smile. A Ladybird billboard in a National Conference T-shirt and robin-crested socks, she waves with both hands. Her stacks of charm bracelets make a tambourine jangle.

The jump ropes fall silent behind her as Avi comes to join us.

"Sasha, Kelsey," I say, remembering my manners and gesturing among everyone. "That's Jaxon. You know Chancho. And this is Avianna's mom, Dame Lorena Silva-Marquez."

"Oh, but my friends call me Lo-Lo!" Tía Lo coos, and takes a moment to hold Kelsey's and Sasha's hands in turn as a way of sizing them up.

In a lifetime of service to the scouts, I'm sure Tía Lo has seen horrors that would never let me sleep and felt tragedies that would tear my heart in half. There must be a reason why she asks Kelsey to hop, why she peeks at Sasha's teeth. You would think that would be the sort of information she would like to share with her niece, but no. I wonder if she doesn't trust me to stick with the scouts long enough to need tricks of the trade. It could be that Tía Lo just never thinks of doing anything that doesn't benefit her directly.

I'd still rather have her here than Mom. Mom would already be sparring and giving out letter grades. Everyone would cry by lunch break, just like when she guest-lectured for my first circle.

Uncomfortable with being inspected, Sasha looks beyond Tía Lo and scans the obstacle course from beneath knit brows. "What does jump rope have to do with me stabbing grubs? I thought this was weapons training."

My heart plummets.

Like everyone else with Abuela Ramona's genes, Tía Lo is short and fine boned. Despite being at least half a foot shorter than the Beast, by dropping Sasha's hands and taking a single step back, Tía Lo stands like an absolute giant. With a dip of her head she takes in Sasha the Beast from the dirty toes of her high-tops to the straps of her layered sports bras.

"Sasha. The criminal inside of the Criminal Element.

You're friends with my Chancho," Tía Lo observes.

Behind her, Chancho's shoulders come up to his ears.

"Now, Sasha," Tía Lo continues, "a Ladybird is light on her feet, quick thinking, and able to defend against any attacker. You could run on a treadmill and pray to gain the dexterity of mind and endurance of spirit that interval training provides, but you would fail. A feeling I hear you are accustomed to." She titters and boops Sasha on the nose like a good dog.

The Beast's mouth turns into an O of surprise.

"No scout is fit to hold a weapon until she learns not to speak until spoken to," Tía Lo says. "We're a sisterhood, not friends or petty thugs."

The Beast stumbles backward, dazedly blinking. Kelsey and Avi edge away from her as though the admonishment could spread to them.

"This obstacle course is a Ladybird standard," Tía Lo explains as she twirls effortlessly between the double Dutch ropes to the other side. "You enter and exit the double Dutch, take the balance beam down to the quintuple walls, then take the stutter-step tires, climb the wall, jump the low hurdles, and finish with the agility ladder."

I check the ground for signs of practice weapons. Dame Debby used to keep them in mason jars, separated by weight. When we were in trouble, we had to carry tiny-gauge knitting needles. Much harder to wield and way more likely to be dropped on the course, sending us back to the start.

"Tía Lo, should I get a knitting needle to use as a baton?" I ask. "Or should the scouts just tag out of the relay?"

"Relay?" Tía Lo throws her head back and laughs at the sun. "Oh, no no no. Each one of you girls is going to run the whole course until you can master it. Any slipup sends you right back to double Dutch."

The slap of the jump rope now sounds menacingly fast. The anticipation hanging in the air starts to sour.

"The whole thing?" Kelsey squeaks. "I've never jumped hurdles before. I could pull a muscle!"

Tía Lo raises an indifferent shoulder. "Then you should start stretching. A Ladybird should always be warmed up."

"Tía Lo-o-o . . ." Diplomacy draws out her name so that it's half warning, half plea. "This is just day one—"

"Of the rest of your lives!" she interrupts. Smoothly, she slips between the double Dutch ropes again, her feet pounding in an easy pogo as she continues. "You don't tip-toe into scouting, ladies! You throw yourself into the deep end and learn not to drown! If you want to be good enough, start now. Dame Prudence will lead by example."

I goggle at her. "Do the whole course?"

"Of course!" she says. "You wouldn't ask your scouts to do something you couldn't do yourself, would you?"

I grit my teeth. "Of course not."

Reluctantly, I slip off my hoodie and fold it neatly on the ground. In a T-shirt, I'm still fairly covered up, but feeling the sun on the length of my arm scar turns my stomach.

The thin puckered skin travels over the bend of my elbow and down to the lump on my wrist. I can feel eyes on the jagged line of it, tracing the doll-like seam. Without looking back, I can't tell if they're the eyes of people who know the story behind it or not.

I stare down the double Dutch ropes, listening to the one-two slap of beads on the ground. When I leap in, one of the ropes hits me across the face. I spin out, sucking in a curse.

"It's okay, Prudence," Jaxon says, still spinning the rope. Built like Tío Tino except too small to be barrel-chested, Jaxon is like a seven-year-old bucket with legs. He wears his hair in the same cool-guy swoosh as Chancho. "Do you want me to show you how to do it right? Avi taught me."

"No, thanks, bud," I say with a wince. Maybe I should have let my mother come in for the day. She might have trained my scouts too hard, but she wouldn't set me up to fail. She would have warned me to put on a sports bra and long sleeves.

"We'll call that one a practice. You'll get it perfect this time," Tía Lo says cheerily from the sidelines. She must sense me seething, because she clasps my shoulder hard and jostles me. "Aww, don't pout, sweetie. You asked me to be here on my *one* day off! But, ladies"—she turns to the others—"this is an important Ladybird lesson! A good scout asks for help when she's in over her head. It'll keep you alive in a pinch, as Dame Prue could tell you."

As she gives my shoulder another squeeze, her thumb digs into the top of my scar, where there is a hard knob of mottled skin. I'm sure she thinks of it as soothing, but the pressure makes me want to pull my arm off. As my brain screams, I count my breath in and hold it. I imagine a wave crashing as I let the breath slip through my teeth. My heartbeat slows. Dad would be so proud.

"You'll do better under more realistic circumstances, I think," Tía Lo says, and I already know that I'm going to hate whatever comes next. Over her shoulder she calls to Avi. "Avianna, will you please give us a monster to fight? It's hardly a Ladybird training without a grub to chase."

Avi hurries over to the supplies under the pergola. Next to Tía Lo's emergency sword is a grub trap. Manufactured and sold exclusively by Ladybird Headquarters, grub traps look exactly like pink plastic reptile terrariums, except that the opening on the top is only as big around as a jelly jar. Or about the distance of from mouth to chin.

With a press of the spring latch, the lid pops open. Avi squishes her lips and cheeks to the trap opening. Practiced, she knows to wiggle her chin to get a tight seal and inhale a lungful of air through her nostrils. Her eyes screw up tight as she exhales a bloodcurdling, whistle-pitch scream. The interior trap lid pops closed, and a moment later a giant white centipede writhes into being.

I hold my breath and don't exhale until I see its black eyes blinking.

A Frightworm.

Kelsey, Sasha, and Chancho all jump backward. Jaxon—who was born without the Sight—picks his nose.

"Does that always work?" Sasha asks my aunt.

"Trapping a scream?" Lo asks. "Have you not read the healthy-living chapter of the Handbook?"

"It's only been two days since they were initiated, Tía," I say. "All we've covered so far is the Ladybird chronicle and grub identification."

"I didn't realize you were on such a leisurely timetable. I thought you were bringing a circle up to snuff as quickly and efficiently as possible to help protect our town. A silly something about life or death. But you'd know better than I do." She turns away from me, going to collect the trap from Avi. "There are a few ways of pulling mulligrubs into our reality for the purposes of training or study. A trapped scream is easiest, but it's a dice roll. You could get literally anything small enough to fit in the cage. You can set up emotional lures with human bait, too. I told a sister scout that I didn't like her idea for our holiday giveaway one year and pulled through a Carnivorous Scranch that ripped apart all the ugly caps she'd knitted—"

"But that's a lesson for another day," I interrupt. I can smell a Ladybird hero story coming from ten miles away, and it's way too soon to teach the new scouts about juicing grubs. "Let me have my second try at the course so that everyone else can go."

Chancho and Jaxon start turning the jump ropes again. I jump into the double Dutch and manage to get out, rip a leaf of Pippy-Mint from the nearest pot, and race down to the balance beams before Lo reaches into the trap and pulls the Frightworm out by the tail. Its hundred sticklike green legs wriggle in the air, its thick white body curving upward to hide its gaping mouth.

"Here you go, honey," Lo says—to either me or the grub, I can't tell—as she bowls the Frightworm at my feet.

It lands on the end of the balance beam with just enough weight that I have to jump off to keep from falling. I can hear the skittering sounds of it chasing me from one quintuple wall to the next—the grub cheats, cutting through the grass—but I can't lose momentum by turning around to see it, or I'll fall to the ground and have to go back to the beginning again. When I get one foot in the first stutter-step tire, the Frightworm bounces again, this time springing at my face.

The scouts scream. Tía Lo smirks. Jaxon yawns, looking at a cloud. Even if he were watching me, there wouldn't be anything for him to see other than me swiping at the air with a mint leaf. And missing.

"Keep going, Miss Prue!" Tía Lo says. "The goal is to get to the end *and* banish the grub!"

I take the stutter steps sideways so that I can focus on not tripping rather than keeping my eyes protected. Claws catch at the hem of my shorts. I push aside the urge to panic or hurry. The rough veins of the peppermint leaf held between my thumb and forefinger are as familiar as the security blanket I was never allowed to have.

"We're light on the balls of our feet," Tía Lo says, her arms up and conducting me like an under-rehearsed orchestra. "And we're smiling! We're having fun! It's just training! You can scowl when something tries to eat you!"

"That centipede *is* trying to eat her!" Kelsey shouts.

"Just a teensy Frightworm," Tía Lo says breezily. "It can't do more than scratch at you and make you un poco sleepy when it gets full absorbing your fear."

The second my feet are free of the tires, I bend down and scoop up the grub as I run for the climbing wall. Its body is water-balloon heavy, distended on my fear of failure. Its rough legs scratch and scrabble against my bare forearms. I jab the mint leaf against the top of its head. As it poofs, I leap vertically to grab the top of the climbing wall and walk my feet up the planks. The low hurdles and agility ladder go by relatively easily with nothing chasing me.

"Three minutes, forty-seven seconds," Avi announces. She holds up her watch to show the timer display.

"Well, at least you didn't set an unbeatable record for your scouts, Dame Prue," Tía Lo says with an encouraging smile. "Now! Everyone line up for a turn. Prudence, you're welcome to have another shot if you'd like to shave off a minute or two—three minutes isn't going to get you back on the leaderboard anytime soon!"

"I'm not trying to get on the leaderboard, Tía Lo," I say, swallowing a wad of hot spit I'd rather hock at her feet. It's bad enough that scouts are responsible for their entire town's emotional well-being. Forcing them to compete against one another on top of that is ridiculous.

Ignoring me completely, Tía Lo turns around, aiming her phone at the outdoor speakers. For someone who hates people knowing how old she is, you'd think she'd stop openly pointing her phone to "catch" the Bluetooth signal. "Let's get some music! I hope everyone likes Justin Bieber! I can't help it! I still Belieb!"

The Beast hands me my sweatshirt as I try not to collapse behind her. As the inferior version of "Despacito" starts, loud enough for the entire neighborhood to hear, I hear Sasha mutter, "I have beheld true evil on this day."

I zip back into my armor and nod. "And no amount of peppermint will ever make her go away."

✝ ✝ ✝

When I hear footsteps on the stairs, I leap off my bed to tidy the heap of sweaty workout clothes that hasn't yet made it to my laundry hamper and kick my shoes under my bed. Mom never comes upstairs after work. She hasn't even changed out of her heels yet. I can hear them digging divots into the stairs.

"Prudence?" she calls the moment before nudging the door open with her hip. She's holding a small cardboard box with the flaps folded down. I watch as she pauses and scans for all the things in my room she wishes she could get rid of.

My windowsill garden of mostly live succulents and mostly dead peppermint.

The elaborate porcelain mermaid-riding-a-dolphin clock sitting next to my bedside peppermint plant.

My fish tank—decorative since Brewster Beta Fish went belly-up last year.

Me.

"Hi, hello," I say, trying to stand casually next to my bed and not look like someone who has just been panic-cleaning. "Welcome home. No meetings today?"

She waves me off with one hand as she sets the box on my bed with the other. "Today was wall-to-wall meetings."

"Right, sorry. I meant after-hours meetings. I know meetings can happen anywhere. Anytime." *Like right now.* "What's in the box?"

She sets her hand atop the cardboard box, patting it as though it is a very good box. "For you. So you can show your scouts what you're best at."

My heart squeezes, imagining the many things I consider myself to be good at that wouldn't fit in a box. I wish I could show the babybirds how to stay soft in a rough world, how to pull the important people close to you and not let go.

Inside the box are strips of pink leather and hard molded

Kydex. While anyone else might be more than a little horrified to get a leather harness from their mother, I recognize the straps as connected to a set of small scabbards.

"Wrist sheaths for your daggers," Mom says. "If you're always going to be in that bulky sweatshirt, you might as well be safe. And you can participate more on patrol."

It's an obligation and an invitation and a present all in one box. The Dr. Anita Silva-Perry special.

"I guess it is time to admit that my arms are full-sized," I say, peering inside the box. "Dame Debby said I should stick to leg harnesses until I got taller, but that ship has probably sailed."

"We are not tall people," Mom says in that way that makes it hard to tell if she's talking about our family or our culture. Sometimes there's no difference between the two, but it's hard to know when. "Your tía says your scouts look promising," she says.

I'm not surprised she's already received a full report. I'm sure Tía Lo was texting before the gate hit her on the way out. Every Dame in her phone will know that she had to come help her novice niece with training fundamentals.

"Although she had plenty of opinions about what they were wearing. I had to remind her that not every child can afford a wholly new wardrobe just to elevate the name of the organization. And do you know what she said to me? She told me to give the schools cuter gym clothes!"

"Cuter? Does she want ruffles? Or glitter?"

"You know she would adore the addition of glitter." Mom covers her mouth, smothering what I'm not sure I dare call a laugh. At something *I* said. "I expect to find a petition on my desk about it any minute."

"Well, her babies have to wear the gym clothes that apparently you, as superintendent, design yourself. How is this season of *Poppy Hills Unified Project Runway* going, by the way?"

"If I were as busy as her, I would have more important things to worry about. Doesn't she have enough on her plate?"

"An important question. For tomorrow's dawn patrol, you should totally open with 'Lo, don't you have a life?' I'll bring the smoothies. You bring the heat."

Her brow wrinkles. I know she would murder me if I mentioned any of this in front of Tía Lo, but it almost feels like we're sharing a joke. It almost feels like having a regular mom, one who doesn't hide behind emotional distance and a whip sword. The kind of mom who could love me more than she was disappointed in me.

The moment passes.

"Don't forget to unload the dishwasher and sweep up the used mint in the backyard. It makes the patio look dirty." She touches the wilted leaves on the nearest Pippy-Mint plant. "You're overwatering again."

I wait for the echo of her heels to fade away before I take the wrist sheaths out of the box. As much as I want to throw them under my bed, I force myself to try one on. The straps don't smell like cow, which either means that the leather is fake or it's extra-super expensive. The Ladybird web store is the only place Mom pays full price.

The sheaths fit perfectly. I have no excuse not to dig out my daggers now.

It's been forever since I crawled into the back of my closet, pushing past the mountain of shoes, the dusty clarinet case, and the kneepads Dad made me get when he found out that Kyle was teaching me to skateboard. At the very back, pressed against the wall, is a beat-up pink corduroy backpack with my name embroidered on it. Skirts and dresses ruffle against my face as I back out.

The backpack is lumpy. Patches of the ribbed fabric are bald from being thrown around during hunts. Seeing it makes my heart hum old One Direction songs I'd never admit to knowing in front of the Criminal Element. Back when I was a proud Ladybird legacy, up all night with my sister scouts, this is the bag I carried in the field.

Beneath the itchy wool scarves I made and old water-damaged charm catalogs, I find the keeping case for my daggers. And beneath that, a Don Collins cigar box.

The wooden sides of the box dig into my thighs as I unlatch the top. Inside is a bottle of my abuela's lemon-oil perfume. Mundillo lace baby booties. A Thanksgiving wishbone torn perfectly in half between Chancho and me. A Happy Meal toy.

A silver heart-shaped locket with the name *Molly* engraved on the front.

The locket is featherlight, as if it's made of nothing at all. My thumbnail digs into the right ventricle. The hinge creaks open.

I've heard that they use school photos for girls whose parents don't truly know why they're dead. Girls who went missing on a "camping trip" or got into car wrecks with no witnesses or simply disappeared, leaving behind too much hope.

Molly was a legacy scout, and her family knew the risk. They provided the picture to Headquarters. It's perfectly her, as she was.

Molly Barry, age thirteen. Under a fringe of reddish-brown hair, her round face is scrunched as she cheeses at the camera. I can almost hear the crackle of her laughter. Pushed up by her chipmunk cheeks, her owlish glasses magnify her closed eyes and deep smile lines she'd never grow into.

Exactly how she looked in the moment just before she died.

12

It is the duty of a scout to keep
safe anyone she knows to be terrorized.

—THE LADYBIRD HANDBOOK

Sardine-packed into Kyle's shedroom later that day, the
Criminal Element take up every seat—be it camping
chair or futon. On the projector screen, a demon-clown
bumps into a mechanical bear, causing minimal damage
but maximum noise from the crowd. The furniture rattles
beneath us as we shout instructions at the players.

Paul punches at the air. "Get them fingies flying!"

"Kill him!" Sasha belches.

"Tear his arms off!" I say, because, in general, tearing
someone's arms off is a pretty definitive way to end a fight,
digital or not.

"Whose arms, babe?" Kyle asks, his curls aquiver with
concentration as he stabs both of his little fingers into the
controller buttons.

"I'm not particular." I take another swig from my

alcoholic soda. This hard root beer tastes like fake sugar and rubbing alcohol. Letting it hit room temp has not helped the flavor. I have to exhale the fumes after each swallow, which makes me feel like a very small dragon. I can't tell if that's positive or negative.

The Criminal Element hasn't been all together since I started giving scout lessons. We're totally overdue for a night of just cheap alcohol Kyle's coworkers bought for us and the very simple rules of Pinkies Only.

Onscreen, the demon-clown makes a suspiciously adroit kick-stab combo. Sparks rain from the mecha-panda's armored neck.

"Hands! Hands! Chancho's using hands!" Sasha howls. One of her Sharpie-blackened nails lifts from the neck of her soda bottle to point accusingly at Chancho's game controller.

"I'm just trying to keep a hold!" Chancho lies, sneakily putting a thumb on the controller.

"Auto-forfeit!" Paul says. "It's Pinkies Only, and you know it!"

Pinkies Only is a time-honored tradition within the Criminal Element, dating back to a campaign of intense video game trash talk among all of us that culminated in Chancho telling Kyle that he could beat him at Super Smash Bros. using just his pinkies. The group collectively called his bluff. It was harder than it looked, so we all ended up trying it. It's stupid and makes rounds take forever, but every time Kyle gets a new game, we have to wonder how hard it would be Pinkies Only.

The controllers get redistributed carefully. There's only enough space in the shedroom for us to sit perfectly in a row so long as no one makes any unexpected movements. One of the other benefits of Pinkies Only is that it keeps movement fairly restrained. On other collab gaming nights, everyone leaves with elbow bruises.

Before Kyle moved to the backyard—before his mom remarried and they even had a backyard to live in—the shedroom was a combination laundry room and potting shed. It's huge by shed standards, nearly the size of a garage and powered by solar panels on the roof. Kyle lives in a slice down the center of the shed—a narrow table carved with graffiti, an old dining room chair, and a futon. The home-made projector screen is a white sheet stretched over PVC pipe hung on the back wall.

The bare boards of the left wall are wallpapered in nerdy posters—a map of cryptids in North America, the ocarina songs from Zelda, a chibi Mothman and Sasquatch cheering up a crying Jersey Devil, various Star Wars blueprints at jaunty angles. The right side of the room is crowded with gray storage tubs, stacked four high so that they don't quite block the single window. Some of the tubs are filled with Kyle's possessions. The rest are Christmas decorations. Up in the rafters, holiday lawn inflatables hang limp, gathering dust and spider eggs above the tiny platform where the Xbox sits.

There are plenty of downsides to living in a shed, or even just visiting one regularly: Bugs. Extreme hot or cold. Having to scurry inside the main house through the sliding glass door to use the bathroom.

The privacy can't be beat, though. No one else in the group has a room where all of us could comfortably hang out. Sasha's apartment has thin walls. Paul's bedroom is tiny. Tía Lo eavesdrops. My house has a ridiculously gendered "no boys upstairs" policy that never troubled my dear queer sister but truly harshes my social life.

So whenever we want to hang indoors instead of in a parking lot, the Criminal Element squish together in the shedroom. Three people on the futon and one in each folding chair. We do our best to keep a decent rotation of who has to sit in the inconveniently small chair, but normally it ends up being Paul because he's the tallest and it's hilarious to watch him have to sit with his knees up to his ears.

I scrape the heel of my hand across my forehead and find it slick with sweat. It's not unusual to overheat in the shedroom, especially during summer with the projector and various electronics whirring above us. Shimmying to keep from knocking into Kyle or Sasha on either side of me, I slip out of my hoodie and use the sleeves to blot my hairline.

"Did anyone bring anything to eat?" I ask, setting my hard root beer on the floor between my shoes. "I think I can actually feel the sugar and the alcohol fighting in my stomach to see which one can make me puke first."

"Don't puke, babe." Kyle sets his controller on the edge of the futon so that he can set a concerned hand on my knee. "We could go down to the bowling alley café if you want."

"Just because you work there?" Paul asks, snatching the controller for himself. "We have to go to *your* place from *your* place?"

Kyle's lip curls, one perfectly pointed canine exposed. "It's just a place where fries come from, man."

"Name three others," Paul snaps.

"What?" I laugh, because it's so stupid a comeback that it has to be rhetorical, but Kyle is already listing.

"Wendy's, the Sonic on West Pine—"

"They do tater tots, not fries!"

"Pretty sure they have both," I say. With some difficulty, I cross my legs and squeeze my knees. If we do end up going out for fries, it'll save me the awkwardness of having to go inside and say hello to Kyle's entire family just so I can pee. It would be super un-Dame-like to bump into Kelsey in the middle of the night when I'm low-key lit. It would also totally ruin my plan to pretend that the scouts don't exist tonight. I deserve a night off. I've lived and breathed nothing but scouts for two weeks.

Maybe that's why my spine feels too sharp. Or is it the bars of the futon frame pressing through the thin mattress? I should just bite the bullet and go inside to get some air-conditioning. If I get any hotter, I'll either have a panic attack or summon an avalanche of Tizzy Lice. Either would be hella embarrassing. Both would be catastrophic, especially since Paul and Sasha have the Sight now.

"Are you stupid?" Kyle asks Paul. "Of course Sonic has fries."

Paul's mouth disappears. "Don't call me stupid, shrimp."

"Hey!" I grab one of the many empty Mountain Dew bottles from beneath the futon and whip one at Paul. A bull's-eye straight at the heart, it pongs off his chest and back to the floor. "Don't talk to him like that."

"Yo!" Chancho says, deepening his voice to enforce his few months of seniority. "No short shit. You know that's against shedroom rules. And, Prue, don't throw things at people. You don't know your own strength."

This hints too much at the truth about the scouts—and me—in front of Kyle. I whirl on my cousin, whisper-screaming. "What is the matter with you? Shut up before I call your mom to come get you because you're drunk."

"Birdshit! Then you'd get in trouble, too," he says. He jerks a thumb at Sasha. "And you're drinking with one of your scouts. Your mom would shit bricks."

I splutter incoherently. How dare Chancho talk about what would or would not piss off our family when he committed the ultimate sin? Dosing two of our friends with the Tea of Seeing is so much worse than anything I have ever done. And I'm the one stuck cleaning it up. Training Sasha and keeping Paul calm are both on me. Not him.

"Don't drag me into this," Sasha growls at Chancho. "If I feel your mayo breath on my hair one more time, I will rip your lungs out. Actually, having met your mom, I'd love to piss her off, so maybe I'll rip your lungs out just for funsies."

"Whoa, what? That's totally unfair!" Chancho leans forward in his camping chair. The back legs lift precariously off the floor. "Don't get pissed because you're the worst at Pinkies Only, Sasha. If you'd just take off those *performative* sunglasses—"

"Chancho!" I gasp. He and Sasha might bicker with each other sometimes—because it's the only way she knows how to talk to people and Chancho thinks it's flirting—but I've never heard him outright insult her.

"*I'm* the worst?" She chugs the rest of her soda and wipes her mouth with the back of her hand. "With *you* here, Chancho Marquez? Your pinkies might as well be made of mozzarella sticks the way you mush them around. Besides, Paul's right. I don't know why we always have to be in Kyle's space."

Kyle strains to look at her over his shoulder, not turning his back on Paul. "You're never in my space anymore! We haven't all hung out in weeks. Everyone's working or babysitting, and the Beast up and joined the Girl Scouts like a pod person."

"Wait, what's wrong with being a scout?" I ask Kyle sharply. "Do you think *I'm* a pod person?"

"No, of course not," Kyle says. "It's just weird for Sasha to join up with something girly—"

Sasha's knuckles pop. "What, I'm not allowed to do girly shit?"

"That's not what I said," Kyle says.

"It's what you meant," the Beast growls.

"And Ladybirds aren't cookie pushers," Chancho adds. "Girl Scouts and Ladybirds are different."

"Ugh, no one cares," I groan. "Your mom isn't here, suck-up."

"Kyle, we're not done," Paul says. "Or are you gonna wait for your girlfriend to fight your battles?"

"At least I have a girlfriend to fight for me, Paul," Kyle says. "You talk a big game for someone who's always alone."

Paul launches to his feet. The small camping chair hangs off his ass, a four-pronged tail. He throws it behind him. "You wanna take this outside?"

Kyle stands and cranes his neck—not so much getting in Paul's face as aiming his face at Paul's face. "Let's go."

Under the sweaty haze and mounting irritation of a joke gone too far, I know this isn't right. Like any friend group, the Criminal Element is prone to squabbles. Most arguments get solved with a quick Google or a mumbled apology over jokes that cut too deep. Once or twice, Sasha has stormed home to sulk and smoke in privacy when she's ended up third wheel on a date with me and Kyle or been told to stub out a cigarette before she was ready. The boys tend to peacock until they all realize it's stupid and pointless and we aren't actually in competition with one another. But no one has ever actually thrown a punch.

Until tonight.

Kyle and Paul aren't even to the door of the shed before there are fists in the air. Knuckles collide with stomachs and kidneys and hip bones as Kyle and Paul grapple through the door and out onto the dry lawn. Kyle launches himself at Paul, using the disparities in their height to his advantage as he jumps on the taller boy's back and weighs him down.

"What the hell?" I shout, leaping over the back of the futon to chase after them. "Stop it right now!"

The sky is dark, leaving the backyard lit only by the glow of life continuing inside the main house. Thankfully, no one indoors is close enough to see Chancho race out of the shedroom and tackle Kyle and Paul to the ground. I think he's going to pull them apart, but it turns out that he's just pulling their hair for an advantage.

"This isn't about you!" Paul says, using his shoulder to land a blow to Chancho's stomach.

"Stop leaving me out of shit!" Chancho shouts in their faces. "You think I don't know you all went and saw the last Fast and Furious without me? Ow, that's my eye!"

Looking for an opening into the fight reminds me of

listening for the patter of double Dutch ropes. If I jump in at the wrong time, I risk taking a punch to the head that I'd really rather not. I could pry them all apart, but not without revealing to Kyle just how much stronger I am than I look.

Out of the corner of my eye, I see a flash of fire. A thin stream of piney smoke drifts overhead.

"They never factor us into their fights," Sasha grumbles, blowing a stream of weed smoke out of the side of her mouth. "We should just go get fries and leave them to it."

"You aren't going to help?" I ask.

"Nah." She takes another pull on her joint, her nose wrinkling with the effort of not showing any effort. She exhales smoke, rolling her shoulders backward and forward. "When they tucker themselves out, I'll be rested and ready to trounce them."

Sasha priorities.

If the fight goes on long enough—or Sasha keeps smoking long enough—for Kyle's mom or stepdad to notice, we'll all get kicked out. I'm *so* not losing access to the shedroom over a Pinkies Only fight.

"You guys," I stress again, keeping my voice quiet but sharp. Being outside makes it easier to breathe. "Break it up and we can all walk down to 7-Eleven for snacks. There's more warm root beer in the shedroom. We can't let it go to waste."

The boys aren't listening. They've rolled all the way to the far side of the yard and pinned themselves against the fence. Chancho has Kyle in a headlock while Paul writhes on the ground, trapped between Kyle's legs. The heels of all of their sneakers are carving tracts in the ground that will be impossible to explain away.

"Okay," I say, louder. "That's it. Last call for being reasonable!"

"Say uncle!" Chancho demands.

"Nooo," Kyle and Paul both gurgle.

Idiots. I cast around the yard for something useful to throw, but somehow I don't think launching a bike at them is the right way to defuse the situation. I settle for turning on the hose. The green rubber coil inflates.

"Hey, uh, Prue," Sasha drawls.

I toggle the nozzle from *flower garden* to *jet wash*. "Kinda busy here, Beast."

"*Dame Prudence!*" she hisses.

I turn to look at her out of sheer surprise. She's never used my honorific before.

When I see what's caught her attention, my stomach drops.

Around the side of the shedroom, beneath the single window, is the Goodwin-Mills family barbecue. It's a standard black kettle. As far as I know, the only food Kyle's stepdad, Tim Mills, can make is charcoal-burnt hot dogs. Which are probably not what is ominously rattling the lid right now.

"Shit." I dig the heel of my palm into each of my eyes, hoping to see something different.

It doesn't work.

Skinny, insectoid legs wriggle through the seam between the barbecue cover and base. The cover falls away, revealing a small Scranch. Standing tall on six curved lavender legs, the grub has a flat face that gnashes its three sets of teeth at us.

Scranch feed on anger by first magnifying all of the irritation within a twelve-foot radius around them. It makes them easy to fight—unless someone hides them, in which case the anger expands, directionless.

"It's got black eyes, at least," Sasha says.

"Thank heaven for small mercies." I sigh, the hose nozzle limp between my hands.

"You have any mint on you?" she asks.

I shake my head, not taking my eyes off the grub. "In the shed. I've got an emergency kit in my bag."

"Too far. What if it gets away and pisses off another group of morons?" The Beast passes me her joint before bending down to unlace the top of her boots. From inside, she withdraws the knitting needles that came with her orientation kit. At my slack-jawed amazement, she grins. "I told you I needed them. Cover me."

"Aim for between the eyes," I say.

She snorts. "You so don't have to tell me how to stab stuff."

Holding the knitting needles at an angle like a slasher-movie knife, the Beast darts to the side of the shed and leaps toward the barbecue. The Scranch's legs contract at the multijointed knees, springing it down to the grass. It scuttles back and forth, cracking its teeth, creeping closer and closer to the giant goth maniac bearing down on it. Sasha's anger must be delicious.

To distract from the giddy sounds of the Beast stabbing to her heart's content, I pop the joint into the corner of my mouth—no time to waste a quick calm-down—and crank the spigot up the rest of the way. The hose inflates in my hands, swishing through the grass like a green Frightworm.

Smoke in my eyes, I take aim at the wrestling mass of my friends. Normally, I would give them a lot more chances to break it up and be reasonable. But also normally, their anger wouldn't be cranked up to feed interdimensional parasites.

So I fire.

The jet of icy-cold water blasts Chancho in the face, forcing him to let go of Kyle to keep from drowning. As Chancho throws himself away from the spray, I move the blast down to Kyle and Paul. They get to their feet, holding their hands in front of their faces as I power-wash the fight away. Their protests are gargles and coughs that I don't bother listening to. It doesn't matter why they think they were fighting. Until the grub is dead, the anger will be impossible to conquer.

I check over my shoulder in time to see Sasha lodge a

knitting needle in the Scranch's head. It disappears, the sound too soft to hear under the hose. She gives me a thumbs-up and slips her knitting needles back into her boot.

Slowly, I relax my grip on the nozzle. Water dribbles threateningly from the tip.

"God, it's like you all have never had a drink before," I say to the boys with fake bluster. "Two malt root beers, and you all turn into full-on WorldStar douchebags. You don't see me and the Beast being mean to each other."

Sasha comes around the corner from her first solo banishment. Cheeks glowing, she forces herself to scowl, but when she takes the joint back, it vibrates between her lips. "Y'all should leave the drinking to the big girls. Hit this shit and cool off. Pinkies Only is ruined."

Paul looks down at the patch of dead grass they tore up. "Hey, uh, Kyle. I'm sorry about the short shit. That was real out of line."

Even in the dark, I can see the livid-red spots on Kyle's freckled cheeks. His chest huffs and puffs before settling into even breaths. Dazed, he rakes a finger through his curls, slicking them away from his forehead.

"It's all right. We just got heated," he says. "I'll go get some towels. Anyone need an ice pack for their face?"

"I'll take a bag of peas," Chancho says. He gently touches his orbital bone. "You've got a strong right hook for a southpaw."

"Must have put my full weight behind it." Kyle rolls his

eyes, but the corners of his mouth tip into a won-over smile. Everyone knows how proud he is of being the strongest in the group. Normally, he'd flex his biceps over his head like a bodybuilder, but the remnants of the Scranch's inflated rage weigh on him. "Lemme get a hit before I go, Beast."

I wait for the sliding glass door to close behind him before I run over to the barbecue. The lid is on the ground, but it isn't empty. Taped inside is a grub cage. It's nearly identical to the one that Tía Lo brought to summon additional obstacles for our course. Except that it's a medium-class size, not a small. Like the one that broke at the initiation ceremony.

Its plastic sides are intact, but the scream chamber at the top is cracked down the side. The only thing holding it together is some shredded glittery duct tape, the kind that girls at Goldfields used to spend homeroom turning into wallets. Sasha peers over my shoulder, leaking smoke into my face.

"Someone did this on purpose," I tell her, yanking the broken trap out of the barbecue lid. I flip it over and see the official Ladybird copyright printed on the bottom. "They're hunting."

Sasha gestures toward the roof of the main house. Above us, a curtain flutters, nearly covering the two stricken faces in the window.

"Man, we're supposed to be fucking sisters-in-arms," Sasha says, exhaling smoke through a sneer. "I can't believe they didn't invite me to their sleepover. Give me that trap. I'm gonna flood their teenybopper butts with grubs."

"No way," I say. "We're gonna have a meeting. Now."

It isn't hard to fake being so mad about the boys' scuffle that Sasha has to walk me home. I can't stop replaying the moment the Scranch leapt out of the barbecue, hungry for my closest friends and the rage it brought down on them. I kiss Kyle goodbye, eat an Altoid from the emergency kit in my backpack, and march through the side gate, where Sasha and I squat down to hide. If I don't cool my head, I'll end up drawing more grubs here. I can't put Kyle in any more danger tonight. Un-Sighted, he's a sitting duck for grubs.

After I send a very specifically worded text message, I rub the tremors out of my knuckles and listen for the sounds of the boys restarting the Xbox to play on without us. They're safe. The Scranch is gone. And, hey, the Beast earned her First Banishment charm.

When I'm convinced no one is going to come barging out of the shedroom and spot us, I lead Sasha around the garage to the front steps.

Avi and Kelsey stand together on the small porch in front of security gate. In bare feet and pajamas ranging from fleecy to flouncy, they huddle together, looking small.

Having to look up at them puts me at a disadvantage, so

I pull a Tía Lo and step back onto the lawn and frown at them from a disapproving distance.

"Prima!" Avi preens, aiming her cheekiest smile at me. "I can't believe you're here tonight, too! Are you here to see your novio?"

"Give me a break, Avi," I say, folding my arms. "We all know why we're here."

"Yeah," the Beast growls behind me. "Because I wasn't invited to the pajama party."

"To be fair," Kelsey says, hiding behind the floppy sleeves of her bathrobe. "That's because you're, like, the scariest person anyone has ever met."

Sasha's shoulders drop into a preening wriggle. "Oh, well. That is true."

"What were you guys thinking?" I ask Kelsey and Avi. "I mean, God, Kelsey, you wouldn't even have a room of your own if Kyle hadn't moved out to the shed. And you repay him by catching grubs right outside his window?"

Kelsey blows a frizzy curl out of her face. "Wait. Are you mad at me as my Dame or as my brother's girlfriend?"

"Both!" I throw up my hands and step toward the porch to keep from shouting. "You ruined my night off and put my boyfriend in danger! What were you thinking with that trap?"

"We're scouts!" Avi says, chest puffed in defiance. "We're hunters!"

"No!" I whisper-shout back. "Right now, you're just

untrained little girls! You don't know shit about fuck! Haven't you heard a word I've said? Scouts *die* doing this job. If you caught the wrong thing, *you* would die. To death!"

Neither one looks scared. Instead, they both fall into hips-cocked, arms-folded defense.

"Then why did you let *her* banish the grub *we* caught?" Avi asks, jerking her thumb at the Beast.

"Sasha is your sister scout," I say, for once not caring how much I sound like my mother. Dr. Anita Silva-Perry might be the only person who could strike an appropriate amount of fear into these overeager tweens. "And she is the only one of you who sprang to action when she saw something that threatened people's safety. She didn't peek from behind the curtains, waiting to see if anyone died!"

"It had black eyes. It couldn't kill anyone," Avi says indignantly.

"All grubs start off with black eyes," I snap, "until they eat someone."

I grip the back of my neck and hold in the scream of frustration building in my throat. Why did I ever think I could reason with eighth graders? I wasn't even good at that when I *was* an eighth grader. I couldn't convince Faithlynn to stop making us all dye our hair pink. I couldn't convince Molly not to attempt a trick out of her skill set.

"Do you understand that you could hurt yourselves?" I ask all three of my scouts. "Do you understand that what you do could hurt other people? Do you know what would have happened if that Scranch had gotten inside the shed with us? Or if it had come into the house? If that amount of anger had hit your mom or your stepdad, Kelsey? Did you even stop to consider what would happen if you pulled through a Carnivore? Not every grub that comes through can just be poofed away."

"My mom even lets Jaxon put a scream into a trap," Avi says.

"Your mom has thirty years of experience. There is nothing Jax could pull through that she couldn't kill. That isn't true for you. It's not even true for me! I don't carry steel. If there was a Carnivore in that trap, I wouldn't have been able to protect you. You can't take a Root shot with fucking knitting needles." The sinus stabbing pain of tears welling in the corners of my eyes is so embarrassing. Dames don't cry in front of their scouts. Dame Debby didn't even cry in front of us at the hospital when we told her that Molly was dead. "I know you're curious, but you have to be smart. Just because you've never seen a White-Eyes before doesn't mean that they can't kill you. Even a Critter could hurt you. Drain your energy. Change in front of you."

Without my asking, my brain shows me flashes of the could-have-beens and yet-to-bes: the Criminal Element taking the fight too far, the babybirds juicing up their Scranch into something unkillable. Noses broken. Blood flowing. Draining. Screaming.

The night is cool, but suddenly I'm as hot and sweaty as I was squished on the futon in the shedroom. As my lungs start to wheeze, my knees give out, sending me to all fours. The position isn't as strong as it is with a yoga mat beneath me. It feels like fainting in slow motion.

"She's having a panic attack!"

"Prudence Perry?"

"Oh God, we disappointed her to death."

People are fluttering toward me. I put a hand out. The worst thing for a panic attack is being touched.

"Stand back," the Beast says.

I'm so thankful for her that I could almost risk the stabbing that hugging her would bring.

Avi and Kelsey stop in their tracks. The worry and confusion coming off them is like a thousand emotional cuts.

I let my neck go limp, focusing on the sharp green blades of grass crushed beneath my fingers. It's so different from the hay-colored lawn in the back.

"This was a bad idea," I confess to the dirt. "This whole experiment of me leading a circle. I wasn't a scout for long enough to learn how to do this part. I can make schedules and brew tea and do the obstacle course, but I can't make you understand what you risk just by having the Sight. If anything happened. To you. Because of you. It would be my fault. And I can't live with that. Not again." Hot tears leak down the side of my face as I force myself to look up at them. "So maybe I should just be done."

"Done how?" Sasha asks, towering over the others.

I dab the wet tip of my nose with my sleeve and sit back on my heels. "Done like I need to quit. I'd rather switch schools than get you guys killed."

"What? Pru—Dame Prudence!" Kelsey stammers to correct herself.

"Oh, boo. You don't mean that," Avi says. "We're legacy scouts, prima. You know that it's our duty to protect Poppy Hills."

"Just because it's *someone's* duty doesn't mean it's yours." It's hard to catch hold of my anger, but I find it and cling to it. It's next to impossible to hyperventilate and rage at the same time. Anger needs airflow. Like a fire. "If you make a stupid mistake like using broken equipment, why would I sign off on you getting a real weapon? It's not like you tried to start with earning all of your basic charms. You still think that it's going to be all monsters and killing. You have to do the other stuff, too. The stuff that's actually in the Handbook. Gardening, community projects—"

"We were just talking about our first project!" Kelsey blurts. "We've spent a whole hour talking about what we want to do for our first act of public good!"

"We wanted to surprise you," Avi sulks.

"Color *me* surprised," Sasha mutters.

I want to walk away from all of this, to go back to a month ago when my biggest worry would have been whether to go home or drag Sasha down to Sonic for a pee break and a s'mores malt. But curiosity gets the better of me. I wipe my nose on my sleeve. "What's the project?"

"A car wash!" Avi says.

My interest instantly deflates.

"So your big plan is the literal first idea listed in chapter four of the Handbook?"

"And it's the cheapest, so we could do it *this week*," Avi says with an exaggerated nod that goes on too long.

"We thought we could send out invites specifically to the other nearby circles," Kelsey says. "Meet other scouts. Hear what it's like."

"Maybe finally meet the circle we're going to be joining at the end of summer?" Avi adds.

"You want to meet the senior scouts?" I ask, taken aback. I honestly haven't considered introducing them to Faithlynn, Jennica, and Gabby. I've been picturing sending them off to Dame Debby's house and waving from the curb like a mom at a sleepover.

I can't think of anything more awkward than having to face my old circle, much less present my hatchling babybirds to them.

"I don't know," I say. "Can I trust you not to set any more unsupervised traps?"

"Yes!"

"Of course!"

"I did kill that grub with zero help," Sasha grumbles. I

stare at her blankly until she gives a petulant stomp. "But I don't want you to quit. So. Sure. Swearsies."

I blow out a long breath and sweep the wetness from my cheeks. "You will have to earn back my trust. I'm talking maximum butt-kissing. You will memorize the entire grub identification chapter. You will earn Arts and Crafts charms. You will make more cookie-brownies because they haunt my dreams."

"Of course! As many as you want!" Kelsey says.

"And our car wash?" Avi asks.

I bite the inside of my cheek, focusing on anything but the queasy flop in my stomach. "Yes, we can schedule a car wash. It's a Ladybird rite of passage. And I'm sure my sister left her buckets and sponges in our garage. But you all are on punishment. Get ready for Go Hunt and burpees."

13

Public service is the act of beautifying
your community from within.

–THE LADYBIRD HANDBOOK

Ladybirds are known for two public-good campaigns:
providing breakfast to high schoolers before the SATs
and free car washes. The car washes, which come with an
interior vacuum and a peppermint-oil carpet spritz, are
more popular. It's a decent start to the second week of our
new circle.

To the surprise of no one, the Handbook has strict rules
about car washes. While scouts should be friendly with
the public, the goal is to sweep the cars for grubs, not to
make friends. The soap must include at least ten drops of
peppermint oil per cup. Scouts washing the cars can wear
bathing suits only so long as their "back and shoulders are
covered."

The babybirds and I have all opted for T-shirts and
shorts. Sasha inexplicably arrived in canvas coveralls with

the arms removed. I'm pretty sure she's humming "Greased Lightning," but it's slightly too quiet for me to make out.

I pull on the stretchy hem of my left sleeve. Today could be considered too hot for long sleeves, but getting dressed this morning, I couldn't bring myself to face an entire day of questions about my scar. Mom forced me to post an announcement to the Dame message boards, but she also had my sister make a graphic to share on social media. Any circle within fifty miles that isn't locked in combat or doing a public-good campaign of their own is going to pass through the Turnip and Beet It parking lot to check out the newbies.

Every car that unloads with cheers of "Hello, sisters!" makes the hair on the back of my neck stand up. So far, we've met scouts from Suisun and Green Valley and retired Dames from as far as Oakland and Sacramento.

No sign of the other Poppy Hills scouts. Yet.

I barely slept last night. In the dark, my brain played everything it could find filed under Ladybirds. Memories of birthday parties and scout milestones and gleeful violence and bone-deep terror kept me up for hours. From our early initiation days, learning obedience and gardening from Dame Debby, to the last day of eighth grade, when I knew I was finally free of them.

Well, when I *thought* I knew.

"Remember," I tell the scouts, "the reason we have car washes is to banish any hitchhiking grubs. If you see something you don't recognize or anything with white eyes, just call out the word *squeegee*, and I'll come help."

To the best of my ability, I don't say out loud. Like any day ending in *y*, all I can do is hope not to run into anything Carnivorous while Mom and Tía Lo are off treating themselves to pedicures on the other side of the plaza.

"Sasha," Kelsey says as she accepts the shop-vac hose from the Beast, "why didn't the Scranch in the barbecue make you go berserk like it did everyone else?"

Sasha looks up from her position, kneeling half-inside a two-door that belongs to a grocery-shopping local, not a scout. "Aww, little bird. I'm always berserk." She unfurls a full Friendly Face, thrusting her lower jaw forward to accentuate her canines.

Kelsey takes two steps backward before getting distracted by a line of cars and minivans turning into the parking lot.

"More customers!" she cheers.

"They aren't really customers if we can't charge them," Avi says, drowning sponges in one of three matching white buckets. "The Handbook calls them 'patrons.'"

The minivans park and pour out a dozen scouts dressed in identical lavender T-shirts that announce them as the MARE ISLAND TECHNICAL ACADEMY LADYBIRDS. They all look Avi's age. She's actually bigger than some of them.

I plaster on a smile and shake hands with the moms, starting with the one in the silver Dame brooch. She's dressed to match her scouts, down to the charm bracelet—although the charms give away her age. One of them is shaped like a landline telephone.

"Welcome to our introductory car wash," I say. "Thank you so much for coming all this way. Please help yourself to a snack."

I gesture to the refreshment table. Kelsey found the recipe guide in the back of her Handbook. Our patrons have their choice between a birdbark granola bar or a less Ladybirdy Rice Krispies treat.

The lavender Dame beams as her scouts pick up sponges and help suds down the vans. "Aww. Look at them, jumping in to help. Sweet darlings. Once they're done with our cars, we'll move them out of the way, but we'd love to hang out for a bit. I can't tell you how excited my girls have been to have scouts their own age around."

"That's so kind. Thank you. Many hands make light work," I say. It's traditional for visiting scouts to help out with a public-good campaign but equally traditional for the home team to make a big deal out of it. "Stay as long as you want. There's a coffee counter inside the Turnip, too. Just so you know."

The moms don't need telling twice. Wholly uninterested in our refreshments, they wave and blow kisses at the Mare Island scouts, who don't seem to notice at all. They've moved on to the most Ladybird activity, showing off charms and telling tales that have Avi's mouth agape.

"Look! It's Pa-roo-dence Perry."

From behind the minivans, the senior scouts step out of the next car in the queue. The voice dragging my name out into a yodel is Jennica Tillerman's. She's always said it that way, from the moment we met at our initiation ceremony. Even when she used to shorten it, she'd end up calling me "Pa-roo," like she was trying to say *Peru* and *Paris* at the same time. She wiggles pink plastic fingers at me as Faithlynn and Gabby walk in stride with her.

Toward me.

At me.

Rooted to the spot, I can't help but catalog all the ways they've changed. And out of my suddenly dry mouth falls, "Wow. You're all gotten so . . . tall."

Three years apart, and this is the best I can do. What am I supposed to say? The last time we were all together was on the minivan ride to the hospital. I quit without saying goodbye, too scared to face the field again. I never thought I'd be forced to regret that.

Unlike when my mom and Tía Lo run into their sister scouts, no one in my old circle rushes to give hugs or kiss cheeks. There is only awkward silence and the tacit understanding of a missing link. We aren't a circle anymore. Circles are a closed loop. The four of us can't close without Molly.

They are a team. I am an outsider.

Rather than the huge matching bows she and Faithlynn used to wear, Jennica's glossy brown hair is now pulled up with a thick satin scrunchie. With her big blue doll eyes and tiny mouth, she looks too delicate to have ever broken a sweat, much less devoted her life to staying at the top of the hunting scoreboard. Her left arm is white under a layer of shimmering bronzer-lotion. Her right arm is pink plastic. The prosthesis was engineered especially for her at UC Davis Medical Center but funded by Headquarters, which may explain the color choice. Looking at it, I have to force myself not to picture the moment the Scranch ate the hand off her wrist or how she cradled the wet stump to her chest as we stumbled into the emergency room.

Gabby Colucci is wearing camo leggings with a matching tank top. When we were younger, being the only mixed-race kids we knew—but weren't related to—made our connection feel special. Italian and El Salvadoran, Gabby is the natural tan that Jennica sprays herself to mimic. This hasn't stopped Gabby from developing a gnarly spiderweb sunburn on her back the size and shape of a scabbard. Anyone else would think it was a racerback tan.

They say that your weapon says a lot about you. Faithlynn isn't just an ax thrower; she's a dual wielder—the Ladybird equivalent to being born a triple Leo, a never-ending silent scream for attention. Like my mother, Jennica has a whip sword—giving her away as an overplanner who lashes out at the first sign of attack. Gabby, a first-generation scout who was recruited for being a gymnast who also read fantasy novels, is a classic sword girl.

Does she miss the weight of her sword out in public now, or is she relieved to have full range of motion? Three years ago, I would have just asked. I would have been allowed. Sisters can ask each other anything.

Quitters, on the other hand?

"Hi, Prudence," Gabby says, still good for breaking into a silence. "Cute hair."

"Thanks. You too." Gabby looks much better with her natural dark hair than the old pastel pink. I push my sleeves up over my wrist bones. My arms have started to sweat. Or maybe all of me is sweating. "Dame Debby isn't with you?"

Faithlynn arches an imperious eyebrow that betrays her true dishwater blond. "No. Is *your* mommy here?"

I have never prayed harder for my mother not to appear. May her pedicure smear and have to be redone. Otherwise, I will have no choice but to hide in the cart corral.

"I just thought Debby might want to meet the scouts I've been training for you guys," I say. I'm ashamed to hear how small my voice is.

Faithlynn tucks her chin into her neck. "Oh, no. She'll meet them when they're steel certified. You don't taste a cake halfway through baking."

I can feel the babybirds paying attention. I wonder what has given away that these are the Poppy Hills senior scouts. Is it the synchronized way they move? Or is it because all the blood has run out of my face to pump triple speed in my heart?

The Mare Island scouts eyes go reverently wide. *Ugh*. I forgot. They all know exactly who these scouts are. Or, at least, they think they do. They're seeing the girls at the top of the leaderboard. The most Carnivore kills in Northern California, blah blah blah.

Faithlynn knows that they know. Smirking, she flicks her eyes at them and gives her charms a jingle. Three full bracelets make quite a racket.

From the way they keep cutting their eyes toward us, I can tell that Kelsey, Avi, and Sasha are wondering what the holdup is with introductions. The whole point of this car wash was to let them meet their future circle. But I don't want to present them to someone who would refer to them as a half-baked cake.

Red-brown hair in the distance makes an infantile part of my brain scream: *Molly!* It seems wrong that any part of me could forget her death long enough to double-take, but I do. Grouped in among the Mare Island scouts is an auburn-haired scout biting into a square of birdbark. But she's not Molly. She's too tall. Too alive. She isn't a dead thirteen-year-old in a Goldfields sweatshirt.

Molly isn't a ghost. Whatever spark defined her was eaten up and turned to fuel three years ago. I've accepted that, but I've never seen the senior scouts all together without Molly, so she's swimming around my mind.

I shouldn't have opened her locket.

In the echoing silence, the senior scouts follow my

glance to the huge flock of babybirds—and Sasha, who has taken control of the hose.

"They're so young," I say. Why is it so much harder to talk to people you used to know than to people you've never known? I almost miss the Mare Island moms.

"They're not as young as we were when we passed over the threshold," Gabby says. The intervening years haven't slowed her speech at all. She talks like she's in fast-forward, like she's afraid of being interrupted.

"Nearly," Jennica says. She inclines her head at the auburn-haired girl, who is helping herself to two of the Rice Krispies treats. "Shelby's twelve and just passed the steel skills test. Mare Island has been drowning in grubs."

"It's the Six Flags," Faithlynn says. "You couldn't pay me to patrol a town with an amusement park. You need a whole circle just to sweep out the Nock Jaws."

Gabby ticks off two more items on her fingers. "Add in a high homeless population and encroaching gentrification . . ."

"Lots of misery," I finish for her.

"Lots of Carnivores," Faithlynn corrects.

"Earlier this year I went and helped their circle take down a six-foot Frightworm on a golf course," Jennica says, flicking her hair over her shoulder with her pink plastic fingers. "A golf course! Can you believe it? That's, like, the *last* place I would go looking for an eff-dubs. People will get deathly afraid anywhere these days! What's next? Dreary Blight at Disneyland?"

This is what passes for humor in Ladybird circles. I'd forgotten. As Gabby and Faithlynn laugh, I force myself to join in.

"It's not a customer or a patron," I hear Kelsey groan. "It's just my brother."

"Ooh, prima!" Avi squeals. "I mean, Dame Prue, your novio is here!"

A white truck pulls into the parking lot.

Oh no, babe. Why now?

My stomach bungees to the ground and back up into my throat. Part of me wishes I could shoo Kyle far away. The other part would love nothing more than to jump into the truck and let him drive me back to normal life. Or Sonic for a malt.

Low to the ground with a permanent squeak in its suspension, Kyle's truck is to a normal truck what a miniature horse is to a Clydesdale. Which should make it easier to wash. Any of the babybirds can easily reach the roof.

Well. Except Avi.

Excusing myself with mostly gibberish, I escape the senior scouts and rush to meet my boyfriend at the end of our line of cars. I do not want him anywhere near the senior scouts. Or any scouts.

"Babe, you have your keys back!" I exclaim.

"Just to drive myself to work. I just fudged my hours to Mom and Tim so I could stop by," Kyle says. His lips make a beeline for mine but veer left at the last second. He jerks his head at the car wash in progress. "Uh, sorry. Is this a hands-to-ourselves situation?"

"They're Ladybirds. They can handle it." I settle my hands on his chest and press up on the balls of my feet. Kissing Kyle Goodwin makes me feel like a princess—until it makes me feel like a Nock Jaw who just wants to devour him whole. That's around the point where I disengage the kiss and gesture to the treat table beyond the minivans. "Can I interest you in a complimentary wait-snack? Fresh from your own kitchen?"

He shakes his head. "I'm good. I had burnt birdbark for breakfast."

"Burning it might actually give it some flavor."

"Still pretty bland, I'm sorry to say." He reaches out and takes my hands. His thumb brushes each of the charms on my wrist so that they tinkle together musically. I notice how thin my bracelet looks compared to Faithlynn's stacks. "So, the other night, when I fucked up Pinkies Only—"

"With help," I say, thinking of the Scranch.

"With help," he agrees, thinking of Paul and Chancho. "It's just that if a night is going to end with everyone going home early, I'd rather you be the one who stays."

"Oh yeah?" I dip my chin into my shoulder to hide my hot cheeks. "Is this conversation going to stay PG-13? I'm at work and there are, like, a million scouts watching us."

He stuffs his hands in his pockets and scuffs an inno-cent heel against the pavement. "Hey, I'm Disney Channel, babe. I just needed to state, for the record, that I'm sorry you felt like you had to leave. I get it. But I'm sorry. And I'd like to make more time for us to hang out. Minus the Criminal Element."

"I'd like that, too," I say, looking down at the toes of his shoes. Kyle and I haven't had as much alone time together as either of us would probably like. "But I don't really own my time this summer. Until I get back out of the scouts, every day is stuff like this. Car washes and tea parties."

"And running," Kyle says. "Kelsey said you've got them jogging your neighborhood. And you're still doing the five-o'clock run with your mom and aunt?"

I can't imagine how ridiculous it sounds to him that I run five miles every morning before dawn just for "quality time" with Mom and Tía Lo. Especially since he's met both of them.

"Yep," I say, hating how much the truth feels like a lie. "I'm, like, peak runner's high all day."

In the distance, Faithlynn is watching the babybirds dry her car with keen interest. I'm sure she's waiting for them to screw up so she can call her mom and tell her what a failure of a leader I am.

"Are those your old friends?" Kyle asks, looking over my shoulder at the senior scouts. Jennica waggles her pink fingers at him like she's on a parade float. "I remember when you used to eat lunch with them at Goldfields."

"You do?" I blink at him. "That's before we knew each other."

"I mean, we hadn't been introduced, but I noticed you," he says. "Chancho's cute cousin with the pink hair. You and the scouts used to walk like you were in a music video. Like there should have been fans on you or something."

He mimes his hair blowing back and I laugh. Sometimes, it still feels like a dream come true to realize that he was secretly watching me when I was secretly watching him. It's weird to remember how mysterious he used to be to me. How I would watch him out of the corner of my eye, not knowing he was watching me too.

"Dame Prue?" Avi calls. "Is there another squeegee?"

Squeegee. They need my help.

Goose bumps run up and down my arms. To keep Kyle from noticing, I kiss him twice.

"Duty calls." I steal a third peck and twirl out of his grasp. I call back to him, "If you go inside and catch my dad, he'll hook you up with some fruit samples. He's been bragging about how good the mangoes are. When you come back, the truck will shine like new!"

Kyle looks understandably confused—I've never tried to pawn him off on fruit before—but he shuffles across the parking lot anyway, curls bouncing. When he waves at Kelsey, she ignores him.

I can't help but rewrite the entire conversation in my

head with Kyle fully filled in. About the scouts. About the Scranch that ruined Pinkies Only. About me.

How different would I feel if I could tell him what today really means to me?

How different would he feel if he knew?

I shake that thought away. It doesn't matter how either of us would feel. At the end of the summer, the babybirds will graduate to Dame Debby's care and I will drink the Tea of Forgetting. I'll never have to worry about hiding anything from Kyle, because I'll be officially out. Done. Forever.

I hurry over, stepping in a soapy puddle in the process. Inside my Keds, my socks squish. Why couldn't Ladybirds have a sponsorship deal with a water-resistant shoe company? Leather shoes would be so much more practical.

The girl whom Jennica called Shelby is wiping her hands on the sides of her legs as though she's trying to smear away invisible spiderwebs.

"You guys are so your own," she says. "I wouldn't take those on without steel. Or maybe a flamethrower."

I push past the cringing Mare Island scouts to find my babybirds shivering together. Kelsey looks distinctly more green than normal. I start to ask why when I see movement in the back seat of the car.

Next to the nozzle of the shop vac on the carpeted floor of Faithlynn's back seat is a pack of Tizzy Lice. Despite their empty black eyes taking up most of their small bodies, they continually knock into one another's figure-eight paths like bumper cars. And as they do, they take beak-bites of orange fluff, cannibalizing one another bit by bit.

Kelsey screams as the victors swell in size.

Avi clamps both her hands over Kelsey's nose and mouth, but not before Faithlynn notices.

"We just got back from a sweep of Solano Park," she calls with a smile that doesn't match the glint in her eye. "We might have tracked some pests into the car."

"Just one or two," Jennica adds with a smile. "Nothing you can't handle!"

Apart from its waltzing gait, the Tizzy Louse defends itself via chemical repulsion. It lets off a pheromone whose effects can best be described as "creeping you the fuck out of your skin." All of a sudden, the idea of its tiny, silly nipple feet touching your skin makes you want to catch fire. Every primal instinct in your body maxes out, wanting to run far in the other direction.

Unless you can remember the flash card with the cherubic tangerine bell with the goldfinch smile and force yourself to act against every instinct lighting up your nerves.

"They d-don't respond to the m-mint," Avi stutters, her arms wrapped around her waist in a self-hug that might also indicate nausea. "I sprayed them and—" She interrupts herself to retch. "And they starting moving *faster*."

"Yeah, once they start eating one another, they grow Roots," I say, cringing. If Mom comes back and sees this many grubs one human snack away from going White-Eyes, I will never live down not wearing my new wrist sheaths today. Paz literally got a scholarship studying the cannibalistic patterns of grubs. "That makes them, uh, hardier than the average Critter. They need to be stabbed."

"Move," Sasha says, already rolling up the legs of her coveralls to show where she's stashed two knitting needles. "I'm the best at stabbing."

The tip of her knitting needle bears down, then stops. Sasha squeezes her eyes shut. Tremors run up and down her arm, but the knitting needle doesn't move. Arm still raised, she slow turns her head to me. Through gritted teeth, she asks, "What the fuck? I . . . I can't."

New Tizzy Lice explode around her feet, bumping clumsily into one another. I turn to the Mare Island scouts.

"Can you take care of those for us?" I ask with tight politeness. "There's extra mint oil in the green bucket. Keep it casual, though."

"We're on it," Shelby says with a sharp salute that I wish I could tell her is so very the opposite of casual.

The Mare Island scouts disperse in all directions, chasing down the Tizzy Lice and bonking them on the head with mint oil.

Faithlynn, Gabby, and Jennica roar with laughter from the refreshment table.

"If Sasha can't stab it, then who the heck can?" Kelsey asks.

She, Avi, and Sasha look at me. The grubs' squeaking gets louder, hitting the back of my skull like the shriek of a fork on teeth. The sound is starting to pull me under, pull me *back*. I can feel Faithlynn, Jennica, and Gabby watching me with hungry interest.

This isn't a test for the babybirds. It's a test for me.

Fuck that.

I look at Sasha, Avi, and Kelsey. "You guys saw me take down Tizzy Lice at the initiation ceremony. You know they can be banished. You just have to remember that all they can do is make you feel bad. They can't hurt you. They can't kill you. They just want to bully you. You have to trust yourselves, even though there's a chemical reaction in your brain telling you lies."

"Trust ourselves," Avi echoes, drawing her knitting needles out of her knee socks. "Right. Right! We got this! We're Ladybirds. If the senior scouts could drive here with these—these stupid nuggets in their car, we can banish them!"

"Yeah!" Kelsey says, scrambling for the bucket of extra knitting needles. "We got this! But what if they explode into goo and guts and—sorry. We got this."

They look at Sasha, who straightens her spine and grumbles. "Yeah, yeah. We got this."

"On three," I tell them. "Ready? One, two—"

"Stab!" Avi cries.

Wooden sticks slice through the air in a minty wind. The three of them rain down stabs on Faithlynn's upholstery. Knitting needles chase down each Tizzy Louse in turn, exploding them as they hit between the eyes. Kelsey mumbles "Gross gross gross" the whole time, but she and the others successfully clean the car. Sasha does the honor of spritzing the peppermint oil to seal the job.

"We did it!" Avi cheers, bouncing up and down so that she's intermittently Sasha's height. "You guys! We really did it!"

While they takes turns high-fiving, I call to Faithlynn, "Your car is ready to go."

Faithlynn takes an extra serving of birdbark from the refreshment table before she leads her circle over. Of course Faithlynn Brett likes birdbark. It proves that she has absolutely no taste.

"Scouts," I say to the babybirds with all the formality of my mother answering a business call. I gesture to the approaching senior scouts. "This is Circle 6986. Faithlynn Brett, Jennica Tillerman, and Gabby Colucci."

"Hello, sisters!" the babybirds say dutifully. Sasha, I believe, just moves her mouth.

Gabby waves with a Rice Krispies treat. "Nice to meet you guys. Great snacks."

Kelsey turns pink with pride and slurps her braces. "Thanks! I made them."

"I love how you ignored the recipes in the Handbook," Gabby says. "The traditional treats can be so repetitive."

Kelsey's flush disappears as she tries to translate whether or not this is a compliment.

"We're looking forward to joining you once we're steel certified," Avi says, turning the force of her enthusiasm on Faithlynn.

"We're looking forward to seeing how you shape up," Faithlynn says. "There's only a few more weeks of summer."

Would it kill her to smile or say something encouraging? Even Dame Debby would have a platitude at the ready. Besides, it's not even July yet. There's plenty of time to get the girls through training.

"A lot can change in two months," I say defiantly.

Faithlynn snaps a piece of birdbark between her teeth. "Let's hope so."

I send the babybirds to start working on Kyle's truck before Faithlynn can shit all over their buoyed enthusiasm.

"We've got a patrol to finish," Faithlynn announces, jingling her car keys. "We can't hang out socializing all day."

"Good to see you again, Prue," Gabby says as she hops into the newly clean back seat. How on earth did she survive the drive here with those Tizzy Lice? Did she make them or just round them up?

"Hopefully, next time it won't take three years," Jennica says, frowning as she slides into the front seat.

Faithlynn finishes her birdbark and towers over me. My head starts where her ponytail ends.

"They're too weak to be scouts," she declares under her breath. "You'll need to toughen them up if you want to pass them off to us. I wouldn't send them to hunt Easter eggs." She jabs two fingers into my shoulder joint and shoves, forcing me to stumble back a step. "And I wouldn't send *you* to hunt anything, quitter."

Anger and hurt keep me rooted to the spot, even as the engine turns over and the car speeds out of the lot. It's not that I don't think the babybirds are soft. They're sweet, and they love baking and sleepovers—but they managed to beat a carful of grubs anyway.

Besides, Ladybirds shouldn't have to be cold-blooded to get the job done. Just because that's the way it's always been done doesn't make it right.

Sasha sidles up to me, thumbs hooked in the pockets of her coveralls. She jerks her head at the senior scouts pulling out of the lot. "I don't like the tall one's face."

"Be nice. Faithlynn's gonna be your sister scout."

"Not if I blow up her car."

"No, Sasha."

She takes out a plastic lighter from her pocket and flicks the sparkwheel with her thumbnail. "All I'd need is a can of dollar-store hair spray—"

"No!"

14

Every charm in the catalog is an opportunity to
become a stronger and smarter scout.

—THE LADYBIRD HANDBOOK

Gathered under the pergola in my backyard for a formal meeting, I pass out everyone's first two charms,
rush-ordered for the occasion, the Identification charm—
a miniature silver Handbook—and the First Banishment
golden robin.

"Congratulations," I tell the babybirds. "Thanks to some
light hazing from the senior scouts and your teamwork
with the Tizzy Lice, you have all earned your first charms!"

"I have waited my whole life for this," Avi squeals,
clutching her charms so hard that the tips of her fingers
turn white. She plants a noisy kiss on the robin's teensy beak.

"I've only been waiting a week, but I'm still hyped,"
Sasha says.

"This explains why there are pliers next to the sugar
bowl," Kelsey says, reaching for the plate of tools. She

squints through the Handbook's little loop. "These suckers are hecka tiny!"

"You'll get good at it," I assure her. "By your fifth charm, you'll be able to snap them on in a jiff. Which brings me to our first order of business today." From out of the same bag, I fish out the charm catalogs. They're floppy magazine paper with two models pretending to be scouts on the cover. I pass them around. "You need to fill your bracelets by the end of summer, and I need to fill in some of the charms I missed back in the day, so why don't we all choose one or two charms and then vote on what we want to focus on for the next week or two?"

"You need charms, too?" Avi asks with a snicker. "But you have a whole bracelet!"

"Bracelets only count if they're balanced," I say, echoing Dame Debby. "You're not supposed to get ten field charms, then quit, like I did."

"Then it's a good thing you're back," Kelsey says, and grins at me.

I peel open the cover of the charms catalog, trying to ignore the sinking in my stomach. "Yeah. Good thing."

GROUP PICK: Entry Point Expert
CHARM: Binoculars

- *Explain the causation of entry-point damage.*

- *Track entry points on a map and note any emerging patterns.*
- *Using either the official Ladybird iOS app or the website, report three different entry points in your town to Ladybird Headquarters.*

"This is what we're looking for, right?" Sasha asks, tromping through someone's rock garden to point at their back fence. There is a suspiciously shriveled wild garlic plant at the base of a warped wooden fence. "Dead plants, wood curved but not broken. This is definitely an entry point."

"It's hard to tell from this side." Avi gets down on her hands and knees in the rocks and presses her eye to the fence. "I think I see something shimmery on the other side. It could be interdimensional iridescence. But there also could be a suncatcher somewhere."

"Hold on." The Beast pulls her backpack off her shoulders. Before I can stop her, she has the emergency ladder hooked on to the fence. She easily loops one foot in the lowest rung and heaves herself up to peer over the fence. "Nope. You're right, Avi. Just a suncatcher and a shitty fence."

"So, what do you think made that?" Kelsey asks, pointing across the street to a tree set between houses, cracked nearly in half with a deep horizontal slash.

If it were a person, it would never survive a wound so deep and jagged across its trunk. The oak's pale insides are striking against its outer bark, especially at its iridescent center. Long-limbed branches twist inward as though trying to hold itself together.

"The split in the bark looks like what was under the Dreary Blight at Goldfields," Avi says, tracing the air in a broken horizontal line. "Only much bigger."

"Which means?" I prompt.

"The grub that came through here is bigger than a wall full of Dreary Blight?" Kelsey says, knowing the answer despite saying it like a question.

"Exactly," I say. "The bigger the grub, the bigger the entry point. Which means *that* tree is definitely something we need to report."

Avi whips her phone out. "I'm on it. My mom got me an iPhone *just* so I could use the Ladybird app."

Kelsey cocks her head at Sasha. "You walk around with a ladder in your backpack?"

The Beast leaps back down to the ground and collapses the ladder like an accordion. "Aren't scouts supposed to be prepared?"

KELSEY'S PICK: Lariat Lady
CHARM: Lariat

- Master use of 30' lariat.
- Demonstrate ability to tie a honda knot.
- Catch a grub with a 10' throw.

My charm bracelet rings as I clap my hands. "All right, you know you can take him down in a group, but let's go one by one. Kelsey, you wanna go first?"

Chancho flings sweat from his brow and turns his cap around. After I count down from three, he sprints toward the back fence. When he passes the Pippy-Mint planter we're using as a distance marker, he starts zigzagging back and forth.

Nylon utility rope flies across the yard. One loop falls short, landing to the left of Chancho's heel.

"Get his feet!" Avi calls.

"The practice log didn't kick this much," Kelsey complains, spinning her lariat overhead again.

"Grubs will kick even harder," I warn. "And they'll be feeding on your energy at the same time."

That's why we aren't training using grubs, even though that's the classic approach. Dame Debby taught me to swing a lariat in the middle of being chased around an obstacle course. Not only did it take way longer for me to master swinging a rope, but I also fumbled the knot and fell out of the stutter steps, twisting my ankle. Being scared just makes you more likely to get injured.

It's easier for the babybirds—and me—to focus on developing new skills when we aren't fighting for our lives.

The rope flies again, this time slipping neatly over Chancho's shoulders. With a tug, the knot pulls tight around his waist.

"Try to get away, Chancho! Don't make it too easy!" Sasha hollers. She sidles up to me and cocks her head as my cousin writhes on the ground. "How much did you pay him to do this?"

"In dollars? Nothing." I fold my arms and take a step backward as Avi's rope flies by, trying to catch her brother's flailing ankles. "I'm going to make Jaxon's breakfast twice a week for the rest of summer."

Sasha snorts. "That is a terrible trade."

"Chancho will trade anything if it means he can sleep in. On Christmas morning, he pays all of his siblings twenty bucks to pretend to sleep until nine," I say with a shrug. "Hey! That's enough. Don't drag him through the grass. Tía Lo will kill us if we stain his clothes."

PRUDENCE'S PICK: Legacy Learning
CHARM: Pair of hands clasped in a handshake

- *Ask an older scout to share a trade secret with you.*
- *Learn about the history of Ladybirds from before your time.*
- *Write a report on the difference between scouts of today and scouts of the past.*

My sister's face peers out from my laptop screen. In the background, her apartment is practically a replica of the Ladybird shrine in Mom's home office. She even has the same framed painting of Ladybird founder Kitty Crosby-Fowler, imperiously holding a hatchet and a teacup.

"Hello, sisters!" Paz says, her eyes crinkling under the force of her smile as she thrusts her face into the camera. "Aww, look at you! My hermana's hermanas! I'm so honored to be your legacy interview."

"Hi, prima!" Avi says. She pushes forward to be the closest to the laptop. "The Handbook says we're supposed to learn about scouts from before our time. Have things changed that much since you went over the threshold? I know you're in college and everything, but it wasn't *that* long ago. Not as long ago as your mom. Or my mom." She shoots me a pointed look over her shoulder, passing along some of Tía Lo's passive-aggression. Like I don't get enough of *that* on dawn patrol.

"Oh, things have totally changed since I started!" Paz says. She pushes her flop of short hair away from her eye. "I was first initiated almost ten years ago, and we were still using the last edition of the Handbook. We weren't allowed to take our steel test until we'd 'entered womanhood.'" She throws up air quotes on either side of her eye roll. "So antiquated and *so* transphobic. First of all, not all girls have periods. And it meant that my sister scouts couldn't all cross the threshold together. I didn't get my sword until sophomore year of high school. Our family are late bloomers. Except for Prue. She started her period the same year I did!"

"Oh my God, Paz, could you not—"

"But then the tenth edition of the Handbook came

out and now scouts take their steel test as soon as they've earned their first full bracelet. Sometimes as young as ten or eleven. Which is good for patrol rotation, but can be really hard on scouts who don't come from legacy houses. Most parents find a retractable sword in their kid's room and they have questions, you know? But that's led to some really interesting innovations in weaponry in the last few years. The umbrella ax and the punch-activated knife-gloves came from an initiative for less conspicuous weapons. It's probably the most important development out of Headquarters since they invented the Tea of Seeing."

"Headquarters invented that nasty tea?" Kelsey asks.

"Oh yeah," Paz says with a nod. "Before they came up with the tea version, Dames had to be born with the Sight so they could guide their circles through a hunt. Scouts would blind-eat part of their first kill to gain the Sight."

"Ew!" Kelsey recoils.

Avi shudders. "I *so* do not want to know what grub meat tastes like."

"Really?" Sasha says. "I do. I've never eaten something from another part of the multiverse."

Avi taps on the side of her nose conspiratorially. "To your knowledge."

Sasha strokes her chin. "That's true. I like how your mind works, Avi."

"Oh. Um. Thanks, Sasha."

"Please. Call me Beast. We're sisters."

AVI'S PICK: Field First Aid
CHARM: Medical kit with a cross

- *Perform in-the-field triage, including (but not limited to) wound dressing, splint crafting, and safe practices for moving an injured person from a dangerous area.*
- *Display understanding of the difference between shock and paralysis related to grub energy consumption.*
- *Earn CPR certification.*

"Thanks a ton for coming to help us out, Paul," I say, watching as he takes down one of Kelsey's cookie-brownies in two bites. A Nike duffel bag thuds onto the table where our tea set would normally be. We're homespun today. "Normally, the first-aid charm is earned when someone gets hurt, but I'd rather not wait."

"Anything for the Ladybirds, man," Paul says thickly, licking the chocolate from his teeth. He's seated at the table under the pergola in one of the wrought-iron patio chairs from Tía Lo's backyard. "Y'all kill shit so no one else has to. Thanks for getting that mad crab out of my yard."

"No problem," I say, brushing off the compliment. Paul's house is on Mom and Tía Lo's dawn patrol route. I only had to steer them toward the obvious entry point. "Just a little Scranch."

The bistro chair shrieks against the concrete as Paul

shoves himself backward. He unzips the duffel. "This here is Rescue Annie, the CPR dummy."

Avi's nose crinkles. "I'm sorry, Chancho's friend Paul, but does your boss at the pool know you stole that mannikin?"

Paul's pretty face twists into an offended scowl. "Does your principal know you wanna walk around with a retractable sword to kill monsters?" From the bag, he pulls out a dummy with beige skin and sculpted hair to match. Its mouth gapes wide enough to fit a deck of cards. "I'm just here to show you all how to practice resuscitating someone on this doll. And, uh, maybe have one of you get rid of something that keeps blinking at me in the showers at work. Pretty sure it's one of your interdimensional aberrations. It looks like a centipede the size of a sausage."

"A Frightworm," Avi and Kelsey titter in unison.

"We can take care of that for you," I tell Paul. "No problem."

While the babybirds take turns pumping Rescue Annie's chest, Paul tips his chair back on two legs and folds his hands together behind his head. His eyes cut over to me and he purses his lips in thought.

"Kyle's getting worried, you know," he says with a sigh. "About you having me and Chancho help out and not him."

I look away from the scouts and lower my voice to a hiss. "I can't have him help out. You know that. He can't See what's going on here."

Paul lifts his hands in a noncommittal shrug. "I'm just saying the dude's getting nervous. I told him you only want me for my mannikin—"

"Oh, and I might need you to come teach the girls how to jump hurdles," I say, biting the inside of my cheek. "My form isn't as good as yours."

"Well, I am the Southie track-and-field GOAT. All-state three years running," he says with a cocky grin. He drops the legs of his chair to the ground and leans toward me. "I normally wouldn't repeat shit that KG tells me in confidence, but he's starting to think you're avoiding him, Prue. Maybe let him tag along and drink some tea sometime. Just so he can see for himself that there's nothing to worry about."

My stomach sinks as I imagine Kyle confiding in Paul and not me. "I'm not avoiding him. I'm protecting him. He doesn't need to be part of the Ladybird world."

Paul lifts his eyebrows. "*Your* world."

"Only for another couple of weeks," I grumble, thinking ahead to the end of summer, when my days will be my own again. When I'm not constantly looking over my shoulder for monsters, I'll be able to give Kyle my full attention. I blow out an irritated breath and look back at Paul. "Have you thought more about whether or not you want to keep the Sight? When I'm done tutoring the babybirds, I can get you a dose of the Tea of Forgetting."

His eyebrows fall back down. "It wouldn't get rid of the monsters, though, would it?"

"No, but I hear ignorance is bliss."

"Tell that to your worried boyfriend. He can't See shit, so he's making up things to be scared of."

SASHA'S PICK: Kick Up Your Heels
CHARM: Can-can dancer

- *Master kickboxing basics.*
- *Win two out of three rounds of sparring with a sister scout.*
- *Train with knitting needles.*

"Cross!" I say, demonstrating with a punch. "Left hook! Jab! Left low kick! Let's see some high knees! Five, four, three—"

Sweat flies off the babybirds as they attack the hot air in my backyard.

"How often are we gonna kick a grub?" Kelsey pants between knee strikes. "Aren't we supposed to stab them and go?"

"What about when you're disarmed? What about when you need to distract the grub?" I ask, circling around the sparring partners. I adjust Avi's posture and step back. "Elbow strike, elbow strike, head kick! Switch!"

"What about when you're a woman alone on a patrol in a world full of its own dangers?"

The scouts use the interruption as an excuse to drop their arms to their sides and catch their breath.

Mom strides out the French doors in her patrol uniform. She's sparkling clean in moisture-wicking shorts and a tank top that shows off the muscles in her back.

"Mom!" I say, for sure sounding too surprised. "You made it! I mean, you said you weren't sure if you'd be able to leave work—"

"The first day of sparring is crucial, Prudence. Proper form is essential for developing new talent," she says primly. Clasping her hands together, she inclines her head toward the babybirds. "Hello, sister scouts. I know I've met each of you in different contexts, but here you can call me Dame Anita. Prudence has spoken very highly of you and your abilities. You should be very proud of all that you've accomplished in such a short time."

Her face relaxes into an affectionate smile that softens her cheeks from catlike to maternal. I truly don't know if I've ever seen that smile aimed at me before. I might have only ever witnessed it secondhand while Paz basked in its glory. It feels like sunshine.

The scouts puff up with pride. And I can't help but puff up right alongside them.

15

For the good of her community,
no risk is too great for a Ladybird.

—THE LADYBIRD HANDBOOK

On the kitchen counter, I have assembled rolled oats, wheat germ, honey, applesauce, and all of the edible seeds my pantry has to offer—from chia to pepita to sesame. The mixing bowls are clean. The parchment paper precut.

The day I have dreaded has arrived.

"Birdbark is a classic scout snack," I tell the group sitting at the kitchen island. I debate mentioning that I have never successfully made a batch and decide that my charm bracelet has already announced this for me. "You can form it into bars to take on patrol or leave it loose to use as a topping for yogurt or ice cream. And I'm pretty sure if we cover it in Magic Shell chocolate at the end, it'll even be edible. Kelsey, you made a batch for the car wash. Anything we should know going in?"

"Oh, uh, what?" Kelsey twitches to attention and slurps her braces. "Sorry?"

Despite being inside in the air-conditioning and gloveless, Kelsey and Avi both have a sudden sweaty nervousness that has me looking for a grub in the room.

Until I notice that what they're trying not to look at is Sasha the Beast, texting under the counter.

"Hey, *Sa*-sha," I say in a cajoling singsong. "Could you, um, not? I'm kind of hosting a baking show here."

The Beast looks up, and my irritation is mirrored back to me in her blacked-out lenses. "It's your cousin. He says you aren't answering your phone."

"Because I don't answer my phone during meetings," I say, hoping to imply that she shouldn't either.

She takes the implication to heart and puts her phone away with a sniff. "He also says it's an emergency."

"An emergency?" I scramble to pull out my phone from under the birdbark recipe open in my Handbook. It has seven missed calls and video chats from Chancho. I text him quickly.

ME: I'm in a meeting. What's wrong?

CHANCHO: I found a grub that needs killing. I'm at The Wooz.

ME: Call your mom?

CHANCHO: I did. She said to call you. Your scouts need more "real world training."

I groan, then give an apologetic smile at the concerned faces aimed at me.

ME: What color are its eyes?

CHANCHO: Black. I'm untrained, not stupid.

"Change of plans," I tell the girls, anxiously biting the inside of my cheek. "We're going hunting."

✝ ✝ ✝

The Wooz is one of Poppy Hills' only non-outlet-mall attractions. Although it is directly next to the outlets. Not quite an amusement park, not quite an arcade, The Wooz is a sort of permanent carnival. The main attraction is a two-story mechanical fun house that exits through a "human car wash." Lots of kids have their birthday parties here. It's a step up from a McDonald's PlayPlace but several steps down from the Six Flags farther along the freeway.

We arrive ten minutes later, red-faced in our tea dresses. Chancho probably walked here. The scouts and I ran, taking the Hillside Trail as a shortcut. Thank goodness we've been doing sprinting drills on homespun days.

Over the main entrance is a huge orange sign, each letter easily as tall as I am. The crooked *Z* on the end looks ready to fall off and crush us all.

"I haven't been here since, like, second grade," Avi says, barely even out of breath.

Sasha sets her hands on her bare knees and coughs a wad of spit between her heavy black boots. "So, a week ago?"

"Be nice," I warn.

"I'm just saying that the all-pink ensemble is a little Baby Gap," Sasha says, waving a hand over Avi's monochrome pastel outfit.

Avi thrusts her hands on her hips. "Excuse you, but the Handbook says that wearing pink helps establish us as a friendly, feminine presence in the neighborhood."

"You know that just because something rationalizes its misogyny doesn't mean you have to participate in it?" Sasha snorts.

"It's not misogynist—it's part of the camouflage," Avi snaps.

"The camouflage is assuming that people don't take little girls seriously," Sasha snaps back.

"There's more than one way to be a scout," I assure them. I hold open the door and usher them inside The Wooz.

"And you know what?" the Beast continues, not paying attention to me. "I'm still mad about that sleepover you two had without me."

"We can always have *another* sleepover, Sasha," Kelsey says.

"If you promise not to smoke," Avi says.

"Or light anything on fire," Kelsey adds.

"You are so fucking square, it's truly tragic," Sasha says.

She turns her nose up at Dizzy Bee, the spiral-eyed mascot that grins maniacally at us from every angle. "And so is this store."

Since only games and rides cost money, The Wooz both opens and closes with a gift shop. Who could possibly need Dizzy Bee bumper stickers or sunglasses is beyond me.

"Remember your combat steps," I murmur to the scouts as we skirt a display of coffee mugs.

"LACE: location, assessment, combat, escape," Avi chirps obediently.

I nod. "Be aware of what's around you. Look for anything out of place. Cracks in walls or wood. Anything warped or distorted-looking. Movement out of the corner of your eye."

"Fangs, too many legs," Kelsey adds. "General creepiness."

"This whole place creeps me out," Sasha sniffs. She picks up a SNOOZE WITH THE WOOZ sleep mask and straps it over her sunglasses. It gives her Dizzy Bee's hypnotic spiral eyes.

"There!" Avi points behind me.

We all turn. With one finger, Sasha pushes up the eye mask. Through the floor-to-ceiling windows, I spy Chancho sitting at a picnic table, nursing a soda in a Dizzy Bee souvenir cup. Jaxon is with him, which is a relief. It would have been weird if Chancho had had the sudden urge to Wooz alone.

Racing through the analog arcade, past the dilapidated

Skee-Ball games and miniature basketball hoops, we pass through the automatic doors and into the enclosed courtyard full of neon-orange tables. Other than my cousins, the courtyard is empty. To one side is the Wooz Café, its three pass-through windows releasing an almost toxic amount of hot-dog-water stench. To the other is a mostly empty carousel and the human car wash.

I can't tell if the mulligrub drove away The Wooz's customers or if this is just a standard day of Woozing.

Jaxon's cheeks and eyes are red. A droplet of snot hangs from the tip of his nose.

"Aww, hermanito," Avi simpers, rushing to her baby brother's side. "What happened, Jaxy?"

He looks up at her, fat tears leaking out of the side of his eyes. "There's an invisible monster, so I'm not allowed to go back into the car wash until it's killed."

"You mean *banished*," Avi corrects.

He shakes his head. "No, I want you to kill it, please. That way it won't come back. I want to go through the car wash twice."

Paying absolutely zero attention to his siblings, Chancho stares at Sasha, eyebrows up so far that they disappear under his hat bill.

"Sasha Nezhad in a dress. I never thought I'd see the day." He leans back, attempting to rest his elbows on the tabletop behind him. It's a move that Paul would pull off with effortless finesse, but Chancho misses twice, looking like a chicken ruffling its feathers. He settles for putting down one elbow.

"You interrupted a tea meeting," Sasha says. One of her hands fists in the skull-print skirt of her dress, which I'm pretty sure I recognize from eighth-grade graduation. It's much shorter now. "Do you have a real emergency, or do you want to make cute fashion commentary?"

"If you think it's cute, I'm good continuing the commentary."

I snap my fingers twice at Chancho, forcing his eyes to focus on me. Left unchecked, my cousin will let the Beast throw insults at him all day just so he can keep batting his eyelashes at her. It's how most of our lunch periods go, both in the cafeteria and when we sneak off campus.

"The grub is in the people wash?" I ask Chancho.

"The people *car* wash," Jaxon corrects. "It's a car wash for people. It has foam rollers and soap and everything."

His older brother sticks his tongue in the side of his cheek in an attempt to appear casual. "It was near the fun house, but it was moving fast. It was just beyond the entrance. I saw the black eyes and got us the hell out of there before we could find out what kind of hungry it was."

"So, you ran away. You're a real hero," Sasha drawls.

"We can't all be scouts, Beast," Chancho says, flicking his eyebrows. "Some of us have Y chromosomes."

"Are you finding those particularly useful right now?"

"Are they flirting?" Kelsey asks Avi in a loud whisper.

221

"Not very well," I sigh.

Avi and Kelsey both burst into giggles. Sasha makes a strangled sound of protest that I ignore.

"Let's go, scouts," I say.

At the ticket booth outside the fun house, I buy six student tickets and keep the receipt to bill Headquarters. The Wooz wouldn't let us explore the people car wash in exchange for all the almond butter sandwiches in California.

The metal stairs clank underfoot. As we pass through the red-painted saloon doors, the bright summer sunlight disappears. Glowing green rope lights guide the way. Once we turn the first corner, I extend my tote to the scouts. Under my wallet and spare water bottle are loose knitting needles.

The girls each draw out a pair and fumble to hold them at the customary chest-high downward angle, squared up like boxers.

I help myself to the last pair of needles. Not knowing what kind of grub we're after almost makes me wish I'd strapped on my daggers. But if it has black eyes, it won't need steel.

I tap my needles together twice and say, "LACE up."

"*Location*," Avi whispers, her footsteps falling within inches of mine. "Dark fun house."

"*Assessment*," Sasha says, pushing her sunglasses up into her hair. "Smellier than expected."

"The water in the people car wash is chlorinated," I say.

"Oh no," Kelsey says with a worried slurp of her braces. "That is going to ruin my hair."

"We'll have to muddle through somehow," Sasha mumbles.

I'm just hoping we survive the *combat* and *escape* parts of the LACE. At the end of the hallway is another set of stairs. As line leader, I'm the first to step up—and find myself sliding suddenly to the right. Grabbing on to the handrail to keep from falling, I let out a small yelp. Embarrassment makes my cheeks hot.

"They're seesaw stairs," I warn the scouts over my shoulder.

"I got you, Prue!" Avi says, helpfully jumping on the other side of the stair to equalize it.

"We'll all bunny-hop to the top!" Kelsey says. "One, two, three!"

We all leap up one stair at a time, four sets of feet landing more or less in unison. Kelsey counts down before each leap. My thighs burn from the strain by the time we make it to the top, but no one else gets thrown from the stairs, so I consider it a win. Ladybirds 1, fun house 0.

"Good thinking, guys," I pant. "That was some real Ladybird teamwork."

They beam at me in return.

The second story of the fun house has barred windows that overlook the courtyard. The thin light illuminates the many signs pointing forward, but reveal no lurking mulligrubs. If Chancho was wrong about seeing a grub in here, I'll have no choice but to kick his ass.

Around the corner we find a pit full of foam cubes. My

toes curl inside my Keds. It's so difficult not to picture grubs lurking at the bottom, teeth and claws poised to strike. The anxiety fire in my stomach grows into a stabbing pain.

"Can't go over it, can't go under it," I mutter to myself as I step down. Instantly, I sink to my waist and curse my short genes.

The three scouts soundlessly slip in behind me. We wade through, pushing cubes aside.

Skittering noises make me stop in my tracks. I hold up a hand, and the babybirds freeze in place. For a moment, no one breathes. The machinery of the fun-house clinks and clanks. The walls vibrate with it. There's the faraway *whoosh* of an industrial fan and the splatter of water on cement.

A wet *swish* draws my attention upward. High above us hangs a Nock Jaw, clinging to the black ceiling with its blunt salamander toes. Its tail ticks back and forth, recreating the slimy sound.

"Oh," I say, choking down my shock. "A Nock Jaw. You guys have seen one of these before."

Kelsey and Sasha bump into each other as they scramble backward.

"Ladybirds move toward danger, not away from it," I chastise, sounding so unforgivably like Mom that I instantly wish I could wash my mouth out. "Who remembers the Nock Jaws stats?"

"They feed on happiness and surprise," Sasha says, idly pushing at the stiff tide of foam cubes around her hips. She frowns as everyone blinks at her. "What? I pay attention to stuff. Don't give it a feast."

"She's right," I say. The words taste foreign regarding the Beast. "If that thing gets much bigger, it'll absorb more of our energy than we have to give."

Avi thrusts her hands on her hips. "You want us to not be surprised? In a fun house? While we're in the dark with a monster that looks like ground pork?"

"Great. I'll never be able to make meatballs ever again." Kelsey gives a full-body shudder.

"Once we banish it, you'll earn a Cool Cucumber charm," I offer.

"How do we get the grub off the ceiling?" Sasha asks.

"I'm pretty sure that if we run, it'll chase us," I say. "Eventually, it'll run out of ceiling."

"Like when we reach the outside where it could feed on lots of people?" Kelsey asks nervously.

"We won't let that happen," I say. "I'm gonna go first, okay? Just like when we run drills. I'll be your pace car. You keep your eyes on the grub. Do not let it out of your Sight. They aren't used to being Seen, so it should make obvious movements."

To get a better grip on my knitting needles, I dry my hands down the sides of a foam cube. I want the babybirds to banish the Nock Jaw themselves, but I'm prepared to step in and be the heavy. I think of the way Dame Debby used to just sit in her car, listening to the radio while my circle hunted. I won't abandon my scouts to a grub that's almost the same size as them.

I wait on the other side of the pit for all of the babybirds to extricate themselves from the cubes. The Nock Jaw takes its time stalking us, its lengthy toes curling and unfurling inch by inch.

"Ready?" I ask the girls.

Avi knocks her needles together, and the others join in, a riot of anticipatory noise that makes my heartbeat flutter somewhere between panic and elation.

A deep breath swells my lungs. I turn and race out of the pit room, down a corridor barely lit with black light. The walls and ceiling are splattered with glow-in-the-dark paint and huge arrows.

Something knocks into me and rebounds off my right hip just as something else crashes into my left side. I lash out with my needles, throwing a spinning back punch that lands with a familiar bounce.

I call back to the babybirds entering the room. "Swinging punching bags! Stay light and protect your faces!"

Metal chains jangle as row after row of the hanging bags sway, obstructing the path. I hear someone take a hit, the *oof* of air pushed out of a solar plexus. I look back, but all I can see is the Nock Jaw blocking out swaths of the luminous paint on the ceiling.

"Bob and weave!" Sasha instructs somewhere in the darkness behind me. "We got this!"

"We got this!" the babybirds cheer back.

The rallying cry makes me smile. Smiling distracts me for just long enough to get hit in the back with a punching bag. I fumble to keep from dropping my needles and my tote. Picking up the pace again, I run at full speed through the next two obstacles, calling out surprises as I encounter them. "Moving floor! Mirror walls!"

"It's not coming down, Dame Prue!" Kelsey calls up to me. "I think the ceiling is its home!"

My toes skitter to the edge of the floor, teetering at the precipice of a yellow tube slide. I hold on to the top of the tube. I really, really hope that I'm not making a mistake leading the grub downstairs. So long as it's inside the fun house, I can control how many people it can feed from. If it gets away from us and outside, it could easily climb the fence and get into town.

I can't let that happen. I trust my scouts. I trust myself. And no matter what Faithlynn Brett says, I trust that we are capable of hunting something bigger than Easter eggs.

"Slide!" I warn the girls. Launching myself into a seated position, I sail down the spiral tube. The rubber soles of my shoes scritch against the plastic, slowing me down just enough that I don't fly out and splatter against the wall. I come to a crashing stop on a squashy tumbling mat. Sunlight is blinding after the dark.

"Land softly!" I shout up the slide and then turn to take stock of the last two rooms.

Across from me is a rotating barrel doorway built into a fake brick wall. The barrel is only big enough for two or three people to fit across. On the other side is the damp cement and spinning rollers of the people car wash. The chlorine smell coming through is overpowering.

The scouts luge out of the slide, one by one. Sasha appears last, her knitting needles folded over her chest like a mummified corpse. She pulls her sunglasses down off her forehead, quickly covering her eyes.

"I think I hear it," she says. "Either that or someone dropped a bunch of wet laundry up there."

"Let's Red Rover this sucker," Avi says, stepping back to stand between the slide and the revolving cylinder. When everyone looks at her blankly, she gestures furiously with her needles. "Make a line so it can't get through us!"

"Right, of course," I say, leaping to her side. I throw my tote to the side. "We'll box it out."

I wonder whether hunting would be easier if we gave names to all the formations. But then the baby-birds would have to forget the names and learn whatever needlessly complicated arrangements Faithlynn has planned for them.

Once we're all shoulder to shoulder, I hold my knitting needles at the ready and wait for the others to follow suit.

"Priority one is making sure that it doesn't get outside," I say. "We need to do whatever we can to stop it from getting through the people car w—"

I've barely wrapped my lips around the *w* of *wash* when a slippery pink blur slingshots out of the slide and soars overhead. We all crane our necks back to watch the Nock Jaw fly above our human shield. It lands with a damp plop inside the churning doorway behind us. Tail whipping back and forth wildly, it scrambles up the side of the cylinder only to find itself on a slow descent toward the ground again. It tries anew to slither to the top but ends up treading in place like a hairless hamster.

Before I can think of an order to give, Kelsey breaks formation and box-jumps into the cylinder. She lands uneasily, her ballet flats unsuited to fieldwork. The Nock Jaw seems to sense her murderous intention; it redoubles its effort to climb, toes and tail desperately slapping the wall. Kelsey runs in place behind it, her pink-and-white-candy-striped skirt fluttering like a hero's cape.

"You got this, Kelsey!" I shout. "Aim for between the eyes!"

"Stop it from feeding on anyone else!" Avi says. "Do it for Jaxon!"

"Send it back to hell!" Sasha whoops.

"Or whatever dimension of the multiverse it's from!" I add. "The Handbook says research on origins is inconclusive!"

"I'm sticking with *hell*!" Sasha says, pumping her needles in the air.

Kelsey's cheeks puff out. To steel herself for the kill or due to the effort of running in place, I don't know. In a clean sweep, she draws both knitting needles up, hops forward, and stabs downward. The moment the tips of her needles make contact with the Nock Jaw's flat black eyes, there's a pop as loud as a champagne cork. Her knitting needles clatter against the side of the cylinder in the airspace where the grub was just a moment ago. She lands on one knee. Shaking the hair out of her eyes, she looks over at us, face shining with sweat and pride as she rises and jumps back out of the cylinder.

When we reemerge from the people car wash into the courtyard, we're sudsy and dripping and giggling. Victorious and silly.

And I think, *See, Faith? Soft girls can still get it done.*

16

In times of peril, there are no dividing lines
among circles; there is only the sisterhood.

—THE LADYBIRD HANDBOOK

"And then!" I gulp down a mouthful of pastelón. Burning-hot plantain scalds my throat. I chase it down with a hurried swallow of water. "And then we had it cornered at the base of the slide and it just *flew* out like a rocket! I mean, it was a huge Nock Jaw, so maybe less like a rocket and more like a hippopotamus tongue."

"A charming image," Mom says, mouth curved up in the corner in an almost smile. It disappears when she blows steam from her fork.

Dad reaches over and refills my water cup from the pitcher. A cucumber plops inside. When your father sells produce, it ends up in *everything*. Sometimes I wish he were a baker.

"How big is a Nock Jaw normally?" he asks.

"The Handbook says they can be anywhere from one

to two feet on arrival," I say. "But this one must have been here for weeks. It was at least five feet long!"

"Who got the honor of the kill? Did Sasha slay the smiley beast?" Dad asks.

"No, it was Kyle's sister, Kelsey! My scarediest scout! I'm so proud of her. I really thought she was gonna quit after initiation, but she's really starting to hold her own. That Nock Jaw was almost as big as her, and she took it down—inside of a moving barrel!"

"Perhaps it's time for The Wooz to get added to the weekly patrol roster," Mom says. "Although who would want to spend that much time there is beyond me. I remember Chancho having a birthday party there when you were little, and the smell left much to be desired. Eat your salad, too, Prudence."

I stab a circle around my salad plate, avoiding the beets Mom forced on me. She doesn't believe me when I say they taste like blood. "I don't know. We had a pretty good time today. Sure, there's a distinct Wooz stank, but taken at a run, the fun house is basically just an obstacle course in the dark. Tía Lo was right—it was really good practice for the scouts."

A knock at the French doors interrupts me. We all turn to look, even though we can't actually see through the glass from here. Besides, a knock on the back door can only be one person. Chancho would text me first rather than interrupt dinner and risk a possible scolding from Mom.

"Sorry. I said Tía Lo was right, and she came running," I say, dutifully eating another bite of salad. "I swear, she's got us bugged."

Mom sets her napkin next to her plate and pushes away from the table. "She doesn't need to. My sister was born with a sixth sense for being the center of attention."

Just before the French doors close behind Mom, I hear Tía Lo say, "God, sissy, you couldn't leave the porch light on for me? I could have twisted an ankle out here."

"Might as well wrap up her dinner now," I murmur to Dad. "You know she's not coming back for at least an hour."

Normally, when Lo comes over after dark, Mom disappears through the cedar gate for all the tea. Sometimes they lock themselves in Mom's office for conference calls with Paz or other legacy scouts. But it's never quick. Mom's dinner gets wrapped in foil and set in the fridge for her to forget about.

"Maybe Lo just needs a cup of sugar," Dad says.

"Lorena Silva-Marquez has not eaten sugar in the last ten years. She doesn't even trust stevia anymore. Our breakfast smoothies are sweetened with date paste."

"Yum," Dad says. "Takes me back to my school days."

"Oh my God, Dad, please don't tell me you were a paste-eater. That's so embarrassing."

"What's embarrassing about it?" he asks as he helps himself to seconds from the casserole dish and licks the spatula—something he would *never* do in front of Mom.

"I yam what I yam. And what I yam is a—"

"Prudence," Mom pokes her head in through the French doors. A deep wrinkle carves a line down the center of her forehead. "Would you join us outside, please?"

I throw a look at Dad and whisper, "Am I in trouble?"

"How would I know?" he whispers back. "I'm just an old paste-eater."

"Eat my beets while I'm gone!"

I walk toward the backyard with all of the heaviness of being summoned to the principal's office. Mom would be so deeply offended by the comparison. Hers is the office that *principals* dread.

Outside, even as the sun is descending behind the wheat-brown hills, the air is thick with nearby grill smoke. Crickets fall silent as I step down onto the still-hot concrete.

Tía Lo is still wearing her work clothes, pink scrubs printed with smiling teeth. The concept of teeth having their own teeth is momentarily staggering. Then again, it could just be the anxiety static in my head, listing all the reasons I could be summoned. *Avianna tattled, Jaxon tattled, Kelsey went home and immediately told her parents all of the scout secrets, everyone is going to find out about Paul and Sasha getting the Sight from my initiation ceremony, Faithlynn Brett has finally found a way to make me prove that my championship Root shot was a fluke . . .*

I push the sleeves up my wrists and fold my hands in an

effort to look contrite. "Is this because Avi is helping with my Charitable Knitting charm?" I guess, my voice fluttering in a failed attempt to sound chill. "Because I swear, she's not supposed to add *any* stitches to my scarves. She just said she'd count the rows to double-check that they were even, and I thought it would be decent practice for *her* Charitable Knitting charm and—"

Mom and Tía Lo mirror each other in brief confusion.

"You aren't in trouble, nena," Tía Lo says warmly. "We simply have Ladybird business tonight. Which concerns you, too."

Surprise eats ten seconds of my brain waves. I'm so used to Mom and Tía Lo and Paz being their own crew, a sort of reverse Criminal Element of do-gooders. Being brought into the fold feels like it should have more pomp and circumstance. A formal written invitation would have been nice. Perhaps a commemorative plaque. Or a hug? I can't remember the last time Mom and I hugged.

"There's been an incident," Mom says. No fanfare for Dr. Anita Silva-Perry. Just the facts rabbit-punched directly into your brain. "One of the Mare Island scouts has been killed in a Carnivore attack in Solano Park."

I can taste the sofrito from the pastelón in the back of my throat, the bell pepper as bitter as bile. "Solano Park? Someone else died where Molly . . ."

I can't bring myself to finish the sentence, but I don't have to. Tía Lo gives a tense nod, her face as serious as her scrubs are ridiculous. It takes all of my willpower to keep my knees from giving out. I clench my hands until I can feel my fingernails digging deep in my palms.

Another dead girl. Another engraved locket. More blood soaking into the hills.

"Her name was Shelby Waters. She was twelve years old, and she'd just . . ." Tía Lo takes a pause, pressing her lips together before spitting out the rest. "She'd just earned her steel. It was a routine outing."

I think of the eager Mare Island scouts at the car wash in their matching lavender T-shirts. One had made me think of Molly. Was that the girl Jennica said had just passed her steel test?

Shelby.

Shelby the dead girl.

"I met her. She helped chase down a Tizzy Louse at our car wash," I say, my voice distant to my ears. "What was she doing in Solano Park? What was a Mare Island scout doing patrolling a place where other scouts have died? We aren't in her territory. They're so far away that Avi couldn't even join their circle, though they're closer to her age."

From the way Mom's frown deepens, I know my tone is too sharp and accusatory. But she uses her soothing educator voice to say, "Because she was the first girl in her circle to gain her steel, she was doing a daylight drill with the senior scouts from Green Valley. We've been keeping an eye on the park since your father's employees went missing earlier this month. But now we're afraid that the worst has happened."

"Something is killing people in Poppy Hills," Tía Lo says. "We have no choice but to take that very seriously."

Not seriously enough to stop sending little girls into a state park with a Carnivore on the loose, I think but do not say.

Mom twists her wedding ring back and forth, holding on to the diamond like a mint leaf. "We cannot protect this town without help. Faithlynn Brett is good, but she's just one girl."

Tía Lo rolls her eyes. "And she's taking a zero period class in fall, so she'll be useless for morning patrol until she graduates."

Mom gives her ring a sharp twist that lets me know that Faithlynn's class schedule was probably shared in confidence. "There simply are not enough trained scouts in Poppy Hills. Every week it seems another scout is dropping off the on-call list. Moving away or getting married or spending more time at work."

Or dying. I wonder how many scouts quit when they're sisters-in-arms die. I can't be the only one.

Can I?

Tía Lo levels me with a soul-freezing stare. "What we're saying, Miss Prue, is that it is time for your scouts to be added to the official roster for daily patrol."

I open my mouth, to argue, to scream, to say no, but Mom speaks first.

"Your scouts are not ready to hunt anything in the Carnivore class, and to tell the truth, you are not qualified to teach them how to handle White-Eyes. But you were saying at dinner that they were showing positive growth in hunting Critters. That will become your sole purview, freeing those of us who can safely fight Carnivores to do so. Your scouts can master banishment and hunting techniques in the field, just as they did today at The Wooz."

That's what I get for telling hero stories. Sharing my excitement with Mom can only ever end in disappointment. The sisterhood always comes first.

Done with our conversation, Mom excuses me with a waggle of unpainted fingernails. "Will you ask your father to wrap up my dinner, please? I need to make some calls to adjust the patrol. Lo and I will need to schedule more sweeps of Solano Park with experienced scouts. Normally, Dame Marcy from Mare Island is the first person to pick up an extra patrol, but in this circumstance . . . Well, she'll be out of commission for a while, I think. It's so hard to lose a scout."

"We'll go in on flowers, right?" Tía Lo asks.

"Flowers die. We'll send a tea sampler. Tea is sympathetic." Mom looks back at me, her eyes a comfortless black. "Headquarters is going to call you about going into the field. And you are going to say yes."

Tía Lo reaches out and clasps one of my hands, squeezing

hard. "We all have friends in lockets, Miss Prue. The sister-hood marches on."

Fear and regret make my limbs feel numb. I stand alone in the backyard long after the cedar gate closes behind Mom and Tía Lo.

My first instinct is to pull my phone out of the pocket of my hoodie and message Kyle. My fingers hover over the screen, wanting to spill everything I was just overloaded with—the dead scout, the Carnivore in Solano Park, the dread twisting through my stomach like Frightworm legs. The betrayal of knowing that my mother will always, always choose what is best for the scouts over what is best for me.

But I can't tell him the truth, so I ask him for a distraction.

ME: Remember September 23?

KYLE: Every second.

ME: Remind me? Tonight sucks.

KYLE: I asked if you wanted to see Wendigo at the IMAX, just the two of us. You said yes even tho you don't like horror movies.

ME: I really didn't think they'd let us into an R-rated movie.

KYLE: We're short but we're obviously old souls. You asked to wear my sweater.

ME: I wasn't that cold. It just smelled like you.

KYLE: Probably like my conditioner. Maybe deodorant.

ME: That's plenty of Kyle smell for me. Now it just smells like
me ☹

KYLE: I could fix that for you. Bring it over here right now and
I'll get my stink all over it. You don't even have to take it off.
Unless you want to ☺

I really would love nothing more than to run to the shedroom. Without the rest of the group. Without a time limit. My mind spins plans, lies, ways to slip away without my parents noticing.

But, once I got there, I wouldn't be able to actually explain why I'm upset. I couldn't tell him that scouts die or how terrified I am that I've recruited Avi, Sasha, and his own little sister to do the same.

ME: I can't come out tonight.
But soon, I promise.

KYLE: Okay, babe. Miss you.♡

ME: Miss you too.♡

Dejected, I walk back inside where the air-conditioning makes my skin prickle.

"Mom says to pack up her dinner," I tell Dad, hardly noticing that he already has the tinfoil out. The beet salad is, thankfully, gone.

"You want me to put yours away, too?" he asks.

"Yes, please. I'm not really hungry anymore." I rest my elbows on the kitchen island. "A scout died."

"Oh no." He sets the foil down. "I'm sorry, munchkin. Someone you know?"

I shake my head. It's not my tragedy to claim. "I met her, but she wasn't local. Not that it matters. Twelve-year-olds aren't supposed to die. Ever. Period."

"That's true. But the world is a scary and unpredictable place," he says. "That's why we have scouts, right? To defend our reality from chaos?"

I examine my hands against the calico granite. There's a scratch running across the knuckles of my right hand. I must have cut myself somewhere in the fun house while my adrenaline was cranked up too high to notice. I don't even know how many hunting scars I have. Aside from the mottled seam on my left arm, there are healed-over gouges on my shins and grub bites on my knees, and a long slice across my back where Gabby once accidentally cut me during a fight with a Frightworm. I hardly think about them until I try to imagine my body through eyes that can't See.

"Dad, how long ago did you drink the Tea of Seeing?" I ask.

"When your mom and I got engaged. Your abuela Ramona wouldn't give her blessing until I took the tea." He touches his head, as though remembering the thick blond hair of his youth. "I guess it's been about twenty years?"

"Did it make you see Mom differently?"

"Of course." He pulls out a long stretch of foil and folds it carefully over my abandoned pastelón. "It made me respect her even more than I already did. When she told me she fought parasites, I never pictured something as big or scary as a full-grown Scranch. I almost fainted the first time one of those things got into the house."

I think of the Scranch leaping out of the barbecue at Sasha. She didn't have the option of fainting. It was banish or be consumed.

"But do you ever regret it? Did you ever wish . . . ? I don't know. That she hadn't made you look at how terrifying the world is? If you were with someone who wasn't a Ladybird, you'd never have to face the monsters."

He balances my plate and Mom's on one arm so he can slide them into the fridge. "Are you asking about me, or are you asking about Kyle?"

"I can have two goals in one conversation. It's called doublethink. My brain is pretty fast."

"I am quite aware." He pulls out a beer and cracks the tab before closing the fridge. He leans on the opposite side of the kitchen island, mirroring my slumped posture. "No, munchkin, I never wished your mom wasn't a scout. Then she wouldn't be your mom."

"She'd still be Dr. Anita Silva-Perry, Ed.D, the youngest superintendent in Poppy Hills history."

He gives me one of those infuriating dad shrugs. "Would

she? Would she have grown up to care so deeply or hustle so hard if she hadn't been raised to banish mulligrubs? The Ladybirds shaped your grandma and your mom and Lo. What you love molds you into who you are. If you took away that mold, who knows who they would have been?"

"Maybe they would have been nicer," I grumble, thinking of the dispassionate way Mom and Tía Lo talk about scouts dying. How they never tear up, no matter how devastating the news. "Mom could have been a delicate fairy princess."

"Your mom is a fairy princess. With a whip sword. I see no downsides there." He takes a long sip of his beer, smacking his lips as his Adam's apple bobs up his neck. "So, why are you worried about Kyle?"

"He can't See what I can. And what if that means he can't really understand me? I have all of these little lies built up. Why I go running with Mom and Tía Lo in the morning. Why I host tea parties with his sister. Where my scars come from. How can he love someone he doesn't really know?"

"Just because he doesn't know the difference between a Scranch and a Frightworm doesn't mean he doesn't know you. And even if he could See mulligrubs, it doesn't mean he'd understand it. You're always saying that scouts do more than just sip tea and rescue people. But it sure looks like there's a lot of tea sipping and people rescuing to me because I'm not there. Sometimes, it's just hard loving someone from outside your group. Even a group that isn't privy to the secrets of the multiverse. If you were on the swim team and he wasn't, you'd worry that he couldn't hold his breath for as long as you."

"That sounds like a better problem to have. It's less life-and-death than the scouts."

"Until the day you needed him not to drown." He takes another drink and glances back at the half-cleared table. "I got a bag of the Tea of Seeing, but I didn't get the Handbook. It can be hard to be able to See but not know what you're Seeing. Thankfully, you and Paz both needed my help with flash cards. I learned a lot from that. But I still have to call in the big guns when I see a grub in the wild."

"You know how to use mint, Dad."

"Barely. I can throw it and hope it works. And I don't know what you do with the knitting needles." He chuckles to himself as he collects the dirty silverware from the table. "I bet I could knit a scarf better than I could stab a grub. Some of those things are so slimy. It makes my skin crawl, just remembering it."

I think of the Tizzy Lice in the back seat of Faithlynn's car. My scouts would have preferred to shear off their skin than to touch them. They had to push through anyway. Not for the good of the community—the senior scouts were more than capable of banishing them—but to prove that they could.

I pick up the water glasses from the table, hugging them

to my chest as I cross the kitchen to set them in the sink. "But, Dad, did you ever ask how to wield mint or needles? Or did you assume a Ladybird was gonna save you the trouble?" Unable to bring myself to see the answer in his face, I examine a drowned slice of cucumber in one of the glasses, trapped under the weight of an ice cube. "Sometimes I wonder who we're protecting with the big secret."

And how you qualify for being protected, I think, feeling the phantom squeeze of Tía Lo's hand on mine. *Rather than being sacrificed.*

17

Working as a team strengthens
a circle from silver to gold.

—THE LADYBIRD HANDBOOK

"Pick up the pace!" Paul blows his lifeguard whistle and shouts, "Get your knees up, Beast, or they're gonna get bit!"

We're back on campus at Goldfields Middle, today on the unpaved running track. The Scranch's sharp-tipped legs cut divots in the dirt as its mouths gnash at Sasha's heels. She only evades getting chomped by bunny-hopping over the traffic-cone hurdle in her way.

"You've got higher hops than that, Sasha!" Chancho calls from between cupped hands. When he gets the finger in return, he quick-glances to make sure his brother is still buried deep in a Magic Tree House book. He is.

In exchange for some of the homespun snacks I've got in the cooler I'm sitting on, Chancho and Paul agreed to come with to help with today's lesson. Paul is our track-

and-field expert. Chancho carried the cooler.

I shake some of the track dirt off the finished end of my scarf-in-progress. The Dame message boards say that it's a good idea to have someone actively knitting during public training exercises. It normalizes having a bunch of girls using knitting needles as batons. And since I still need to get my Charitable Knitting charm so I can buy the Tea of Forgetting, working on my project seemed like a no-brainer.

In practice, however, I can barely concentrate on knitting and purling. The yarn trembles in my hands as I think about another girl dying in the same place as Molly. How can I bring the babybirds into the field, knowing that there's a Carnivore on the loose?

How am I supposed to tell them that the sisterhood will march on even as scouts die?

"Can we *please* banish it now?" Kelsey pants as she trots past me, her normally peaches-and-cream complexion now closer to ripe strawberry. Sweat-drenched curls not long enough for her ponytail stick like wet vines to her cheeks as she huffs for air.

"Not till you reach the end of the timer," I remind her, shoving my knitting into my tote bag. I wipe the sweat from my brow with my sleeve. "You're luring it somewhere to fight in private. You can't let just anyone see you with your needles out."

"It's definitely getting stronger," the Beast wheezes.

Her sunglasses bobble up and down her nose. "And we are getting weaker."

"Where do you think its energy is coming from?" I ask. If I have to take them into the field, they have to be stronger. They have to be prepared for how exhausting patrol can be. I fetch a La Croix out of the cooler and crack the tab. I take a deep, refreshing sip and call out, "It came here for someone else's anger, but now it's only got yours to feed on."

"That's not fair!" Avi gasps, clumsily jumping the highest hurdle as the Scranch swerves to follow her.

"Uh-uh!" Paul whistles. "Get that trail leg up, Avianna! You're gonna get *bit*!"

Chancho's babysitting time-out timer buzzes, making Jaxon cringe. Chancho holds the digital timer over his head and calls out, "Time!"

In clunky unison, Avi, Kelsey, and Sasha pull the knitting needles out of their pockets. Still gliding over the hurdles, they turn their attention inward instead of forward. They encircle the Scranch, keeping pace with one another until they're close enough to skid to a stop and cross their ankles into a protective circle. Shoe to shoe, they hold the Scranch in place so that Avi can rear back and hit it between the eyes. It disappears, and the three of them go slack with mission-accomplished bonelessness.

They drag themselves toward the bleachers, reaching for their water bottles. Sasha coughs into the dirt and holds her hand out for my La Croix. When I pass it to her, she pours it over the back of her neck.

"That sucked," the Beast growls at the ground, although I think she's mad at me, personally. "Do you know how fucking hot it is out here?"

"I do know." I nod, getting myself a new drink—for drinking rather than bathing in. "That's why the trap can only pull Scranch. It's too hot to feel anything nice."

Avi rests her hands on her knees, her back heaving. "I thought we were moving into chapter five this week, prima. Chapter five is circle bonding!"

Kelsey wipes her face in the hem of her shirt and gives a mournful slurp of her braces. "It's where the Baking charm requirements are."

"You already know how to bake," I tell her, my jaw tense. Baking won't keep any of us alive. It's part of the Ladybird cover story, totally unrelated to fieldwork. "You need to shave some time off your sprints before we get deeper into the Handbook."

Avi throws her hands up. "We have all summer to shave seconds off! You're not even logging our time with Headquarters. Who cares?"

"Wait, this isn't being recorded?" Sasha stands up to her full height. "Then what's the point?"

"I'm logging times," Chancho says, holding up his phone. "That's why I'm timer guy!"

"I'm not sending times into the leaderboard," I explain

to the scouts. "It pits you against one another when you need to be focused on being a team. Different scouts get different results. You aren't clones. And if you want to outlive a grub, you'd better be able to outrun one for more than five minutes! So, drink some water and then get back to the first hurdle. Jax, bud, can you give us another scream in the trap?"

Without even looking up from his book, Jaxon provides a new Scranch, this one slightly bigger than the last—probably because he's deeper into his story and more annoyed at being interrupted. My stomach reels as I scoop it out of the trap, my bare hand clamped around its kiwifruit fuzziness, squeezing tight to keep its teeth inside its mouths.

Lined up at the pink starting cone, Sasha, Avi, and Kelsey stare at me—and the Scranch—with a slack-jawed terror that seems a little over the top for the situation. If they're really too tired for a second try, I can always banish this Scranch so we can dig into the peanut butter cups in the cooler before we go another round.

"Pa-roo-dence Perry!"

Skin crawling, I turn around, purple Scranch legs waggling between my fingers like wilted claws. The senior scouts are standing on the other side of the field in patrol athleisure. From the bulges pressed against their windbreakers and jogging skirts, I can see that they're fully armed.

Jennica gives a homecoming-queen wave to the assembled crowd. "Do you mind if we join this round?"

I glance back at my scouts, already red-faced and sweating. No matter how much I want to tell the senior scouts to back off and leave us alone, I know I can't. The babybirds will be their sister scouts soon enough.

The Scranch in my hand swells.

"Sure, yeah. Many hands make light work and all that. We're running covert drills," I say. The senior scouts are already walking past me, their matching mesh Keds kicking up dust.

Instinctively, the babybirds take a generous step back from the approaching scouts. Although, I also wouldn't be surprised if Faithlynn hissed at them to move so quietly that I couldn't hear it. She used to control my circle with whispers in front of other people. And yelling in private.

When I throw the grub at the track, Paul blows his whistle and Chancho starts the timer. Faithlynn, Jennica, and Gabby burst out of the starting line, a wave of synchronized motion that gazelle-leaps over every hurdle with no visible effort. Behind them, my scouts fumble to keep up. Giving chase, the Scranch knocks over two of the starting cones and one of the hurdles. But, for once, it doesn't bother with Sasha at all. It cuts across the center of the track, galloping toward the senior scouts, running beside them, keeping pace with them hurdle for hurdle.

Except that the Scranch isn't running as fast as they are. They must be slowing to keep pace with the grub. Because when the timer dings, their speed is an explosion. They get far, far ahead of the Scranch and the babybirds, then tear the weapons out of their holsters. Jennica's belt rips off to showcase the razor edge of her whip sword. Faithlynn's two axes unfold from hot-pink handles. Gabby's retractable sword comes out of her back harness; with a press of her thumb, the steel shoots forward.

Light-years ahead of crossing their ankles and aiming their knitting needles, the senior scouts repel away from one another, fanning out as they change direction and run *toward* the Scranch. All the babybirds can do is slow to a stop and watch.

In one flick, Jennica's whip sword tears the legs from the Scranch and drags it forward through the dirt. Faithlynn calls a warning, then launches her axes. Both blades crack into the Scranch's jowls, pinning it to the ground like a scientific specimen.

It's a Carnivore kill on a grub too small to require it. Gabby comes in for the Root shot, her sword aimed low and level. Even as the Scranch pops away, too flimsy to have Rooted to this dimension, Gabby's sword carves a circle in the air. If the Scranch had been a Carnivore, its Root would have fallen neatly between Gabby's shoes, ready to be scooped up and measured by Headquarters.

The senior scouts march off the track, crunching through the dead grass toward the bleachers.

"Wow!" Avi says, her fingertips holding her jaw in place. "That was absolutely holy-moly wow!"

Sasha gives an approving nod. "So many different kinds of stabbing."

"That was fun!" Jennica says, smiling like she maybe even means it. "We never hunt for fun anymore."

"We're a little busy hunting *all* of Poppy Hills' aberrations," Faithlynn says, talking to Jennica but looking at the boys on the bleachers.

"All of the aberrations in North Town," I correct her. I gesture at Avi with my thumb. "Our family has run the southern boundary since the nineties."

"Actually, that's why we're here!" Gabby says, skipping toward me until Faithlynn holds up a hand signal that makes the other senior scouts freeze in place.

She digs her Keds in and sinks to one hip. "Who are the Boy Scouts, Prudence?"

Chancho hurries to get to his feet on the bleachers, taking off his hat like maybe he's going to doff it, then smoothing his hair swoop and cool-guy nodding instead. "Hey. It's been a minute, Faith."

She crinkles her nose at him. "Oh. Right. Prue's brother."

"Cousin," Avi corrects. "He's *my* brother, Constantino, but everyone calls him Chancho which means p—"

"The boys are just moral support," I assure Faithlynn. "They're like legacy cheerleaders. They have the Sight and other special skills."

"Except Jaxon," Kelsey says, sneaking toward her water bottle. "He's just cute."

"Oh, so are you Jaxon?" Jennica asks Paul, whose eyebrows go up.

He leaps to his feet, adjusting his tank so that the LIFEGUARD logo is prominently displayed. "No, I'm Paul Blair, South Hills High Track and Field. And who are you, other than perfect?"

"Jennica Tillerman, North Hills High Ladybird Scout." She gives him her prosthetic hand to shake, and he cups her pink fingers.

"Thank you for your service to our community, Jennica."

The Beast shoots me a look over the top of her sunglasses. I concur. *Yikes.*

When Paul starts flirting in earnest, we're normally looking at losing him to another social group. He'll follow a girl into whatever clique she came from and forget about the Criminal Element entirely for a month or two, then show back up, single and ready to chill.

Usually, it doesn't bother me at all—as long as he checks in sometimes so we know he isn't being brainwashed into a for-real cult—but it would be very bad news for him to get mixed up with the senior scouts.

Bad news for me.

What if he told Jennica how he got the Sight? What if he told Kyle how he met Jennica? What if Jennica uses him to gas up grubs for her to fight, manipulating his emotions for her personal gain?

"Are you guys here about the Carnivore attack in Solano Park?" I blurt.

It does work to puncture Paul's and Jennica's heart eyes, but only by replacing them with horror at my distinct lack of tact.

Chancho shies back toward the bleachers. "There's a Carnivore in town?"

Avi rubs her arms and shudders. "It ate a scout from Mare Island."

"What?" Kelsey gasps, forgetting to slurp her braces and dribbling spit down her chin.

Chancho glares at his sister. "How do you know that?"

Avi wrinkles her nose at him. "Mom told me. It's scout business."

The Beast glowers at me. "Were you gonna mention that to *your* scouts, Prue?"

I ignore the question, guilt sinking like a stone in my stomach. Standing up straight, I address Faithlynn directly. "Is it a Scranch?"

"It is Scranch weather," Faithlynn says like it should be obvious, like there aren't other monsters to face. "Headquarters needs *us* to track down the grub and eliminate it. Which means we need *you* to pick up the slack. Your circle can take on Gabby's neighborhood patrol. It's the closest to your house."

I know exactly where Gabby lives. I could walk there in my sleep.

I glance back at the babybirds. "They aren't steel certi-fied yet."

"That's totally okay. They can patrol in needles," Gabby says. Her topknot quivers as she rushes to add, "There hasn't been a Carnivore spotted in my neighborhood in, like, two years at least, and that was only because there was a fight at a backyard wedding. The combination of Scranch and Nock Jaw made this gnarly hybrid—"

"Fine," I say, cringing away from hearing the details. It's one thing to go around knocking back all the mulligrubs in town, but another to have to hear the story behind every single one. It feels like a privacy violation to dissect the whys just because we're the only ones who can. I wouldn't want anyone analyzing my grub patterns. "Do you have a boundary map or . . . ?"

Gabby pulls out her phone. "It's everything between the cemetery and the drive-thru Starbucks. I'll text you the Headquarters map now. You have the same number, right?"

"Right," I say, uneasily. I don't have any of the senior scouts' numbers saved in my phone. When the text comes through, I hold up my phone as proof that our interaction can now come to a close. "Got it. All set."

"Time for us to get back to hunting," Faithlynn announces, to my great relief.

"Fight the good fight," I say, waving my bracelet in half-hearted goodbye.

"Nice to meet you!" Gabby says to the boys.

"You too! Especially you, Jennica Tillerman!" Paul calls back.

Jennica bats her lashes at him before she swishes her ponytail into step between Faithlynn and Gabby.

"When we join their circle," Kelsey asks, "are we going to have to learn to walk like that?"

"Oh yeah. One hundred percent. They take the walk very seriously," I say, remembering how Molly and I used to make fun of it, pointing out to each other every time it was in a movie or TV show, further proof that Faithlynn was using us as her own little Barbies to live out weird popular-girl fantasies. Molly would always toss her hair too hard or take steps too small, just to make Faithlynn mad. Which would make Jennica mad. Which would rile Gabby up enough that we'd end up pulling through a grub big enough to fight.

What a mess we were. Who would ever let us call each other sister?

And yet I find myself worried about them going back into Solano Park, going up against the same type of monster that ripped apart our circle three years ago. Which is ridiculous. They've spent the intervening years perfecting the hunt. They could probably take down a Carnivorous Scranch with one hand tied behind their back. They protect Poppy Hills from the big bad monsters every day. By comparison, cleaning up Critters in Gabby's boundary should be painless.

I sit down on the bottom bleacher with my knees up, careful to keep my skin away from the hot metal. "Congratulations, scouts, we've been called into temporary active duty."

"Our very own patrol route!" Avi swoons, her head dipping toward the ground. "I'm gonna need new shorts and a fanny pack and a visor and pink running socks—"

"All you *need* is more practice," I say, pointing at the starting-line cones, "without the senior scouts poaching your grub to show off."

18

Social relationships are an essential part of
a scout's life. It's important to find a balance
between friends and sister scouts.

—THE LADYBIRD HANDBOOK

For the first time all summer, I don't wake up before the sun. Since my circle is meeting up to patrol Gabby's boundary, I didn't have to run the dawn patrol with Mom and Tía Lo. I could definitely get used to sleeping until ten thirty, even though my phone is full of sad faces from Chancho, who had to make breakfast for himself and Jaxon this morning. Avi, I assume, fed herself something gluten- and sugar-free, just like her mom would want her to.

I take my time picking out my patrol clothes since these will actually be seen by humans, not just family members and monsters. I don't own any of the chic bird-shit the senior scouts have—my closet has zero wind-breakers or tennis skirts, and I don't have a sports bra I'd be daring enough to wear as a shirt. I settle for pastel-blue bike shorts and a tank top that should look fine with my hoodie.

After a moment's hesitation, I pull out the new wrist harnesses Mom got me. The leather rubbing against the scar on my left arm not only makes me a little too aware of it but also makes it hard for me to bend my wrist enough to buckle the straps on my right arm.

But there's a Carnivore on the loose, even if it was last seen on the far side of town. I slide my daggers into the Kydex sheaths.

When I hear the doorbell, it's just early enough that I have to throw my sneakers down the stairs and follow them in my compression socks. Thank God I don't have to style my hair anymore, or I'd never be on time to anything.

I throw open the door and stagger back a step when I find Kyle on the other side. His hair is damp from a shower, and he's wearing a blue alien shirt the same color as his eyes. When he steps inside to pull me into a hug, I notice Kelsey on the front step, eyes wide like she's trying to apologize telepathically, and Kyle's little white truck parked on the street.

"Babe!" I squeeze his neck, inhaling the clean smell of him, then remember my wrist sheaths. Distracting him with a kiss, I pull back and set my hands gingerly on his shoulders.

"Mom got tired of being the only one who could bring me to meetings," Kelsey explains, standing in the doorway.

She holds on to the straps of her backpack with white knuckles. "I tried to explain to him that Mom doesn't normally hang out."

Kyle frowns at her over his shoulder. "You let Paul and Chancho hang out, didn't you?" He looks back at me and says, "I don't have work for another hour. I know you guys aren't drinking tea or making cookies today, but I could help out with whatever you're teaching."

My heart drops as I imagine Kyle on patrol, Sightless and vulnerable. "Today really isn't that exciting. We're gonna run the Hillside Trail behind the cemetery. Maybe look at some trees? Paul came to help with the track-and-field stuff," I explain quickly. "The girls were working on a Teamwork charm and needed help with a relay."

"And hurdle jumping." Kyle nods. "Kelsey was talking about it at dinner. It sounded cool. I didn't realize scouts had to be so athletic."

Kelsey's shoulders creep guiltily toward her ears. I try not to aim my annoyance at her. I can't expect her to give her family zero information on the twenty hours a week of scouting we do. It's not like she mentioned the monsters chasing her around the track. Hopefully.

"The Handbook says staying active helps keeps your mood stable, but I think it makes us too tired to feel much of anything," I say with a nervous laugh. "You don't want to get sweaty with us before you put on your uniform. You still smell all dreamy and coconutty."

"The coconut conditioner is mine," Kelsey says, bursting that bubble.

"It's communal," Kyle assures me.

I hear the back door open. "Happy patrol day, sisters!" Avi calls. "I'm here, and I brought everyone a protein shake! You all better be ready to kick butt and drink—" She comes around the corner and sees Kyle. The four reusable cups in her arms droop for a second in surprise before she crushes them to her chest extra hard. "Hello, Kelsey's brother, Prue's boyfriend, Kyle."

"Hi, Chancho's sister, Prue's cousin, Avianna," Kyle says with a grin. "Do you need some help with those shakes?"

"Oh, here." Kelsey swoops forward to help keep Avi from dropping the cups.

"What's patrol day?" Kyle asks me, snaking an arm around my waist so he can closer inspect the silver crest pinned above the Sasquatch patch. His eyes crinkle with teasing laughter. "Is this your sheriff's badge, Miss Perry?"

"Patrol day is nothing," I say, not even lying. The Handbook calls for *daily* patrol of town. I twirl my arms overhead to keep my daggers from touching Kyle through my sleeves. "We're working on a Nature Patrol charm today, and every day is 'happy something day' to Avi."

"Yesterday was 'happy day before Nature Patrol charm day,'" Kelsey adds, unhelpfully.

"Tomorrow will be 'happy we got Nature Patrol charms day,'" Avi says in a rush.

"If all goes well," I say, making a face at both of them to stop helping. I tuck one of Kyle's curls behind his ear. "You should come back on a tea day. Or when we go to plant mint in the park, we could definitely use the truck to haul shovels."

"Okay, as long as I can be helpful somehow," he says, looking disappointed. He swoops down to catch my lips in a quick peck. "I'll let you guys get to your smoothies and Nature Patrol charm day."

I trace his jaw with the side of my hand, wishing I could keep him here and shoo everyone else out. "Come back soon."

"I'll steal you away for Sonic sometime," he promises. He kisses my cheek and starts for the door. "It's like real summer vacation now that I've got wheels again."

Once the door closes behind him, Kelsey rolls her eyes. "Now maybe he'll stop tracking grubs into the house while he and Mom fight about him being grounded."

"I know, right?" Avianna says with an eye roll that moves her whole head. "At least your brother can't See his grubs. Chancho made this huge knot of Dreary Blight in the living room that even started to wiggle like it might grow feet. And I was like, 'I'm sorry you flunked your driver's test *again*, but could you, like, pick up a mint leaf and clean up your own mess?'"

I accept my protein shake and hazard a chunky sip. "Did he?"

Avi scoffs. "No way! Once it started to move, he freaked out and ran away. I covered my nose with one of the couch pillows and stabbed it with my knitting needles."

The front door flies open. Sasha the Beast pants in the doorway, her sunglasses falling down the sweaty bridge of her nose. She bares her teeth in a hyena grin.

"I found an entry point! A big one!" she gasps.

"It's our first day patrolling the western boundary," I tell her. "We have to go check Gabby's neighborhood for grubs."

"No shit," the Beast says, jerking a thumb over her shoulder. "I told my mom to drop me at Starbucks an hour ago. You know I like to know the lay of the land, Prudence Perry. And I found a big-ass entry point, so hurry up, we gotta go back."

✝ ✝ ✝

The Hillside Trail is a paved bike path that starts behind the cemetery and follows the western boundary of Poppy Hills. In middle school, my circle used it whenever we snuck out of Gabby's house. Faithlynn saw the path—miles of empty pavement—as her own personal runway, a place where she could make us rehearse our hunting formations and walking in a line.

At the end of the trail, miles beyond the drive-thru Starbucks that marks the end of the western boundary, is the entrance to Solano Park.

Sasha assures me we aren't going that far. She leaps off

the path, racing downhill toward a tree with a huge bough hanging limp in the dirt.

The hair on the back of my neck stands up. There's no fracture point on the branch. Connected to the trunk, it twists toward the ground. As though it's taffy, not solid black oak. Across the trunk, a horizontal slash.

Sasha mashes her thumb inside the arboreal wound. "See?" she says. "It's hella fresh. The inside hasn't dried out at all. This grub came in, like, today."

"Who's having feelings all the way out here?" Kelsey asks, looking around at the bike trail and sparse trees.

"Probably someone who lives in that neighborhood," Avi says, pointing at the wooden fences that butt up against the grove.

"Grubs go where the people are," I concur.

I fiddle with my sleeves as we step out into the neighborhood. The houses here are older, and there are tons of cars in the driveways, which suggests either retirees or stay-at-homes. The Handbook says that you can tell the difference by lawn care, but that doesn't account for people who aren't physically or financially capable of prioritizing green grass in a drought state, so I tell the babybirds to ignore the dandelions and only look for grub activity and eyes watching us through windows.

Avi falls into step beside me, her knitting needles clutched at her sides. "Do you think this is the same grub that ate that scout Shelby?"

"Not if it came in today," I assure her. "It shouldn't be bigger than a Critter."

"But you're wearing your daggers," she notices.

"It's prudent to be prepared. You can run into anything on patrol," I say with an indifference I don't feel. The new wrist sheaths are more comfortable than the old saddlebag scabbards, but my daggers are an unfamiliar weight under the sleeves of my hoodie. Any shift in my hands makes the dagger handles press greetings into my wrists. Part of me worries that I should have practiced more before strapping them on, maybe even taken a refresher steel test.

Another part of me worries that I haven't forgotten how to wield them at all.

Following a muddy smear in a sprinkler-soaked flower bed and a recently collapsed side of chain-link fence, we end up turning a corner into the expansive parking lot of WinCo Foods.

"Look, something pushed over those carts," Kelsey says.

Inside the roundup, all the shopping carts have fallen to one side, leaning heavily on the metal railing. "It wouldn't go into the grocery store, would it?"

"It's where the people are," Avi says.

"And there are lots of emotions inside," Sasha says. "Have you ever been here when they only have one cash register open? Chaos reigns."

On the other side of the automatic doors, I'm surprised first by the blast of cold air, meant to keep flies from getting in, and second by the sheer size of the place. Apparently, WinCo is a warehouse store. Red metal shelving towers overhead. I crane my neck to see plastic-wrapped pallets of baked beans stacked twelve feet high.

"Wow," I say. "The food goes all the way up to the ceiling."

"Wait." Kelsey stops in her tracks and grabs my arm, digging one of my harness buckles into my scar. "Have you never been to WinCo before, Dame Prue?"

"Nope." I gently remove my arm from her grasp. "My dad works for Turnip and Beet It. This is enemy territory."

"Only if your enemy is savings," Sasha says, eyeballing a display of Doritos. She snags a snack-sized bag of Cool Ranch and starts to pop it open, only to have her knuckles rapped by one of Avi's knitting needles.

"Ladybirds don't steal!" Avi hisses. "If we get kicked out, we won't know if the grub was here!"

Sasha's nostrils give a threatening flare. I brace to throw myself between them—the Beast is almost twice Avi's size—but Sasha surprises me by tossing the bag back onto the display.

"I could have paid for it," Sasha mumbles with a surly frown.

"But you wouldn't have," Avi says, skipping ahead into the produce section with Kelsey.

"I miss the Criminal Element," Sasha grumbles at me. "Those ding-dongs are appropriately scared of me."

"It's hard to scare a sc—" I start to say.

"*Squeegee!*" Kelsey screams from around the corner.

I sigh. "At least, it's supposed to be."

Worrying that I should maybe have instituted a non-car-wash-related code word for today's patrol, Sasha and I rush into the produce section. Here, there are actual shoppers, their carts blocking the way through bins of apples and potatoes. It takes a moment for me to spot Avi and Kelsey standing in front of a barricade of WET FLOOR signs. Behind her are bulk food barrels, many of which have been overturned. Rice and cornmeal spill out across the floor, with a long, flat trail cut through the center.

"It's gotta be something with a tail," Sasha observes. "Scranch make holes in the ground."

"Did you see it?" I ask Kelsey.

She shakes her head. "No, but the path looks like it's going toward—"

A crash of twanging metal and a yelp of alarm from our left leads us to find two employees in matching WinCo polos cursing while surrounded by dented cans of green beans and corn.

"Are we having earthquakes or just shitty luck?" one asks, scooping up an armful of cans.

"It was like this last night, too," the other says, replacing a can of yams on the shelf. "We had two sheet cakes fall on the floor, and all of the greeting cards, like, exploded. I've never been more exhausted after a shift. One more mess, man, and I'll quit. Work somewhere that isn't open twenty-four fucking hours." They look over at us and straighten up. "Oh, sorry, did you girls need help finding something?"

"No, we're okay," I say, scanning the aisle for a flash of tail or fangs.

Leaving the employees to pick up their vegetables, the babybirds and I tiptoe into the next aisle.

An old woman stands alone in front of a wall of breakfast foods, reading the nutrition facts on a box of Hershey's Kisses cereal. Her cart is heaped with what I would guess to be visiting-grandkid food—Capri Suns, frozen chicken nuggets, a tower of Lunchables. It almost distracts from the mulligrub hiding on the cart's bottom rack, its green sticklike legs curled around the metal to hold itself steady.

"Is that a Frightworm?" the Beast asks me under her breath. "It's almost as big as Avi."

"It's big because it's been terrorizing the store all night," I whisper back. "We need to banish it without drawing attention to ourselves."

The Frightworm's big black eyes observe us curiously for a second before it rears its head back in warning, showing the horribly sharp mandibles over its open mouth.

Kelsey swallows an alarmed squeak. The Frightworm shivers in pleasure, feeding on the fear.

"Sorry," Kelsey chirps when Nana Lunchables looks up at her, concerned. Kelsey grabs blindly at a box of cereal and holds it out, blocking the woman's view of the cart. "I just think that Oreo O's are so much better than Hershey's cereal. Have you ever tried it?"

Slithering out from underneath and climbing into the cart, the Frightworm's many legs push over the Lunchables tower as the grub makes its way across the groceries and jumps onto the old woman's back. The weight of fear makes her shy away from Kelsey's proffered box of Oreo O's.

The Frightworm shudders and swells before leaping over the shelves into the next aisle.

"Think about it!" Kelsey says, tossing the cereal into the cart with the Lunchables.

We hurry around the corner in a huddle.

"To try to get more fear to feed on, it's going to be unpredictable," I tell the scouts. "But if we show up at all the messes the grub makes, it'll look like we're the ones making them. We need to hold it in place long enough to banish it."

"What about luring it outside?" Avi asks.

"There's too much for it to eat here. More people showing up every minute," I say.

"I have my practice rope in my backpack," Kelsey says. "We could lasso it."

I shake my head. "Lassoing inside would draw way too much attention to us. My circle tried it against a Nock Jaw in the McDonald's PlayPlace once. We got thrown out before we could stop it from exploding all of the ketchup dispensers."

"We could try to trap it with a mint barrier," Sasha says. "The Handbook says that Critters can't cross a peppermint barrier, even when their hides get too thick to pierce with a leaf. It won't banish it, but it should hold it in place long enough for someone to stab it."

Avi bounces up and down. "There's peppermint in the produce aisle! I'll be right back!"

"I'll help!" Kelsey says.

In its leap to the other side, the Frightworm knocked over several packs of toilet paper. Swishing its tail, it's now flinging the packs all around the aisle. Those creepy Charmin bears are spinning across the high-gloss floor in a whirl of color, running into shelves and the toes of our shoes. To someone without the Sight, it would be a scene out of *Paranormal Activity*. With the Sight, it looks like a fat white centipede being annoying in hopes of getting a treat.

When Sasha and I don't feed it any of the fear it's hungry for, the grub stills. It trains its eyes on us. Considering. Assessing.

"Oh, I do not like that," the Beast says, lifting her knitting needles. "Why do I feel like it's memorizing me?"

My thumb settles on the safety latch of my wrist sheath. "It's eating your emotions. Like a real jerk."

The Frightworm rises up and lets out a gurgling whistle. Sasha lunges at it with her needles, but the grub stands on its back legs and tail, gliding backward away from her on the polished white floor. Its many front legs paw at the air.

Avi and Kelsey run back into the aisle, their fists fat with greenery. They look like they're in the middle of a salad robbery. The leaves are dripping wet, drowned under the produce misters. My dad would be appalled.

I start throwing fallen toilet paper packs back onto the shelf to make room on the ground. "Make a circle around it."

Damp peppermint slaps against the ground as Kelsey and Avi throw their bounty. The rest of us hurry to kick it into a tight perimeter before the Frightworm can slip through a gap. The grub throws itself toward the boundary, screeching and skittering away from the peppermint leaves like a moth flapping into an electric fence. The vibrant green mint ring withers to brown dust where the grub touches it.

Sasha executes a strong ax kick, her heel slamming down on the Frightworm's tail. It wheels around, legs waggling menacingly in her face as it shrieks at her.

I find my daggers in my hands, wrist sheaths flapping open under my pushed-up sleeves. My blood sings in my ears, shushing reason and passivity. I don't think about how the kill should be Sasha's or that the babybirds need to practice. I don't worry about Nana Lunchables seeing me with a pair of five-inch daggers, my name engraved in the Connecticut steel. I only want to get this grub away from my friend.

Before I can move, Avi front-flips into the crumbling peppermint circle. With a roar of fury, she sends both of her knitting needles down, into the Frightworm's head. The grub vanishes, leaving Sasha falling backward. The impact of her butt hitting the floor scatters the dust of used peppermint and empty twist-tie tags.

Kelsey and Avi help Sasha up, giggling and congratulating each other.

Unused adrenaline makes my fingers tremble as I sheath my daggers. It takes me a couple of tries to redo the safety latch. I swallow the hitch in my throat. Nothing went wrong. Everyone is safe.

If only I could guarantee that every hunt would end like this, in celebration instead of terror. If it always went the way it was supposed to, staying in the sisterhood would almost be worth it to feel this dizzying sense of accomplishment.

Almost.

I adjust my sleeves down over my wrists again. "Awesome teamwork, scouts! We should celebrate."

"With cookies?" Kelsey asks.

"With pizza bagel dogs?" Avi asks.

"Why not both?" I say. "Is anyone down for a sleepover?"

Sasha's face erupts into a genuine smile for just a moment. She forces it away, scrunching her nose and pushing up her sunglasses. "Only if we can get Doritos."

19

Camping gives the modern scout a
chance to gain deeper respect for the
pioneering Ladybirds who fought for the
emotional health of their community.

—THE LADYBIRD HANDBOOK

Two months ago, if I had announced a last-minute
sleepover with three girls who had every intention of
invading the kitchen, sparring on the tumbling mats in the
garage, and eating three WinCo bags packed with junk
food, my mother would have banished me to my room
and pretended not to know me when the girls in question
arrived at the door with their pillows and pajamas.

However, since our guests are Ladybirds, Mom greets
everyone with a warm "Welcome, sisters!"

Even after weeks of meetings in my backyard, the babybirds are shocked by the sheer amount of scouting non-
sense tucked into the corners of my house. They count
seven Pippy-Mint plants downstairs—including the one

on the top of the toilet tank—and fawn over Mom's collection of emergency weapons mounted inside the coat closet. Avi points out the limited-edition Ladybird American Girl doll behind glass in the forbidden room, complete with miniature charm bracelet.

Mom gives a tour of her study, showing off her collection of vintage charm catalogs and the huge framed photo of Abuela Ramona meeting the great-great-granddaughter of Ladybird founder Kitty Crosby-Fowler. Among the trophies and blue ribbons pinned to the wall, Sasha finds a medal for ax throwing with my name on it, which is how we end up watching old videos of the Regional Conference obstacle races while we eat pizza in the living room.

"Holy fuck," the Beast says, mozzarella falling out the side of her mouth. "Look at baby Prudence Perry flinging axes!"

Kelsey rocks forward on her knees, squinting at the grainy image. "Is that really you, Prue? Your hair was so long! It's almost touching your butt!"

"Super impractical in the field," I say, reaching up and brushing up the back of my hair against the grain. Just looking at my younger self's braided pigtails makes my neck ache.

On-screen, my younger self sinks three bull's-eyes in a row. When the third one hits, little me starts jumping up and down, thrilled to have earned the medal. My sister scouts, waiting their turns to compete, applaud but don't rush out to greet me. Except for Molly, who runs forward—faded pink hair streaming behind her—to high-five me with both hands.

"Prudence?" Avi asks, her tone implying that it's the second time she's tried to get my attention. "Are we going to learn ax throwing this summer?"

"Oh, uh." My thoughts feel far away. I stuff my face with pizza to buy time, then swallow. "Ax throwing is an advanced maneuver. You really only need it to hunt Carnivores. Throwing your weapon at a Critter is literal overkill."

"The hatchet is the most traditional Ladybird weapon," Mom says, in repose on the couch. She is, of course, *not* eating pizza. "For a hundred years, scouts had only the hatchet to choose from. There wasn't always a weapons catalog. There was just the same hatchet you used for food and fuel."

"I read a book about that in fifth grade!" Kelsey says. "But it was about a boy who gets a hatchet from his mom."

My mother rolls her eyes grandly. She has opinions about *that book.* "My mother could have gifted her ax to any one of her daughters or granddaughters when she retired from fieldwork. Instead, her last request was to be buried with it. No Ladybird would ever leave her ax to her *son.*"

I try to imagine Jaxon wearing Tía Lo's knife-gloves. Right now, his hands are so small, I don't think he could even punch-activate the inside safety button. Chancho could. When we used to play scouts, he would put sticks between his fingers and swipe at the air in uppercuts while complaining about the neighbors. Just like his mama. But while Paz and I got to test out the gloves and Mom's whip sword before we chose our own weapons, I'm sure Chancho has never been allowed to wield any Connecticut steel.

Does he ever wonder about it? Or resent it?

After dinner, Kelsey helps the rest of us earn a Baking charm by whipping together a batch of birdbark in minutes so we can focus on helping her perfect her chocolate-and-potato-chip cookies.

"I put peanut butter cups in last time, but it made them too sweet," she explains, crunching Ruffles into the bowl of the stand mixer. "They're supposed to be equally salty and sweet, soft and crunchy. The perfect PMS food, basically."

Avi sets her elbows down on the kitchen island and wrinkles her nose. "What if you don't have PMS? Yet, I mean."

Kelsey's cheeks flush. "Oh, sorry, Avi. I didn't mean to leave you out. I didn't realize you hadn't—I mean, it's just a cookie. My brother and stepdad liked the peanut-butter-cup ones."

"Periods don't make you a girl," Sasha says. "And lots of people don't menstruate at all. Prue's sister said that's why they had to update the Handbook, remember?"

Avi gives a weak nod. "That's true. It just sucks waiting

to catch up to everyone else. I'm already the smallest and the youngest, and the only one in middle school."

"Then don't think of it as catching up," I say, unable to stop myself from thinking of Molly. She was the smallest member of my original circle, even shorter than me and plagued by baby-fat cheeks that made her look even younger than she was. She died in a training bra. "Being the youngest is going to have to be something you get used to because you can only get older a year at a time. You're not going to wake up one day and be exactly the same as your sister scouts. You don't earn your charms the same way or carry the same weapons. You're different parts of a whole."

"'We are all on the same journey taking many paths,'" the Beast intones, trancelike. She winks at Avi over the rim of her sunglasses. "They made us say that at the beginning of group therapy at County Day."

Kelsey bites her bottom lip with the clear brackets of her braces. "Sasha, why did you set the Old Navy outlet on fire?"

"They only carry plus sizes online," Sasha says. "Your brother can't buy pants there, and neither can I. How fucked is that? It's fat segregation."

"Discrimination," I correct.

"Oh, that isn't fair," Kelsey says.

Sasha scoops a fingerful of dough out of the bowl and pops it into her mouth. "And, man, those double-extra-small T-shirts went up like flash paper. Rayon burns *fast*."

Dad helps us get the tent set up on the back lawn. Avi runs between the cedar gate twice to bring over pillows and blankets.

Kelsey hitches an owl pillow-plushie under her arm. "The second we get the inside of the tent set up, I want to look through the weapons catalog!"

Sasha takes her garbage bag of clothes and bowls it inside the pink-and-lavender tent. She chucks herself in after it, shouting, "Daggers and Doritos!"

Kelsey and Avi echo, "Daggers and Doritos!" and run into the tent behind her.

"Sleeping in a tent together is good circle bonding," Mom tells me over the sounds of the scouts oohing and aahing over the large interior of the Ladybird brand tent. "Just remind Sasha that polyester is very flammable."

"I will," I promise. "In the morning, we're going to go out early and patrol Gabby's boundary so I can give them the afternoon off. They've been pushing themselves hard."

Mom regards me with a pleased glint in her eye. "I had my doubts, Prudence. But you've shown yourself to be a capable leader. I look forward to seeing what you do next."

She claps her hand on my shoulder. It is practically a Dr. Anita Silva-Perry bear hug. I don't know how to imprint this moment on my soul other than to wish extra-super hard that I never forget the squeeze of Mom's pride. At the end of the summer, it will all disappear like a run-through grub. She'll never be proud of me for anything other than putting scouts in the line of fire.

Which is fine. I lived most of my life without Mom's approval. And Dad is good for actual hugs—so long as he's using real deodorant and not the weak stuff he gets from the Turnip.

But for this one fleeting moment, I don't feel inferior to my sister or like a disappointment to our legacy. Today, I am fit to be my mother's daughter.

At the end of the summer, I hope I can remember that it was a choice—not my destiny—to be the black sheep.

Inside the tent, the girls have turned on the camping lanterns and set them at either end. The mesh skylight is zipped open so we can see the fading twilight. Once we get the chips opened and the warm cookies distributed, we gather around Avi's tablet and log into the Ladybird merch store.

"I already know what I'm going to get. I have the paper catalog at home," Avi says. She swipes past pictures of plastic-handled weapons so fast that they become a colorful blur. She lands on a long-handled ax. The website points out that both the handle and the leather sheath can be personalized for an additional charge.

"Look! It comes in pink or teal. Teal!" Avi swoons into Kelsey's shoulder. "It will match my Keds!"

Kelsey pats the top of Avi's head with a giggle. "Are we

supposed to pick our weapons based on cuteness?"

"The Handbook says that your weapon is an extension of your personality. Like astrology, with knives," I say, smoothing down my mint-print sleeping bag. I've never had a sleeping bag that didn't come from the merch store.

Crunching a fistful of chips, Sasha knits her eyebrows together. She swallows with a wince. "I like that teal ax, too. But maybe I should go double swords. I'd hate to be a copycat."

"Double swords?" Avi shakes her head. "I always pictured you as a halberd, Beast."

"A who what?" Sasha leans forward to see me from around Avi's shoulder. "Am I offended?"

"A halberd," Avi repeats, swiping again until she finds the long-handled weapons. She enlarges a matte black halberd and holds it out to the Beast. "It's an ax on a pole, with a spike on top. So you can chop or stab. Your two favorites. Of course, the Ladybird ones are retractable."

Sasha sucks the Cool Ranch dust from her fingers before accepting the tablet. "Oh my," she breathes. She sets her damp fingertips delicately on the screen, as though trying to touch a lake without making a ripple. "It's *beautiful*."

Avi's smile presses her cheeks into her eyes. "And that one's from the stealth collection, so you can get it in all black to match your clothes."

"I don't know what kind of weapon I am," Kelsey says, squirming into her plushie owl pillow. "Is it wrong that I sort of want to keep my knitting needles?"

"It's not weird," I reassure her. "That's how I ended up with my daggers. I knew I was good with my needles, so I wanted something that felt similar. But dual wielding means that you're carrying twice the weight as someone with just one weapon. When you're choosing weapons, you also want to look at what your circle needs from you. Kelsey, you're the strongest with a lariat, so you could go whip sword or you could get a smaller weapon and upgrade your practice rope. One of you will be in charge of carrying a first-aid kit in the field, and once you upgrade to hunting Carnivores, you need to have evidence bags on hand, too."

"Evidence bags?" Sasha asks. "I'm not working for the fucking pigs, man. All cops are bastards."

"You don't send evidence to the police. You send them to Headquarters," I tell her. "When you banish a Carnivore, you're supposed to cut out its Root to be processed. Headquarters likes to keep track of anything higher than us on the food chain."

"Chapter seven of the Handbook has instructions for taking samples of dead predators," Avi says. "Headquarters has a lab where they study all the different types of grubs. I'd give anything to go see it."

"I hear it's cool," I say. "Headquarters is open to any active sister scout. You can run the obstacle course during gym hours. My mom and sister went for Paz's eighteenth birthday."

"You didn't get to go?" Sasha asks. "That's bullshit."

I reach for a PMS-chip cookie and stretch out to eat it. "I'd already left my circle. Quitters are not welcome at Headquarters. Or anywhere, really. They only let me be in charge of you guys because the real scouts are too busy killing Carnivores. I'm not a scout. I'm just repaying a debt."

"That's not true!" Avi says. "You're a great scout."

"And a great Dame!" Kelsey adds, scooting closer to me. She pouts her lower lip. "Scouts won't be the same without you. You should come with us to our new circle!"

"Just because it's going to change doesn't mean it'll be bad," I assure her. My stomach sinks as I picture myself sticking around, asking Dame Debby for a place in her circle. Or, more likely, having to ask Faithlynn. She'd laugh in my face so hard, it'd leave a mark. "Besides, I wouldn't be welcome with the senior scouts. No one likes a dropout. And I would prefer to never hunt a Carnivore again. If you can't protect your town, you can't be a Ladybird."

"But you do protect your town!" Kelsey argues. "You banished that Nock Jaw on initiation day!"

"Without you, we couldn't have cleaned up The Wooz or WinCo!" Avi adds.

I shake my head. "Those were all Critters. Stuff too small for the senior scouts to worry about."

"But they affect people! Just because it's not life-and-death doesn't mean it's not important," Avi says, setting aside her tablet. "The Handbook says that thirty percent of grub-related deaths are Critters taking more energy than people have to spare. You could protect thirty percent of Poppy Hills!"

"When you're a scout, you're supposed to outgrow chasing Critters," I tell her. "You hunt Carnivores for the rest of your life. But after my last hunt, I *couldn't*. I couldn't go back into the field. That's why I can't come with you when you join Dame Debby's circle. I'm not just a quitter to them. I'm a traitor. They hate me for being too weak to fight."

"They sound like shitty sisters," Sasha says.

"Yeah," Kelsey says, tipping her chin up. "If you were too scared to leave your house, we'd just meet you here."

"Or kill the thing that was scaring you," Sasha says darkly.

"That's not your job." I shake my head. "Scouts aren't supposed to protect their Dame. It's backward."

"Okay," Kelsey says, setting her chin in her hands. "But friends are supposed to protect one another. So you can be our Dame second and our friend first."

"You can be my Dame third," Avi assures me. "And my prima second."

Warmth spreads through my chest, a happy glow that wants to believe that the sisterhood could actually feel as simple as this. The babybirds make it so easy to be a Ladybird. No competition, no emotional manipulation. Just actual belonging.

If only I had the courage to tell them that once the summer is over, I have no intention of staying in this world I've shown them.

The Beast sits up, folding her long legs into a careful pretzel. With deliberate slowness, she pulls the sunglasses off her ears and sets them aside. Kelsey and Avi freeze as the Beast blinks. It's so rare to see her unmasked and even rarer for her to lean forward to focus her bare eyeballs on my own.

"What made you quit?" she asks. "What happened on your last hunt that was so bad?"

I meet her gaze. She, Avi, and Kelsey deserve to know why there's an empty space in Dame Debby's circle for them, why I refused to go back into the field for so long.

I owe them the truth.

I owe it to Molly, too.

After a moment of hesitation, I slide my arms out of the sleeves of my hoodie. Twisting my left arm, I let everyone in the tent see the full line of scar tissue puckered from shoulder to wrist.

"Three years ago, my circle started hunting Carnivores."

20

Failure is the ultimate teacher.

—THE LADYBIRD HANDBOOK

THREE YEARS AGO.

In order to find anything worth killing, my circle had to beat all the other patrols. Back then, my sister was leading a circle with a huge crew of eight scouts. By the afternoon, they'd picked clean anything but the smallest Critters. That meant if my circle—the five of us—slept in too late, there was almost no chance of running into something big enough to actually fight. We were tired of running the after-school patrol, waiting for run-ins with small black-eyed grubs manifested by kids walking home.

We had real, true Connecticut steel burning a figurative hole in our harnesses. What was the point of tossing peppermint leaves at Critters anymore?

Then one day, at five in the morning, Gabby's alarm clock played Taylor Swift to wake us up. We all leapt out of our sleeping bags and into shoes and weapons.

If we'd spent the night in a Ladybird legacy house, we wouldn't have needed to sneak out. But Gabby's house had the best snacks. Mrs. Colucci didn't know a mulligrub from a mogwai, but she made sure we had giant tubs of popcorn mixed with M&M's and never asked to tag along on our patrols, so it was worth it to have to tiptoe across the roof and shimmy down the deck to where we'd stashed our bikes next to Gabby's dad's moped.

Faithlynn referred to our escape route as "formation eleven" because we only had ten hunting formations and she's never been very funny.

Once we were all safely out of the neighbor's yard, we jogged in formation up the bike path toward the state park.

The Handbook says the easiest place to hunt is the forest, and Solano Park was the closest thing we had to a forest. Its trail wound up through the hills, passing oak and walnut trees that we'd heard might be showing signs of grub disturbance. Entry-point lashes. Branches inexplicably bent but not broken.

Mom and Tía Lo said that the influx of campers must have pulled the Carnivore through. There were rumors about people coming out here in the middle of the night to party. If it was a party monster, it'd most likely be a Nock Jaw, which we'd gotten good at taking down during Christmas break.

We were going to hunt the Carnivore ourselves. Carving

out its Root would definitely put us on the leaderboard.

Obviously, we hadn't confirmed this plan with anyone else. Faithlynn was positive that my sister would try to swoop our kill by bringing in her circle of senior scouts. So, I kept my mouth shut. I didn't even tell Chancho. I couldn't risk him telling Tía Lo, who was always talking about how my circle was getting "too big in the britches." She thought we were too cocky to be Ladybirds. And we probably were. We walked around the bike trails, just begging for grubs to fight. We'd bait traps with screams, pick fights with one another, all to see what we could banish.

We thought there would be fewer lectures when we proved that we were better by eighth grade than most scouts hoped to be by the end of high school.

As we parked our bikes and walked into Solano Park, we flicked on our flashlights. If anyone thought it was stupid to hike in the dark, no one said so. Gravel and grass crunched under five pairs of sneakers. The tips of my twin dagger sheaths peeked out under the hem of my shorts, bouncing against the sides of my legs. The harnesses chafed, but I thought they looked very cool.

"Gabby, if you don't stop singing that fucking song, I swear I'm gonna chop your head off," Faithlynn threatened.

"I'm sorry!" Gabby squeaked, caught mid–Taylor Swift song again. She'd already spent our entire bike ride humming off-tune. "It's gonna be stuck in my head all day."

"It's creepy," Faithlynn said. "It sounds like it's about a haunted doll."

"No, it doesn't," I argued. At the time, I had a Taylor Swift poster on my wall—not that anyone in the circle would have known that but Molly. The *Reputation* era really spoke to my secret inner Goth. "It's about how people who have been manipulated forever eventually snap."

"Whatever." Faithlynn gave an exaggerated yawn to end the conversation. "Jennica, did you remember the evidence bags?"

"Got them!" Jennica said pertly. She held our field bag, which had extra flashlight batteries, the first-aid kit, and enough mint to make tea for fifty. Or to slow down one Carnivore, we hoped.

"Did you hear that the Ladybirds in Sacramento caught an eight-foot Frightworm last week?" I asked the group. Talking would keep my mind off the hot coal of anxiety burning in my stomach. Either there was a huge grub nearby or I was so scared of seeing one that I'd pull something else toward us. Gossiping about other circles always kept my mind busy.

"Oh my blob! They are so lucky," Jennica chirped, unironically—she can't help being stuck in an embarrassingly dated flashback.

"Eight feet long or eight feet wide?" Molly asked, and tripped on a pothole in the dark, bumping into my back. Thankfully, not with her sword. "I guess it doesn't matter with a worm, huh? Otherwise it'd be a pancake."

I yawned until my eyes watered. "I'd love to fight a pancake. It'd be so much easier to run across it for a Root shot."

"Those Sacramento scouts only had rope and their knitting needles," Faithlynn said. If this had been two years before, she would have started that sentence with *My mom says*. But she was in high school now, which she'd never let anyone forget, and she'd decided to pretend like all of Dame Debby's ideas were her own.

"Was . . . the Frightworm . . . Carnivorous?" asked Gabby, cracking her gum between words. If she didn't chew during a fight, she forgot to breathe. We'd learned this the hard way in fifth grade when she fainted while fighting a Nock Jaw behind Target.

"I mean, they said it was," Faithlynn said, successfully hijacking yet another conversation. "But apparently it all happened so fast that they didn't have time to take any samples for Headquarters so we'll never really know."

Jennica tried to comb the bedhead out of her bangs with her fingers. "They're *so* gonna get the Biggest Grub Award at the Regional Tea Gala."

"No way," Faithlynn said. "Not with the top of the Root shot leaderboard here."

Flashlight filled my eyes, Faithlynn blinding me for sport as she pretended to laud me for making the scoreboard on the Headquarters app. I'd found a sweet spot in killing large-scale grubs that I didn't have with grubs my own size. Like many of the stunts on the leaderboard, the Root shot is a high-risk trick. Sort of like a slam dunk in basketball. Except instead of a ball, you have a weapon made by a secret society in Redding, Connecticut, and instead of a basket, you're splitting a grub's skull open, tearing out its Root, and landing safely before the monster gets sucked back into its own dimension. Being small, I had the unique advantage of being able to pull off my Root shot with a rear approach—running up a Nock Jaw's tail and cutting my way down—which is how I'd ended up on the leaderboard.

That stunt had earned me the only charm I'd gotten without the circle's help. And Faithlynn's unending disdain because she hadn't been able to replicate it.

I pointed my flashlight northeast. Blackened, withered trees leaned away from one another, creating a path away from what was designated by the signage. Our flashlights made rainbows out of distant iridescence. "Entry points."

"Great job, Pa-roo-dence," said Jennica, adding in the extra syllable that made me hate the sound of my own name.

"Fighting formation five," Faithlynn called, taking her axes out of her holsters.

Gabby stamped her heels. "We can't hold flashlights in formation five."

"Then we'll fight in the dark," Faithlynn bit back, taking her position as the apex of our triangle formation. "Do you think that the original Ladybirds had LEDs? Grow up, Gabby."

"The original Ladybirds fought by candlelight," I said, grudgingly setting my flashlight between two skinny trees. I left it on, hoping the light would lead me to it on our way back. "And mostly died of smallpox and malaria."

"But not because they didn't have a fucking flashlight," Faithlynn said, beaming at me like I'd proved her point.

My fingers itched to just throw hands, to finish all our conversations with a spar. It was impossible to reason with Faithlynn, impossible to ever be anything but her sidekick. Ever since we'd entered the field, hunting was the only language she spoke. And even then, she only respected it as long as she wasn't outshone.

We started up the side of the hill, passing between the shriveled oak trees. I rolled my shoulders. It was hot out. Scranch weather.

"Thanks a lot, Prue. All I can think about now is pancakes," Molly sighed. "Gabby, do you think your mom will make us some?"

"As long as we sneak back in before she wakes up," Gabby said.

"Excuse me," Faithlynn said, cracking the handles of her axes together like huge drumsticks. "Trying to save the world here! Anyone else?"

"The world?" Molly giggled. "I thought the grub was just eating drunk campers."

The ground trembled, and the silliness fell out of our postures.

Our formation tightened to the exact measurements prescribed by Dame Debby's playbook. Spines straightened, weapons raised, even as we could feel the shudder underfoot of something coming at us, gaining speed in the dark. It got closer, revealing knotted lavender legs tipped in sharp spikes.

Definitely not a party monster. It was a Carnivore-class Scranch, nearly seven feet tall, with a body as wide across as a compact car. It looked down at us with eyes like white sunlight made out of pure hydrogen and human rage. Impossible to stare at directly. Impossible to look away from.

"Oh, fuck this," Gabby whispered. "Let's go back to the sleepover, please. I'll make the pancakes myself!"

"Shut up, Gabby," Faithlynn snapped. "And hold your damn positions."

"It's huge," Molly whimpered. Caught in the white light of the grub's eyes, she was already ghostly, as pale as she'd been the day we'd been told we were going to be initiated two years early. "Did you know it was gonna be that big?"

I hadn't known. I was sure that if I had, I wouldn't have agreed to the mission. But it was too late now. Ladybirds aren't allowed to back down from a fight. My knuckles popped as I tightened my grip on my daggers.

The Scranch hopped forward. Not in a menacing, sleek predator way. Like a pogo stick. Like it should have boinged.

That's when we should have run.

Instead, Gabby laughed—out of nerves, I think—and we all ran forward. The first objective in fighting something bigger than you is to cut it down to size. Jennica was already wrapping her whip sword around the leg nearest her, pulling it hard in an attempt to tear it away from the hip joint. We'd never fought a Carnivorous Scranch before, didn't know how much harder their shells were than the black-eyed ones. The Handbook says they get stronger, but it doesn't tell you that they get almost impenetrable.

They want you to think you have a chance.

Gum cracking, Gabby swung her sword into a leg, succeeding only in bringing two of the Scranch's mouths toward her. Hundreds of teeth rattled in the darkness.

I broke formation, leaving the back legs standing so I could pull the grub's attention away from Gabby. I leapt up, using my daggers to stab into the Scranch's farthest jowl and pull myself upward on its torso, ice-pick style.

"God, Prudence, way to hog the Root shot!" Faithlynn said, somewhere below my swinging legs. "Are you so determined not to share the spotlight?"

"I'm not hogging anything!" I shouted down at her. My forearms shook as I held myself off the ground by dagger handles and force of will. "We're trying to get rid of it, aren't we?"

The moment my concentration broke, the Scranch swung hard from side to side, dislodging me and, unfortunately, only one of my daggers. I tucked and rolled, my spine landing against one of the warped oak trees. I got back on my feet and rushed forward to help Jennica pull her whip sword back. It took both of us to tear off one leg.

As we ran toward the next leg, I was jerked backward by the pigtails, feet momentarily off the ground, pain exploding through my head. I was sure that it was Faith—yanking my hair to keep me from climbing the back of the grub—but when I reached up, I could feel only the sharp spines of Scranch leg. Molly ran to my rescue, setting a hand on my shoulder to keep me still as she started using her sword to try to cut me free.

"Hang on there, Rapunzel," she said, "You're leashed to this leg! I think I'm gonna have to try cutting the hair and not the spike."

"You know, I've always wanted a bob," I said, feeling loopy with fear as the grub was momentarily distracted by our sister scouts. "Try to leave me enough to show under my tea hat or my mom will flip out!"

Faithlynn was shouting. New formation numbers. The rest of us limped forward into position. With only one pigtail, I felt lopsided. I was so scared, every footstep felt like walking in space. Floating, untethered.

I tripped over something shiny. My other dagger on the ground. I picked it up and squared my shoulders. In my mind, I thought about being six and playing Ladybird in the backyard with Chancho. How had that felt more real than actually facing down death in the field?

"Now," Faithlynn said, addressing all of us and the grub in the same voice of fourteen-year-old dictatorship, "*I* am going to go for the Root, and *you* are going to get those fucking legs off."

"Isn't that what were we doing?" Gabby asked.

"That's what you were *failing* at," Faithlynn said. "It still has four of its legs!"

Agitated with us, the Scranch hunkered low to the ground and dragged its belly through the dirt. It roared. Its breath was curiously cold and stank of rotten eggs. I thought of a passage in the Handbook: "If you're close enough to smell, you're close enough to taste." I'd never realized it was a warning. Or possibly a threat.

The grub sprang forward. It snapped at Jennica, who screamed and fell back. A leg dragged Faithlynn forward. Faith welcomed the momentum, letting the Scranch pull her halfway to its mouth before she barrel-rolled over the leg and thrust her axes into the grub's haunch. She succeeded in pulling it downward, the veins in her arms bulging with the effort.

When Molly made the run around the back, I knew exactly what she was going to do. We all did. As Faithlynn pulled the Scranch to the ground by sheer force of will— and Gabby and I followed formation, doing our best to pin down the other two legs—the grub would be in easy position for someone to get its Root.

A Scranch isn't made for standing on; its knobby body is like a giant's fist, all knucklebones. Molly ran up the back easily enough, though, her Scotchgarded Keds taking its spine like a balance beam. She cranked her sword as she went, proudly displaying her hand-me-down steel for once.

"*Look what you made me do!*" she sang out, her sword lifted to the sky. "Root shot!"

The leg that Faithlynn was holding tore away from the body and fell toward me. One of the burrs clipped me in the shoulder and knocked me into the dirt. I thrashed beneath it, feeling my skin tear as I tried to free myself.

Easily pulling out of Gabby's grip, the Scranch flipped itself over onto its back, sending Molly toppling. It caught her out of the air, pinching her between the tips of its two remaining legs. Sharp claws pressed into her stomach. It looked like it might spin her in a web like a spider.

Molly didn't cry out or curse God. In the spotlight of the Scranch's eyes, one moment she was held aloft.

The next, she was stuffed, unceremoniously, into the centermost mouth.

Face-first, thank God.

Legs kicking figure eights, she fought like a Ladybird all the way until the end.

But then it was the end.

In the Scranch's jaws, the lump of her shattered.

The sound was awful. Beyond awful. So loud that I couldn't hear my own screams. Fear like I'd never known flooded my system.

And the Scranch was still moving. Turning every particle that had been Molly Barry—her goofy laugh, her taste for pepperoni-and-pineapple pizza, the red roots under the pink hair she wore to match us—into fuel for killing. And all I could do was lie on the ground, frozen, watching it happen. Despite my years of training, the legacy status in my blood, the charms on my wrist, there was nothing I could do to save my friend. There was nothing any of us could do.

The air started to shimmer around the grub. There was a molasses-in-a-vacuum sucking noise and brief, intense heat, like an oven door open too long. All around us, tree trunks burst open with vertical slashes. The Scranch was swelling. Growing. Getting stronger.

Gabby helped pull me to my feet. Jennica was sobbing and babbling about losing her charm bracelet, her sweatshirt bundled around her arm.

Faithlynn called for us to retreat.

The light of our dead friend's soul burned behind us, illuminating our way out of the park. We left our bikes and staggered into the street. Faithlynn flagged down a minivan—a mom on a predawn Starbucks run—to take us to the hospital.

I don't remember us talking to one another until we were standing alone in front of the ER. At that moment

—before Jennica removed the sweatshirt from her wrist and we realized that it wasn't her bracelet that the grub took, but her whole hand and most of her wrist

—before we were rushed into separate triage rooms

—before I fainted while trying to count the staples in my arm

—before Gabby's parents put out a missing persons warrant for her but not for the rest of us

—before Dame Debby showed up with one of the Grand Dames from the regional clubhouse to take an official report

—before the police's birdshit report about a mountain lion protecting its cubs—

the only thing anyone said aloud was "Molly must have thought she could make the Root shot because Prudence did."

†††

"After that," I say shakily, focusing on the white light of the nearest camping lantern. "I knew couldn't be a scout anymore. I was supposed to return to the field when my arm was healed, but I started having panic attacks just seeing Critters around the house. I couldn't go to school. I was afraid of going to sleep because I didn't want to see grubs in my dreams. When I got diagnosed with PTSD, my dad and my psychiatrist talked my mom into letting me officially leave the scouts. I didn't—I don't—want to

face another Carnivore. Scouts are supposed to keep people safe, and I proved that I couldn't."

"Prudence," Kelsey says with a soft slurp of her braces.
"I had no idea."

"Oh my heart." Avi sniffles and wipes her wet eyes
before launching herself at me, hugging my shoulders
tight. "Prima, I'm so sorry that happened to you."

"No, I'm sorry," I say, patting the top of her head. "I
should have told you the day of the initiation ceremony.
I shouldn't have let you get this far into training without letting you know exactly how dangerous scouting can
be. What happened to Molly could happen to anyone.
A Carnivore killed a scout a week ago. All Headquarters
does is send out memorial lockets and train new recruits.
Because there are always more grubs, the sisterhood has to
keep going."

The Beast lurches forward on her knees, picking up her
sunglasses and crawling for the tent flap.

"I need some air," she grumbles, shoving her sunglasses
back on her face.

"Sasha!" I call after her. When she doesn't slow down—
or zip the door behind her—I carefully disentangle myself
from Avi's grip and leave the tent.

There's no sign of the Beast in the backyard. Ahead, in
the darkness, I can hear the scrape of the trash cans being
shoved aside and the front gate creaking open. I jog toward

the noise, slapping past the Pippy-Mint bushes that line the side yard.

The motion sensor light clicks on over the driveway as a stream of vape smoke raises from between my parents' cars. The Beast paces and puffs, looking like a bull getting ready to charge.

"Sasha," I start, unsure if I want to apologize for not telling her exactly what risks she was signing up for or admonish her for smoking in clear view of the front window.

"There was no mountain lion attack?" she snarls. "You've been lying to me for our entire friendship?"

"What?" Surprise makes me stagger back a step. Of all the things she could have been mad about—the danger synonymous with being a Ladybird, the truth of how the senior scouts and I failed Molly, even the idea that I used to sneak out of the house way more readily than I do now—the mountain lion cover story was not what I was expecting. "Yes! I mean, only as much as I've had to lie to anyone who isn't a scout. Kyle and Paul heard the mountain lion story, too."

Sasha takes another agitated pull from her vape, shaking her head in disbelief. "Yeah, but that's them! I've been doing this Ladybird shit with you all summer! Were you ever gonna tell me the truth? I thought we were best friends, dude!"

My hands curl into fists at my sides. "We are!"

"Not if you're keeping shit from me!" She crosses her arms and glowers at me. "What else haven't you told me?"

"Tons!" I burst out. All of the anxiety that I've kept to myself comes bubbling to the surface, overflowing out of my mouth. "I wish you'd told me before you joined up. I think you are going to *hate* joining Dame Debby's circle. When you get something wrong, she hits your knuckles with knitting needles, which hurts like hell. And I am absolutely terrified about what the senior scouts will turn you into." My sinuses pinch as tears start to form in the corners of my eyes. "I don't want to see you, Avi, and Kelsey pitted against one another so you can make it on the leaderboard. I don't want you to become cold-blooded hunters who only care about birdshit—like Faithlynn Brett and Tía Lo and my mom!"

"Then don't quit!" she growls. "If you're our Dame, then you can make sure we do more than hunt! We don't care about keeping score. And we don't care about joining those snotty seniors. All of us like being part of *your* circle. So why not just keep running it after summer's over?"

"Because everything I have done this summer is so that I can finally just Forget . . . all of this!" I sob, tears spilling down my cheeks in hot rivulets. I feel too exposed out here, unarmed without my hoodie. "All of the horrible shit that being a scout has put in my brain!"

Sasha throws up her hands. "Why are you talking like

it's all bad? We've had *fun* this summer, and you just want to bail. So you can—what?—go back to killing time with the Criminal Element, sneaking into the movies, hooking up with Kyle, and hotboxing the shedroom?"

I wrap my bare arms around my stomach, stung. Because I have been dreaming about exactly that—my scout-free life, where my biggest concern is scraping together enough money to chip in for weed and malt liquor and worrying about whether or not the movie theater is finally going to make good on their promise to perma-ban us. Until tonight, I'd assumed Sasha was happy doing all that stuff, too. Except for making out with Kyle, of course.

"I just want to be safe," I say in a small voice. I rub my wet nose on my bare wrist, leaving snot marks on the thin skin of my scar. "I want a life that isn't fully prescribed by the Handbook."

Her lip curls. "Then why don't you just show us something that isn't in the Handbook?"

I open my mouth, to tell her I can't, that it's too late, that I've already promised them to Dame Debby.

But then I stop. I've been teaching the Handbook my way already. Without corporal punishment, without pitting the scouts against one another.

What if I could also teach them how to stay soft, even when I'm not there to lead them?

The sun is barely up when I wake the babybirds and push them all out of the tent. The air is cool, the grass dewy damp against the hem of my pajama pants.

"Please tell me something needs killing." Sasha yawns until her jaw cracks. "It's too early to be alive."

"Are we going on dawn patrol?" Kelsey asks, rubbing the dried drool on her chin with the heel of her hand.

"Oh my gee," Avi says, bouncing beside me. Unsurprisingly, my baby cousin is a morning person. "I've always wanted to get invited to join Mom and Tía Anita—"

The back door opens, and my dad steps out in his usual Lululemon regalia, his yoga mat tucked under his arm. He blinks a few times in obvious surprise.

"You girls are up early," he says. His forehead wrinkles the same way Mom's often does. "But Anita and Lo left for patrol about an hour ago. They went out the front door so that the back gate wouldn't wake you."

Avi visibly deflates. I step in front of her.

"Actually, Dad, last night Sasha and I were talking about stuff that isn't in the Handbook, and I thought it might be a good idea to add yoga into our training. If you wouldn't mind taking us through that ocean-breathing vinyasa sequence you showed me?"

"Well, sure, munchkin!" Dad says brightly. "We don't have enough mats for everyone, but let me pop inside for some beach towels! I'll be right back."

Leaving his mat propped against the wall, he dashes

inside. I wonder how long he's been waiting to be more helpful to the Ladybirds than just buying flowers and staying out of the way.

Kelsey cocks her frizzy head at me. "Yoga? Is there a charm for that?"

"Nope," I say with a shrug. "But I think we should start working on emotional regulation. The Wooz Nock-Jaw and yesterday's Frightworm both got bigger as we fought them. You'll be safer in the field if you can keep calm. Smaller grubs are easier to banish."

The Beast gives me her friendliest Friendly Face, her teeth glinting in the early morning light. "Good idea, Dame Prudence."

Fieldwork is the backbone of our organization.

—THE LADYBIRD HANDBOOK

It's been three days since we took over Gabby's boundary, and the senior scouts still haven't caught the Scranch that killed Shelby. According to the daily regional email blast and Mom's dinner gossip, Faithlynn, Jennica, and Gabby are stationed in the campsite at Solano Park, refusing any offers to take a shift off to go home, see their families, sleep in their own beds. Presumably all they've done is hike-hunt the Scranch and make sure it doesn't eat any other campers.

"I hope they're not just out there gassing it up for points," I say, helping myself to more cauliflower rice and pigeon peas, forgetting for a moment that we've got family over for dinner who actually listen to the things I mutter under my breath. Or, at least, don't pretend not to hear them.

"Prudence!" Tía Lo snatches the bowl away from me, chest-passing it to Tío Tino, whose plate is buried under four charred chicken breasts. "Ladybird scouts would never prioritize charms over people's safety."

"We earn charms in order to make people more safe," Avi says, in a way that is neither agreeing or disagreeing. She reaches for the heavy glass pitcher of mint ice water on the center of the table and carefully refills both her own and Jaxon's cups. Jaxon, whose face deep inside a book with a dragon on the cover, doesn't notice.

"Right," I say as Avi and Tía Lo wield their forks and knives in the same mincing manner, like they're playing tiny violins rather than cutting meat. "But that means that if a scout wants to upgrade their weapon or to gain more field experience or even to qualify for a scholarship to college like Paz—"

"They would not choose to think about that when a sister has so recently died in the field," Mom interrupts, the white streak in her hair trembling with indignance. "Shelby Waters's memorial lockets have just been pressed, for God's sake."

"I wasn't trying to dishonor the memory of a dead scout," I say. My face is hot, and the corners of my eyes start to burn. I take a deep breath, hold it, and pray not to hear a grub pop up at my feet. Tía Lo hates when grubs run into her mint garden—it makes the leaves wither.

Across the table, Avi clears her throat. "I think what Prudence was trying to say is that it's taking an unusually long time for the senior scouts to complete their mission."

I send her a grateful look, and she gives me a nose-wrinkling smile in return. Since the sleepover, Avi has almost felt more like my friend than my baby cousin. Before hearing the story of how Molly died, she never would have risked taking my side in a family Ladybird argument.

"Last week, we saw them take down a small Scranch in two seconds flat," Chancho says. He rips the flesh off a drumstick and whips the bone around, miming the senior scouts closing in on a grub. "Just *boom boom*, hatchets, sword. Poof!"

"Not every problem can be taken down on the stab. Sometimes you have to regroup and try again," Tía Lo says.

Mom nods. "That's the growth mindset."

"Does that mean Chancho's taking his driver's test again?" Avi asks.

"Not in my car, he's not." Tío Tino laughs and elbows my dad in the side. "You know how much it costs to put a new bumper on a Cadillac?"

My dad laughs along, even though he drives an electric car that looks like a cheap toy next to Tío Tino's Escalade.

Chancho sneers at his sister. "Don't you have a sword test to study for?"

"It's a *steel* test," Avi corrects with a haughty toss of her hair. "But we've been too busy to have a regular meeting. We're focusing on sweeping our patrol boundary and learning yoga and meditation for emotional regulation."

"Yoga and meditation?" Tía Lo throws an accusatory look at Dad, knowing this is his influence. "Where is that in the Handbook?"

"Maybe it'll make the eleventh edition. Scouts are always evolving," I say, parroting something I've heard my sister say. "When the senior scouts get back, we'll start the Life Skills chapter."

"Oh?" Tía Lo is suddenly alert, her head cocked toward me as if I've said some secret passcode. "Do you need some help with your weapons unit, Miss Prue?"

I realize now that this whole dinner was probably a setup. Tía Lo wasn't happy just coming to one meeting, even though she swore she was too busy to help at all.

"Headquarters has some videos everyone is supposed to watch to prep for the steel test," I say, doing my best to sound cavalier. "I was just going to send out the link for some independent study—"

"Traditionally," Mom says, dabbing the corners of her mouth with her napkin, "before the steel test, legacy scouts come in to demonstrate the different options—"

Across the table, Dad makes eye contact with me and grimaces almost imperceptibly. He knows, as well as I do, that this is a plan that has already been constructed. All I'm allowed to do is say yes.

Resigned to this new meddling, I make myself hold my chin up and smile at Mom and Tía Lo. "I wouldn't want to ask you to take time off from work—"

Mom beams back at me. "Then we'll schedule for after four."

And the trap clicks shut behind me.

Thus begins a week of patrol *and* meetings. Every single day, Sasha, Avi, and Kelsey arrive at my house by noon and go home for dinner. Measuring time in sunscreen and water bottles, we get comfortable running the Hillside Trail, memorizing the bends and potholes in the pavement. Our eyes start to glaze over the entry points we've seen, no longer needing to refer back to the Ladybird app to tell us what we've already reported. Between patrol and working through the Handbook, we practice the yoga sequence my dad showed us.

> Back under the pergola, Tía Lo shows
> up with a box full of pink
> and announces, "Patrol uniforms!
> I couldn't resist! I know
> you all love to wear your PE clothes
> in public, but these
> shorts are from the merch store
> and they have pockets for
> your knitting needles! Isn't that darling?"
> The Beast holds up her pair of 2XL
> spandex bike shorts.
> Her upper lip curls. "The things a
> woman has to do for pockets."
> She refuses to wear the matching T-shirt.

We spend a morning chopping Dreary Blight
off the front wall of the cemetery,
then come back the next day
to plant a peppermint garden. With Kyle
lugging bags of fertilizer for us, the ground
between the wrought iron gate and the stone wall
transforms from dry stems and foxtails
into a usable mint barrier.
Kyle doesn't even notice
when the babybirds disappear
to chase a Frightworm
between headstones. To him, they're
dancing in the sprinklers.

Stretching in the sunshine together,
we push up from a plank
and bend backward into cobra.
"Remember to breathe into each pose," I say.
"In through your nose, out through your mouth."
Kelsey's arms start to wilt. "Ow," she groans.
"I am not feeling very centered, Dame Prue!"
"Breathe through it!" Avi reminds her.

The last chapter of the Handbook
before the steel test is Life Skills,
where most of the advanced hunting
techniques are learned for charms.

Tía Lo borrowed Dame Debby's
ax-throwing setup, a familiar set of
scarred pink boards and matching
practice axes. She sets the targets
in a circle and throws the first round
blindfolded. It's not a good
lesson, but it is very impressive.

Everyone in the circle accidentally earns
a Bait and Switch charm while examining signs
of an entry point on someone's front porch.
When the door opens, there's an old man,
yelling at us for sneaking around his property,
and a Scranch clicking on the tile behind him.
While I apologize and pretend to
want to know what kind of
dead cactus is potted next to the mailbox,
Sasha quickly shoves Avi off the porch.
The Scranch surges forward, rushing outside
to eat Avi's indignance as she lands, butt-first,
in the dead grass. The door slams closed,
and the Beast stabs the Scranch between the
eyes with a knitting needle.
"Sasha, what's the rule?" I ask
as Kelsey helps Avi back to her feet.
The Beast looks grumpily at her feet.

"Only use my own anger as bait."
"That's right."

We sit cross-legged in the grass around
a tight circle of peppermint leaves.
"Beast, when you pushed me off the porch,
I felt disrespected and unsafe," Avi says.
In the center of the peppermint leaves,
the small Scranch I trapped trembles,
flexing its legs as though considering its own weight.
Kelsey eyes the grub uneasily,
her hand inching toward her knitting needles.
"Breathe through it, Sasha," she says.
"Remember, anger is just a wave
on your feelings ocean."
"How do you know it's *my* fucking anger
making it grow?" the Beast growls.
The Scranch gnashes its teeth and swells between us.
"Because I'm not angry," Avi says haughtily.
"Just disappointed."
"Jesus Christ," Sasha grumbles. "*Fine.*
I'm sorry I pushed you, Avi. We're all on
the same team."

In the backyard, Mom shows off the
trick shots with her

whip sword that earned her a dozen
trophies. Cutting a pencil
in half. Slicing the cap off a water
bottle. When she snuffs the
flame of a taper candle in my hand, even
Sasha joins the riotous applause.
"Now, I know you're starting to
prepare for your steel test,"
Mom says as she reattaches the whip
sword to her purse, where it
acts as the crossbody strap.
"And I hope some of you will consider
becoming whippers. Even
though your Dame will make a strong
case in favor of dual steel."
"Not me," I assure her. "I just want
everyone to choose the weapon
that makes them happy. What works
for me won't work for everyone."

Deep inside his goalie-mask suit made
of pillows, Chancho makes
a gurgle of protestation as his back
slams into the mat again.
Off to the side, behind the
punching bags and scouts

waiting for their turn to prove their
self-defense competence,
a Tizzy Louse bursts into being
that, for once, I didn't make.
Avi looms over her winded brother,
arms folded. "If you're going
to get your feelings hurt, too,
then you can't play."
"I'm. Fine," Chancho wheezes from
the ground. "Just give me a
breather before we try more groin stuff."
Sasha snorts. "That is assuredly what she said."
"I'll go get another you another
pillow," I offer. "And an ice pack."

It's so hot outside
that we take our cool-down
stretches to the living room,
where we follow a guided meditation
on YouTube. Then fall down
a baking video rabbit hole.

The table under the pergola has all of
the weapons my family has
to offer. Tía Lo's vintage '90s house
swords—one pink, the other green—
and her daily punch gloves, a practice

halberd Paz left in the garage with a
collection of multicolored lariats,
Mom's beginner whip sword—
concealed inside of a brown leather belt—
and an umbrella-sword from
last year's weapons catalog I had no
idea she'd ordered for herself.
My daggers complete the arsenal,
but none of the scouts
reach for them. Sasha immediately
grabs the halberd, Kelsey
a whip sword, and Avi two swords.
They bounce on the balls of
their feet waiting for me to pull a
grub out of the trap for them.
The Dame message boards say trying
out weapons is supposed
to inspire the scouts to
study for their weapons test,
but I'm pretty sure it's inspiring all
three babybirds to consider
stealing a practice weapon. For once,
I do not blame Mom and Tía Lo
for staying to supervise.

Alone in the backyard, I pack up the ax boards and fall
mats to make space for tomorrow's double dose of patrol

and parkour basics. The mats scrape the cement as I sled-push them off the grass and up against the side of the house. There's no danger of rain, but Dad's too proud of the lawn to let me kill it out of laziness. I crack my back and rub a cramp out of my abs.

Behind me, the cedar gate opens. Instead of a family member walking through, it's Gabby Colucci, my old sister scout. Oddly all by herself.

"Don't you have initiates to do that for you?" she asks, nose turned up at my hunched-over posture. She glances back at the pergola, where there's a water pitcher I haven't yet taken inside. Mint leaves stick to the inside, no longer weighed down by ice cubes. Gabby loops her hands in the straps of her backpack. "I guess I missed the tea party. Your aunt told me you were back here."

"We were homespun today. You only missed hatchet practice, which I'm sure you don't need." I gesture at the general mess of the backyard, half lit by the fading sun, half lit by the unnatural yellow of the kitchen. "You guys caught the Scranch?"

"Oh yeah," she says with distracted disinterest. She reaches up and scratches at her ponytail with an embarrassed squint. "I was going to drop the evidence bag at the post office, but I thought your babybirds might want to see the Root. They haven't fought a Carnivore yet, have they?"

I shake my head. "Your neighborhood was all Critters, just like you said it would be."

"Did you guys hit The Wooz?" she asks.

I struggle to remember the boundary map she sent me. "We did a couple weeks ago, but not since we've been on patrol. It's in my mom's territory, isn't it?"

"Yeah, but adults never pay attention to kid places, so we usually end up sweeping those, too," she says with a sigh. "Anyway, do you wanna see the Root?"

She's already swinging her backpack around. It's a serious charcoal gray and made out of swishy industrial nylon.

"REI?" I ask her. "That's not the backpack I would expect from a girl who brought a Louis Vuitton suitcase to sleepovers."

Gabby looks at me from under brows I once helped pluck in two. "It's a camping bag. My family think I got all super-outdoorsy environmentalist when I got promoted to senior scout because we're always going on these long hunts. I get so many REI gift cards for Christmas now, it's ridiculous."

Out of the serious camping backpack, she pulls out an evidence bag and hands it to me.

It's been years since I saw a Root. The Handbook likens the grub's single organ to a two-legged carrot. This one is as big as one of my daggers, its bottom twisted twice—presumably the number of people it ate. I hold it up to the light to see the trapped iridescence inside the lavender plastic.

"That's how they make the teas, you know," Gabby tells me, pointing at the base of the Root, where the legs have wispy hairs coming out the bottom. "They regrow the Roots, then shave them down like truffles."

Curious, I bring the Root closer to my eye. The bottom reminds me of the whiskers that grow out of green-onion bulbs. "Do they grow in dirt?"

"No, they're more like air plants. They'll just keep growing until you mint them. There's a glass orb garden full of them on the Headquarters tour. I went for my sweet sixteen. My brother got a car."

"My sister took a birthday trip to Headquarters. Now they're paying for her to hunt in the desert and pretend to care about college."

I hand the bag back, noticing that the front has Faithlynn's name written on the *pursuant scout* line. A Root this size must be worth a bundle of points on the leaderboard.

"I heard Paz is so devoted, she only dates scouts now, too," Gabby says.

I hold my breath, waiting for her to tack on something shitty and homophobic—it's what Faithlynn always did. Paz has been out since before we were initiated, and Faithlynn never missed an opportunity to point out how weird it was that there was a gay Dame. I could never make her understand that when she said *weird* she really meant *not heteronormative.*

But Gabby just waits for me to say, "She says she doesn't have enough in common with 'civilian' girls," before she shrugs and says, "Maybe she's right."

I keep waiting for her to mention Faithlynn or Jennica—to factor them into her decision to be here or their opinion on being alone with me—but instead she surprises me by pointing at the ax boards still on the lawn and asking, "Do you wanna play?"

My stomach squirms. I look back at the French doors, wondering if my parents have noticed that there's someone here. Not that they'd care. It's a scout.

"Come on," Gabby says. She drops her backpack unceremoniously on the ground and grabs an ax from the bucket. "We won't keep score. Unless you want to?"

The ax droops in her hand. She must see the hesitation on my face. And I don't have a good reason to turn her away, other than paranoia that whatever I say to her, I'm also saying to the rest of the circle.

Of course, the senior scouts are the only people who already know my big secrets. Nothing I've done in the last three years is worse than inspiring Molly to get herself killed, then having a full-fledged nervous breakdown and dissolving all my friendships.

I pick up an ax. "I'm not as good as I used to be."

"Just rusty, I bet," Gabby says. She lines up her shot, extends her arm, and throws. It lands right of center. "See? I don't use a throwing weapon. Can't you throw your daggers?"

"They're kind of big for throwing," I say. Not that I like the idea of flicking my weapons around willy-nilly. What if they fell in a hole or off a bridge or something?

"Tell me all about your cute little civilian life. Like the white boy with his hands in your pockets at the car wash. Is he your boyfriend?"

"Oh, yeah, that's Kyle," I say, unsure of how much I like the idea of my civilian life being "cute" or "little." "He's going to be a senior next year—"

"An older man? Go, Miss Prue!" Gabby titters, and throws another ax. It lands at a sharp angle.

"I've barely had time to see him with scouting," I say, hurling my hatchet at the board. "His sister is in my circle, but he doesn't have the Sight, so it's . . . complicated. You know?"

"Um, yes, I know," Gabby says. She presses an offended hand to her clavicle as she goes to yank her axes out for the next round. "I'm from a non-legacy house, remember? No one in my family can See. It's like you're dating my idiot un-Sighted brother. Except less weird. Because Carlos is a super slacker who is never going to move out unless my dad makes him."

"My boyfriend is like the opposite of that," I say, thinking of Kyle picking up a job at the bowling alley to pay for his own car insurance. "He'd be in his own apartment already if he could be. He moved into the backyard so he wouldn't have to share a room with his sister. He and his stepdad turned their shed into a tiny house with no plumbing."

She gives me an approving, wide-eyed nod. "Wow, a senior with his own place! You really were living the dream before you got dragged back into all *this*, huh?" With an ax, she motions at the boards, the mats, and herself.

"I didn't know how good I had it," I admit.

"Well, I hope that your scouts pass their steel test soon," Gabby says, landing the first bull's-eye and turning back with a big smile. "Then they'll join us, and you can get back to real life."

I realize that in the last week, I've barely thought about giving the babybirds to the senior scouts. Between patrolling and yoga and feelings circles, they've felt more like *my* circle rather than initiates I'm tutoring for someone else.

But now I remember that the babybirds aren't mine, not really. Every patrol, every feelings circle, every cup of tea is bringing us closer to the day I have to give them up. And they won't be my sister scouts anymore. Just like Gabby and Jennica and Faithlynn aren't.

The Tea of Forgetting can take the monsters out of my world, but will it also take my friends? Will they start to look at me with the same disappointment my mom did for three years? Will they learn to call me quitter?

I heave the hatchet in my hand, and it lands with a crack next to Gabby's in the bull's-eye.

"Right," I say with a weak smile. "My cute little civilian life."

22

In order to complete her training,
every fledgling scout must display her ability
to think, fight, and comport herself as a
Ladybird under every extreme circumstance.

—THE LADYBIRD HANDBOOK

The Ladybird steel test is actually four different tests. Studying the Handbook, I'm furious to realize that there's no official rule that says that all of the tests need to be done at the same time. Back in the day, Dame Debby scheduled our steel test to be done in the middle of her annual Christmas party, so we were trying to hunt and banish the various grubs that had been set loose among her un-Sighted guests. Molly and I nearly knocked over a punch bowl full of eggnog trying to catch a Tizzy Louse, and Gabby lost points when she stabbed through a Nock Jaw and nicked the table.

With some help from the Dame forums on the Head-quarters website and a dozen unasked-for texts from my sister, I plan steel test activities to coincide with our usual schedule of meetings.

Day One: Unarmed Combat

From the moment we're done with our warm-up stretches and start a light jog around my neighborhood, the baby-birds are nearly as jumpy as they were during our threshold-crossing field trip. Even with their pockets stuffed with mint leaves and emergency Altoids, I can see their fingers scrabble for knitting needles that aren't there.

"Doesn't the Handbook say that a Ladybird is never supposed to be caught unarmed?" Sasha the Beast asks, out of breath. Running has never been her favorite, but she's taking running-with-zero-prospect-of-stabbing as a punishment.

"Yes, but you aren't defenseless. You have plenty of mint," I tell her. I hope I don't look as nervous as I feel. Paz was furious when I told her that I didn't have a clipboard to carry around the grading rubric papers with me, but I'm pretty sure I can remember to look out for the automatic fails: screaming, crying, and allowing anyone to be fed upon without acting.

Kelsey slurps her braces twice in nervous succession. "What happens if we don't find a grub today? Does our whole steel test get pushed back?"

"It's very unlikely that there isn't a single Critter-class grub loose in Poppy Hills right now. We just have to keep looking," I say.

"Why don't we set a trap?" Avi asks.

"Yes! I've got a belly full of screams just waiting to be monsters," Sasha says.

"It's not a trapping test," I say. "Sometimes, patrol is just a long walk. Or run, if you want to get it done faster."

Out of the corner of my eye, I can see movement on a nearby front porch. For a second, I think it's a small white dog. Until my stomach drops to my feet and my hands shake. I press my lips together, watching the babybirds for signs of recognition. The Beast frowns and wipes her forehead. Kelsey tightens her ponytail. Avi starts running faster.

A Frightworm explodes out of the bushes up ahead at the same time a car turns down the street.

"We've got eyes," Sasha warns her sister scouts.

Without missing a beat, Avi drops down to one knee on the sidewalk, pretending to tie her shoe. As the Frightworm gallops toward her on its many green legs, she fumbles with the stretchy spandex pocket built into the side of her running shorts. Kelsey and Sasha come to a stop, behind her on either side, mint leaves peeking out between their fingers as reinforcement.

The Frightworm leaps into the air, ready to throw its full weight onto Avi when she surges upward, a leaf burning to ash in her hand as it pops the Frightworm out of existence.

The car passes us. The driver doesn't even turn their head.

"These are really good," Kyle says, biting a tea sandwich in half. His curls poke out from beneath an unseasonable black beanie. "It's really just cucumber and butter?"

"That's the whole recipe. It's in the first chapter of the Handbook," I say. I pass the last cup of tea to my right so that it lands in front of Jaxon, who is reaching for another lemon cupcake. He eats all of the frosting off the top in one messy yellow bite.

"Hey," Chancho chides his brother. "Pass me one, dude. Before your hands get any stickier."

It's eighty-five degrees under the pergola, which makes the idea of diving into the steaming cuppa in front of me less than appetizing. Because this isn't a real meeting—only a decoy for the scouts' second test—I could have served anything. Iced tea or root beer floats or Mexican Cokes with peanuts in the neck.

But the boys seemed genuinely excited at the prospect of our "thanks for helping" luncheon being a regular tea meeting. After they spent days blowing up our group chat asking what hats they should wear, I didn't have the heart to not boil water for them.

The babybirds don't complain, but I catch Sasha sneaking some of the ice cubes out of her water glass into her tea. She's using her teaspoon and not her gloved fingers, so at least I don't have to deduct points from her score.

I could. But I won't.

When Kyle turns to pass the sugar bowl down to Paul, I lean forward in my seat and remove the cloche set between the cucumber sandwiches and the fruit salad. Underneath, on a pink plastic cake stand, there's a Nock Jaw. As I slowly lower the cloche again, before Kyle notices what to him would be an empty stand, the Nock Jaw slithers down and hops onto the sandwich plate, knocking crustless white bread to the ground.

Unlike on initiation day, nobody screams. Which is good, because it would be an automatic disqualification. Sasha puts an elbow on the table to bar the grub from getting past her to Paul, who has started talking twice as loud trying to act like he can't See the monster on the table. Avi asks Chancho to pass her the fruit salad spoon, using his reach to bar the grub in the other direction. Kelsey's eyes dart back and forth for a moment. I can see her deliberate options—needles would be too obvious, the closest mint plant is farther than a stretch from her chair, if she doesn't move quick, she'll lose the chance—before her hand closes on the Nock Jaw's head, holding its mouth closed as, with one quick tug, she dunks it into her teacup.

It poofs away, leaving a slimy sheen on the top of her cup.

Day Three: Speed and Agility

The obstacle course is back and eye-wateringly pink as ever. Tía Lo and Mom stand shoulder to shoulder, mirror images of folded-arm rigidity. Next to them is the largest plastic grub cage we own.

Mom gestures to the cage. "Prudence, would you like the honors?"

I don't know how honored I am to press my face into the scream chamber, but I do it anyway. Repeating *No white eyes, no white eyes* in my head, I fill my lungs and let out a muffled shriek into the plastic cube. The cage rocks side to side as an explosion of Tizzy Lice burst into being.

"I'm sure I should be surprised," Mom says. She taps her foot, waiting for the grubs inside the cage to start eating one another into something big enough to fight. Rocking the cage to agitate them, she manages to get two swollen-pumpkin-sized Tizzy Lice.

First up, the Beast psychs herself up, bouncing on her feet and cracking her neck and her knuckles in a series of clicks and pops. After a moment of consideration, she removes her sunglasses and hands them to Chancho at the double Dutch rope. I'm pretty sure they touch his heart before they make it to the pocket of his shorts.

When Mom releases the grubs from the cage, the timer starts and Sasha jumps into the double Dutch ropes. The Tizzy Lice seem overwhelmed by the amount of anxiety in the air and bobble toward me, Avi, and Kelsey—until Sasha has to jump out of the double Dutch and gets nervous enough to be interesting again.

Leaping from the balance beam to the quintuple walls,

Sasha the Beast glances over her shoulder and finds the Tizzy Lice hot on her heels. They swell in size, and she slips down the last wall, her heel catching the grass. A lost point.

"You got this, Beast!" I cheer. "Keep those heels up!"

"Don't get tricked by their yucky pheromone!" Avi calls out.

Sasha leaps into the stutter-step tires. The Tizzy Lice crawl clumsily behind her. Approaching the climbing wall, the Beast notices the grubs slowing behind her. One falls into the center of the last tire.

Kelsey claps. "You got this! You're scarier than them!"

"Watch your time!" Mom cautions.

Sasha turns and pops the first Tizzy Louse between the eyes. In order to grab the rope on the climbing wall, she has to drop one of her knitting needles.

"That's okay!" I call out. "Finish strong!"

Aware of the timer counting down, the Beast throws herself over the climbing wall and gallops over the low hurdles, face reddening with visible effort. The remaining Tizzy Louse slips on the grass behind her. With the last obstacle coming up, Sasha reaches behind her, scoops the Tizzy Louse like she's palming a basketball and chucks it, full force, at the nearest peppermint planter. Mint explodes into a puff of ash as the grub disappears. Chancho drops the double Dutch ropes to applaud.

Mom and Tía Lo confer silently, then give an approving double nod.

"Unconventional, but effective," Mom says.

"Excellent aim," Tía Lo says.

The Beast punches the sky in victory.

Day Four: Teamwork

At my mother's insistence, I've invited Dame Debby and her scouts to watch the final round of the steel test. I was hoping they'd say no—they should be doing their regular sweep of Solano Park today—but instead they agreed to have Mom and Tia Lo patrol the park for them.

They arrive in tea-party full dress, skirts crisp and gloves clean. The ringing of charm bracelets falls silent as they take their seats beneath the pergola, turning their chairs to face away from the table so they can watch the lawn. Eyes glassy, fingers drumming, they all look bored, even as the large Frightworm comes roaring out of the trap.

In the grass, the babybirds fan out, making sure to keep the grub from heading over the fence or toward our guests. Kelsey pockets her knitting needles and slides the practice rope down from her shoulder. She must be scared about getting the knot right because the Frightworm hisses at her, rearing back. She throws the lariat over its head and tugs hard, shearing off a dozen of its spindly legs. The Frightworm screeches and writhes, its mandibles chittering in pain.

The sound is horrible, but Dame Debby seems more interested in the construction of the chocolate-dipped birdbark squares on the table. She bites off a corner, smiles, then passes the square to Faithlynn, who tries to turn it down and keep her eyes on the test. Dame Debby reaches across her daughter, holding the bark square out to Jennica.

Sasha mounts the back of the Frightworm, using her body weight to ride it to the ground, following the Handbook regulation to keep the grub off its powerful back end during combat. Needles drawn, Avi scurries around to the front of the grub, going for the kill shot. She stumbles over the wriggling green legs, falling forward and accidentally puncturing the Frightworm in the side.

It bursts into banishment before anyone can tag it between the eyes. All three babybirds collapse into the newly empty grass.

My stomach sinks. This was not exactly the impressive display I'd hoped to present to the senior scouts. They're already exchanging knowing looks.

But who cares if the babybirds aren't perfect? If Dame Debby won't take them because they aren't absolutely flawless, then we'll just train harder and show the senior scouts exactly what we're capable of.

Dame Debby stands up, dusting birdbark crumbs off her skirt.

"Good job, scouts," she announces. "Your first meeting will be scheduled after your weapons arrive. We'll be in touch through the app."

She takes one more chocolate-covered birdbark square

and leaves through the front gate. The senior scouts file out behind her without a word.

I know I should be happy that Dame Debby isn't demanding the same level of perfection that she used to. No one got screamed at or had their knuckles rapped. But it still feels wrong. The test was supposed to end with the grub being tagged between the eyes, so how did we scrape by with an accidental banishing?

Pushing aside my hesitation, I turn back to the baby-birds and clap. "You did it! You passed!"

It's not every day that you have to sign for a giant FedEx box of weapons.

Despite the box having the Ladybird crest on the side, Mom insists that cardboard is tacky and makes me transfer the new steel to a pink steamer trunk from her office that's normally filled with old National Conference posters. Chancho has to help me carry it out to the pergola.

For our last meeting, instead of a tea party or home-spun celery sticks, the table is set with sparkling waters and a plate of cookie-brownies I made myself. At everyone's usual place setting, there are the last charms they need to fill their bracelets. My wrist is slightly heavier with a Knitting charm I possibly fudged—my hat ended up fitting Jaxon, he just didn't like it—and a Baking charm rolling pin that matches Kelsey's.

"Happy last day of training!" I say in my best Avi impression when the scouts arrive.

Everyone is in their normal clothes, and I'm surprised to remember that before this summer the Beast was only ever in ripped jeans. Avi's faded old Ladybird shirt must be a hand-me-down from Paz—it's from a Conference from when Avi was still in diapers. Kelsey's tawny hair is flat-ironed sleekly over one of her eyes.

It's weird how much they've changed in just a few weeks. At the start of summer, the three of them could barely speak to one another. Now they throw the good pliers back and forth across the table as they fasten the charms to their bracelets and talk about ways to get a Dreary Blight infestation off the roof of the gazebo downtown. I'm surprised by how sad I am imagining them and the senior scouts going on a mission to basket-toss Avi up into the Dreary Blighted ceiling. Will the senior scouts toss Gabby up to see who could do it better? Will they even bother throwing Gabby anymore when there's someone smaller and lighter on the team?

What kind of team will they be, my old sisters and my new ones—without me?

My nose burns. The last thing I want to do is cover the pergola in Dreary Blight. I knew this day was coming. I ran toward it all summer. I can't be surprised that it's here.

One last ceremony and I'll be free, just like I wanted.

I push my chair back from the table. "You've all worked

so hard this summer," I say, looking out at my scouts. My friends. "I've never seen anyone work through the Handbook this fast. Not the circle you're joining, not the scouts my sister trained. Nobody. I'm so proud of you. I hope you're proud of yourselves, too."

The pink trunk opens on silent hinges. From the top of the pile, I pick up the teal plastic handle of the only ax in the bunch and its matching backpack scabbard.

"Avianna Marquez." I hold the ax out to my cousin. "You have earned your steel."

She takes the ax in both hands. "Thank you, Dame Prue!"

Next in the trunk is Sasha's matte-black halberd with hip holster.

"Sasha Nezhad, you have earned your steel."

Sasha eagerly gets to her feet, rushing around the table to take her weapon by the staff. Swishing it toward the lawn, she presses the release button and the halberd extends to its full length and clicks into place.

"Kelsey Goodwin." I pass her a lavender lariat and matching single dagger. "You have earned your steel."

Kelsey and Avi join Sasha in the grass. The three of them take turns swishing and posing with their weapons, taking pictures, looking at them, then deleting them since the Handbook forbids it. Too risky.

"We came to drink tea and banish grubs," Avi says, posing with her ax unsheathed and the Beast's sunglasses on.

Kelsey snaps her lariat and slurps her braces. "And sometimes turn those grubs into tea."

"You only drink the grub tea once," I tell her, taking the picture, then handing Avi her phone back. "It's important to me that you know that. Don't repeatedly ingest grubs."

Kelsey turns to me, lower lip jutting out. "Aww, Prudence, this means you aren't our Dame anymore!"

"Nope. My time in the sisterhood is over," I say, opening my empty hands. "Again."

Another pang of sadness hits me. Being connected to the whole sisterhood I can definitely do without. I don't need the Bretts in my house or the senior scouts watching me with their triple Scranch mouths. But I have to admit that I will miss the babybirds. I'll miss baking together and teasing one another and pushing one another to be better without it being a competition as to who's the best. I hope I've trained them to be a better kind of Ladybird—a nicer, more well-rounded scout who can be a nontoxic sister to her circle. Scouts strong enough to stand up to the corrupting influence of Faithlynn Brett and the leaderboard.

A tear splashes down my nose. "I'm gonna miss seeing you guys every day," I admit. "I had a lot of fun with you."

"Oh, it's okay, prima!" Avi says. Dropping her ax in the grass, she wraps arms around my shoulders in a boa-constrictor hug. "You can still see me whenever you want! I'm just one fence away!"

"And I'm one fence and one text and one ride away!"

Kelsey hugs me from the other side, ducking down to put her head on my shoulder.

"I don't hug, but, yeah, BFFs or whatever," the Beast says. She looks at me over the rim of her sunglasses. "You're one of us, Prudence Perry. For life."

23

Beyond her time as a school-age scout,
the legacy Ladybird can continue to be
a champion of her community by taking
up a boundary patrol, training new scouts,
or deescalating grubs in the workplace.

—THE LADYBIRD HANDBOOK

On my first scoutless day of summer vacation, all I do is sleep and watch TV. I text my thoughts on the later seasons of *Great British Bake Off* to Kelsey, who has lots of opinions whenever the British contestants are tasked with making American-style desserts. She also informs me that for the babybirds' first meeting today, Dame Debby has tasked them with teaching the senior scouts how to make the chocolate-dipped birdbark squares.

That's my scout legacy, I guess. Abuela Ramona once saved an entire nursing home from Carnivorous Dreary Blight that had taken over the cafeteria. And I added Magic Shell to birdbark.

Still. It's an upgrade from being an anxious quitter.

I'm tempted to text Sasha and Avi for more details of their first meeting at Dame Debby's house. I want to know if Debby still has all-white furniture and if they have to do pushups when they speak out of turn and whether or not any of the older girls mentioned that the babybirds passed their last test on a technicality.

But I don't. It's not my business anymore. I did what I was asked to do: I tutored new recruits, and I handed them off to a more seasoned circle.

It's time to start de-scouting my life.

The hats and tea dresses go back to my sister's room. My daggers and charm bracelet go back into the pink backpack of secrets at the rear of my closet. The Handbook is shoved onto a bookshelf between *The Anxiety and Phobia Workbook for Teens* and a cryptid atlas I borrowed from Kyle and never read. The planner goes in the trash, full of unused meeting minute sheets. I finally take the silver crest pin off my hoodie. It leaves a hole in the cotton, above the Sasquatch patch. I toss it into my jewelry box, along with all of the earrings with lost mates and monogrammed necklaces that have never been my style.

Lastly, I check my account with Ladybird Headquarters. My digital charm bracelet is fuller than it was before, and my status has updated from *Tutor* to *Dame*.

My heart rate triples. Hands shaking, I open the merch store. Scrolling past commemorative pins and scarves, obstacle course pieces, tea sets in wicker baskets, and grub cages in every imaginable size, I find it.

The Tea of Forgetting. One dose.

It's free other than the five-dollar shipping charge. I guess Faith was right. Headquarters doesn't actually want people to walk around with all of their secrets.

I think of Paul, telling me that Forgetting won't take the monsters out of the world. I think of family—Mom and Paz, Tía Lo and Avi—all of them bonded closer together because of the sisterhood. When I deactivate my account with Headquarters, I'll go back to being an outsider.

How much worse could it be to be Sightless? Jaxon manages just fine. Sure, he's in the second grade, but he's probably read more books this summer than I did all of last year.

Before I press the order button, a video chat request from Kyle comes up.

I bounce on the edge of my bed, eager to give him the full heat of my attention again. Undivided and undistracted for the first time since the last day of school.

"Hey, babe!" I answer, checking my hair in the camera for a second before noticing the white screen behind Kyle's shoulder. "I thought you were working tonight?"

He pulls his phone back so I can see the full scope of the shedroom behind him. "No, they had us double-booked for Glo-Bowl tonight, and it turns out it really doesn't take two of us to rent shoes."

"Even on a Friday night, huh?" I ask. Bowling isn't for me, but surely it's for somebody. Why else would almost every town have their own place to do it?

"There was a birthday party and some old guys," he says with a sad shake of his curls. "They were losing money paying me to sit on the counter and pretend not to see Josh watching TV on his phone. So, I got to come home early! What are you up to?"

"It's a very cool night in the Perry household," I say, aiming my camera at my overflowing closet. "I've been cleaning my room for fun. Putting away all my Ladybird stuff now that I'm re-retired."

"It's weird seeing Sasha and Avi with Kelsey without you," Kyle says, frowning. "Earlier, I walked into my kitchen and the Beast was there. Making smoothies."

"What evil have I unleashed upon you?" I ask, saying it dramatically even though I do genuinely wonder.

Kyle laughs, his smiling lips forming a perfect heart shape. The way his blue eyes sparkle, just for me, I'm overwhelmed with remembrances. Kissing him, rubbing my nose against the roundest parts of his cheeks, inhaling the smell of his skin.

"What if . . . ?" I say before I can second-guess it. "What if I came over tonight? Just me."

"Yeah?" His eyebrows go up.

The sun is already setting. I've never offered to go out after dark before. Not by myself. Normally, I'd be scared of getting caught. The official rule is home by ten—unless I'm hunting.

This is the last time I can use the hunting excuse. Once I order the Tea of Forgetting, I'll have to deactivate with Headquarters. Early curfew forever. Avi will be up later than me, even as I finish high school.

I should take this taste of freedom while I've still got it.

"Yeah," I say, feeling more confident the more I think about it. Did I really spend all summer fighting monsters just to go back to being scared of the dark? I should have a little bit of summer vacation before school starts again. Something more than trips to Sonic and Pinkies Only with the crew. "It's only a few blocks. If I cut through Gold-fields, I can be there in, like, fifteen minutes. I ran farther than that every day with the scouts."

"For sure! I don't doubt that you can get here and I'd love to see you." He sounds like he's going to throw a *but* onto the end of that sentence—like *but you've always been too anxious to try this before*. Instead, he asks, "You don't want me to drive you? I could come pick you up on the corner."

"That's more likely to blow my cover," I assure him. Mom recognizes Kyle's truck on sight. It'd be way too easy for her to peek out her bedroom window and notice the suspension she thinks is too low. "I'll be right there. Don't go anywhere."

His smile is blinding. "Pretty sure if I move, I'll wake up from this dream, but okay."

I check my bra for cuteness, my armpits for deodorant —fail both tests and hurry to recover—before pulling on shoes and socks and walking through a heavy spritz of ocean-scented body spray.

For good measure, I send my parents a white lie.

ME: Don't worry if you hear the gate! Babybirds asked me to come see a trap they set. BRB

As long as I have knitting needles in my bag, I have plausible deniability. The tracker app on my phone will even show me going to a scout's house. If I have time, I could even pop in to see Kelsey and ask more about her first meeting at Dame Debby's. Win-win-win.

Confident, I leave through the back door. The night is cool enough that I actually need my hoodie, which feels like a good omen. I zip up to the neck and jog along the street, running toward the last of the late sunset.

It's odd to run alone after a summer of patrols. There's no one to keep pace with, no sound in my ears except for my own short breaths. Under my arm, my tote bag flaps against my body, knitting needles and water bottle and phone rattling together as I cut across the Goldfields soccer field.

Running toward the hills means losing more and more sun the closer I get to Kyle's house. Here, the streets are lit by open garages and TVs in the window. The Handbook points out that it's needlessly dangerous to walk alone in the dark, so I veer toward the cemetery, where the streetlamps are bright.

A dog starts barking as I cross the street. The break in silence makes me lose my footing and stagger from a sprint to an awkward skip

"Sorry." The dog's owner holds up an apologetic hand, the other wrapped tight around the leash of a very unhappy Jack Russell terrier. "Guess he wants to go home."

I force an awkward laugh as my stomach knots. Drying my forehead with the back of my sleeve, I decide to continue onward at a walk. Spiking my adrenaline and getting anxious-sweaty is only going to ruin my sneaking-out date. Ladybirds run their patrols for efficiency. I no longer owe anyone that efficiency.

Under the lamplight at the cemetery gate, I stop and drink from my water bottle. Inside the darkness of the cemetery, I can hear the *click-click-click* of sprinklers and remember watching Sasha, Avi, and Kelsey take down a grub in the open here. My eye wanders to the ground, to the row of Pippy-Mint I know we planted two weeks ago.

It's all gone. Torn out by the root. Only mounds of dark brown fertilizer are left behind.

Who would tear out brand-new plants?

I can feel my anxiety flaring. The tremble in my hands. Thickness in my throat. Mounting paranoia that someone purposefully damaged my mint plants.

Did I even care about these plants yesterday?

Finding it hard to swallow, I put my water bottle back into my tote and fish around my memory for the next closest mint garden. The Ladybird app would tell me, if I looked it up. But would it also tell me that this safeguard was still here when it wasn't?

I'll feel better when I've made it to Kyle's house. Just two blocks up and three blocks over. Easy.

A breeze ruffles my hair. The cold sends prickles down my scalp, traveling the full length of my nervous system, demanding the most primal part of me to start running.

Instead, I look up.

Into the white-hot eyes of a Carnivore I've never seen before. Livid red skin and a beaked mouth, rising up from behind the cemetery wall on legs made of Dreary Blight.

Its beak lunges for me.

And I run.

24

A circle is only as strong
as its weakest communicator.

—THE LADYBIRD HANDBOOK

Flying on adrenaline, I run like I've only run once before in my life. Blowing through stop signs. Dodging in front of cars. All of the noise around me drowned out by screaming that I pray is only inside my head.

When I worry that I can't make it, that I'll die from the panic, I see the porch light on at Kyle's house. The side gate is rough on my palms. The grass crunches underfoot.

I fall through the door of the shedroom, gasping for air as my lungs burn and my legs give out. The cement floor is freezing cold against my hot skin. I wrap my arms around my knees, curling myself into the fetal position.

An unclassified Carnivore.

If I'd stayed a minute longer, I'd be dead.

It's not one of the core five. I'd recognize it if it were. They wouldn't let me train scouts all summer if I couldn't identify basic grub types.

White-Eyes in the middle of town.

Kyle calls my name. Appears above me. I can't open my eyes enough to see his face, but I can feel his fear when he repeats my name.

If I hadn't been able to See the grub, I'd be dead. I would have just stood there and let it crack my skull open with its beak.

"Babe, I need you to tell me what happened," he says, suddenly down on the floor with me. Not touching me, but not leaving me alone. "What happened? Are you hurt?"

Wetness slides around my cheeks. I have to touch it and look at it to know that it isn't blood. The grub didn't touch me. I got away. I'm not hurt.

I shake my head, open my mouth, and wheeze. I can't take in enough air to make words.

"Prudence," Kyle says, his trembling voice doing its best impression of soothing. "Focus just on breathing. Air in, air out. You gotta start with one deep breath, okay?"

I open my mouth again and suck in a breath. My stomach constricts, as though it could puke up oxygen.

"In and out," he says, encouragingly. "In and—do you want me to get you the vape? Sometimes your anxiety needs to reset and—"

I swing my head. I don't have the privilege of getting high right now. I can't turn off this feeling. I have to do something. "No, I have to tell someone—"

"Tell *me*, Prudence," he begs.

But I can't. I need someone who understands. Someone who can See. I need an adult.

No, I need a scout.

"I have to talk to my sister," I splutter. I can taste mucus in my mouth, I throw my hands in front of my face, humiliation starting to creep in along with the panic. "I'm so sorry. I'll go outside, I don't want to kick you out of your own room."

"It's okay," Kyle says. He gets to his feet. "I'll go inside and get you some water. I'll be back in a minute."

My hands are shaking hard enough that it takes two tries for me to call Paz. Leaning against the wall of storage tubs, I press the phone to my face.

Paz answers on the first ring, sounding worried. I never call her.

"There's some kind of Carnivore in the Hillside Cemetery," I whisper-scream, cupping the phone to my face. "I snuck out to see Kyle, and I only have knitting needles with me."

"So, sneak back home and get your steel," she says. "You're a Dame, Prudence. You can take down a Carnivore. I know the last time you tried was traumatic, but you've successfully taken down White-Eyes before. You have a Root Shot charm—"

"No, no! You're not listening! This wasn't, like, a big Scranch. I don't know what it was! I've Seen grubs my entire life, and there are five kinds, that's it! This had a

347

beak—like a Tizzy Louse—but it wasn't orange or furry. It was on huge legs that looked like Blight, but that never grows a face—"

"You think it's a hybrid?" Paz asks. "Are you sure?"

"No, I'm *not* fucking sure!" I fold in half again, blowing out another breath of pure panic. "If I were sure, then I wouldn't be calling you in the middle of a panic attack. I would call Dad so he could tell me everything is cool and safe. I've read the Handbook cover to cover this summer and there is *nothing* in it about hybrid grubs."

My sister sighs. "Don't swear at me, Prue. It's not very Ladybirdy. Hybrids aren't in the Handbook yet because the information isn't ready. All of the research I've been doing is for the eleventh edition. Right now we're calling them Cannibal class because they're the product of Carnivores eating other Carnivores. They used to be super rare, too rare to study. Because Carnivores are attracted to apex emotional flareups, and how often would two different seismic shifts happen so close together? That would be like having more than one national tragedy happen in a week. An earthquake at the same time as a wildfire. A mass shooting the same day as a riot."

My heart sinks as I realize that she's describing exactly the kind of world we live currently live in. "Oh. So now it happens all the time?"

"I mean, not every day, but it's definitely not rare anymore. That's why we have to be so diligent about daily patrols. Critter sweeps are important, sure, but we really have to make sure that Carnivores don't roam around far enough to run into other Carnivores. The extra grubic energy makes them mutate, take on aspects of one another."

"Whoever wins, we lose." I bite the inside of my cheek and shake my head. "But there hasn't been a major traumatic event going on in Poppy Hills, Paz! The only Carnivore that's been reported this summer was taken out by Faithlynn Brett a week ago. I saw its Root in an evidence bag!"

"I don't know what to tell you. You said yourself that Dreary Blight never grows a face. But the cemetery would be a super-weird place for a Cannibal class to show up. They're normally in rural places, neglected boundaries. Not in the middle of town, where scouts would pass it every day."

I bounce my head against the lid of a storage tub, rattling the Christmas ornaments inside. "I have to do something."

"You could call Mom. She'll go easier on you if you leave out the part where you were sneaking out to see your boyfriend."

The idea of having to talk to Mom while my anxiety is peaking makes me queasy. Worst-case scenario, she'd tell me to go kill the grub myself to prove that I was worthy of my new Dame status. "I'm not calling Mom. She'll just tell me that panicking is risking pulling more grubs through."

"Well, if you can get a Cannibal Root out intact, it would really help my research. And it's worth, like, a million points on the leaderboard."

My hands curl into fists, and my eyes squeeze shut. "Please don't talk to me about the leaderboard right now. I already feel like I'm going to puke."

"Then report it to the app and let boundary patrol take care of it. Flag it as an emergency. Headquarters will make the call."

This idea actually calms me down. This is what Headquarters is for. They can send out the emergency alert that wakes up Mom or Tía Lo, not me.

After thanking Paz and hanging up, I sit down on the edge of the futon and open the Ladybird app. The town map is pinned with active and deactivated entry points and peppermint gardens. Zooming in, I see that there is a mint-leaf icon over the cemetery, indicating that there's a garden there that isn't.

Clicking on the cemetery, I fill out the pop-up Emergency Sighting report.

Number of Mulligrubs Being Reported

■ 1 _____

Mulligrub Type (choose one):

☐ Nock Jaw

☐ Dreary Blight

☐ Scranch

- ☐ Frightworm
- ☐ Tizzy Louse
- ☑ Unknown/Unclear

Known Carnivore?
- ☐ No
- ☑ Yes

Reason for Reporting Scout Declining to Take Action:
- ☑ not armed for advanced combat

Additional Notes:

POSSIBLE HYBRID GRUB

When I hit *submit*, a dialog box pops up, thanking me for my service to the sisterhood. It feels sarcastic.

I lay my head back against the futon's metal frame, breathing in slowly, holding it, and exhaling. My heart still feels like it's beating too fast, but it's no longer pounding painfully against my ribs like it wants out.

Hearing footsteps in the grass, I hurry to wipe my face, already feeling ridiculous for how hard I panicked. Minus ten covert ops points for sure. Totally failing at my namesake.

Kyle comes in, hugging two clear plastics cups of ice water to his chest. He looks over his shoulder at the main house, shaking his head. "What is going on tonight? Everyone is running around screaming, but nobody will tell me anything! Did the Purge start?"

Sniffling, I sit up on my heels so I can see him better over the back of the futon. "What do you mean everyone is running and screaming? I—I just got scared on the way over and—"

"And then all the Ladybirds left!" he says. Collapsing on the futon next to me, he holds out my cup of water. "My mom's pissed. Kelsey told her they had 'scout business,' and they all went running. I had to get out of there before she asked why I was getting two cups."

I freeze. "What Ladybirds?"

Kyle gets tired of holding the cup out to me and sets it on the floor. A wrinkle of concern creases his forehead. "I told you. The Beast was here making smoothies. She and Chancho's sister have been here since, like, four for a sleepover—"

"No. No!" I say, reaching for his shoulders and holding on to them tight. "When did they leave? Five minutes ago? Ten?"

"Literally one second ago," he says, examining my face with worry. "I assumed they were coming back here to see you, actually, but they went out the front door—"

A wave of dizziness hits me, making my vision spotty as a Tizzy Louse pops up at my feet. Headquarters wouldn't put out an emergency bulletin to three brand-new scouts, would they? Did it go out to all of the town scouts? The cemetery borders the south and western boundary, much closer to my family's patrol route than Gabby's.

But in an emergency, there are no boundaries. Just the sisterhood. And whoever can get to the grub first.

I let go of Kyle's shoulders and push myself to my feet, lurching toward the door.

"I have to go after them," I declare, sounding ridiculous even to my own ears. Just me and my knitting needles and that towering skinless monster. I pull my bag up my arm. The Tizzy Louse at my ankles knocks over the full cup of ice water on the floor. "I'm sorry. I know I just got here, but I can't let them—"

Kyle leaps over the futon arm, chasing after me in two strides. "You're leaving? Prudence, what the hell is going on? Are they in trouble? Are you? Can you please just tell me what's going on? I've barely seen you all summer, then you come in here freaking out, and now you want to chase after my sister in the middle of the night?"

"I know. I'm the worst." Fresh tears well up in my eyes as I reach for the doorknob. "I'm sorry, I really am, but I can't make you understand!"

"You could try!" He fists his hands in his curls. "Don't run out of here. Please, let me try to help you. I—I just, God, I love you, and I wish that—for once—you would let me help you!"

My fingertips fall away from the doorknob, my heart beating so hard that I couldn't leave if I tried. I look back at him. "You've never said you love me before."

He grunts, nervously rubbing his neck. "I've been trying

to find a way, but for weeks you've been acting like you don't need me anymore. I thought tonight was going to be different, but once again, you'd rather go after your friends—including my little sister—than be alone with me for five minutes. I don't know if it's this new fitness thing you're on and all of a sudden your fat boyfriend can't keep up—"

"That's not what this is!" I scoop his hands between us. His fingers twine through mine, holding tight. "Kyle Goodwin, of course I love you. Everything about you. But that doesn't mean I can make you . . . See."

Out of the corner of my eye, I watch the Tizzy Louse toddle out from under the futon's metal legs.

Unless I can.

I press my forehead to his, staring deeply into his eye. "How much do you trust me?"

He frowns. "How much do I need to trust you?"

The pads of my thumbs trace the lines of his cheeks. "More than you've ever trusted anyone."

"Is this about when I went out with that girl Sophie? Because that was so long ago, we didn't even—"

"Nope, not that," I interrupt, wincing as two more Tizzy Lice pop up at my ankles. I reach down to grab the nearest one. Its body squirms, fuzzy and light, in my palms.

"I am going to pass you something," I warn him, struggling to keep my voice steady. I can't start crying now. One false move and the Cassandra paradox will kick in—Kyle will think that I'm delusional and never trust me again. I'll lose the love that I just found. "Something invisible. And I am going to ask you to eat it."

"What?"

"Just one bite," I promise. Squid-black eyes stare up at me moments before the Tizzy Louse's beak bites into the flesh under my thumb. I yelp, and Kyle looks extra terrified. Because, to him, his girlfriend just mimed being scared of solid air. "And then you'll understand everything. Okay?"

I start to hold out the grub writhing in my hand, but Kyle takes a step away from me.

"No, Prudence. It's not okay. What the fuck are you talking about? You want me to pretend to eat an invisible—"

"Not pretend," I say firmly, closing the distance between us again. "It's invisible the way that infrared or ultraviolet is invisible. Your body just hasn't learned how to See it yet. Which is why when I put it in your hands, you are going to take an actual bite of it. Or I am going to leave and go save my scouts without you. Understood?"

I've never spoken to him like this before. Could he learn to love someone who talks like a scout?

He extends his hands. The Tizzy Louse does not like being hot-potatoed. It wriggles and shudders as I set it firmly into my boyfriend's cupped palms.

Kyle's head snaps up, suddenly alert. He can feel the thing he can't See. The bristling fur. The nubby feet. The hummingbird heartbeat. The amplification of my fear and his.

"Babe," he breathes.

"You have to take a bite," I plead.

I know that this is how it used to be. I know that scouts used to have to dose their loved ones with alien meat in order for them to truly See and be Seen. I know that Headquarters would just slice off a piece of Root and have me brew it in a pot for him.

I never wanted this for Kyle. For me.

If this fails, it fails the most. He could get sick. Or die. Or burn me at the stake.

Drawing the Tizzy Louse to his mouth, he fumbles a bite, aiming at empty air. It's all I can do not to slap the grub out of his hands. To leave him here, un-Sighted and safe.

He takes a generous bite, and his face seizes up. I set my hands on both his shoulders, grounding him.

"You're almost there," I say. "Hopefully one bite will do it."

"Hopefully?!" he chokes through a fuzzy mouthful.

I shrug helplessly. "This isn't really how we do things anymore, but desperate times . . ."

He gulps down the bite and sticks his tongue out. Green blood stains his teeth.

"I don't know how long it takes this way, but—"

He gasps and drops the Tizzy Louse on the ground.

"What the fuck? What the fuck did I just eat, Prudence?"

One of the two-by-fours that frame the wall cracks as a Frightworm blinks into existence beside me.

Kyle gasps, pulling his curls far away from his face. "That's a Mongolian death worm!"

"No, it isn't," I say sharply. "It's a Frightworm. And it's here to eat the fear in the room. Your fear actually."

I dig through my bag and grab my knitting needles. I stab through the Frightworm and the remaining Tizzy Lice in three pops.

"Now please get your truck keys because your sister and the scouts just left to go up against a monster three hundred times that size."

†††

ME: Did your mom get an emergency Ladybird call?

CHANCHO: I don't think so. It's close to Ambien o'clock.

ME: I need you to get her house swords and bring it to the Goldfields sign.
The babybirds went after a hybrid Carnivore and I don't have my steel.

CHANCHO: You want me to steal my mom's weapons?

ME: Would you rather try breaking into my room for my daggers?

†††

Kyle doesn't stop talking the entire drive. "So, what *are* mulligrubs? Bugs? Sea monsters that evolved to breathe air? Aliens? Prudence, please don't tell me you kill aliens."

"They're not aliens," I say, sending a third *do not go to the cemetery* text to all three of the babybirds. "They're interdimensional aberrations, but we call them mulligrubs because it was code in colonial women's magazines that stuck. The Handbook didn't get updated for the first hundred years. Then there was a scouting boom and cheap printing, and now they change the rules every couple of years to stay competitive."

"So, for two hundred years you've been killing these invisible aberrations?"

"Not me personally," I say, dividing my attention between him and my phone. The Ladybird app still has the cemetery listed as an active point. I have to stop picturing the babybirds running there faster than the truck can drive. "My family's legacy only goes back two generations, and I was retired until this summer. But the sisterhood, yeah."

"The sisterhood?" he repeats, cutting his eyes at me. "Is it a cult? Did you induct my sister into a cult?"

"It's more of a secret society. Or a clique with a merch store." I point out the window. "There's Chancho!"

Next to the metal Goldfields marquee, Chancho has a bulging backpack slung over one shoulder. I barely wait for the truck to slow down before I'm unbuckled and out the door.

"Thanks, primo, I owe you."

I reach for the backpack, but he holds it out of my reach.

"I'm coming, too," Chancho says. He lifts up his hands. I'm horrified to see that he's wearing his mom's Leisure-line punch-activated gloves.

"No way," I say. "If you want to play Ladybird, you are not doing it going up against something that isn't even in the Handbook! You'll get yourself killed."

"I've been to more trainings than your boyf has!" Chancho says. He swings one pink puffy hand at Kyle climbing out of the driver's side. "How is Kyle supposed to fight something he can't See?"

"Oh, I am Seeing shit, dude," Kyle says. "But I'm not convinced that any of it needs fighting."

"What?" Chancho and I ask in unison.

"Just because something invades your space doesn't mean it needs killing," Kyle says. "What research has been done into coexistence? What if the extra emotional energy we're carrying around is *supposed* to be eaten?"

Chancho looks at me, bug-eyed.

There's no time for this. "Just give me the swords and stay behind me."

25

Ladybirds are the leaders of their community,
acting where others fail to do so.

THE LADYBIRD HANDBOOK

Carrying Tía Lo's vintage house swords—one pink, one green—my thumbs on the steel releases, I lead Chancho and Kyle across the street to the cemetery. The front gate is spotlit in overlapping pools of streetlamp light. It's also locked.

Punch-activating his right glove, Chancho uses the four extended claws to point up at the sign: POPPY HILLS CEMETERY HOURS: DAWN TO DUSK.

"So they couldn't get in," Kyle says. "Crisis averted."

"If the Beast wants in, she gets in," I remind him, squinting through the wrought iron gate into the darkness beyond. "I'm sure they have the emergency ladder with them. We need to find a second entrance. Or a shorter gate."

Jabbing the air and bouncing on the balls of his feet, Chancho shadowboxes forward, clearly relishing the sound of the claws slicing through the empty air.

"The lack of screaming is comforting," he says.

"No," I tell him. "It isn't."

Around the corner, away from the fancy brick-and-wrought-iron front, the fence turns to shorter chain link. Much easier to climb. I throw the swords first before swinging my legs over. Chancho struggles to maneuver with the gloves on, accidentally punching the claws on and off twice as he heaves himself over. Kyle complains about the likelihood of being stabbed by Chancho, a point I cannot argue with.

"Don't be mad because you're the only one unarmed," Chancho says, dusting himself off with his claws out. "It's not my fault your girlfriend won't share her *two* swords with you!"

"First of all, I'm a certified dual-wielder, thank you so much for remembering." Doing my best not to step on any headstones, I flick open the swords. The steel slides into place with a satisfying *shink, shink*. "And second, Kyle isn't unarmed. The Handbook considers knitting needles weapons as long as they've been recently treated with mint oil. Which those have."

Kyle awkwardly holds up the knitting needles I gave him out of my bag. "Is that why you always smell like peppermint? I thought you just ate a lot of Altoids."

"I do," I assure him.

"They'll banish a grub in a pinch," Chancho adds.

"And bad breath every time," I say.

The cemetery stretches out a full block, the paved driveway up the center lined with tall pointed cypress trees that block our view of most of the grounds. Not seeing any movement or any signs of the grub's bright white eyes makes the anxiety burning in my stomach double. Am I leading Kyle and Chancho into a danger I can't save them from? Could the Cannibal grub have already eaten the scouts and escaped into town? Is it possible that I imagined it to begin with?

I call desperately into the darkness. "Squeegee! Avianna! Kelsey! Sasha! *Squeegee!*"

"Who's Squeegee?" Chancho asks me.

"Do all scouts get code names?" Kyle asks. Curls bouncing, he trots to catch up to my side, despite clear orders to stay *behind* me. "Wait, is Prudence not your real name? Kelsey said you were named after the Ladybird Handbook."

"There are no code names," I say, walking twice as fast to stay ahead. The deeper we get into the cemetery, the shallower my breaths become. It's getting harder not to hyperventilate. "And if I was going to have a code name, don't you think I would have picked something more this century than *Prudence*? My mom's just a big fan of the mission statement. If she'd had a third kid, she would have had to name it Public Good Perry."

"Or Bien Público," Chancho offers.

The evergreen trees quiver, even though there's no wind. I think I see a glimmer of a light between branches. My stomach drops. I hold out both swords, making Kyle and Chancho stop in their tracks.

Tizzy Lice rush out from underneath the trees, like rats from a sinking ship, moving too fast to even bother trying to eat one another. Two of them bump into my planted feet. I slice through them with my swords.

"Tag the rest of them before they start eating each other!" I tell Chancho and Kyle.

Or get eaten by the Cannibal grub, I think. We can't risk that thing getting any bigger.

As I push through the close-together trees, sap-sticky branches catch against my sleeve, making my skin go cold. I hold my breath until I'm through to the other side.

Light flashes. My swords are up in a defensive diamond over my head before my eyes have a chance to adjust and make out the shadowy shape of a body.

"Prima?" Avi asks, lowering a flashlight to her side. In her other hand, the exposed blade of her ax droops toward the ground. "Why are you answering the emergency call?"

"I *made* the emergency call," I say. I start to ask her where the others are, when a scream answers for me.

In the back corner of the cemetery, the hybrid grub writhes underneath a rope too plain to be Ladybird regulation. Its glowing white eyes make searchlight sweeps, briefly lighting the girls struggling to hold it in place and the emergency ladder swaying against the brick wall. Kelsey and Sasha hold the plain rope at either end, their hands protected by white tea gloves while they run in opposite directions, maypole-wrapping the hybrid's raw red torso and Dreary Blight legs, momentarily immobilizing it. When its beak swoops down toward a terrified Kelsey, a snap from Jennica's whip sword keeps it from taking a bite.

The grub screams like a girl. Literally. Out of its open beak is the high-pitched shriek of a young girl, echoing forever, too cacophonous to be real. It hits my ears like an ice pick.

Holding up two flashlights to illuminate the proceedings is Paul, shirtless and in swim trunks. Iridescent spores float off the grub's flailing legs, shining like soap bubbles in the light and disappearing before they hit the ground. I assume from the way that Paul's weeping that he's inhaling most of them.

"I'm supposed to be keeping a lookout," Avi sighs, pulling my attention back to her. "In case my mom or your mom shows up to answer the call—wait, who is that?"

Bursting out from behind the trees, Kyle runs forward, his knitting needles held perfectly upward like two Olympic torches. He skids to a stop in front of Paul, his head swerving all over as he examines his friend for signs of injury.

"Dude, are you okay? Did it get you? Are you bleeding?"

"I'm good, man," Paul sniffles. "Just in the middle of a weird date. What are you doing here?"

Kyle points a knitting needle at the writhing grub. "Holy shit, a chupacabra!"

Jogging to catch up, Chancho frowns at him. "Hey, man. Maybe let the Puerto Ricans tell *you* what is or isn't a chupacabra, okay? That's a mulligrub."

"Wait, Kyle!" Paul's eyes light up. "You can See this shit?"

Avi glares at me. "You brought your boyfriend *and* my brother? You're even worse than Jennica."

"You answered an emergency call when you've only had your ax for a *day*?" I glare back. "You're even worse than me."

"We're just supposed to hold it down until—"

The hybrid grub screams again, wagging its body backward deeper against the wall. Straining against the rope, its craggy calcified legs push even more spores into the air. Kelsey throws an elbow in front of her nose, but the Beast is too late, inhaling a lungful. She pitches back, sobs racking her body, shaking the sunglasses off her face. They crunch under her feet. Swearing and crying, she fumbles to keep hold of her end of the rope.

"Sasha!" Kelsey calls. "Breathe through it! We got this!"

But they *don't* got this. Other than the rope, they're unarmed. The hybrid grub is favoring Sasha's side now, pushing its red beak under the loops and twisting its head. To get free or eat Sasha, or both, I can't tell.

When I rush forward to help, there's a crack of metal. A patch of grass explodes at my feet, making me jump back just in time to not get the laces sliced off my sneakers.

Jennica retracts her whip sword with a grimace. Her hair is up in a soggy ponytail, and her patriotic tank top is actually a one-piece bathing suit worn under shorts. A pair of white platform flip-flops have been kicked off next to her. She definitely wasn't planning on hunting tonight.

"Sorry, Pa-roo-dence, but you need to get the heck out of here. This is our grub, not yours. We already claimed it on the app."

"Then take the Root shot before someone gets hurt!" My knuckles burn as I grip the handles of the swords. "You've got brand-new scouts out here with no steel!"

Jennica takes a moment to scan me, sizing me up as a possible threat. I can tell the second she decides she can take me. Her posture shifts forward, catlike, and her smile changes to something much closer to the Beast's Friendly Face. "This really isn't your business, Pa-roo. Just take the boys and go. Paul only came with me because I drove us to the pool and he wanted to feel useful. Why don't you all go home and play video games or something more your speed? We have three more years' experience than you do."

"And I've trained three more scouts than you have."

"You really want to brag about that right now?" A jerk of her head indicates the babybirds clumsily holding down the hybrid grub. Avi has rushed in to help. The three of them are coughing, eyes running. "They don't even have scores registered with Headquarters yet."

"Then maybe someone should carve up a Cannibal-class grub and send it in with their names on the bag," I growl.

I dart past her before she can decide to whip me back again. Swords drawn, I fly toward the White-Eyes. The ground underfoot releases a familiar cold sigh. I look down to find a hastily planted ring of mint, most of the leaves withered and blackened from where they've been touched by a grub. There are too many to just be the ones we planted out front.

"Prudence!" Kelsey exclaims, struggling to keep hold of the end of the rope as the grub swivels and yanks, hoping to free its beak. Her eyes are puffy from crying, the tip of her nose blistered red.

A branch of Dreary Blight reaches for me, squeezing itself between coils of rope. I chop it in half.

"Where are your weapons?" I ask.

"In the field kit," Kelsey says. "Jennica said it's not ready to be banished!"

"Well, it's ready to kill someone!" I say. Another chunk of Dreary Blight leg falls to the ground, shriveling to dust upon impact. I hold my breath, but I can still feel the spores burning the corners of my eyes, wriggling under my lids. Sadness blooms in my chest, sudden and horrible.

Feelings are a wave, I remind myself. *The ocean is.*

"Hold it still," I tell the babybirds.

"We're *trying*!" Sasha says through clenched teeth. Her

eyes are so bloodshot from crying, they're as livid as the Cannibal's skin.

The emergency ladder wobbles as two hands grasp the top. Faithlynn leaps over the wall, landing in front of the grub and unsheathing the axes from her side in one fluid motion. In the white light of the Cannibal's eyes, she's a vengeful ghost with blond pigtails.

"Go home, quitter! You're interfering with another circle's hunt!" she warns, pointing a blade at me. It feels like the old days, when sparring to solve problems was the only answer.

The tips of Tía Lo's swords drag across the tops of gravestones, which sounds cool but is totally an accident. These swords are much, much heavier than the daggers I'm used to. "The Handbook clearly states that the sisterhood is stronger than any one circle, Faith."

"In times of peril!" she quotes back at me.

Behind us, Gabby jumps down from the ladder and unfurls an enormous blue tarp that crackles like plasticky thunder. The handle of her sword waggles in her backpack but stays sheathed as she stakes the tarp to the ground with a rubber mallet, calling to Sasha and Kelsey, who hurry to help pull the free corners of the tarp over the grub.

Faithlynn's blades clang against mine, the metal ringing from my wrists all the way back to my molars.

I dig my heels into the dirt, holding my position even

as my arms start to shake. "If a Cannibal-class hybrid isn't peril, then what is?"

"It's our fucking jackpot, so back off." Faithlynn pushes me hard, sending me skittering into an angel headstone. "It's been feeding here for years. It's gonna have a Root so big we're going to break the leaderboard. We're gonna be legends. Headquarters's gonna have to give all of us a scholarship to any school we want."

"You've been juicing it for points?" I gasp. If I live through this, the absolute first thing I'm going to do is tell Tía Lo I was right. Faithlynn Brett hasn't changed a bit since the day Molly died. She's the same points-obsessed narcissist she's been since elementary school. "Do you really think I'm going to just stand aside now and let you keep feeding a monster?"

Faithlynn howls a laugh that's almost as terrifying as the grub's scream. "Let us? You? A know-nothing quitter? You have zero authority here, Prudence. Why don't you just fuck off and finish Forgetting about us?"

"I'd love to, but you're putting my friends in danger and keeping a monster as a pet in the middle of town!"

I throw my swords up so that Faithlynn has no move except to block with both axes. As they cross in front of her, I lift my heel and kick it as hard as I can into her solar plexus. Feinting to the right, I charge toward the grub squirming beneath the tarp. Under the blue plastic, all I can see now is its free beak, hacking into the dirt. If it can feel the sizzle of the peppermint plants turning to ash around it, it doesn't show it.

Gabby throws herself between me and the hybrid, arms out. "Wait! Don't!"

"Yeah, Pa-roo-dence!" Jennica says, rushing to help Faithlynn stand. "If you cut the Root wrong, you'll ruin everything! Three years of hard work for nothing! Just let Gabby do it!" She glares at her sister scout. "We really should have put it down after what happened to Shelby."

Gabby folds her arms across her chest. "There's still no proof that was because of Mulli!"

"*Stop calling it that,*" Faithlynn hisses. "If there was a second Carnivore in Solano Park, we wouldn't have had to camp for so long while we waited for one. It's been long enough. We made a hybrid no one's ever seen before, and we kept it around for as long as we could. Now, as long as it's one of us who takes the Root shot, I'm fine. But the bag better have all three of our names on it. I worked too hard to let someone else get the points."

"You take it, Faith," Jennica says, stepping back. "It was your idea."

"Gladly." Faithlynn cracks her neck. Lowering her head like a battering ram, she warns the rest of us, "Move unless you want to get carved up, too."

"No!"

Pushing the tarp back, Gabby grabs hold of the top and bottom of the mutant grub's beak and forces it open. I instinctively reach out to stop her, but she's already pushing her face close. She screams into the grub's mouth, the way she would into a trap, and steps back.

From deep within the grub's throat—or maybe deeper— a faraway voice calls, *"Look what you made me do!"*

Molly's voice.

26

The experiences a scout has in the field
will shape her for the rest of her life.

—THE LADYBIRD HANDBOOK

I stagger backward, ears ringing.

No matter what we thought we just heard, it's wrong.

"If that thing can talk, it has advanced sentience," Kyle says in the following silence. "That makes killing it murder."

"Shut up, Kyle!" Kelsey says. "You shouldn't even be here!"

"It's not possible," Jennica whispers. She goggles at Faithlynn, searching her friend's face for answers. "It's *not* possible, right?"

Horrified, my eyes are stuck on the long red beak that used my dead friend's voice. The swords in my hands sag toward the ground. "No. Molly's not in that grub. She's dead. We watched her die."

"And we felt some kind of way about it. Remember

when we saw something huge surface? Sparkly lights, lots of broken trees?" Gabby gestures awkwardly between the still-struggling grub and the rest of us, like we're going to be partners on a group assignment. "This is what we made."

"This is just what we found when we went back," Faithlynn says, spitting a mouthful of Blight spores behind a headstone. "After Prudence fucking quit and Jennica was stuck in the hospital, Gabby and I went back to Solano Park and found this. A hybrid White-Eyes living on grubs coming out of the campsite. It was close to where Molly—" She swallows hard but won't say *died*, even in the middle of the cemetery. "But the Scranch that got her was taken down by the last circle of senior scouts. Its Root wasn't even impressively big. Not like this one is going to be."

Gabby looks shocked. She shies backward, toward the grub. "You heard her in there, Faith. Molly's memory is literally alive in there. You can't just kill it."

"Yes, you can," I argue, shocked to find myself on Faithlynn's side of the argument. "It's a fucking giant monster!"

"We've been managing it just fine for the last three years!" Gabby argues.

"Until you weren't," Sasha says, shying back toward the emergency ladder. Underneath is a lumpy bag that I'd bet dollars to donuts has her halberd inside. The Beast can smell a fight coming the way cows smell rain.

"Move out of the way, Gabby," Faithlynn says, cracking her neck. "It's time to finish this."

"No!" In a blur, Gabby's sword is unsheathed and aimed at Faithlynn. "You said we were going to find a new place for her to live, somewhere she could rest quietly!"

Faithlynn laughs at Gabby's bare steel. "I know you're only a junior still, but God, you can't be that naive! We can't move this thing back and forth forever just because you put enough of your feelings in it to teach it to sing! There are no bonus points for that!"

"Stop talking about points! I don't care about points or scholarships!" Gabby lunges forward with her sword.

Tendrils of Dreary Blight explode from underneath the tarp, shooting out in every direction, unraveling over head-stones and shrubs, encasing the emergency ladder and all of the cement wall behind it. The tarp flies backward, stakes yanked from the ground like weeds. The Cannibal grub rises upward on legs that continue to grow and stretch. The snap of Jennica's whip sword only assists in tearing through the last of the rope.

Finally free, the Cannibal snaps its beak at us, pushing us away. But Gabby moves toward it, her hands up like she thinks she's a velociraptor trainer. When the grub swoops at her again, she blocks with her forearm and falls back shrieking as the Cannibal's beak pecks her.

"Mullifucker!" Gabby screams.

"Fall back!" Faithlynn calls, turning away from the Cannibal to point her axes at Jennica and the babybirds. "Get the fucking civilians out of here!"

But, I realize as I stare around in terror, there is no way out. Just locked gates and tall fences covered in increasingly more Dreary Blight. It's everything I've been terrified of for the last three years. Trapped between a Carnivorous mulligrub and everyone I love the most.

And it's my fault.

I shouldn't have let Kyle and Chancho tag along. I shouldn't have agreed to train Kelsey and Sasha. I should have fought harder against Avi taking my place in Dame Debby's circle.

It's too late to run. We fight or we die.

We could fight *and* die. Just like Molly did.

Above us, the grub's body swells until it's bigger than the ten of us put together.

"Look what you made me do!" it screams again in Molly's voice, scaring the bats out of the trees. And then it charges.

In the rush of fear that follows, Frightworms burst into being all over the cemetery, only to immediately get eaten by the huge Cannibal now scuttling forward on legs made out of crystallized sadness. The Cannibal lights its own way, bright eyes illuminating everything below. Everyone is moving so fast, I can only catch them in strobing glimpses.

Gabby, arm blood soaked,
fumbles with the field first-aid kit,
tearing gauze with her teeth.

Avi throws the weapons bag to Kelsey,
who pulls out her lavender lariat and dagger.

Faithlynn and Jennica gazelle-leap
over headstones like hurdles, taking a wide berth
as they run to intercept the grub head-on.

Sasha twirls her halberd overhead to extend it,
accidentally cutting down
part of the nearest evergreen tree.

Chancho ducks
to avoid being decapitated by Sasha's halberd.

Paul and Kyle rush for the chain-link fence, one pair
of knitting needles split between them.
While Paul bends down to stab every
Tizzy Louse and Frightworm that comes his way,
Kyle kicks them full force
into the darkness.
I've never seen a pacifist in the field before.
It'd be cute if it weren't so stupidly dangerous.

The Cannibal follows the line of punted grubs, gobbling
them up in an appetizer trail that ends with my boyfriend

and his mostly unclothed best friend. I'm left with no other choice but to pull some very stupid solo maneuvers I haven't attempted since middle school.

Like trying to climb a grub while holding two swords.

Scaling Dreary Blight in shorts is not unlike swimming naked in a coral reef. Every time I lose a foothold or the Cannibal tries to shake me off, a layer of my skin is shredded. But every chop at the Dreary Blight banishes a segment away, and if I hold my breath, it stays gone.

Unfortunately, even if I could stab-and-climb the next six feet up the legs, there's no way I could stand long enough on its elongated head to hit between its eyes. Not without immediately getting snapped up by its beak.

"We got you, prima!" Avi calls from the ground.

"We need to close its beak and pull it down to the ground!" I shout back. "The tarp would be useful!"

"On it!" I hear the Beast somewhere on the other side moments before the Cannibal takes a sharp dive to the right. The glint of steel at the end of Sasha's halberd swishes through the air, hacking through boughs and offshoots of moving red Dreary Blight.

"Heads up!"

Purple rope flies through the air. Kelsey's lavender lariat sweeps by my ear, landing around the Cannibal's beak and yanking it sharply to the left and throwing me off-balance. My ankle is dragged raw against the Dreary Blight as I fall to the ground.

Landing hard on my back knocks the wind out of me. My diaphragm seizes as I struggle to sit up, unable to breathe. Avi calls my name, rushing toward me to check that I'm okay. I wave her off, pointing toward the grub trying to tug free of the lariat. It hasn't even registered the loss of my weight.

Get up, scout, my mother's voice barks in my memory.

Planting a sword in the grass for leverage, I wobble back to my feet, doing my best not to look at the blood seeping into my socks. All of me stings.

In the distance, steel strikes against steel as Gabby stands between the senior scouts and the Cannibal's lariat-leashed beak. The white gauze on her arm is already soaked through with blood, and more oozes down her elbow as her sword flashes against every blow from Faithlynn's approaching axes and Jennica's whip sword. Even injured, she won't let her sister scouts near the grub's Root.

Its mouth momentarily muzzled, the Cannibal diverts its energy through its limbs. Rather than continuing to chase, it shoots its arms of Dreary Blight into every direction, cracking through marble grave markers and wrapping around trees. Kyle trips over a branch and is quickly swept underneath hard veins of Blight, pressing him deeper into the grass. Struggling beneath it just shakes more and more Dreary dust onto his face.

I scream his name, but Blight rises up between us, a wall of briars holding me back. Through the thicket, I can see

Paul stabbing wildly, attempting to free Kyle, but his single knitting needle can only banish an inch at a time and he's huffing so much dust, he's likely to start drowning in Blight himself.

Tying the end of her lariat around an obelisk headstone, Kelsey runs over to help Kyle, her small dagger cutting through the red tangle holding down her brother's arms.

"Kelsey, I'm so sorry," Kyle cries. His face is covered in a thick coating of iridescent spores. "I shouldn't have said I couldn't live with you. I was just so mad at losing my own room, and Mom and Tim got married so fast—"

"It's okay," she says, brow furrowed in concentration as she saws through Blight branches. "You love the shedroom. It's just the grub feeding on you. It happened my first day, too."

"I'm not a good brother," Kyle sobs. "I didn't even know you had a lasso. You're Wonder Woman!"

"It's a lariat," she tells him. But he can't hear her. His eyes flutter closed. She shakes his shoulder, getting no response. "Kyle? Kyle!"

"Someone grab that lariat!" the Beast shouts. She points her halberd at the lavender rope starting to slip down the headstone.

Paul leaps up, grabbing the lariat and pulling hard to keep the Cannibal's beak shut. The Cannibal turns, catching Paul in the full light of its eyes. A Frightworm bursts to life in front of him. Four claws explode through the top of its head, obliterated in an instant by Chancho, who is so proud of himself, he accidentally conjures a Nock Jaw. In the instant it takes for him and Paul to both banish the Nock Jaw, the lariat goes slack in Paul's hand. The Cannibal yanks itself free with a triumphant scream at the sky.

I have to get to my friends. I have to protect them. But I can't go over the grub. And I can't go under it.

I need it to turn around.

Gripping my swords hard, I take a second and let all of the feelings I've been trying to hold back rain down on me.

I did this. I made the emergency call. And even before that, I brought all of these people into this world. It's my fault that every non-legacy in this cemetery can See. Jennica may be Faithlynn's preschool bestie, but Gabby was recruited from my gymnastics class. Molly died attempting a stunt she watched me do half a dozen times.

Underneath a bramble of Dreary Blight, all I can see of Kyle is his unconscious face. He had been so peaceful before I dragged him into this. He was so much happier believing that the mysteries of life were added value, not actual nightmares.

I let the truth of the feeling fill me up. The guilt, the regret, the fury, the *grief* of it all. Until the Cannibal stops in its tracks, scenting me.

Achingly slowly, it begins to turn around to face me.

Yes, I think. *When you need someone to save the world, call an empath.*

I will feel the sadness of everyone in the cemetery, everyone in Poppy Hills, if it will keep these nine people alive. I can handle it. It's what I was born to do. To be the ocean that lets every wave of emotion crest. To feel so deeply, so entirely and know that the feelings won't kill me. Because it's not for points, it's not for the reward. It's to show people that it can be done.

One way. Not the only way.

"Get the tarp!" I shout.

The tarp flies over the back of the grub, smashing its torso into the ground. On one side, Paul and Chancho pull as hard as they can. Avi, Kelsey, and the Beast strain to keep their side down. Although most of the Dreary Blight dust is trapped underneath, a low tide of spores glints in the light.

"*LOOK! What you made me DO!*" the grub screams in my face with breath like sulfurous ice, sounding less and less like Molly. It's just a memory of her, a fragment in time. Not her proudest moment, or ours. Just one of a million bits. The part that makes us the saddest.

Gabby sobs on the other side of the grub. "Prudence, please!"

I shake my head, refusing to give in to her pleading. This grub has to be banished. Even if a shadow of Molly lives on inside of it. Because this isn't how we should remember Molly. She was so much more than this, more than just the moment she died. She was small and scrappy and sarcastic.

She was glasses and freckles and the chipmunk cheeks that she hated. She was hopes and dreams and play-pretends about the future. She was jokes about Faithlynn and elaborate victory dances and the first one asleep at sleepovers. She was a person. She was my best friend.

"I didn't make you do it, Molly," I tell the grub's white eyes. "And neither did the sisterhood. You made a choice. You made the wrong choice at the wrong time. And I wish you hadn't. Or that I could have stopped you. I wish we'd known then that there are so many other ways to be a scout." I glance at my friends, who are holding down the tarp with all their strength. "We're allowed to ask for help."

Rearing back, I stab the green sword through the grub's beak, pinning it closed. Knowing it won't hold for long, I retreat three steps and run at a diagonal, gaining enough speed to flip onto the top of the grub's head. Sweat burns my eyes as I struggle to keep my balance. Clutching the pink sword in two hands, I crack down into Cannibal's skull, between its eyes. Dame Debby taught us that taking out a Root is like carving a jack-o'-lantern. Saw the sword up and down in a circle. Reach in to pull out the guts.

The moment my hand wraps around the Root, the white eyes burn out and the Cannibal grub shatters into nothingness under my feet. Dreary Blight spores burst into the air like confetti, only to disappear before the wind can pick them up. The tarp drifts to the ground, useless.

My butt lands in the dirt. Even in the sudden darkness,

I can tell that the Root I'm holding is unlike any I've seen before. Thick as a parsnip, it's a twisted, multicolored mass with four legs. Touching it makes my skin crawl. I let it drop, leaving it next to a bouquet of dead yellow roses on a gravestone.

"Prudence!" Chancho calls. He's kneeling next to Kyle. "I don't think he's breathing."

Panic has me up and racing for Kyle in an instant. He's lying unconscious between two graves. My knees skid in the dirt as I push past Chancho and set my ear against Kyle's chest. His heartbeat is a whisper.

"Babe, I need you to wake up," I beg, pushing the curls back from his forehead. Dozens of tiny scratches on his face are leaking blood. "Kyle, you didn't get the Sight just to die your first time in the field. I won't let you!"

Opening his mouth and pinching his nose, I press my lips to his like he's the scream chamber on a grub trap and exhale all of my adrenaline into his lungs.

"Two breaths, then compressions," Paul reminds me, leaning down on the other side. Behind him, I can see Avi and Kelsey hugging each other nervously. "Nice even pushes, Prue."

I interlock my fingers and thrust my hands against Kyle's chest. He's so much more solid than the Rescue Annie mannikin and yet so much more fragile. I can feel his rib cage under my hands and the soft swell of his belly. My eyes burn with tears that want shedding, but I blink them back, blowing two more deep breaths into Kyle's mouth.

His body shudders, head lolling to one side as he lets out a deep, wet cough. Dreary Blight spores pour from his lips and sink into the ground as he hacks and heaves the sadness out of his lungs.

His eyes flutter open, blue eyes sparkling up at me. "Okay, babe," he croaks, hands fumbling for mine. "I get why you have to kill them."

Laughing in relief, I grip his fingers, crying and kissing his knuckles. "Headquarters prefers the term *banish*. It's friendlier."

"Hey, sorry to interrupt," the Beast says. Her halberd is raised, pointing at the senior scouts edging closer to the fallen Root. "I am wholly stoked you aren't dead, KG, but what does the Handbook say to do with traitors? Ship them to Headquarters? Duel to the death?"

After the fight we've just had, I'd like nothing more than to wash the blood off my body and rest. I'm not equipped to dole out punishment for harboring a dangerous monster and juicing it for points. I don't even know what Headquarters's penalty is for scouts who endanger their community rather than protect it.

But I know who would know.

I blow out a breath. "Let me call my mom."

27

When making any choice, a scout must
ask herself: What is most peaceful, prudent,
and public-minded?

—THE LADYBIRD HANDBOOK

Dr. Anita Silva-Perry is less than thrilled when she climbs the emergency ladder into the cemetery and finds the senior scouts lariat-leashed to the pedestal of an angel statue. I can only imagine how much more pissed she'd be if I hadn't convinced Kyle to drive Paul and Kelsey home before she arrived. Best to keep my mother's wrath contained to the legacy scouts. And Sasha, who refused to leave.

"Prudence!" Mom shrieks. She's decked out in patrol clothes and a jogging headlamp that hides the white streak in her unbrushed hair. I can tell that my phone call woke her up, because her running leggings don't match her T-shirt.

"Hey, Mom. Thanks for coming." With a wince, I lift myself off the headstone I've been resting on. My legs ache, but none of the scratches seem deep enough to need stitches, which is definitely an improvement over my last Carnivore hunt.

Behind me, Jennica is changing out the soiled gauze from Gabby's arm, the field first-aid kit open between them. Faithlynn is sulking, her left eye starting to swell. She wouldn't put her axes down without a fight, which the Beast was all too eager to provide.

Ladybirds may spar, but from the way Faithlynn went down, I'm pretty sure she's never been headbutted before. The Beast has been standing guard over her ever since, waiting for another excuse to drop her halberd and throw hands.

"What in God's name is happening here?" Mom asks. She grips the whip sword on her shoulder, her head swiveling. "Where's the reported Cannibal?"

"I told you on the phone. We banished it." I step over the pile of weapons the senior scouts more or less surrendered. The Cannibal's Root sits neatly in the circle of Jennica's whip sword. I pick it up and toss it to my mother, who catches it—one-handed—out of the air.

The emergency ladder starts swaying again, making me pause. Before I can worry about a new grub coming through or a threat from our own dimension—it's probably illegal to gather inside a cemetery after hours, right?—I see a flash of pastel pink. Tía Lo swings over the wall and down to the ground in a three-point superhero landing, lamb-print pajamas fluttering in the breeze. Without waiting a moment, she flies at Avi and Chancho.

"Constantino Marquez the Fourth! Are you wearing my jogging claws?!"

Chancho takes a step back so that he's poorly hidden behind his much shorter sister. He puts his puffy-gloved hands in front of his face to keep from getting swatted. "Ma, I had to! It was for the public good!"

Tía Lo glares at him before dropping to her knees and checking Avi's face for signs of injury. "Avianna, are you okay? Are you hurt?"

"I'm fine!" Avi says, bringing up a shoulder to deflect her mom's licked thumb coming in to clear a dirt smudge from her face. "I earned an Emergency Signal charm *and* my first Carnivore Hunt charm!"

"Oh, I'm so proud of you, nena," Tía Lo says. Her arm shoots out, stopping Chancho before he can creep into the shadows. "Not so fast, young man. Gloves off. Now!"

"God, Mom," I say to my own mother, hating the whine in my voice. "I told you that the grub was gone. You had to bring Tía Lo?"

"When my younger child calls me from the site of an active hybrid Carnivore scene?" Mom huffs, shaking the multicolored Root at me. "You're lucky I didn't call every active scout in the county. Did you learn nothing from your last Carnivore hunt, Prudence? Sneaking out with under-trained scouts—and uninitiated *boys*—you're lucky to even be alive! If it weren't for the senior scouts—"

She takes a step forward, like she's considering freeing the senior scouts from their bonds. Sasha hits a defensive stance, her halberd extending to its full length across her chest. Without her sunglasses, it's too easy to see the bloodlust twinkle in her eyes.

I get between them.

"If it weren't for the senior scouts, we wouldn't be in this mess," I snap, standing on my toes to make Mom look at me—just me. The blaze of her headlamp blinds me, but the single LED bulb is wan compared with the memory of the Cannibal's hydrogen-fire eyes. "And I wasn't just lucky, Mom. *I* banished the Cannibal grub. The senior scouts are the ones who have been keeping it alive. Look at the number of coils on that Root. Their pet ate more than just other grubs and Shelby Waters. They've been juicing it for points for *three years*."

Mom finally takes notice of the Root in her hand and its bulky abnormalities. The twists reveal a sickening number of deaths. The whiskers growing out of its four twisted legs are long and bushy. The candy-corn striation is Dreary Blight red and Tizzy Louse orange and Frightworm white. Mom turns it over twice, then calls for her sister to take a look.

Tía Lo takes a break from worrying over Avi and berating Chancho. She plucks the Root from Mom's hands and holds it up to the headlamp beam. Their silence tells me what I already know. There's no mistaking it for a normal Root.

Mom points her headlamp at the senior scouts. "You did this?" she asks in a rough whisper.

I don't think I've ever heard so much raw emotion in her voice. She sounds like someone close to tears, although her eyes are in the shadow of the headlamp, so I can't see for sure.

"You fed innocent lives to a hybrid aberration?"

"No! We didn't feed anyone to it!" Gabby protests, one hand clamped over the gauze wrapped thick around her arm. "We only gave it other grubs! We had it penned in a Pippy-Mint circle, up in the hills above Solano Park. It was away from the campsite and the trail. When we found big enough Critters in town, we'd drive them out to Solano Park. And if there weren't enough grubs, I fed it my own screams. It never should have gotten hungry enough to eat a person."

I remember the day of the car wash when the senior scouts pulled up in Faithlynn's car, the back seat full of Tizzy Lice. No other scouts would ever be comfortable driving around with grubs loose in the car. It'd be too draining, too distracting. I should have known then that it was common practice for them to chauffeur monsters around.

"But it *did* get hungry," Jennica says softly. She winds a strand of hair anxiously around her prosthetic index finger, sending a sidelong glance at Faithlynn. "It must have.

There's another girl in a locket because of us."

"What were those scouts even doing that far from the path?" Gabby asks shrilly. "It was a routine patrol! They should have stayed in the campsite!"

"Your grub used Molly's voice to scream," I say. The memory of it makes me queasy. "It lured them. They probably thought they were saving someone."

"Does Dame Debby know that you were keeping a grub alive?" Avi asks the senior scouts. She looks at her mom and mine and tucks her chin sheepishly into her shoulder. "We only found out about it tonight. Faithlynn told us to wait here to claim the emergency call, since we were closest. Prudence told us what happened on her last Carnivore hunt. We wouldn't have come otherwise, I super swear."

"*I* probably would have," Sasha mumbles.

"Where is Dame Debby?" Mom asks the senior scouts, folding her arms imperiously. "Even for experienced scouts, an uncategorized Carnivore is exceedingly dangerous. She should have answered the emergency call with you."

"Or was juicing a grub her idea to keep you at the top of the leaderboard?" I ask.

Being first on the leaderboard would all but guarantee Faithlynn the merit scholarship, and her mother would have been praised for having trained the strongest scouts. Their legacy would have continued to be revered, even after Faithlynn went off to college. I can totally imagine Dame

Debby planning this whole thing, desperate for her circle to be the best, no matter the cost.

So I'm shocked when Faithlynn starts to laugh.

"Oh please," she says derisively, her upturned nostrils flaring wide. "That old bitch has no fucking clue what goes on in the field. She's been pretending to be a scout for years."

"What?" I ask at the same time Tía Lo gives a shocked "Language, Faithlynn, please!"

Jennica scoots awkwardly to lean around the marble pedestal and face her sister scout. "Faith! We swore we wouldn't tell."

"And what good did it do us?" Faithlynn bites back. "We cover her ass, and we're the ones who risk our lives. I don't see *her* getting tied up by a quitter and her fucking loser brigade."

"We'll untie you when you start answering questions," Sasha says, pointing the spear end of her halberd at Faithlynn's stomach.

"Dame Debby can't See grubs anymore," Gabby announces suddenly. "After Molly died, she decided to Forget."

Jennica looks at me with unmistakable pity. "She took the dose that was supposed to go to Prudence."

My skin goes cold. I knew, of course, that Dame Debby had ordered a dose of the Tea of Forgetting for me. I remember how furious Mom had been at the idea, as though following protocol and erasing my Sight would dishonor our legacy.

I never imagined, though, that Dame Debby would take it herself. Forget and yet remain the leader of a circle of scouts? How could anyone be so reckless? She couldn't help her scouts even if she wanted to, not without being able to See what they were up against.

Faithlynn glowers at me. "She thought it would get rid of her nightmares. But it just made her afraid of her own shadow, and even more useless than she was before." She spits in the dirt and jerks her head at Sasha and Avi. "That's how we ended up with three initiates who didn't even really pass their steel test."

Stunned, I picture Dame Debby sitting in my house, sipping tea, making decisions on behalf of Headquarters, talking birdshit about other legacies while she couldn't save herself from a grub if she wanted to. That's why she passed the babybirds on a technicality. She couldn't See them fail.

"Un-Sighted? This whole time?" Mom gasps. "How?"

Tía Lo's eyes are bouncing as though invisible calculations are swimming around her head. "It doesn't make any sense. She volunteers at the regional clubhouse! She attends National Conference every year!"

"You don't need the Sight to go to tea parties and show off your battle scars. She shows up for the nostalgia," Faithlynn says. "Headquarters leaves the real fighting to senior scouts. Everything that happens in the field falls down on us. While everyone else grows up and moves on, gets jobs and boyfriends, we're stuck in the shit. Cleaning up the emotional messes the old legacies think are beneath them." She presses forward against the purple lariat, sneering at Mom and Tía Lo as she lowers her voice down to a growl. "The two of you patrol your neighborhood so you can talk shit and peek in the windows, but you know where the real monsters are? Schools. Amusement parks. Anywhere parents ignore and kids are left alone to fend for themselves. How do you think we found enough food to keep a hybrid alive for this long?"

From just one summer of patrolling, I know there's too much of our town left untouched by dawn patrol. I think of the Scranch we found in the fun house at The Wooz. The Dreary Blight covering the portables at Goldfields Middle School. The Frightworm in the dressing room at the public pool. All places adults would avoid. Places my circle and my friends had no choice but to face.

"You don't want to know how we do what we do. You want to see our names at the top of the leaderboard and feel safe," Faithlynn continues. "Do you really think we're the only circle in the country that's been keeping a grub to juice? How else are we supposed to earn the points to upgrade our steel? Giving out almond butter sandwiches? Hosting car washes? No. Headquarters wants results. And that's what we give them."

Much to my chagrin, I can sort of see her point. Faithlynn is exactly what a legacy scout is supposed to be:

completely devoted no matter the cost. If I hadn't quit after Molly died, if I had doubled down on my allegiance to the sisterhood and become the kind of scout my mother wanted me to be, I would probably be just like Faith. A hunter first and a person second.

With no life outside of the scouts, how would you even know what people were supposed to be like? The Handbook only teaches you how to spot people at the height of their emotions—the best and worst. But life is mostly in the middle. Scouts don't know what to do when the stakes aren't life or death.

"She's right," I say. When everyone looks at me in surprise, I shrug. "Not, like, morally right. I don't think juicing a Carnivore is good, even if it does have the memory of a dead sister scout living inside it. But the rest of it makes sense. The competition. The secrecy. The weight of it all. It's too much. The world gets harder and harder to protect, and in return Headquarters wants scouts to get harder, too. Wouldn't it make more sense to actually get softer?"

Mom and Faithlynn make identical snorts of disdain, but Tía Lo narrows her eyes at me and asks, "Softer how? You can't cuddle a Carnivore to death, Miss Prue."

I cross my arms and stand up as tall as I can, refusing to be shamed into silence. "No, but you could hit the grubs where it hurts the most: in the food supply. If we spent as much time training scouts how to handle their emotions as we do teaching them how to pour tea, then we might actually draw fewer grubs to our dimension. If we didn't pit the scouts against one another on the leaderboard, how many fewer Scranch would show up to feed on the jealousy? Instead of car washes, our public good could focus on mindfulness meditations and yoga. Not just making people feel good to distract them from a quick banishing, but actually trying to make them less tempting to grubs in the long term. We could teach legacy boys with the Sight how to banish their own grubs." I glance back at Chancho, who is quietly swishing his mother's house swords like green and pink lightsabers. "What if the next evolution of scout isn't a fearless hunter? What if it's a friend?"

"That's all very interesting in theory, Prudence," Mom says with a sniff. "But taking focus away from the leaderboard, changing our core mission from hunting to counseling, adding males to the sisterhood—it would take years to convince Headquarters to allow even one of those things, let alone all of them. You're asking for a lot of radical change."

"Yes, I am," I say, lifting my chin. "Because without radical change, you're going to get more nights like tonight. More burned-out scouts who put their community in danger because no one ever asked them about their grief." I look at my former sister scouts, and my voice cracks. "I have missed Molly every day for three years. But we don't need a grub to remember her by. And we don't need lockets. We're supposed to keep other people from dying the same way she did. That's what they mean when they say the sisterhood marches on." I turn back to Mom and Tía Lo. "But it's supposed to march on and *get better*. It's supposed to evolve. And so are we."

The Beast jerks her halberd, collapsing its telescoping handle. "Look, Sister Chancho's mom, Sister Prue's mom."

I rub my aching eyes and groan. "Sasha."

"Sorry! *Dr.* Sister Prue's mom." She saunters forward, swinging her halberd at her side. "Let me tell you something I heard a lot at County Day. You may have been dealt bad cards, but you choose how to play them. Seems to me that the tenth edition of the Handbook is a hand of bad cards. Too much focus on charms and points and that shitty granola you people love—"

"Birdbark," Avi corrects in a squeak.

"But it sounds like the Handbook before was even worse," Sasha says. "Having to wait to get your period before you could earn your steel makes zero sense. My uterus doesn't make me any better or worse at stabbing shit. And Chancho did a decent job of fighting off grubs tonight, without a uterus or any training."

Surprised, Chancho nearly drops the swords he's holding. "Hey, thanks, Sasha!"

"So, I don't see why the eleventh edition of the Handbook shouldn't be able to make some big changes. Bring in some boys. Teach anger management. Get rid of the points-hungry idiots who wouldn't know public good from the hole in their ass—"

"All right, Sasha," Mom says. "You've made your point."

"I haven't, actually," Sasha says. "Not yet." She cuts her eyes at me, the corner of her mouth curling into a lopsided smile. "It seems like the only way to keep the whole sisterhood from collapsing is to change it. And that means having Dames who give enough of a fuck to start changing before Headquarters gives them the go-ahead. That's what real leadership is, right? Not just having 'the Sight,' but being able to 'see' what a circle actually needs?"

My chest tightens. After spending so much of my life trying to escape my Ladybird legacy, could I really spend high school leading a circle of scouts, like all of the women in the my family before me?

Except it wouldn't be exactly the same. Every Dame in my family has taught out of a different edition of the Handbook, wielded different weapons, made their own changes. Paz is making sure the next generation of scouts knows about hybrids. Mom makes sure there are scouts employed in the school district. Tía Lo changed the free sandwiches to almond butter, which probably did help people with peanut allergies.

The mission of peace, prudence, and public good can

obviously mean different things to different people—just look at the senior scouts using it as an excuse to feed Critters to a hybrid for three years. I could make sure that doesn't happen again. Or, at least, I could try.

Forgetting didn't save Dame Debby.

Quitting again won't save me.

28

A scout's legacy lives on in
all of the lives she's touched.

—THE LADYBIRD HANDBOOK

It's more crowded under the pergola than it used to be. I had to borrow a new tea set from Tía Lo to accommodate everyone.

The table is laid with a full spread in celebration of our first integrated meeting. Heaps of cucumber sandwiches, PMS-chip cookies, and birdbark made with Rice Krispies, Kelsey's newest creation.

At the far end of the table, Avi pours Pippy-Mint tea from a second teapot and passes it to Chancho.

"Don't add too much milk," she warns as he accepts the cup and saucer. "It dilutes the active menthone."

My sister told me that the fastest way to get things done through Headquarters is to let Tía Lo start making a fuss. So while we start the Criminal Element boys on chapter 1 of the Handbook—tea and grub identification—Tía Lo is calling every legacy she knows, asking if their sons have ever expressed an interest in being a Ladybird. *Think of what it could do for recruitment!* she said when she heard about the boys helping take down the hybrid. *We could finally trounce those cookie-pushers!*

My mom is less thrilled by the idea. Probably because it means when I say I'm going hunting, she can't guarantee that I'm not also going to see Kyle. But she did order a bench seat for the outdoor table so that we could squeeze more people together, which means she's at least coming around to my new initiates.

The Beast shows Chancho and Paul how to clip the golden robins onto their slightly extended charm bracelets.

"How can you even see that ring?" Paul asks, squinting at his bracelet while Sasha affixes his charm. He's wearing a Panama hat that I bet he borrowed from Jennica. He is definitely *that* super-obsessed boyfriend. Last year, he wore a girl's diamond stud in his right ear until it got infected. I am slightly worried that if Jennica gets picked up by a new circle, he'll want to join it, too.

After Mom and Tía Lo reported the doings of Dame Debby's scouts to Headquarters, Faithlynn, Jennica, and Gabby were given a choice: They could leave the sisterhood entirely or be demoted back down to initiate level, losing all of their charms, their steel, and their leaderboard records until they worked their way back up under the guidance of a new—Sighted—Dame, one who isn't related to any of them. Faithlynn and Jennica apparently chose demotion, but they haven't yet been able to find a new circle that will take them in. I certainly won't. Not just because they called me a quitter and juiced a grub for three years but also because Paul and Jennica are still seeing each other and the circle can only handle so many couples at once. Even so, Jennica gave Paul her Handbook to study since she has it memorized.

Gabby retired outright. When I saw her last week, she said she was looking forward to starting her own cute little civilian life, away from the scouts. She looked more normal than I'd ever seen her—in jeans and chunky boots rather than workout clothes. The camping backpack she'd had before was traded out for a white leather purse. She gave me her Handbook and her sword so I could use them for training the boys.

She also gave me a tea bag in a wrapper the color of Scranch legs, stamped with the Ladybird crest.

"Dame Debby took your chance before. Just because you want to fight today doesn't mean that you'll want to fight tomorrow," she said, reaching out to touch Molly's locket, hanging at my neck.

I've been wearing it, sometimes. When the memory of her or the Cannibal grub is too strong.

Gabby's eyes watered. "Keep your options open, Dame Prudence."

So I put the Tea of Forgetting, still in its packaging, in the closet cigar box, along with the smell of my abuela Ramona, a broken wishbone, and other things I thought I couldn't live without. After facing down the Cannibal-class grub, I'm pretty sure I'd rather be able to See what grubs are after me. And what grubs I'm attracting.

Kyle's curls poke out adorably from beneath a cap that makes him look like a charming chimney sweep. I steal a kiss from him as I hand over his cup of tea.

Kelsey bangs her teaspoon against the cake cloche. "Hey! That's not Ladybird behavior!"

"We're trying to have a civilized meeting here!" Chancho jeers. "No tonguing each other at tea!"

Blushing, I sink back in my seat. "Sorry! He's just so cute. He makes me forget the rest of you are here."

"Boo!" The Beast throws a cucumber slice at me. "Breathe through it!"

"Okay, scouts." I pull the cloche off the pink cake stand, revealing three toddling Tizzy Lice, nipping at one another with their tiny sharp beaks. "Today we're going to focus on keeping your cool in the field. It doesn't help to banish grubs if you're just making more."

None of the boys could find white gloves, so out of fairness, I let the babybirds keep their hands exposed, too. The glove rules were definitely made by East Coasters, who have never heard of a hot September. I've even left my hoodie draped on the back of my chair for the meeting so I can enjoy what little breeze there is in the air.

Above my charm bracelet, the thin skin of my scar is fully on display, getting its first sunburn.

ACKNOWLEDGMENTS

This book would not have been possible without:

Laura Zats, my agent and friend.

Erik Hane, cofounder of Headwater Literary Management and king loon.

Tiff Liao, Kate Farrell, and Mark Podesta, my wonderful editorial team.

Erin Duffey, a true-blue Ladybird (just kidding, she's a Girl Scout and weirdly proud of it).

Tehlor Mejia, my sounding board for all things.

A. R. Capetta and Cory McCarthy, for their rousing encouragement.

Sabba Rahbar, who asked her mother for Farsi swears I didn't end up using.

Sylvia Sudat, who lured me out of the house with Korean food.

The Rats in the Alley circa 2006, who never asked (to my face) why I was always around.

The many named groups I was part of as a teen that either dissolved or evolved: the Harbor Kids, Team Monkey, Cuddle Party, and the Girls.

And my Camp Fire troop, who probably think this song is about them. It's not. Mostly. (But, for real, the appropriation was OFF THE CHARTS.)